Praise for *Rising Danger*

"*Rising Danger* grabbed me from the first chapter and never let go. Don't miss this edge-of-your-seat story of suspense and romance."
> —Christian romantic suspense author Patricia Bradley

"Fast-paced, explosive thriller. I couldn't turn the pages fast enough."
> —Carrie Stuart Parks, award-winning, bestselling author of *Relative Silence*

JERUSHA AGEN

RISING DANGER

LOVE INSPIRED

INSPIRATIONAL ROMANCE

LOVE INSPIRED®
INSPIRATIONAL ROMANCE

ISBN-13: 978-1-335-40187-8

Rising Danger

Copyright © 2021 by Jerusha Agen

This edition published by arrangement with Harlequin Books S.A.

For questions and comments about the quality of this book, please contact us at CustomerService@Harlequin.com.

Love Inspired
22 Adelaide St. West, 40th Floor
Toronto, Ontario M5H 4E3, Canada
www.Harlequin.com

Printed in U.S.A.

Recycling programs
for this product may
not exist in your area.

To Mom, my still waters

Soli Deo Gloria

Acknowledgments

This book wouldn't be what it is today without the wonderful people God has used to bless me. To thank everyone would fill up a book itself, so I'll have to limit myself to just a few here.

Thanks to Emily Rodmell and everyone at Love Inspired Trade who made this publication possible.

Amanda Dykes, thank you for putting me in touch with Erika Nordstrom, the source I desperately needed to learn about dams. Erika, thank you for helping me depict river dams as realistically as possible. Because much of this information is protected, I took fictional license wherever needed and any errors that exist are entirely my own.

Michelle Griep, thanks for your help with Minneapolis local color and details.

Wendy Lawton, my dream agent, thank you for being my champion and cheerleader. I'm so thankful to partner with you on this journey.

Emily Conrad, my critique partner and friend, you know how much you've done for me and that "thank you" could never say enough. I'm so grateful to have you in my life.

The Quotidians, a fabulous group of writers and friends, thank you for letting me be part of such a special community.

Stephanie Gammon, my fellow suspense author, thank you for your friendship, for being "unoffendable" and for the love you bring into my life.

Jeanne Bader, thank you for your faithful and powerful prayer support. You've taught me much and given me much.

Dad, thank you for making my dreams possible.

Mom, thank you for being my best friend and always believing in me. Because of you, I know what real love looks like.

To my Lord and Savior, Jesus Christ, thank You for these blessings and so much more. I am in awe of the privilege You've given me to create with the Creator.

Or who shut up the sea with doors, when it brake forth,
as if it had issued out of the womb?
When I made the cloud the garment thereof,
and thick darkness a swaddlingband for it,
And brake up for it my decreed place, and set bars and doors,
And said, Hitherto shalt thou come, but no further:
and here shall thy proud waves be stayed?
—*Job* 38:8–11

RISING DANGER

Chapter One

Chaos assaulted her as soon as she opened the door. For a moment, just one second, Bristol Bachmann wanted to retreat into the Jeep and shut out the sounds of panic and terror that threatened to conjure the same emotions in her.

Her hiking boots landed on the faded blacktop of the parking lot as she forced away memories that clustered like a mob of shadows at the back of her mind. She shot a glance at the Minnesota Falls Visitor Center as she moved to the back of her Jeep.

People poured out of the tourist complex, exiting the main entrance in semiorganized fashion and then scattering, some yelling and screaming.

Flashing lights of police squads and fire rescue trucks painted a dizzying spectacle of color against the backdrop of gray, cloudy sky.

She swiped her hands together, sweat dampening her palms as if this were her first bomb threat. But symptoms like that had disappeared after her first day with the Minneapolis Police Department's bomb squad over two years ago. She tried to ignore the real reason for her unusual nerves as she opened the liftgate and reached inside to release Toby from his crate.

The seventy-five-pound black Labrador retriever dropped out the back to the pavement of the parking lot, wriggling as she checked his harness. She straightened the harness for his comfort, the Phoenix K-9 Security and Detection Agency's logo resting on both his shoulders, along with Explosives Detection identification and a warning: Do Not Pet. Toby panted and pranced around her, more than ready to get to work.

She snatched the fanny pack that housed his necessities and the essential tennis ball attached to a rope. She snapped the pack around her waist under her open windbreaker as she and Toby hurried toward the brick-and-concrete visitor center, positioned above the famous Minnesota Falls.

Crowds still rushed through the glass doors at the front of the building, their faces a study in terror.

Her stomach clenched.

If there was a bomb here, as the anonymous threat had indicated, there were a lot of people who could get hurt if it detonated. The $42 million complex constructed last year had been built to make Minnesota Falls a tourist destination. But today, it seemed only to have created an easy target for maximum casualties.

The sound of water rushing over the falls reached her ears, swishing the anxiety in her stomach. Her gaze was pulled to the Mississippi River. She could see it clearly to the left of the building.

The water was choppy, moving fast and disappearing behind the building where it crashed over the Minnesota Falls Dam with audible power.

Her pulse ratcheted up. The water level looked higher than normal against the banks. They'd had so much rain this spring.

If a bomb detonated here, now...

It wouldn't. Toby would find it.

Someone bumped against her arm as she reached the fringes of the fleeing crowd.

A high-pitched sound cut through the shouts and voices.

Bristol paused, heedless of the people brushing past. Was that crying?

Toby perked his ears, and Bristol followed the direction of his gaze.

A toddler stood in the middle of the streaming crowd, sobbing as people bumped into him. He could get knocked down and trampled.

"Clear the way!" Bristol's shout and Toby's plowing body cut a path through the crowd.

They reached the boy just when another panicked adult thudded into him. Bristol grabbed the child as he started to topple and hefted him in her arms.

"It's okay, buddy." Bristol used her best soothing tone as the little boy sobbed in her ear.

Toby charged ahead and led the way out of the crowd, probably as eager as Bristol to escape the jostling and bumping.

"See the doggy? Look at the doggy."

The boy stopped the painful screaming and sniffed, his blue-eyed gaze drawn to the black dog pulling them ahead.

They emerged in the open air outside the fleeing mob. "Toby." Bristol's one word brought Toby back to her side, the dog reaching his nose in the air to sniff the boy's dangling foot.

Bristol spotted a female police officer posted at the entrance to the complex. Not ideal to take the child toward the bomb, but it was the fastest option when speed mattered. "Officer!"

She moved toward the shout as Bristol headed her way. "Lost child?"

Bristol nodded and handed the boy over. "Would you find

his parents? And I need to get in. Explosives detection." Bristol pulled out her private investigator's dog handling license as ID.

"Go ahead." The officer pointed toward the glass door she had been standing at before, the farthest left of the entrance doors. Must be locked from the inside or partitioned off, since none of the visitors were using it.

"Thanks." Bristol walked quickly to the door just as a German shepherd emerged from the crowd, an MPD officer in tow. The fortysomething man's familiar sturdy build and five-foot-six height that matched hers brought a smile to Bristol's lips. Officer Rick Miles and his K-9, Duke.

Her smile faded as quickly as it had come. She couldn't be sure what kind of reception she'd get from her former coworker, even though they'd been close enough friends that he and his wife had hosted her for dinner a couple times.

She opened the door and held it for the other K-9 team.

"Hey, Bachmann. Good to see you." Miles gave her a smile as he passed through with Duke.

"You, too, Miles."

Toby wagged his tail but held true to his training and didn't try to smell the other dog as they followed Miles through the entryway and second set of doors.

They rounded the barricade blocking the entry from the escaping people and stopped in the lobby where the crowd dwindled to a trickle as the remaining visitors exited.

"I'm glad the sergeant called the Phoenix K-9 agency to bring you in, too." Miles's green eyes pulsed with his characteristic insatiable energy. "Nick is out with an injury."

"Oh, no." Heavy blow to the MPD Bomb Unit, losing the K-9 star of their most experienced detection team. "Is it bad?"

"Just a sprain. Training injury. I'm glad we have backup now with your new partner." Miles grinned at Toby.

"Me, too." Relief washed through her. Maybe Miles understood why she had left MPD's bomb squad to join the private K-9 security and detection agency owned by Phoenix Gray. "So what have we got here?"

Miles dropped his smile. "I was told the threat indicated an intention to blow up the dam, so there could be one or more devices anywhere in the building. Or in the dam itself."

Nerves twisted her insides. She'd hoped the target was the new visitor center, not the actual dam. She swallowed hard. "Wouldn't that cause flooding?"

"Probably. The safety supervisor for the dam is supposed to meet us—"

"That's me." The masculine voice with a hint of roughness singed her ears. It couldn't be…

"Sorry to be late."

She turned to see the source of the voice.

"I was overseeing the evac…" Remington Jones stood six feet away, his sentence dying off as his gaze locked on her face. He'd grown a closely trimmed beard and his golden brown hair was longer on top, but there was no change in those un-mistakable chocolate brown eyes or the grin that slowly curved his mouth. "Bristol Bachmann."

The sound of her name on his lips stirred her nervous stomach as though fish decided to take a swim in the tension pooling there.

"You know each other?" Miles cut in like a life preserver.

"Very well." Rem gave her a too-familiar grin, as if they were still dating and she hadn't learned his true character.

She tightened her abs, forcing away her silly schoolgirl flut-ters. She may have fallen for him six years ago, but she never made the same mistake twice. Apparently, she needed to make that clear. "*You're* in charge of dam safety?" A pointed blow that was supposed to shoot down his grin.

"Surprises me, too." He didn't miss a beat and kept the smile.

They didn't have time for Remington's immaturity or his unreliability. "Officer Miles and I need to search the structure with our K-9s immediately."

"Right." The grin finally disappeared. "I can escort one of you past our security into the dam's interior."

"You take the interior." Miles repositioned Duke's leash in his hands as he looked at Bristol. "We'll get the upper level. If we don't find anything, we'll switch."

Officer Hank Stevens and a young-looking officer Bristol hadn't seen before entered the building and hurried to them, carrying duffels that held their explosive ordnance disposal suits.

Bristol nodded at her former Bomb Unit partner, probably the best technician on MPD's squad.

"Bachmann." Stevens's long face appeared even longer thanks to his dour expression. Evidently, Miles was the only one with no hard feelings. "We'll wait here, centrally for the two K-9 teams, and you can send a runner to get us if you find an explosive device." Stevens aimed the directive at Miles, but Bristol assumed she was to follow the same procedure.

Unfortunately, they couldn't phone or radio, which would be faster. But they couldn't risk the radio signals with a bomb possibly nearby.

"I'll take Craig as my runner." Miles nodded to an officer Bristol recognized who was guiding a few people toward the exit.

"I can be Bristol's runner, since I'm going with her, anyway." Remington's tone held too much eagerness for her taste.

Bristol opened her mouth to protest, then shut it. They didn't have time to waste.

Miles turned away, giving Duke his signal to search.

Bristol met Remington's gaze head-on, stifling any reaction to those eyes by reminding herself who they belonged to. "Which direction?"

A flicker of something she didn't recognize sparked in his gaze, then disappeared. "This way." He set a quick pace to a windowless steel door off the lobby as Toby and Bristol followed on his heels. He swiped a pass card through a magnetic reader on the door and opened it. "After you." He held out his hand in a gallant gesture like he used to when he would open her car door for her on their way to dinner or after a day of training at the police academy.

She steeled herself against his charm. "Toby, seek." She brushed past Remington, focusing on her dog and the job at hand. Lives were at stake. Especially with the dam involved. Her throat started to close as she followed Toby up the narrow hallway. If the dam was breached, how big would the flood be? How many lives—

No. This was not an out of control situation she couldn't do anything about. She was here with Toby, in time. They were ready for this. They would find that bomb and disarm it before it could go off.

Remington's rough-edged voice found her as her courage returned. He was saying something she didn't catch.

"What?" She didn't look back as she watched Toby carefully, though the hallway was empty of anything visible.

"I said it's strange meeting again like this. I didn't expect to see you when I went into work today."

She bit back asking if he'd expected a bomb threat, which was all he should be thinking about right now. He obviously still didn't take things seriously when he should. She paused by the closed door at the end of the hallway that boasted another magnetic card reader.

Remington came close to her in the small space to slide his pass card through.

She resisted the urge to back up, keeping her gaze locked on the reader instead of giving in to the ridiculous desire to look at him.

He swung the door open. "I can't believe you're here, doing this kind of work." A wave of damp, musty air flooded her nostrils from the next room as he turned to face her with his eyebrows lifted.

"Why? I'm not the one who got kicked out of the police academy."

Toby pulled Bristol through the doorway, providing an easy excuse to leave the silenced Remington behind.

Even in Rem's wildest dreams, he never would have thought a bomb would bring Bristol Bachmann back into his life. He had been pretty sure he'd never see her again, no matter how much he wished otherwise.

He followed her fast descent down the stairs into the mechanical room, her black Lab easily traversing the narrow, almost ladderlike stairs. How could she suddenly be here, at one of the dams in his charge?

And did she have to be exactly the same as he remembered? She still told it like it was, no matter how much it hurt to hear. Her swinging ponytail revealed she still had the same long, wavy brown hair with hints of mahogany, though he couldn't see the highlights of color in the murky belly of the dam. That adorable hint of a cleft still nestled in her chin, and her gray-blue eyes drew him in like a magnetic storm cloud.

A cloud that had unloaded on him the last time he'd seen her. The memory of her fury rained on his mental walk down memory lane. He had deserved no less then, but right now he didn't need her to remind him of his past failures. He lamented those every day as it was. He had enough of a burden to carry today, dealing with a bomb threat on Minnesota's most famous dam, which happened to be in the heart of Minneapolis.

He rolled his shoulders and shifted his gaze to her dog as he mentally reviewed the evacuation procedures, double-checking he'd done everything he could to get all visitors and staff safely out. *Lord, please let this be a hoax. Let there not be any bomb so no one will get hurt.*

The dog—Toby, he thought she'd called him—drew Rem's attention with his ecstatic movements. His floppy ears stayed hiked above his forehead as he smelled along the walls, crevices, around pipes—wherever Bristol directed him to search with her hand, pointing and touching specific items.

Bristol walked quickly to keep up with the fast-moving dog. Energy rippled off Toby, while Bristol was a study in quiet concentration. She had worn that same expression at the academy in classes, drills and during exams, when Rem had watched her instead of doing his work.

It was the look that said no one and nothing was going to distract her from her mission. Even him.

She was so driven. So sure of what she wanted to do with her life. Like his dad. A born cop. Born hero.

"Keep looking for something unusual." Her voice halted his thoughts. She was actually looking at him. For a second. Then she switched her gaze back to her dog as they moved toward the junction box along the dam's north wall. "You'll know it better by sight here than I would. Look up at the walls especially. Toby will have a harder time scenting the explosives if they're a distance up."

Rem did as she said, not noticing anything out of the ordinary on the dark, damp walls, other than a few surface cracks he already knew about.

"What would happen if a bomb detonated here? How badly would it damage the dam?"

"Depends on where it is." The possible grim scenarios running through his head had him silently praying again. *If this is real, please help us find it in time.* "If it's close enough to the dam structure to cause a breach, it certainly wouldn't be good, given how high the river is right now with the snow runoff and spring rains. We're nearly at record-high water levels."

He glanced her direction in time to catch her watching him before she turned away. Her ivory-toned skin looked paler in the shadows of the dimly lit mechanical room, but that couldn't be a reaction to what he'd just said. She'd always had nerves of steel and more guts than most of the guys in training at the academy. Maybe she shared his uncertainty this time. "I'm praying we'll find the bomb in time or it will turn out to be a hoax."

She threw him a glance, eyebrows raised. Because he'd mentioned prayer or she didn't think it was a hoax? She turned away to climb the short metal staircase that led to a raised platform along the wall.

He stayed at the base of the stairs, looking up to watch as concern cinched his throat tighter. The longer they took, the more likely a bomb would go off if there was one. "I'm leaning toward a hoax myself." He forced a confident tone, hoping she might agree with him and he could relax. "This dam has pretty decent security and safety procedures in place. An unauthorized person would have a tough time getting inside to plant a bomb."

He stepped away from the stairs to check behind the boiler where Toby had already searched, hoping what he said was right. This dam hadn't implemented all the security measures he'd suggested, but he hoped what they did have in place had been enough.

"I wasn't told anything about the caller." Her voice floated down as she returned to the stairs. "But such threats do often end up being false alarms."

"I hope you're right." Despite the confidence he'd tried to fake, the feeling he'd gotten from the phone call said otherwise. Maybe she needed to know that. He drifted back toward her as she reached the bottom with Toby. "The guy sounded pretty serious, though."

"You spoke to the caller?" Those blue-gray eyes turned on him for a second, then disappeared as she turned to head for the closed door that led to the hydropower room.

"Not exactly. I only said, 'Hello,' and then listened."

"But he called you?"

"No." Rem rubbed a hand against the back of his neck. "He called this dam and asked to speak to the person in charge. I was here for a safety meeting, so someone forwarded the call to me."

"I see. This room is clear." She paused at the unlocked door and opened it.

He reached above her to hold the door while she went through with Toby into the much louder, larger space that housed hydropower turbines.

"What did the caller say?" She threw the question over her shoulder as Toby pulled her toward the nearest turbine.

Rem extended his stride to keep up. "He said he wanted to unleash the river from its shackles, to let it be free and natural again."

"An environmental terrorist."

He barely caught what she'd said as she signaled to Toby to search around the base of the huge turbine. "Sounded like it. Sometimes they don't want to hurt anyone, but just want to get attention, right? I'm hoping that's all the guy has in mind and he isn't really a bomber."

"You always were optimistic." Like with their relationship, her sardonic tone implied.

She continued without looking his way for a reaction. "I was told the threat didn't indicate the location of the device at this dam or number and type. Did you tell Dispatch everything when you called?"

As if he would've held information back. Rem pushed his fingers through his hair, reining in irritation. It was his fault her opinion of him was so low. "He only said he was going to start his mission with the Minnesota Falls Dam by blowing it out of the river they never should have tried to hold back."

She glanced at him as Toby led them to the next turbine. "Is that word for word?"

"Pretty much." He'd scribbled down the exact words as soon as he'd realized it was a bomb threat.

"So he didn't say anything about a bomb specifically?"

"No." Just what was she getting at? That he'd called the police for no reason? "The police seemed to think it qualified as a bomb threat when I called them."

"Yes, it does. I just hoped he might have given us more to go on, even if unintentionally."

His irritation cooled as he let her get ahead, disappearing around the turbine with Toby. Why was he being so sensitive?

The answer followed easily enough. Because it was Bristol. And it stung, way down deep, to be reminded of how much he'd damaged her trust in him.

"Jones!" Her shout broke through the machinery noise.

He lurched into a run around the curved turbine wall, stopped when he saw Bristol.

Toby sat in front of her by the turbine, his front paw lifted in the air.

Rem's gut twisted with the deduction he didn't want to believe.

Bristol met his gaze. "Toby's found the bomb."

Chapter Two

Bristol's heart rate held steady and calm as she stared at the improvised explosive device, nestled in the corner where the turbine's giant supporting limb met its outer shell. The device appeared to be homemade, pretty simple. Probably built by the environmental terrorist himself.

Low-tech could be worse—more unstable and unpredictable.

An exposed timer counted down from ten minutes, thirty-six seconds.

"Good boy, Toby." She pulled his tennis ball rope toy from her fanny pack and let the dog tug on his reward. But her fingers itched to get to work disarming the device.

She looked at Rem, who stared at the IED with a mix of fascination and alarm in his widened eyes. "Get Stevens, fast. The timer says we have ten minutes, but it might be inaccurate."

He turned his attention to her. "I'll stay behind and show them where it is. You should leave, get to safety."

Was he kidding her right now? Bad time to feign responsibility. "I worked on the bomb squad for two years, and I can disarm the device myself if I have to." She kept her fanny pack stocked with her basic explosive ordnance disposal tools, just in case.

He stared at her, an unreadable expression on his face.

"You're wasting time."

"Right." He turned away, then looked back. "Please be careful."

"Go!" Her shout spurred him into action, and he took off at a faster clip than she'd expected, his sprint athletic and easy. Good. He should reach Stevens with enough time for the bomb tech to get down here and disarm the device.

She let Toby have his toy, and he lay down to chew on it as she approached the IED. She squatted to see it better.

This was going to be the tough part of working at Phoenix K-9, a private agency, instead of with the MPD Bomb Unit. Because they weren't law enforcement, she and the three other women who worked for Phoenix Gray had more flexibility and freedom from regulations in some ways, but when it came to bombs, she could only search for and locate them now. She wasn't authorized to disarm them.

She rose and spun toward Toby. "Bring it here, Toby. Time to clear the rest of this room."

He popped up at her voice and trotted over with the toy, which he dropped into her hand. She stuffed the wet rope and ball into her pack. "Toby, seek."

They quickly searched the remaining two turbines while Bristol's mind fixated on the device. At least an explosion in the hydropower room instead of closer to the actual dam should mean the river wouldn't run out of control. Or would it? She should've asked Remington. Anxiety fluttered in her belly again.

If the dam remained intact, there would be no flooding. She brought Toby back to the IED, releasing him from search mode as she crouched to check the timer.

Six minutes, fifty-four seconds.

She reached for the zipper to the pocket of her fanny pack that held wire cutters. There would not be a flood. Not on her watch.

She moved her hand away and stood, letting out a long breath. She could disarm the device in less than five minutes if she had to. She'd seen enough to know that. This situation was under control.

The unsettled swirl in her stomach dissipated as she shoved aside images of rising waters and instead focused on the IED, her strategy for disarming it. If Stevens didn't show soon…

A noise drew her away from the turbine to where she could see the door. Toby followed, brushing against her leg.

The door opened and Remington charged through, Stevens and the young officer following behind him in their green bomb suits.

They covered the ground quickly, no robot with them. Remington must've conveyed the time constraint.

And she knew Stevens. He'd take contact ops over the robot any chance he got. Maybe that was where she'd learned the same approach.

Stevens gave Bristol a nod as they came close, his clear face mask pushed up onto the thick, black helmet. "Show me where the device is, and you can go." His tone carried the clear inference that she would have to leave.

She showed him the IED with as few words as possible, aware he'd want to assess the device on his own and disarm it his way.

Remington met her gaze as she turned from Stevens and the other tech.

"We need to go now." She resisted a lingering glance at the device as she and Toby followed Remington out of the hydropower area and back through the darker mechanical room.

She mentally rehearsed the steps Stevens might be taking to disarm the IED, hoping he did it correctly. But she'd learned from him, so of course he would. Didn't make her like the feeling of leaving the job in someone else's hands, though.

"Must be weird for you." Remington's voice startled her as he headed up the skeleton stairs that led to the exit.

She trailed after him with Toby, surprise infiltrating her Remington Jones defenses. He couldn't possibly be talking about the same thing she was thinking. He couldn't read her that well.

"You're probably used to disarming the bombs yourself."

She lifted her head as she reached the top of the stairs, meeting Remington's perceptive gaze. An uncomfortable warmth seeped into her chest as he watched her. "We should go."

He looked away to open the door, which he held for her to pass through.

She ignored his proximity as she brushed past and hurried up the narrow hallway they'd been through before. She opened the next door before Remington could beat her to it.

The bright lighting of the visitor complex stung her eyes as she scanned the area for Miles, checking the empty entryway nearby on her left as well as the lobby to her right.

She didn't have to look back to feel Remington's presence as he stepped away from the door behind her. "You can go ahead outside where it's safe. I'm going to look for Miles and Duke, see if they need help clearing the rest of the building."

Remington came up beside her. "I want to check to make sure everyone's been evacuated."

At least the man wasn't a coward. Then again, he'd always leaned more toward foolish risks than safety.

"Fine."

They drifted apart as they walked farther from the entry-way, in the direction of the stores and restaurants lining the wide—

A boom shook the air.

Her breath halted.

But the sound had been muffled, distant. As if outside the building.

"What was that?" Remington froze, stared at her.

"A bomb." She took off for the entryway, Toby kicking into a run with her. Had the bomber planted another device somewhere else?

Remington pushed through the glass doors beside her, emerging into the cool outdoor air at the same time.

She searched the sky. Nothing to the south. She looked north.

A cloud—billowing in gray, tan and black—marred the overcast sky in the distance.

"Dear Lord, no."

She barely heard Remington's whisper as horror exploded in her chest.

Rem watched Bristol's hands clutch the wheel as she drove them to the Leavell Dam in Whitlow Heights where the second bomb had reportedly detonated.

Her knuckles whitened while her voice grew tighter. "Are you there yet?" She'd been talking on a Bluetooth earpiece to someone named Cora for the past five minutes.

She'd mentioned victims, the search for survivors.

Every word fell like a blow on his searing conscience. *Please, God, don't let anyone have been hurt. And please don't let it be my fault.*

Probably the fifth time he'd prayed that in the last few

minutes. What if it was his fault? The thought sliced into his gut. Clearly, his safety and security measures that he'd led the dams in the state to follow hadn't been enough. They'd broken down. But how?

Leavell Dam was a tricky one. It was so open to the public, thanks to its location in Whitlow Heights Regional Park. Far from being blocked off and secure, there was a popular pedestrian walkway across the length of the dam that connected to the park's well-used trails.

The weather was finally warm enough—only the second week of temps in the fifties—that the walkway could have been extremely busy. He prayed it wasn't so. That no one had been there.

He'd taken the call from the bomber—had he missed something?

The bomber hadn't said anything to indicate a second bomb or dam. Rem was sure.

He pulled from his pocket the scrap of paper where he'd scrawled the bomber's threat. No, nothing that suggested—

A jingling ringtone punctured his thought process. His phone. He pulled it out and checked the caller ID.

Calvin Bestrafen.

He stifled a groan at the sight of his resentful coworker's name. Just what he needed at a time like this. But under the circumstances, he'd better answer.

"What happened?" Calvin barked in Rem's ear.

"I don't know. I'm headed to Leavell now."

"You better find out fast or this will be the end of your brief career. You might even end up in court."

"I have to go, Calvin." Rem punched the end button, cutting off more of Calvin's angry threats.

Silence reigned in the Jeep.

He glanced at Bristol, who had discarded her earpiece and apparently ended her call.

"Who were you talking to?" Her voice held a suspicious edge.

No doubt it didn't help he'd needed to bum a ride from her. She likely thought he was his old self—still too irresponsible to save enough money for a car. Probably didn't believe his car was in the shop.

He cleared his throat. "A coworker." He looked out the windshield as she took the exit for Whitlow Heights. "Who were you talking to?"

"The same."

He turned to gauge if she meant that as combatively as her tone indicated.

Her face had turned as white as her knuckles.

He'd never seen her like this. She looked either sick or... scared. Couldn't blame her. He felt nauseated himself. He wanted to ask about the survivors and victims she'd mentioned on her call, but his throat closed.

He turned his head to check the dog in the back instead. The Lab sat in a large wire crate, panting heavily, though Bristol kept the interior frigid with air-conditioning, never mind the outdoor temp was only fifty-six. "Why aren't you and your dog with the police?"

She stared out the windshield without even a twitch in response.

"I figured you for a career cop. Never thought you'd leave the force."

She still squeezed her fingers on the wheel. Maybe he shouldn't press, but she needed something to distract her from the stress that was clearly getting to her.

"Or did the bomb squad change your mi—"

"This isn't exactly the time for catching up." She pinned him with a glare. "And if it was, I wouldn't want to."

Ouch. But he deserved no less. "You're right. This isn't the time for small talk. I just wondered how someone like you couldn't cut it on the force. If *you* couldn't do it, there's no hope for anybody."

Color infused her cheeks with hot anger that flashed in her eyes. "I excelled as a cop with MPD for five years. Leaving was my choice."

That was the Bristol he remembered. A beautiful firecracker... who had once let him come close without getting burned.

"You're in charge of dam safety and security, right?"

His stomach tightened. "Yes."

"Then what happened?" Same question Calvin had screeched at him. But somehow her softer tone packed more of a punch.

"I don't know."

"This should've been prevented." She glanced his way before mercifully giving the road the full force of her accusatory glare. "Don't you have security measures in place to stop terrorists from getting inside the dams?"

"Of course we do. I revamped our security measures with my predecessor before he retired. The new regulations include terrorist attack prevention."

"Well, they didn't work."

The understatement of the year pressed on his chest.

"Stuff like this shouldn't happen." Her voice took on a huskier tone, thick with the remorse that started filling his insides.

"No, it shouldn't." He nearly choked on the words. *God, forgive me if it is my fault. Please.*

He felt her gaze on him, and he turned his head to catch the surprise registering in those amazing eyes—the color of the sky in the transition that happened just before a storm, a shift from blue to charcoal.

She looked away. "There were people on the dam when it exploded." Pain thickened her voice even more.

The same pain tore through his chest. "Who told you?"

"Cora Isaksson. She works at Phoenix K-9 Security and Detection. My boss, Phoenix Gray, is coordinating the search and rescue efforts." She swallowed, her fingers trembling on the wheel just before she tensed them again.

Was she scared? She'd been a cop for five years. And she'd just insisted on staying with the bomb at the Minnesota Falls Dam when he went for help. She hadn't broken a sweat then. She couldn't be scared now.

But the signs indicated she was.

He was, too. Scared to death of what they'd see when they reached the dam still marked by a pillar of smoke rising above it, like something out of a movie. Or a nightmare.

Chapter Three

Bristol pressed the gas pedal as she drove away from the MPD officer she and Remington had shown their IDs to. She passed a few more parked squad cars before she spotted what she was looking for—the white cargo van with Phoenix K-9 Security and Detection emblazoned on the side.

As she headed toward the vehicle, Phoenix, Cora and Amalia Pérez came into view, standing behind the van as they pulled on backpacks and adjusted their dogs' harnesses.

Bristol swung her Jeep past the van to park in the empty spot next to it, along the edge of the hill that appeared to plunge at the border of the gravel lot.

"God, please, no." Remington's anguished words made her blood freeze. He looked out the passenger window.

She couldn't see past him, but her clenched chest wouldn't let her breathe until she saw what he meant.

She shoved open her door and dropped to the ground, jogged around the front of the Jeep as Remington got out on his side.

The sight at the edge of the hill slammed into her like an aftershock, the devastation buckling her knees.

The Leavell Dam, which had crossed the Mississippi River, was now a pile of concrete rubble that waters rushed over as if on an unstoppable mission of death and destruction.

Realization mixed with fear as she pushed her gaze farther and saw how much the water had flooded beyond the dam, overflowing its normal banks and leaving trees in standing water that looked at least two feet high.

How severe had the initial flood been when the dam had exploded? Toppled trees and debris carried far away from the dam gave her a terrifying answer. Her stomach lurched as memories from the worst day of her life threatened to wash over her with the same force of death as the river below.

She forced herself to assess the situation in front of her. Rescuers and emergency workers, some in dive suits, worked their way down to the destruction. Spots of color dotted the rubble above the rushing water in the river. Were those people?

Bile surged up her throat. This couldn't be happening. Not here.

A scream pierced her ears.

The terror of memory crashed in.

Her mother's screams, stinging Bristol's ears as the water from Hurricane Katrina filled her second-floor bedroom.

Water splashing against her chin.

Her hand slipping from Mom's as she tried to follow her out the window.

"Bris?" Riana's voice, the sweet call she thought she heard from somewhere across the water that was drowning the world as far as her eyes could see.

A touch on her shoulder. "Bris, are you okay?"

Bristol turned to look, her gaze falling on the delicate features and pale complexion of Cora.

Not her sister.

Cora's bright blue eyes lit with compassion as she gently rubbed Bristol's upper arm, tendrils of her light blond hair reaching down from her updo to brush her snow-white cheeks.

Her golden retriever, Jana, matched the sweet demeanor of her partner, sitting at Cora's side and looking up at Bristol with soft, dark eyes.

No, Bristol wasn't okay. This shouldn't have happened. It could have, should have, been prevented.

She swung her attention to Remington, ready to let loose her surging anger.

He stood ten feet away, still staring at the destruction. His features contorted with pain.

Her heart squeezed. Did he know someone who'd been at the dam?

"We've got people to find." Phoenix's strong voice prompted Bristol to turn to see her boss standing with Dag, her sandy-colored shepherd mix, at the hood of the Jeep.

Phoenix's honey brown hair was swept back in a ponytail under a charcoal baseball cap, the brim hiding even more than usual of the unreadable expression that neutralized her symmetrical features. "Get Toby and let's head out."

Cora gave Bristol's arm a gentle squeeze that matched the empathy in her eyes.

Bristol took in a breath. "Right." She moved to open the Jeep and release Toby. She couldn't let her past get in the way. There might be survivors she could find, she could save. She wouldn't think about the high waters, the flooding. Or the memories that threatened to paralyze her.

This wasn't New Orleans and Hurricane Katrina. This was a preventable act of a violent person. And she'd do everything in her power to make sure he didn't claim any more victims.

★ ★ ★

The ringtone called to him in the nightmare. Rem pulled out his cell from the pocket of his khakis on autopilot, turning his head in time to watch Bristol walk away with her dog and the other Phoenix K-9 women. "Hello?"

"Remington." The relief in his mother's voice flowed over his pain. "Are you all right? Are you hurt? We heard about the dam on the news."

"Yeah." The word came out as a croak. "I mean… I'm not hurt. But…" He turned to look at the rushing waters below, the patches of color he desperately wanted to believe weren't people—bodies—caught in the debris. "I think people were killed."

"Oh, sweetie." Emotion thickened her gentle tone. "I'm so sorry. I'm so glad you weren't hurt. We both are. Your father was worried, too."

A different kind of pain pinched his chest. "Nice try, Mom." He knew what his dad was thinking. That Rem had failed again. So much for earning his father's respect, or even getting him to acknowledge Rem's existence. But at the moment, his dad's blame couldn't worsen the remorse ripping him apart from the inside.

"Sorry, Mom. I have to go. I need to see if I can help."

"Okay. Be careful. I love you."

"Love you, too." He stuffed the phone in his pocket and turned away from the horrific view.

"Remington Jones?"

He glanced toward the source of the voice, a petite woman in a dark jacket and pants marching his way with a winner-takes-all expression.

She flipped open a wallet to flash an FBI badge as she stopped in front of him, somehow effectively blocking his path with the disproportionate magnitude of her attitude. "Special

Agent Katherine Nguyen. I need to talk to you about what happened and how to contain the situation. We need to know how long it will take for the floodwaters to recede and details of potential hazards with the remaining structure."

"How bad is the damage beneath the surface?"

"Extensive. There's no portion of the dam that can be accessed anymore. What remains of the underwater portion has been completely crushed and flooded."

Rem's heart plummeted. He'd hoped the damage was less than it appeared. "What happened to the two men working at the dam?"

"Rem!" A man jogged toward them, hand lifted in a fixed wave.

Joe. Hope surged in Rem's chest. If one dam operator had survived, maybe they both—

Joe Millington crashed into him with a hug.

Rem returned the embrace, blinking as the usually stoic man caught a sob on his shoulder.

Agent Nguyen watched them without a word.

"I just came back from lunch." Joe pulled away, wiping at wet tracks that coursed through dirt on his cheeks. "I brought a sandwich…for Tom." He broke down again, sobs racking his thick torso.

Rem put his hand on Joe's shoulder, tears moistening his own eyes. *Please, God, help us.* He waited until Joe's sobs subsided, then swallowed back the lump clogging his throat. "What happened, Joe?"

Joe wiped his dirty shirtsleeve across his nose. Looked away. "It just blew up. It was all gone. In a second."

The next question threatened to choke him, but Rem had to get it out. "Were there people on or near the walkway?"

Joe met his gaze with watery brown eyes. "Maybe twenty, thirty. Not sure." He sniffed. "I saw the explosion, but it knocked me over. When I got up, I saw that." He nodded toward the view off the edge of the hill. "Except the water was higher. Biggest wave I've ever seen. Dragged everyone away. Screaming." Joe stared at a fixed point somewhere in the distance. Or at nothing. He looked like he was in shock.

"Have the EMTs checked you out?"

He didn't move.

"Joe?"

"Huh?" He looked at Rem, his eyes clearing. "Yeah, sure. I'm good." His work-roughened skin crinkled on his forehead. "What happened?"

Rem glanced at Agent Nguyen, who stood still as a stone and offered just as much help with her unmoved expression.

He met Joe's waiting gaze. "We received a bomb threat. But not for this dam." Despite the truth of his words, guilt crawled up his throat. "I didn't know." But could he have prevented it somehow? Like Bristol had said?

"We have to go now." Agent Nguyen took two steps toward them, effectively backing Joe away.

"Go?" Rem wasn't leaving. He needed to stay, do what he could to help.

"I need to take you offsite where we can talk."

"Why? I don't know anything. Nothing helpful."

"You talked to the caller with the threat, Mr. Jones. You may know more than you think."

Joe trudged away, going toward the taped-off perimeter. People pushed at the boundary, shouting, asking about names, probably family members or friends in the park. Maybe the people on the dam when it had exploded.

He shook his head. "I have to stay here and help. I can look for survivors."

Agent Nguyen put her small hands on her hips, her almost-black eyes narrowing. "The first responders and the Phoenix

K-9 team are taking care of that. You can do the most good now by telling our task force everything you know while it's fresh in your mind. And giving us intel on what we're dealing with underneath all that rubble."

Rem pushed his fingers through his hair. "That can wait." He looked at the crowd, the worry and grief on their faces. "If you won't let me search, I can at least try to comfort the families, make sure they're being informed."

Tom Elliot's wife. He should call her. Rem pulled out his phone. Unless she was already here.

He walked toward the people clamoring for information behind the tape. He scanned their faces, half-afraid he'd see Tom's wife there. What if he was partially responsible for making her a widow?

A tight grip on his elbow stopped him. "You need to come with me, Mr. Jones." Agent Nguyen's tone held a steely edge.

He met her unblinking stare. "My place is here."

She glanced at the crowd, then lightened her grip and expression. She jerked her head to the side, suggesting, rather than demanding, he should move away with her.

She dropped her hand and let him make the choice to follow her a few feet back.

He stopped in front of her and leaned his head down to catch her quieter words.

"We need to know which dam is going to go up next."

The idea hit Rem as hard as if she'd punched him. "Another one? You mean there's another bomb?"

She glanced to the side, as if checking to make sure he hadn't been overheard. "There certainly could be. If not today, soon. Unless we can stop the bomber." She stared up at him, not releasing his gaze. "You are one of our only leads at the moment who might give us a clue. We need your help."

Rem nodded and numbly followed the agent to a black

sedan with one emergency light on top. Dread curdled in his stomach as he tried to grasp the possibility that the horror had only begun.

The sloshing sound of water against Bristol's galoshes and the touch of raindrops on her cheeks played with her mind.

Houses with water up to their roofs appeared in front of her eyes.

Then she blinked away the memory and saw the trees and plants of Whitlow Park, buried under only six inches or so of water this far from the river.

Toby panted in front of her, leading the way and air-scenting with undaunted excitement. Concern for what his paws could hit under the water occupied one part of her divided attention. But Phoenix had said no booties because they would get waterlogged. She was right.

It didn't stop worry from stealing half the air from Bristol's lungs. Or maybe it wasn't worry.

"Bris!" Her sister's desperate cry pierced her ears.

Dad tried to pull Riana from the car as the waters poured in and over it.

The images she'd later imagined were as real as if Bristol had been with her father and sister instead of waiting on the roof of their house with Mom, clutching loose shingles to keep from sliding off, crying and praying to be saved from the sudden ocean around them. Helpless.

A crackle brought her back to the forest. The radio on her waistband snapped again, then a voice emerged. "Cora to Bristol."

Bristol lifted the radio, which Phoenix had supplied when they realized cell reception was poor in the park. The bag over the radio had collected drops of rainwater that added to the wet coating on Bristol's hand. "Cora, this is Bristol." She hoped Cora couldn't hear the tremor in her words. "Go ahead."

"How are you doing, Bristol?" Cora's soft voice seeped into Bristol's consciousness like a soothing dose of reality.

"Fine." She should be. She was safe, on dry land. Well, land where the waters weren't extremely high. And it was a park—empty forest. Not a residential area where the damage would be far more catastrophic.

"Any sign of victims yet?" Cora and Jana searched nearest to Bristol and Toby in the grid they'd mapped out, but Bristol couldn't see them anymore.

"No." Bristol and Cora were to move away from the river with their K-9s, searching up to a mile out. The initial blast and resulting flood had carried people far and caused damage to the forest. There could have been people on the trails of the park who were impacted. They could be stranded, injured. Or drowned.

Bristol's throat closed.

"Neither have I, thankfully. I'm praying there are few casualties."

Bristol resisted telling Cora her prayers wouldn't change a thing. Their friendship was new, and they had to work together. Cora was free to believe what she wanted and grab whatever comfort worked for her.

"I'll leave you to the search. I lost visual contact with you about ten minutes ago, so don't forget to check in every fifteen minutes."

"Right, thanks. Out." Bristol hooked the radio on the waistband of her jeans and focused on scanning the area. She needed to keep her senses alert, hearing primed, gaze constantly moving, searching for details. But the wet landscape in front of her was too familiar.

Fear started to press on her chest, shortening her breath.

No. She shook her head. This wasn't like the past she fought to keep at bay, the day her world crumbled around her and she couldn't do anything to stop it. This wasn't a natural flood or a storm. This was a bomb. It was isolated, preventable. Controllable. It wouldn't happen again. She would see to that.

But right now her job was to recover the people she could here, today. She needed to keep a grip on her emotions. Stay focused.

Like Toby was, his nose in the air as he scented with energetic concentration, intent on finding survivors. Or victims.

Phoenix had found two survivors and radioed the news to Cora and Bristol a half hour ago from the opposite side of the river. The two adults had burns from the explosion, and one had crushed ribs.

But they were alive. Which meant survival of the blast was possible. The longer it took to find the other people, though, the less likely they would be to have the same positive results.

Bristol wiped at the water dripping down her forehead to her eyes. Her cold, rain-soaked hand didn't help. She could've put up the hood housed in the zippered collar of her windbreaker, but she knew the fabric over her ears would hinder her ability to hear survivors if they called out. She'd have welcomed the extra warmth since the temperature had dropped with the rain.

Toby splashed in the water, picking up speed and pulling at the leash. He'd caught a scent.

She let out the slack of the long line, and Toby catapulted to the end of the twenty feet. She hurried as quickly as she could behind him, slowed by the awkward overshoes and water.

Her heart pounded as she scrambled over a downed tree, barely avoiding the snare of branches. She pushed past thick brush, raindrops pelting her face.

Toby barked and pulled against the line. But she didn't

dare let him go. He'd disappear too quickly with his youthful speed and enthusiasm. Phoenix, the one who had trained Toby and all the agency K-9s, had said he couldn't be trusted that much yet.

Bristol pushed herself faster, water splashing her thighs and windbreaker as her feet slapped through to the ground.

Adrenaline pumped through her veins. They could have their first rescue—a person saved thanks to Toby and their teamwork together.

A sound reached her amid the wind noise, manufactured by her fast clip.

Crying?

Her heart lurched, limiting the oxygen she needed to keep up her pace.

She peered through rain and branches in the direction Toby ran.

Nothing but trees, some leaning on each other to stay partially upright.

But she was as sure it was crying as when she'd heard the boy that morning at Minnesota Falls.

Toby sped even faster, and Bristol made a choice Phoenix probably wouldn't approve. She let him loose.

She sprinted to keep him in sight, almost losing him behind some trees.

Then she spotted his wagging black tail. He'd stopped by a large tree that still stood erect.

Something caught her eye a few feet from the foot of the thick trunk. Pink. Clothing?

A person.

Bristol panted, trying to catch her breath as she slowed, nearing the person.

A woman, wearing a pink jacket, lay facedown in the standing water.

Bristol hurried to her and rolled the woman over.

Dark eyes stared lifelessly up at Bristol. The woman looked to be in her thirties. Lacerations marked her face and hands. Her hair and clothing clung to her slim frame, soaked.

Her face was pale, lips blue, skin cold. Bristol knew even as she felt for a pulse that there wouldn't be one. The woman was dead.

A whimpering sound, nearly drowned by the pounding of rain, drifted to Bristol.

Chapter Four

Toby pranced at the base of the tree, looking up.

Bristol stopped her fruitless search for a pulse and sloshed over. She peered into the branches.

A girl of about six or seven perched in the tree, clinging to the thick branch she rested on as she sobbed.

"It's okay, sweetie. You just stay where you are, and I'll come get you." Bristol bent to quickly pet Toby and tell him he was a good boy. Finding a child would be a better reward than a toy for the kid-loving Lab.

"Mommy... Mommy." The girl's trembling cry cut Bristol to the quick.

The woman must have been the girl's mother. Anger heated Bristol's cold limbs as she slipped her arms out from the straps of her backpack. This shouldn't have happened. If only she'd known about the second bomb. They could've found it in time. Avoided all this tragedy.

She yanked the radio off her waistband and called Phoenix.

"Good work, Bristol. I'll send the rescue team to your location." Phoenix's deep voice shot through the radio with the same commanding confidence she conveyed in person. "Stay put until they arrive, then continue your search."

"How's Toby holding up?" Cora's gentle voice contrasted with Phoenix's like sunlight after night. "Does he need a break?"

Bristol looked at Toby, who stared earnestly at the child in the tree as if trying to figure out a way to climb up and get her himself. "No, he's holding up fine."

"Do you need help getting the child down?" Phoenix's transmission crackled, an unfamiliar voice saying something in the background.

"No, I've got it."

"Good. Rescue team is on its way. Radio when they arrive or if you need help."

"Got it. Out." She returned the radio to her waistband and crouched by her backpack to unzip it. She pulled out a coil of red climbing rope and stepped closer to the tree. With the nearest rock climbing over an hour away, she hadn't packed carabiners or climbing harnesses. She looked for a branch to start up, but the closest one poised out of her reach.

The deceased woman appeared to be about Bristol's height. How had she gotten the girl up so high?

"I want my mommy!" The girl delivered the shout with a loud cry. She shifted her legs on the branch.

"No, no. Hold still, sweetie." Bristol held up a hand toward the girl. "What's your name? Can you tell me your name?"

The girl sniffed. "Megan."

"Megan. That's a pretty name." Bristol stepped around the tree trunk, and a white patch about a foot up from the standing water caught her gaze. A branch had apparently broken off, likely in the initial rush of higher floodwater. The girl's mother must have used the limb to step on to reach the branch where she had put her daughter.

Had a wave hit the tree, swept the branch out from under her, and she'd fallen to her death? Her open eyes suggested she'd hit her head immediately when she fell. Probably drowned in the water after that, or the blow had already killed her.

"I'm just looking for a way up the tree, and then I'll get you down. Okay, Megan?" Bristol stepped around the curve of the trunk and spotted a branch within easier reach of a tossed rope. "Okay, I'll be on my way up in a few seconds. Don't move, Megan."

She quickly looped the rope and chucked it over the limb, hitting the mark the first time. She slackened the rope enough so the loop swung within her reach, threaded the end of the rope through and cinched the loop tight around the branch.

Her wet palms wouldn't be much use on the rope. She dug in her backpack, hoping she hadn't removed the winter gloves she'd used in the recent cold weather. She puffed out a breath as her fingers closed on them. Climbing gloves they were not, but the light grips sewn to the palms would be better than her slick hands.

She tugged the gloves onto her wet skin, then gripped the rope and started to climb.

Toby barked from below as she made progress, her arm muscles straining under the unfamiliar need to heft her entire body weight.

Her biceps started to burn as she neared the branch. She reached up with one hand and managed to plant her palm on top of the limb. *Hold on.* Willing her muscles not to relax, she took a deep breath and in one motion released the rope and clapped her other hand over the branch.

Her arms screaming, she swung her body side to side, then used the momentum to throw her legs on top of the branch.

Toby barked more rapidly as she climbed up.

She straddled the thick limb, pausing for a second to catch her breath. "Toby, enough."

He stopped vocalizing and wagged his whole body with broad sweeps of his tail as he grinned up at Bristol.

She looked higher for another branch, spotting one almost level with the limb the girl sat on. She stretched to heft herself onto it.

"Megan." Bristol mustered a smile for the terrified girl who stared at her mother below as she trembled. "Megan, I need you to look at me."

She lifted her head, dark eyes leaking tears down reddened cheeks.

Bristol couldn't risk joining the girl on the same branch. Their combined weight would probably be too much. And Megan didn't seem coherent enough to manage tying a rope around her own waist. "I need you to reach for me, okay? Reach out your arms, sweetie."

Reach for me, honey. The man's voice echoed in Bristol's memory, bringing the image of his hands and arms, reaching from the boat she was supposed to get into without falling into the rising water that had swallowed her world.

She blinked away the memory, the fear, the terror.

Megan leaned out, tilting toward Bristol.

She caught the girl, swung her against her chest. "Good job." She spoke the words into the girl's wet, strawberry hair. "Hang on tight. I'm going to get us down."

Bristol guided the girl's arms to wrap around her torso. "Ready?"

A whimper against her neck was the only answer Bristol was going to get.

"Hold on to me." She started down, carefully retracing her route up the tree. When she reached the lowest branch, she pulled up the slack of the rope still tied to the limb. She tied the rope around Megan's waist and started lowering her.

"Mommy!" The girl squirmed as she neared the water-covered ground.

"Megan, wait. Hold on to the rope." The rope burned Bristol's hands through her gloves as she slowly let it out by inches.

"No! Mommy!" She started to kick, throwing her body in a swinging motion.

Bristol gritted her teeth and held tight, the burn sharp against her palms.

"Mommy!" Megan kicked again, reaching and flapping with her arms. She threw her whole body toward her mother.

The force yanked the rope and ripped a glove off Bristol's hand.

Her heart jumped to her throat as she lunged to catch the rope, Megan dropping.

The girl hit the ground, splashing forward onto her knees in the water.

Toby was instantly at her side, and Megan grabbed the dog's neck to stand more quickly.

Bristol breathed again. The girl was okay.

Climbing down from the tree as fast as she could, Bristol caught up with Megan at her mother's side, the red rope still tied around the girl's waist.

"Mommy!" She threw herself on the woman, trying to hug her. She pulled back, staring at her mother's face. "Mommy?"

Bristol dropped to her knees next to Megan, ignoring the inches of water that soaked through her jeans. "Megan, sweetie." She could barely push out the whisper. "She's…" How could she say it?

They're gone. Both of them.

Her own mother's broken announcement tore through Bristol.

"Mommy!" The scream ripped from Megan's lips.

Bristol reached to take her in her arms, but the girl pushed away, crying, screaming.

Megan laid her head on her mother's chest, the girl's small frame quaking with sobs.

The same sobs Bristol had cried as she'd pushed away her mother, who'd tried to hold her, tried to explain, to console. But there was no explanation, no consolation, that could stop the pain. She'd never see Dad or Riana again, and there was nothing she could do to change that.

Toby gently licked the girl's cheek, then lay down beside her, heedless of the water.

Sorrow pelted Bristol with every cold raindrop that hit her face. This wasn't supposed to happen here. She was supposed to be safe from this kind of horror in this place.

But a terrible premonition, shuddering through her body, told her no one would be safe for some time.

Chapter Five

Rem shifted in his chair, a restlessness tickling his ribs as Agent Nguyen talked to someone on her cell phone, her straight black hair brushing the shoulders of her white shirt while she paced along a wall covered with a large projection screen. It seemed wrong to sit here at the Minneapolis FBI office when people needed to be found and rescued. But the agents and cops at the meeting had assured him that others more qualified than Rem had that effort under control.

At least no more bombs had gone off. Yet.

All area dams had been immediately warned and the staff at each, along with the MPD Bomb Unit, were searching their premises. No more explosives found so far.

Agent Nguyen lowered her phone and scanned the task force that occupied the conference room. Some of them stood, taking messages and calls on their phones, and a few sat at the long table in the center of the room along with Rem.

Agent Nguyen had told him who they all were, or at least which branches of law enforcement they represented, as they'd assembled earlier in the day. An MPD police lieutenant and a sergeant, a Homeland Security agent and three FBI agents besides Agent Nguyen.

The odd ones out were Calvin Bestrafen, brought in as the Department of Natural Resources chief civil engineer to consult on the damage of the Leavell Dam, and Franklin Mason, head of the Minnesota DNR Waters team. The presence of their boss seemed to be taming Calvin's more vocal criticisms, though the engineer took every opportunity to send Rem judgmental glares across the table between them.

"As of yet the lab doesn't have any leads from the bomb the Phoenix K-9 team found." Agent Nguyen's commanding tone called the attention of the distracted task force. "No fingerprints and nothing obviously unique about the materials used to build it. Common homegrown components anyone might have access to."

A woman shorter than Agent Nguyen entered the room and handed the agent a slip of paper.

She read it in one second or less and started in on Rem again. "Let's review the call one more time." She'd said *one more time* the last four times.

Rem bit back his irritation. The exhaustion of the day and being at this chaotic center of activity, not allowed to do anything, for over six hours was getting to him. But if it helped find the bomber, he'd repeat what he knew a hundred times.

"You said the caller blocked the phone's caller ID, correct?"

"Yes." Rem leaned forward, resting his elbows on the smooth table.

"Was the voice a man's or a woman's?"

He had to keep himself from shaking his head at the way Agent Nguyen rephrased the same questions every time, as if he hadn't already told her the facts. Was she trying to catch him in a lie? "Like I said, I think it was a man because of the low register, but it's impossible to be sure because he—the person—used a voice changer."

Rem's cell phone, which he'd taken from his pocket and set on the table, dinged.

"Check that. Could be important."

Her assumption he needed her permission rubbed against his raw nerves. He'd already looked at every other text from the dams without getting her okay first. He let out a breath as he read the text from Brady, an operator at the Crownover Dam. He needed to chill before he said something he'd regret.

Crownover Dam searched, top to bottom. K-9 didn't find anything.

Rem lifted his gaze to Agent Nguyen, who watched him, too much like a predator with prey for his taste. "Crownover Dam is clear."

She jerked a nod. "I'd like you to tell me what the caller said, as precisely as you can."

Again, something they'd already asked him several times, and she held the paper—the computer printout of his statement— that proved it. Maybe she simply wanted to see if he'd remember more or something different. Or she was trying to catch him in a slip. Pretty clear Agent Nguyen didn't trust him.

But a good law enforcement agent didn't trust anyone until proven otherwise. He knew that. Needed to stop taking this so personally and do his best to help. He took a calming breath. "After I said, 'Hello,' the caller said, 'Libertas is here. The time has come to unleash the river from its shackles, to let it be free and natural once again. This is the mission of Libertas. I will begin my great mission today at the Minnesota Falls Dam. I will blow it out of the river they never should have tried to hold back. Nature must be free.'" Rem fingered his watch as he rested his wrist on the table. "Then he hung up before I could say anything else."

"Okay." Agent Nguyen looked at her team again. "Anything pop out at anyone from that?"

"Environmental terrorist." The Homeland Security agent moved his thin lips up and down as if chewing on his thoughts.

"Or someone who wants us to think he's an environmental terrorist." An FBI agent with her hair in a knot so tight it seemed to be stretching her skin back clipped out the words while looking at her phone.

"Good." Agent Nguyen nodded, apparently unoffended that everyone else was barely looking at her.

"The press is asking for a statement." The knotted-hair agent glanced up from her phone, where she must be getting messages, too. "It's strongly suggested you give them one within the half hour."

"Then give me something to say, people. I don't want to go out there with no one and nothing." Agent Nguyen stalked to the chair opposite Rem, pulled it out and sat down, pinning him with a dark-eyed stare. "We have to find out who this guy is and what he's up to before he can strike again, Mr. Jones. Who do you think this bomber is?"

He blinked. "How would I know?"

"I thought you might have some idea from the fact the bomber accessed both dams, undetected." A hint of accusation laced her tone and infused her gaze.

Just doing her job. Nothing personal. He breathed again to curb his natural defensive reaction.

"I'm wondering that, too." Calvin.

Rem glanced away from his interrogator to see his co-worker's smirk.

"How exactly did this happen—" Calvin leaned over his

elbows on the table "—given your new safety plan you forced on everyone the moment you took over?"

Agent Nguyen observed their interaction closely, like a behaviorist documenting animals fighting in the wild.

"The safety plan wasn't all my own. The former safety and security supervisor had already formulated a good portion of it when he brought me in to help." Rem looked at Franklin for support.

His gaze met Rem's through thin-rimmed glasses. He shifted. "It's true." His already quiet voice came out even softer than normal, but Rem couldn't blame him. This was an intimidating setting, to say the least. "Graham Middleton, Remington's predecessor, worked on the new security plan for a long time, and Remington did all he could to implement it." His mouth turned down as if he'd eaten something sour. "It was a sound plan."

Not an impressive speech, but at least Rem had one supporter present.

Movement at the door caught his attention and sparked hope he'd be saved from more interrogation by the distraction.

A woman with long blond hair under a baseball cap, the one he'd seen with a tan dog at the explosion site, entered the room.

"Phoenix, good." Agent Nguyen rose from the chair with the first smile he'd seen from her.

Someone followed Phoenix.

Bristol.

His heart tripped.

She'd let down her hair and it fell onto her shoulders in strands clumped together, darkened close to black, as if it had gotten wet and maybe still was. She looked tired, a frown shaping her full lips, and her skin pale. But her natural beauty still took his breath away.

Seemed he wasn't the only one who noticed the loveliness of the new arrivals. The men at the table perked up, and those standing quickly moved to take chairs as Bristol and Phoenix sat at the far end.

The women's outdoor clothing, streaked with mud and still wet, bore evidence of what they'd been through. As did their grim expressions.

He watched as Bristol took in the room and its occupants. Her gaze found his, her blue-gray eyes sending a surge of awareness through him. She looked away quickly, but not before he saw the aching sadness in her eyes.

His heart squeezed. What had happened out there?

"Thanks for coming in. Everyone—" Agent Nguyen raised her voice slightly "—this is Phoenix Gray, founder of the Phoenix K-9 Security and Detection Agency. Several of the agency's K-9s double as search and rescue dogs, so she's coordinating the search efforts. With her is Bristol Bachmann, the handler of the K-9 who found the bomber's first device at Minnesota Falls."

Agent Nguyen swung her attention back to Phoenix. "How did the search go?"

"We ran our dogs until dark." Phoenix answered in a strong tone, surprisingly deep for a woman. "Other volunteers from the state arrived and are covering the overnight shift. My team will start again in the morning."

Agent Nguyen nodded. "Numbers?"

"So far, nineteen survivors, eight dead."

Nausea churned in Rem's stomach, climbing up his throat.

Calvin glared at him, an expression that wouldn't make a dent in Rem's psyche if it wasn't for the sense of guilt already building.

Rem was in charge of making sure the state's dams were safe for the public. He was supposed to ensure this kind of thing didn't happen. He'd failed. And this failure was a whole lot worse than getting kicked out of the police academy.

Then again, maybe his selfish lifestyle when he was at the academy had led to all of this. If he hadn't made the stupid choices he had back then, he'd be a cop now instead of the person overseeing dam safety. Someone else would have had this position. Someone who wasn't being punished for his past mistakes.

"Mr. Jones?" Agent Nguyen raised her dark eyebrows. Had she asked him something?

Bristol's gaze was on him, along with everyone else's.

"I asked if you have any records of previous threats made against the dams."

"No."

"You should." Agent Nguyen turned and started walking away.

"There haven't been any threats since I became the safety and security supervisor. Until now."

"I see." She stopped at the head of the table and faced him again. "How long have you been in charge?"

"Eight months."

"We'll have to get a list from you of your personal enemies."

Calvin snorted. "That'll be a long list."

Bristol's gaze swung from Calvin to Rem, like she was deciding who to root for.

As if Rem didn't feel guilty enough, now Agent Nguyen was suggesting the bombing was because of some personal vendetta against him?

"How do you think the bomber got through your security measures at two dams?" Agent Nguyen's question hung in the air like an explosive that would detonate if he touched it.

He swallowed, minimal moisture scratching his dry throat. "I haven't had time to think about it with all the chaos."

The agent's hard stare said he better start thinking about it now.

Bristol watched him, her expression indecipherable.

Frustration rose in his chest. She probably thought he was the same guy he used to be, the guy who cared more about having fun than doing his job well. He moistened his lips. "Only employees have access to that area of the dam."

"So you think it's an employee?" Agent Nguyen kept her uncomfortable attention on him. "Disgruntled employee, perhaps."

"I don't know of anyone who would have a grudge of that magnitude." Except maybe Calvin, but his seemed aimed only at Rem.

"Check your records and get back to me tomorrow."

Rem nodded.

"What types of passes or keys are used to gain access to the dams?" Phoenix peered at him from under the gray baseball cap that cast her eyes in shadow.

"It differs at many of the dams. But all employees at the Minnesota Falls Dam and Leavell have pass cards they run through magnetic readers. They get a fresh set every week."

"Outsourced." A statement, not a question, from Phoenix.

"Yes."

She turned her head toward Agent Nguyen.

The agent nodded. "We'll look at the company." She swung her attention to Rem. "The dams should be using more advanced technology, like thumbprint or retina scanners."

"I know, but it wasn't in the bu—" He stopped himself, glancing at his boss before he finished saying he wasn't given the budget to fund such security measures. Though dam owners should have funded the equipment themselves, few wanted to spend that kind of money when they didn't think it was necessary.

Franklin watched Rem closely, his green eyes cautious behind his glasses.

Rem picked his words carefully. "The dam owners might be willing to cover the cost of security improvements now."

"As if that will fix the problem." Calvin glared. "You shouldn't blame others for your own deficiency."

"I wasn't trying to pass blame." Why did Rem's gaze automatically go to Bristol when trying to defend himself? "I was only explaining why more technologically advanced security measures weren't already being used."

A loud throat-clearing brought everyone's attention to Franklin. "The DNR is in a complicated position with these dams." He gripped the earpiece of his glasses to shift them up. "Some are privately owned, and others are owned and operated by the Army Corps of Engineers. We have certain safety requirements that must be met, but the details of security and some safety measures are left to the dam owners to either follow or disregard, as they see fit."

Thank the Lord that Franklin was there to back up Rem.

"I see." Agent Nguyen's focus held on Franklin for the moment. "As I speak to the dam owners, I'll advise them to consult with Phoenix on implementing tighter security measures."

"I'll be in contact with all area dam owners, as well." Rem spoke before he thought through the consequence of drawing attention to himself again. "I'll emphasize the need for specific security measures and changes, and I can help them with those."

Agent Nguyen skipped her gaze from him to Phoenix and Bristol. "Along those lines, we're contracting Phoenix K-9 Security and Detection to provide services for the dams until we can catch the bomber."

Agent Nguyen scanned the faces of her team. "Their K-9s

and experience make them an asset and will free us up to focus on this investigation with all the manpower we have."

"Exactly what kind of services are you talking about?" Calvin gave her the suspicious look he usually reserved for Rem.

The agent leveled Calvin with a hard stare that nearly brought a smile to Rem's face. "The Phoenix K-9 agency currently has seven working dogs handled by an experienced team of five agents. They specialize in protection and security, narcotics and explosives detection, search and rescue, and water rescue for the Twin Cities and surrounding areas. Their cooperation with law enforcement has proved invaluable in the past, so I've asked Phoenix and her team to patrol the Minnesota Falls Dam with their protection K-9s. The bomber tried to damage it today and failed, thanks to Ms. Bachmann and her K-9."

Agent Nguyen removed her heated gaze from Calvin to nod toward Bristol. "But we can guess he'll try again. Hundreds of visitors are there every day, and it's centrally located downtown. Collateral damage of an attack would be high. I want it guarded 24/7. I'll verify the dam also adds additional security and MPD will swing by frequently. But we're all short-staffed, as always."

"We're bringing in our wardens from other sectors to add a greater security presence at the dams overnight." Calvin smiled as if the idea had been his instead of Rem's.

Agent Nguyen's hands went to her hips. "Since MPD's bomb squad cleared the remaining dams, the additional security should be enough to keep the bomber from planting explosives tonight. But we're not taking anything for granted."

She shifted her focus to Bristol. "MPD's bomb squad will search the dams for explosives daily, as they're available, but they only have one K-9 team at present. And they could get called away if there are threats elsewhere. So, Ms. Bachmann, we need you and your K-9 to perform daily searches at all the dams in the Twin Cities area. Under the supervision of Mr. Jones."

Bristol swung her gaze to Rem, her eyes widening. She glanced at Phoenix, whose placid expression didn't falter.

Rem's pulse thumped as warmth heated his torso. He and Bristol would work together? See each other every day?

A dash of color infused Bristol's cheeks, and she turned back to Agent Nguyen. "I don't need any supervision." The sharp edge to her tone broadcasted her displeasure.

"Since you're a civilian, you'll need Mr. Jones for access to the dams and secured areas within them."

Bristol's jaw clenched as her face turned a deeper shade of pink.

"You'll have to start tomorrow."

"What about the search for survivors?" Her big eyes held a glint of desperation as she looked at Phoenix the way a child looked at her mother when begging to escape a punishment.

The anticipation firing his belly cooled a bit.

"We've got it covered." Phoenix's answer was just what Rem wanted to hear, but the disappointment that sagged Bristol's shoulders added a sting. "We have three other K-9s for search and rescue, but only one bomb detection K-9. Toby's more needed to make sure there aren't future explosions."

Phoenix switched her attention to Agent Nguyen, seemingly unaware that Bristol obviously disliked her assignment. Or just the thought of doing it with Rem. "We'll start security patrols at the Minnesota Falls Dam tonight."

"I'm sure you two will need to coordinate your schedule for the searches."

Rem had to pull his gaze from Bristol as Agent Nguyen spoke to them. Not that Bristol was willing to look at him, anyway.

"You're both free to leave and do that now." Agent Nguyen's tone indicated she was finished with them. "Phoenix, would you stay?"

"Of course." Phoenix leaned toward Bristol and whispered something to her.

Bristol's frown deepened as she shoved her chair back and got to her feet in one quick motion.

Rem stood and hustled to catch up. He had the feeling she might run off if given the chance. Like she had the last time he'd seen her. When he thought he would never see her again.

What a miserable situation. Bristol kept her gaze pinned to her phone's screen as she heard Remington exit the FBI conference room and join her in the hallway. The text from her grandmother blurred as she seethed over Agent Nguyen's unexpected plan. Phoenix clearly hadn't been surprised, but she didn't know Remington like Bristol did.

Proactively searching for explosives made sense. Needing to do it with Remington Jones did not.

"So what time would you be ready to start tomorrow?"

"Probably a lot earlier than you." The words came out quicker and with more bite than she'd intended. Though she was only stating the truth. Partying most nights and showing up late in the mornings had been his pattern at the academy until she'd pushed him to be more responsible.

"How about seven-thirty?"

She was almost certain she heard a smile in his voice, but she refused to look to confirm it.

"Fine." She rapidly typed an answer to her grandmother's worried text. I'm safe. I'll stop by on my way home.

"I'm starving, and I'm guessing you haven't had a chance to eat yet, either. Want to finish this conversation over dinner?"

Surprise popped her gaze to his. A jolt shot through her

chest at the impact of his warm eyes. Exactly what she was afraid of. That and the way her pulse skipped at the smile that curved his mouth.

His beard and the hair he kept pushed off his forehead and collected in a stylish wave had an unfortunate effect. They only enhanced the appeal that had drawn her to him at the academy.

She needed to put the kibosh on her swoony reaction and the interest swimming in his eyes. "I don't think we need to make that mistake again."

The charming smile dropped as his darkening gaze locked on to hers. "Is that what you think we were?"

Her heart stuck in her throat. The heart she'd had to put back together, piece by broken piece, when she learned he wasn't the man she'd thought he was.

He cleared his throat in her silence. "I only meant dinner as professionals, anyway. As partners."

Partners? "We're not partners, and we never will be." Who was he kidding? Irritation heated her limbs, cold under the wet clothes she hadn't had a moment to change out of. She could never be partners with someone so dishonest and unreliable.

"Look—" he stepped closer to her, and her rebellious body heated even more "—I get that you don't want to work with me." He ran his fingers through his tumble of hair.

She'd forgotten how thick his hair was, so—

"You think you can't depend on me."

The accurate admission caught her renegade thoughts short.

"But I've changed. I promise I'm more responsible now." The earnestness in his eyes was new, but she wasn't going to fall for his empty promises again.

I'll take things seriously. One of the many lines he'd fed her at the academy echoed in her mind. *I won't go to another party, and I'll ace the academy. You watch. I can work hard if I'm doing it for you, Bristol. I won't let you down.*

She looked away from the more mature face that threatened to be just as convincing and took a fortifying breath. "Let's not make this about us or our past." She forced her gaze back to his. "We have more important things to deal with. Like a terrorist. We need to get organized." And Remington Jones was certainly not the person for that task.

A hint of humor quirked his lips as he watched her. If he was trying to distract her with that cute smile like he used to, it wasn't going to work.

She met his gaze without a trace of amusement. "The Bomb Unit can search pretty well, but if the bomber manages to get past the security, Miles and I will have the best shot at finding bombs with our K-9s. We need to get the most coverage we can from our two teams. How many dams are at risk?"

Remington crossed his arms over his chest. "I'll have to check with Agent Nguyen, but from her description I'm guessing she's thinking of the five or six located in the more populated areas in the Twin Cities and suburbs."

"We'll need to be more precise than that."

He shrugged. "I'll ask her later."

She knew it. He hadn't changed a bit. "I'm not doing this in your haphazard way. Disorganization and procrastination lead to chaos, which lead to days like today."

His mouth creased into his beard as his lips pinched. "I only meant I've been dismissed along with you from Agent Nguyen's meeting in there." A glint flashed in his eyes. "I have her number, and I can call her. I'll verify the dams she wants us to search and know where we're going by seven-thirty tomorrow morning, on the dot. I'll also contact the bomb squad's K-9 team to set up a rotation between our team and theirs, so we spread the K-9 coverage as much as possible."

She fought the instinct to let her jaw drop at his serious tone and take-charge demeanor. She'd never seen him with anything but a goofy smile and flippant attitude at the academy. Well, except when he'd looked at her and let her see the man she'd thought he could become.

But even a stand-up comedian would be serious on a day like today. Didn't mean he'd changed.

She straightened as she realized what he had said. "I was going to contact Miles. It only makes sense because I worked with him and I have the other K-9 team."

Remington shook his head. "I'm in charge of safety and security. It's my job to make sure that's covered."

A flush of frustration traveled up her neck as she opened her mouth to respond—

"Besides, you'd program every last detail down to the second."

"What's wrong with that?"

"You'd be giving the bomber a nice schedule to follow to know when he could plant a bomb the K-9 unit wouldn't have a chance to find."

She gritted her teeth. He was right.

"This is one time when organized chaos might give us an advantage. And that's my specialty." The corner of his mouth twitched.

Was he laughing at her?

She was right. He hadn't changed at all.

She turned away, exasperated by the flutter in her stomach that evidenced something far more annoying. When it came to Remington Jones, she hadn't changed, either.

Chapter Six

Toby wagged his whole body at Bristol's side as she inserted her key in the front door of her grandmother's house. Bristol pushed open the red-painted door. "It's just me, Grandma." Her call carried through the entry and hallway.

"Didn't you bring my boy?"

Bristol grinned at her grandma's response as she bent to unclip Toby's leash.

He took off, trotting through the first doorway off the hall.

Bristol followed, smiling at the sight of Toby already getting the attention he'd anticipated, his front paws planted on the sofa where Grandma sat as he reached to lick her face.

Grandma laughed, ignoring the lit TV across the room to pet her eager friend. "You're my good boy, aren't you?" Her pitch elevated higher than normal as she baby-talked to Toby. "Are you hungry?"

"He already ate dinner in the Jeep."

She looked at Bristol, her glasses reflecting the light from the lamp in the corner. "A little snack won't hurt him. Put some kibble in his dish."

Still smiling, Bristol walked closer to the sofa. "I will not. He won't be able to help anyone if he gets out of shape."

Toby lowered his feet from the cushion and went to the bed Grandma had bought for him, kept in the corner of the living room. He spun in quick, tight circles three times, then plopped down, resting his head on the bed's bolster with a contented sigh.

Bristol chuckled. "Sometimes I think he likes it better here than at my house."

Fine lines of concern deepened the worn marks of Grandma's familiar face. "Sit down, sugar." She patted the cushion beside her.

A mixture of warmth and tension created an unsettling blend in Bristol's stomach as she sat. Exhaustion tingled through her body, traveling from her head to her toes.

Her attention drifted to the TV, the volume low. Images from a news channel flashed on the screen.

The Leavell Dam explosion.

Bristol's ribs squeezed inward.

The TV went dark.

Grandma set down the remote and rested her hand on Bristol's knee. Her blue-gray eyes looked through her glasses, into Bristol's heart. "I saw you and Toby on the news. You both helped a lot of people today."

Bristol's gaze dropped to her grandmother's hand, the familiar wrinkles and moles, the blue veins that crisscrossed under the soft, pale skin. Bristol swallowed, her throat almost too dry to do it. "Not enough."

Grandma moved her hand in a comforting stroke. "You rescued that little girl. I was so proud when I saw you with the reporter, and the girl with her arms around Toby."

Bristol tilted her head back and looked up at the ceiling

she'd repainted last spring, trying to use gravity to force the tears away from her eyes. "Her mother was already dead when I got there."

Toby's panting filled the silence that hung between them.

Grandma's touch stayed on Bristol's knee. Safe, comforting. Patient.

Bristol lowered her head and turned to Grandma.

She was waiting, her gaze washed with glistening moisture that had yet to fall. "You can't save everyone, sugar."

"But she shouldn't have died." The rising pain in Bristol's chest lit with an angry spark. "This shouldn't have happened. It didn't have to. I could have—" The words choked in her shrinking throat. She swiped at a tear that escaped and raced down her cheek. If only she could wipe away the encroaching memories that easily.

Grandma cupped Bristol's cheek in her hand. "My sweet, sweet girl. I know you want to keep everyone from going through what you did." Her lips lifted in a sad smile. "But you can't save everyone. Only God can. And that's a good thing because He is so loving and merciful."

"Then why doesn't He save everyone? Why doesn't He stop stuff like this from happening?" The sharp questions exploded before Bristol could stop them.

Her grandmother lowered her hand. "Only He knows the answer to that. But I know His reason is good."

His reason was that He was obviously not interested in doing anything with this mess of a world. Just start it and let it go. Like a bomb-maker who enjoyed building things and watching them blow up. Bristol pressed her mouth shut to keep from voicing the thought. Grandma was only trying to provide some comfort.

"I should get going." Bristol glanced at the clock on the wall—8:36. "I have an early start tomorrow."

"Looks like he'd rather stay here." Grandma gazed at Toby.

The dog dangled his head over the side of the bed with his mouth partially open and his eyes closed.

A smile found Bristol's lips at the goofy sight.

"Why don't you stay the night?"

It would be a shorter distance to the DNR office in the morning from Bristol's house. But her depleted body screamed not to get up again. Or maybe it was her mind and emotions that were sapped, leaving her in a mental state that craved comfort.

The comfort of her grandma's wise eyes and soft lavender scent. The comfort of someone who knew and understood. Who hadn't forgotten and moved on as her mother had.

"You look like you're going to go to sleep right here." Grandma patted Bristol's knee. "I insist you stay the night." She used her hand on Bristol for leverage to push off the sofa as she stood. "I'll get your room ready."

Bristol smiled as she followed her grandmother into the hallway. The room was always ready for Bristol's overnight stays, but Grandma had to check it, anyway, as if little house elves appeared to sabotage her housekeeping when she wasn't looking.

The jingle of dog tags signaled Toby had risen, too. He shoved past Bristol as she stepped through the doorway of the blue-toned bedroom.

Grandma leaned over the bed, perfecting the placement of decorative pillows. She cast a critical gaze across the rest of the room. "Your pajamas are in the dresser, of course. Did you bring your bag?"

"It's in the Jeep. I'll run out and get it." The extra set of clothes she always packed in case she got messy in the field would work for tomorrow's outfit. She'd had to stay in her wet clothes so long today that they'd dried on her. "I think I'll take a shower and turn in."

Grandma turned her gaze to Bristol. "Will you search for more survivors tomorrow?"

"No, the FBI agent in charge of the task force contracted us to patrol the Minnesota Falls Dam and me to search for explosives at all the Twin Cities dams."

Grandma shook her head, her halo of white hair undisturbed by the motion. "Sounds like you and Toby will have your work cut out for you." She reached to pet the Lab, who gently brushed against her leg, wagging his tail. "I'll pray for you."

If only that would help.

Grandma's keen gaze went to Bristol's face. "There's something else bothering you."

"Not really." Bristol pushed her fingers into the back pockets of her jeans and watched Toby circle and drop to the carpet next to the bed. She blew out a breath. "They've assigned Remington Jones to go along with us on the searches."

"Now that's a blush I haven't seen in a long time." A smile curved Grandma's closed lips.

Bristol's jaw slackened. "I'm not blushing."

"You always did whenever you talked about him. I've missed that."

"You never met him, Grandma." Thankfully. "Do you remember what happened?"

"I remember you dated while you both attended the police academy. Several months, wasn't it?"

Three and a half months. Such a short time to fall so much in love. Bristol shrugged instead of trying to voice her thoughts around the regret filling her throat. Whether it was regret their relationship had ended or regret she'd let herself get involved with him in the first place she was in no mood to figure out.

"And I remember he made you very happy."

Happy? Bristol's cheeks warmed at the twinkle in Grandma's eyes and the memories that flitted in her mind. The laughter, the fun, the plans they'd made for the life they would have together.

Bristol shoved the distracting thoughts aside. "Did you forget he got expelled for cheating?" That should douse the twinkle.

But it didn't. "Yes, I remember. A real shame." A smile crinkled the wrinkles at the corners of her eyes. "But it sounds like he must have turned his life around if he's in a position to give you security clearance to these dams."

"I wouldn't be so quick to jump to that conclusion. He only managed to get a job as the head of dam safety and security for the Minnesota DNR."

"Impressive."

Bristol tilted her head and lowered an eyebrow at her grandmother's meaningful tone. "Don't go getting any ideas, Grandma. I would never make the mistake of falling for Remington Jones again."

"It's been six years. People can change."

Bristol shook her head. "Not Remington."

Grandma's smile faded. "Because you couldn't change him?"

A twinge punctured her chest. "I guess."

"Sugar—" Grandma touched Bristol's arm "—never underestimate the power of God to change people." Something peculiar glinted in her eyes. As if she had another meaning hidden in that statement.

The traditional ringtone of Bristol's phone sounded from her pocket. She pulled it out and checked the screen.

Cora.

"It's work."

Her grandmother nodded with a gentle smile. "I'll let you talk. I'll leave a sandwich in the kitchen if you're hungry."

"Thanks." Bristol put the phone to her ear as Grandma left the room. "Hey, Cora."

"Hi. How are you doing?"

Bristol took a moment to process the unexpected question and the genuine tone behind it. She should be used to Cora's caring ways by now. In the three months since Bristol joined Phoenix K-9, she'd talked to Cora the most, since she seemed to be the agency's one-member welcoming committee as well as communications manager.

"I'm okay. You?"

"Tired, but sleep will help that. You and Toby must be even more exhausted, after finding the bomb and then the girl."

"Just doing our job, right?"

"Yes. But the job can be very hard sometimes. Especially when we have to see things like the tragedy we witnessed today. It can take a while to recover from something like that."

Had Cora noticed how rattled Bristol had been during the search? How she'd barely kept her raw emotions from overflowing when she'd had to talk to the reporter about the rescue?

The soft understanding in Cora's tone conveyed no judgment, just a sympathetic kindness that made Bristol feel more uncomfortable than if Cora had told her to toughen up.

"I don't mean to call late—" Cora mercifully broke the silence herself "—but someone phoned the office this evening, wanting to talk to you. An Agent Moses from Homeland Security. He said he needs to speak with you tonight."

Bristol stifled a sigh and sat on the patterned white and navy-blue bedspread. "Okay. What's the number?"

Cora gave her the number with a Saint Paul area code.

"Thanks, I'll give him a call."

"I hope it doesn't take too long. Try to get some rest."

"You, too." Bristol ended the call and pushed off the bed as she punched in the digits she'd kept in her mind. She went into the hallway, Toby popping up to catch her.

"Do you have to go out again?" Grandma turned away from the kitchen counter as Bristol passed by, thumb poised over the green call button.

"No. Just getting my bag. I'll be right back." Bristol held the phone to her ear as she stepped out into the dark night.

Clouds shifted over the moon, signaling the rain was only taking a short break before dousing them again.

She headed for her Jeep in the driveway as the phone rang, the sounds of barking dogs and a motorcycle engine reaching her ear away from the cell.

The third ring cut short.

"Hello, Bristol." Why did the man's voice sound so strange?

And how did he know it was her right away? He couldn't have her number yet since he'd called the PK-9 office before. Maybe hers was the only call he was expecting. But that would be even stranger for a Homeland Security agent.

She unlocked the door of the Jeep and pulled it open. "Is this Agent Moses?" She stretched over the driver's seat, letting her foot come off the ground to reach the bag she'd left on the passenger side.

"That's what I told your friend."

A voice modulator. That's why he sounded weird. A tingle shot up her neck as she froze.

"You can call me Libertas."

The statement brought both feet to the ground with a kick to her pulse.

"You stopped my bomb today. That was very wrong of you."

Rage surged to overtake her surprise. "No, it was wrong of *you*. You killed people today."

He chuckled, a sound contorted by the voice changer. "You're clearly on the side of those captors who want to keep the great river constrained and forced to do their bidding. Nature must be free. The river is only the beginning."

Was the guy reading from a cue card? Sounded like a scripted speech. Maybe she could force him to go off-script. "Don't you care that you hurt innocent people? Blowing up the dams does that. People who had nothing to do with putting the dam there in the first place."

"That's the price of the evil that's been done. The river must be freed, no matter the cost."

Her blood heated. "I won't let you hurt any more people. If you want to blow anything up again, you'll have to get through me."

He laughed. "I knew you were my enemy the moment I saw you on TV with your dog. The cute little dog who found my bomb."

TV. The news coverage on the rescue of the girl. That was probably how he'd discovered she was with Phoenix K-9 and knew to call there to get to her.

"I welcome the challenge." His voice firmed. "Nothing can stop my mission. You may have scored a point this time, but I assure you—Libertas will win."

The small bit of noise in the pauses, maybe from wind, stopped.

She looked at her phone.

Call ended.

A crack behind her.

She whirled away from the Jeep.

The dim yard stood empty. The bottom branches of the

thick tree near her could have made the sound by clacking against each other in the wind.

Must have. Bristol pulled out her bag, shut the door and locked the Jeep with the remote, inhaling deeply.

The bomber was trying to get under her skin, but that didn't mean she'd let him. She'd never had a bomber contact her before. A few perps she'd arrested as a cop before the bomb squad, though, had given her the usual threats.

If the bad guys were happy, she wasn't doing her job right. This was good. She reached the front door and went in with a smile that was halfway genuine.

The bomber had made a mistake when he called and singled her out. But he was right about one thing. She was his enemy. And she couldn't wait to take him down.

Chapter Seven

Bristol glanced at her phone on the nightstand as she sat on the edge of the bed. Still no response from Cora, but it had only been about fifteen minutes since Bristol had called to report her contact with the bomber.

Toby rested his head in Bristol's lap, and she stroked his smooth head. "Time to go to sleep, buddy."

He turned away as if on cue and circled a few times before lying next to her feet.

Her mind reviewed the call with the bomber again, analyzing every detail to make sure she hadn't missed any clues. They had the phone number he'd given, but it was almost certain to be from a burner phone. And with the voice modulator, she couldn't ID him.

He hadn't used a voice changer with Cora, apparently realizing she would detect he was a fraud if he did. But Cora had never heard his voice before and there was nothing distinctive about it that could lead to identification.

Her phone's screen lit up on the nightstand. Phoenix.

Bristol grabbed the cell. "Hi, Phoenix?"

"Cora told me what happened." Phoenix never did seem to waste time on pleasantries. "How sure are you it was the bomber?"

Bristol could almost feel her boss's piercing gaze through the phone. "Can't be positive. Could be someone who just wants attention after seeing everything on the news. But the wording he used in this call and the name matches what he supposedly said to Remington Jones earlier." She grabbed the pad off the nightstand where she'd written down the bomber's words while they were still fresh. She read her notes to Phoenix, then waited.

"Sounds like the real perp. Could you identify anything about the voice?"

"I think male, though it's hard to be sure. He used a voice changer again."

"I'll relay the info to Katherine. She's working around the clock with the task force. If she wants to talk to you, I'll have her go through me."

Handy that Phoenix apparently had a close friendship with Agent Nguyen. Bristol resisted asking Phoenix how that had come about. The woman wasn't just a closed book—she was sealed shut and covered in a shroud of mystery that Bristol had the impression no one was allowed to disturb.

"I don't like that he singled you out and threatened you."

"It wasn't exactly a threat."

A pause. Just long enough to make Bristol question what she'd been thinking in contradicting her boss so overtly.

"I'd like to loan you Apollo until we know what's going on."

Phoenix's Doberman protection dog? Bristol didn't think Phoenix ever parted with her dogs even for one night. But she couldn't imagine explaining the big Doberman to Grandma, especially when it wasn't necessary. "I'm actually at my grandmother's house for the night. I'll be fine."

"You're right, he'll likely look for you at your main residence first. But I wouldn't stay with your grandmother for long, either."

Was she implying Grandma could be in danger because Bristol was with her? Worry started to balloon in her chest. "I don't really think the bomber is after me personally. He just wants to blow up dams and free rivers."

"And you're standing in his way." Phoenix's quick answer reversed the calming effect Bristol's reasoning was having.

"Are you trying to scare me?" She tried to inflect the question with a lighthearted tone.

"Denying the danger never helps anyone. You need to take steps to keep you and your loved ones safe."

"Better safe than sorry."

"Exactly."

Wonderful.

"I want you to think about taking Apollo. He'd tolerate Toby if Toby can keep from trying to play with him."

Bristol gave a half-hearted chuckle. "That'd be a trick."

"Then we'll have to get you your own protection dog ASAP."

At least that was a familiar proposal, one Phoenix had mentioned several times since hiring Bristol. According to Cora, Phoenix wanted all the women at the agency to have protection dogs, at least for their homes if not for professional protection work. Phoenix herself had three protection dogs— Dag, Apollo and Birger, a Great Pyrenees she kept for home guarding.

Amalia and Nevaeh Williams had the agency's other two professional protection K-9s. But Cora said she had resisted Phoenix's insistence about needing a protection dog for years because she didn't think she could handle a canine that could become aggressive, whether it was warranted or not. Though Bristol didn't share Cora's concern about handling a protection dog, she didn't see the need for one in her own life. With her training and experience, she could protect herself. She held back telling Phoenix again that she'd rather not have a protection dog.

"But that doesn't help us with tonight." Phoenix moved on without needing a response.

"I have my Glock." Bristol pulled out the drawer of the nightstand where she'd tucked the weapon in its holster.

"Keep it close. Get some sleep."

Bristol's eyes were far too wide open after this conversation to make sleep a possibility. She'd sleep like a baby if it were just her, but Grandma… Maybe Bristol shouldn't have stayed here tonight.

"We'll talk in the morning. If you think anything's off, call me. I'll be there in five with the boys."

Bristol could just picture it—Phoenix busting into Grandma's house with two fierce protection dogs in the middle of the night. The incongruity of the image relieved some of the tension in her muscles. "Got it. Thanks, boss." Amusement made her borrow Nevaeh's favorite name for Phoenix without thinking.

"You know I hate that." A hint of humor filtered through the phone. "Call me in the morning before you head out so I know you're safe."

Bristol paused this time, the precaution catching her off guard. Did Phoenix care about her that much? They hadn't known each other long. About four months since the day Phoenix had asked Bristol to join Phoenix K-9. She hadn't been warm in her approach then, either. Just enticed Bristol to leave the bomb squad by listing a few straightforward advantages— that were exactly what Bristol had wanted. Even when Bristol had said yes a week later, Phoenix hadn't betrayed a bit of emotion.

Bristol kept her questions out of her voice as she answered. "Will do."

"Don't worry, Bristol. We've got your back." Phoenix's firm tone made the statement sound like a promise.

Warmth seeped into Bristol's chest. But she tamped it down as she thanked Phoenix and ended the call.

She lay back on the bed and stared at the ceiling, willing her heart rate to calm. She didn't need anyone's help. Phoenix had to be wrong in her assumption the bomber would get personally violent. Bristol had the situation well under control.

Rem wished he'd skipped the extra doughnut this morning as he knocked on his boss's closed door, his stomach flipping over.

"Come in." Franklin's underwhelming voice still made it through the door.

Rem hesitated a second, then entered.

Though gentle and silent far more often than he spoke, Franklin was still Rem's boss, and being called to his office first thing in the morning was probably not a good sign.

When Rem took the chair opposite the desk, he had a hard time meeting Franklin's gaze. The anxiety churning Rem's belly was uncomfortably reminiscent of the day Sergeant Standish had summoned him to his office at the police academy. That meeting had ended with Rem getting expelled.

But this time, he hadn't cheated or done anything wrong. At least not intentionally. But that truth didn't banish the sense of guilt he'd been carrying around since yesterday. And if he got fired now... The thought nearly choked him. The idea of calling home, telling his mother. What she'd tell Dad. It would seal the nails his father had already put in the coffin of their relationship. Or maybe it would just bury it completely.

Look him in the eye like a man.

His father's familiar admonishment made Rem force himself to face what he had coming and meet his boss's gaze.

A distant expression, though not an unkind one, lurked there. "I understand what happened is not your fault. I want you to know that."

Rem's shoulders dropped as his breathing resumed. Maybe he wasn't getting fired, after all.

"Graham felt confident in your abilities to take over this position, even though you lacked the DNR experience of some other staff members."

Meaning Calvin. Rem's muscles stiffened again. Where was this going?

"I know Graham gave you training and guidance before he retired, and I respected his wishes that you fill this position. However…" Franklin clutched the arms of his chair and shifted his body.

Rem had the feeling this was where the positive effect of his predecessor's favor and mentorship ended.

"After the attack yesterday, we're under a great deal of scrutiny."

Rem nodded. "And pressure." Evidently.

The lines of Franklin's face relaxed slightly as he looked at Rem. "Yes, a lot of pressure. We need to publicly appear that we're making changes in response to this incident that will prevent such a thing from happening again. Do you understand?"

Rem opened his mouth to respond, but Franklin continued, leaning forward and bracing his arms on his desk.

"It's crucial that we regain the public's confidence in us and the safety of the remaining dams as soon as possible." Franklin watched Rem, as if his actual meaning was completely clear.

Rem bit the bullet. "Are you saying you're letting me go?"

"No, no." Franklin pushed off the desk, waving his hand back and forth in the air even though his cheeks reddened. "No, I don't want to do that."

But that was clearly what Franklin was being pressured to do. Was the pressure coming from Calvin or the public? What if Calvin was saying things to Franklin or others behind Rem's back to make him appear as the best scapegoat for the bombing disaster?

"You've done a good job so far, and you have a lot of fresh ideas."

Rem tried to unclench his fists and focus on Franklin's words instead of Calvin and possible sabotage. God was in control here. Rem needed to trust Him.

"I know how hard it is to get all of the dam owners to follow what you're asking them to do. But given what happened, I'm going to keep suggesting that we give you a chance to implement reforms. You need to overhaul our safety and security measures to ensure this never happens again." Franklin's goldfish-like lips opened and shut, then opened again. "If no more incidents occur and I can show positive reforms are being made, and if I can swing the public our way, then no heads will need to roll. If you'll pardon the expression." He attempted a weak smile.

A lot of *ifs* in that semipromise. "How long do I have?"

Franklin pointed at Rem with another try at a good-humored smile. "That's what I've always liked about you. You don't beat around the bush." He glanced upward as if the answer to Rem's fate were scribbled on the ceiling of the DNR office building. "I'd say two weeks. Give or take."

Give or take how much? Frustration demanded he voice the

question, but Rem knew there was no point in asking. Franklin was shooting in the dark with the estimate—all based on public opinion, Calvin and an unidentified bomber.

Rem pushed out of the chair and swung toward the door.

"Rem."

He stopped, turned halfway back.

The fake smile was gone, replaced by a worried furrow crunching Franklin's brow as he removed his glasses. "No more incidents. I'm counting on you."

Rem nodded, but the truth gripped him with a warning. Unless the bomber was caught soon, preventing another incident—another bombing—might be entirely out of Rem's control.

Bristol pulled into the parking lot of the DNR's small office building, Toby panting with excitement in the back of the Jeep. Probably hoping he was getting out to work here.

The clock on the dash read 7:05. Maybe she could drag Remington out of here early. They could have saved time and met at a dam if Remington would actually get a car of his own and be more organized.

But she didn't expect anything better from him. No doubt he still spent ninety percent of his time goofing off.

The door of the building swung open, and the man of her thoughts stepped through with a wave. He swung a jacket over his shoulder, dangling it from one finger while his long legs made quick work of the distance to her Jeep.

Her stomach fluttered as she took in his blue button-down shirt tucked into belted khakis, emphasizing his broad shoulders and trim hips a little too well. Maybe the eggs she'd had that morning weren't agreeing with her. She clung to that make-believe answer for her stomach's behavior and steeled herself against her usual reaction to him.

He rapped his knuckles on the passenger window with a grin that sent her heart into a cartwheel. "Going to let me in?"

She fumbled for the unlock button as she resisted the urge to give herself a good smack. She was a professional, and he was an ex-boyfriend from her past. So what if he'd broken her heart? She was over him. End of story.

He slid onto the passenger seat, filling the Jeep with a masculine presence and scent of woodsy cologne she didn't remember him wearing before. "Morning, Toby." He lifted his hand in a wave toward the back, where Toby watched him with ears perked and a panting grin.

Bristol's lips tugged upward at the friendly gesture to her partner, but she suppressed the reaction. She couldn't let him get past her defenses again.

Remington angled back toward her and flashed the teasing smile that used to turn her knees to mush. "Thanks for letting me in." His eyes twinkled behind trendy black-framed glasses. He must be taking a day off from contacts like he used to do occasionally. "I figured you'd be here early."

"And I figured you'd still be sleeping." She hid her racing pulse behind the quip and started the engine. The guy even made glasses look incredible. She cleared her throat. "Where are we going?"

"Minnesota Falls first."

She nodded as she turned the Jeep around and headed for the street. At least she could agree with that decision. The Minnesota Falls Dam should be the first priority, though security overnight had hopefully prevented any additional bombs. "What's the schedule for the day? And where are Miles and Duke going to search?"

She caught the amused angle of his mouth as he propped one arm on the door, the rolled-up sleeve of his shirt exposing a muscled forearm.

"There are five dams to cover, and both teams—us and Miles—should be able to search every dam once a day. Each team is assigned a different starting point daily, but we're not going to schedule times or search the dams in any fixed sequence, or the bomber would be able to predict where we'll be and when."

Made sense. But didn't mean she had to like not having more predictability. "Where are we going after Minnesota Falls today?"

He grinned again. "Don't worry, I've got a plan." He tapped his head. "It's all in here."

"I'd prefer it was somewhere safe."

He laughed, a deep sound with a slightly rough quality that was distinctively Remington. And did distinctively odd things to her pulse. "There's the Bristol I know and I—"

Was he going to say *love*? Her heart stopped. Then lurched ahead as a blend of fear and anger rushed through her veins.

She knew without looking that his grin was gone. Could hear his tense breathing. Feel his gaze on her.

"Bristol—"

"Don't."

He dropped his arm from the window. Sighed.

She braced herself for him to turn on the charm, to try to get her to laugh off what he had done like it didn't matter.

"I'm sorry."

Her gaze jumped to Remington's, which was locked on her face. An apology? Hadn't predicted that.

"I know I let you down when I cheated on the tests at the academy." He looked away and shoved his fingers through his hair. "I let a lot of people down."

A residue of the pain she'd felt six years ago sliced her heart. "You didn't just let me down. You betrayed me, my trust. You betrayed the police force and everything it stands for." She squeezed the steering wheel. "You told me you were going to take things more seriously and be someone…" Her throat clogged with the words.

"You could depend on. Bristol, I—"

"They said you cheated on almost every exam. You were doing it the whole time we were dating. Even though you promised me you'd changed. That you were working hard and being responsible. You made a total fool out of me."

"That's never what I meant to do. I loved—"

"Stop." She held up her hand, palm out toward him. "I can't do this right now." She tensed her jaw, letting anger win out over the hurt. "The bomber called me last night."

"What?" Vertical lines appeared at the inner corners of his eyebrows.

"He left a message at Phoenix K-9 yesterday, pretending to be with Homeland Security. I called him back and learned he was the bomber. Or at least he claims to be."

Rem's eyes darkened. He leaned toward her a few inches. "What did he say?"

She jumped her gaze back to the road, away from the intensity she hadn't expected. She managed to get out a brief review of the conversation.

His mouth tightened. "So the bomber knows who you are and now has your phone number?"

"Yes."

"What's the FBI doing about it?"

She moistened her lips and forced a shrug, trying to cover the chaos of her system this man was causing. "Nothing major. Agent Nguyen grilled me over the phone on my way here. I'm sure they'll dissect everything he said, but there's not much else to be done at this point. The number he gave me to call led to a dead end, of course. Probably a burner phone he chucked right away."

Rem pushed his fingers through the wave of hair on top of his head, leaving a tendril falling forward to touch his forehead.

Her fingers flexed with an appalling urge to push the wayward clump back into the styled tousle where it belonged.

"I don't like that the bomber threatened you, that he contacted you personally."

She cleared her throat and watched the road. "It might be a good thing. Maybe I can smoke him out if he keeps trying to engage with me."

"It's not a good thing from where I'm sitting."

She risked a glance. Her gaze collided with his intense one, a protective flash sparking the dark orbs like when he had said he'd walk her to her car from the academy every night, so he knew she was safe. Did he still care about her? Her pulse skittered.

But this was Remington Jones. He'd convinced her once before that he would change for her. That he'd become someone she could rely on in good times and bad. But he couldn't even be responsible enough to graduate from the police academy the honest way. He'd chosen an easy, irresponsible shortcut that ended any chance they'd had at a future together. She would never understand why he had thrown that away.

The Minnesota Falls parking lot appeared on her right, just in time to get her thoughts and emotions back on track.

She nodded toward the visitor center complex as she pulled into the lot. "We have work to do."

She exited the Jeep and got Toby out as rapidly as possible, trying to shake the sadness and hurt that cloaked her heart. If only she could go back to her normal life as it had been yesterday morning. A life in which Remington was a distant memory.

He may be concerned a bomber had her number, but in her educated opinion, Remington Jones was far more dangerous.

Chapter Eight

Clouds gathered in the sky, forming a cluster of gray like a reflection of the worry shadowing Rem's thoughts as he approached the entrance of the Minnesota Falls Dam, Bristol and Toby walking a few feet away.

After Franklin's warning earlier that morning, Rem had buried himself in security procedures and guidelines, racking his brain for ways he could get the dam owners to implement the suggestions he'd already made. He'd thought a little about the weaknesses the bomber might have exploited to gain access and plant his bombs, but if Rem had known about Bristol's conversation with the perp, he would've spent a lot more time solving that problem.

The threat of losing his job dimmed in comparison to the possibility that a man who had killed people was now targeting Bristol.

She stopped by the new security guard posted outside the entry, and Rem waited while she spoke with him briefly. The guard used his radio to report their arrival to the other security personnel as Bristol turned away.

Rem stepped ahead of her to hold the door open for her and Toby.

She didn't look at him as she passed, but Toby did, reaching a wet nose toward Rem's hand.

Rem smiled and petted the dog's head.

Bristol stopped and looked back at Toby pulling toward Rem.

"Oh, maybe I'm not supposed to pet him while he's working?"

Her frown started to curve the opposite direction. Was that humor threatening to break past her guard? "Would you stop if I said no?"

He grinned. "Probably not." He rubbed the sides of Toby's face and ears between his hands as the dog wagged his whole body, eating up the attention.

"Okay, boys. Time to work."

Rem chuckled as he gave Toby one more stroke and straightened. "Yes, ma'am." He made a sweeping gesture toward the lobby. "After you."

He stifled a pitiful sigh as she walked away and told Toby to seek, beginning the search of the spacious lobby.

How was it possible to feel all the same emotions about a woman he hadn't seen in six years? The truth was, though he had let her down and she'd clearly gotten over him, he had never gotten over her. And he'd never forgiven himself for not trying harder to become the man she had wanted him to be. The man he should've been.

Bristol clearly hadn't forgiven him, either.

But God had. Thanks to Jesus, he was a new creation now, freed from his old self.

Didn't mean there weren't consequences. Like the way Bristol felt about him.

There was no going back. He'd have to live with his just punishment for the way he used to be.

He walked toward the Italian restaurant and stopped near the gated entrance as he waited for Bristol to come that way. He slid his hand down his beard.

Even if she didn't like him much, he wouldn't let anyone hurt her. As soon as they were done with their searches today, he'd spend whatever time it took to figure out how the bomber had gotten into the two dams. And to find out who he was.

What she'd said yesterday was right. It shouldn't have happened. He would figure out how it had and hopefully ID the bomber so he could be captured and leave Bristol—

"Hey, Bris." The female voice drew Rem's attention to a slim woman headed for the lobby with what looked like a rottweiler on leash. Her red windbreaker with *Phoenix K-9* on the back answered his question as to who she was.

Bristol turned and greeted her with a smile. A small smile, but still more than Rem had seen since their surprise meeting yesterday.

He pushed his hands into his pockets, avoiding a pity party by sauntering over to the two ladies.

"We've been on about an hour. Nothing weird so far." The woman jerked her head to watch Rem, the movement drawing his attention to her riot of black curls and the three long spirals that hung down to brush the brown skin of her forehead.

"Hi." He smiled.

She didn't smile in return, just switched her gaze to Bristol, then back to Rem.

"Nevaeh—" Bristol shifted a hand toward him "—meet Remington Jones, safety and security supervisor. Remington, this is Nevaeh Williams, protection and security specialist."

"Please call me Rem." He reached out for a handshake, noticing her dog watched his arm carefully. Hopefully not about to take a chunk out of it.

Nevaeh looked him up and down, her full lips frozen in a neutral position. "So you're him." She took his hand in a hard shake that she ended quickly.

He let out a chuckle that probably sounded as awkward as he felt. "I get a feeling that's a bad thing."

She lifted one shoulder. "Depends."

"Can I meet your dog?"

Nevaeh shot a glance at Bristol, whose mouth angled in what he could imagine was the hint of a smile. Maybe.

Nevaeh put her hand on the dog's large head as he stood quietly by her side, staring at Rem. "His name is Alvarez."

"Such a handsome guy." Rem grinned at the powerfully built dog with black and brown markings. "Okay to pet him?"

She shrugged both shoulders this time. "I guess."

He let the dog smell his hand, then scratched him under his chin.

Alvarez swished his tail and leaned his square head into Rem's palm.

"Don't most rottweilers have short tails or no tail?"

Nevaeh frowned. "People dock them. But he's a rottie mix Phoenix rescued from a shelter."

Alvarez licked his hand with a big tongue.

At least the dog liked him. He wasn't doing so well with the ladies today.

"We need to get back to the search." Bristol's abrupt tone suggested she thought he was goofing off again. "Who's covering patrol tonight?"

"Phoenix and Apollo. He should be rested up after getting to nap all day."

"Rested from what?"

Nevaeh's dark eyebrows drew together. "Patrolling your house last night."

Bristol's eyes widened. "Patrolling my house?"

"Yeah. In case the—" she cut another look at Rem like she thought he was a spy of some kind "—you know."

"But I don't—" Bristol flattened her mouth into a straighter line. "Never mind. I'll see you later."

"Yeah."

Rem tried one more smile. "Nice meeting you."

Nevaeh gave Rem a nod before heading for the entryway, probably to patrol outside. A nod was an improvement, anyway.

He turned to face Bristol, but she and Toby already waited by the closed steel gate of the Italian restaurant.

"Let us in?"

Toby pranced around her legs, as excited as Rem remembered his childhood dog getting before a walk.

Rem covered the distance in long strides, pulling a set of keys from his pocket. He quickly found the key for the restaurant and lifted up the gate. He'd leave it open while they were inside, since there weren't a lot of visitors at the dam this early in the morning.

"So much for tightening security." Bristol glanced at the keys in his hand before letting Toby pull her into the restaurant. The seating area was illuminated by morning light that streamed through floor-to-ceiling windows on the far wall, offering a view of the Minnesota Falls.

"They have improved it for access to the dam's galley." A little. Rem needed to push them to accelerate the time frame for the additional security measures he'd recommended.

"That's a relief." She wove between chairs with Toby, the dog sniffing under, on and around every table and piece of furniture.

"So does Toby do the guard stuff, too? He doesn't seem to have the cautious demeanor Nevaeh's dog has."

She chuckled, looking at Toby. "It's called protection work. And no, Toby would welcome any stranger as his new best friend. Phoenix, Amalia and Nevaeh handle all the protection and security jobs."

"But some of them also do search and rescue?"

"Yeah. A number of the PK-9 dogs are dual-purpose, like Toby. He does search and rescue, which we call SAR, along with explosives detection. Cora's golden does narcotics detection and SAR. Amalia covers protection and SAR with her German shepherd and water rescue with her Newfoundland. Phoenix has three working K-9s, including Dag, who's kind of a superdog expert in SAR, human and animal tracking and protection."

Rem let out a whistle. "I didn't know the agency offered so many services. Are the other dogs from shelters, like Alvarez?"

Bristol nodded. "They're all rescued in some way. Phoenix believes in giving dogs a second chance at life, so she finds dogs others don't want that can be trained for this kind of work." She gestured to Toby, who ran his nose along the floor by the wall. "She got Toby from a shelter. He was surrendered because he was destructive and had been returned twice. He probably would've been euthanized, but Phoenix found him and trained him to use all that energy for good."

"Oh, hey, Rem." A man's voice from behind.

Rem turned.

Jackson Haile, a shift manager for the visitor complex, leaned in. "I saw the gate open and thought I better check."

"Hey, Jackson. Good call." Rem gestured to Toby and Bristol, who went behind the bar counter. "We're doing a search."

Lines appeared on Jackson's forehead as his mouth tensed. "Looking for more bombs?"

Rem nodded. "Don't worry. If there are any, Bristol and her dog will find them in time."

"Right." He stared at the skilled team as if waiting for good news.

"So, how's Clare?"

Jackson turned to answer Rem's question, enthusiasm for his newborn daughter chasing away some of the anxious lines.

Rem kept him busy with small talk while Bristol and Toby disappeared into the kitchen area.

Jackson threw glances at the door to the kitchen as they talked. He drifted into silence when Bristol emerged and headed for them.

"Clear in here." Bristol looked at Rem, but he suspected the statement was for Jackson's benefit.

Jackson's tense features relaxed into a half smile. "I guess I'll get back to work. Later, Rem."

"Have a good one, man."

Jackson hurried up the wide hallway, veering off into the children's Discoveryland while Rem and Bristol also left the restaurant.

Rem closed the gate and hurried to catch up with Bristol and Toby.

They set a fast pace, cutting an angle across the hallway to the open souvenir shop. Bristol cast Rem a glance when he reached her side. "I suppose a lot of the staff are nervous."

"Yeah. It will help to see you and Toby here."

"Or make them more nervous." Toby scurried around the corner immediately inside the shop, Bristol and Rem following as the dog sniffed along the row of magnets, key chains and other knickknacks that bore the Minnesota Falls Dam logo.

Bristol's thick ponytail swished against her shoulders as she glanced back at Rem. "Has the task force figured out how the bomber got in yet?"

The very problem he'd been mulling over for the last forty-five minutes. "I don't know, but I had some thoughts when I was drafting new security recommendations this morning."

She cast him another look, this time with her eyebrows lifted in skeptical surprise.

Did she think he never worked at all? Probably. He hadn't at the academy except when she'd pushed him to.

"So, what's your idea?"

At least she wasn't shutting him down. "Could be what your boss was getting at—that the bomber worked at TWR Global where we get our security pass cards, or he pretended to be an employee here. Or maybe paid one off."

They turned to walk in the narrow space between shelves of mugs and chocolates. She didn't say anything, obviously underwhelmed by him borrowing someone else's idea.

He could risk voicing the alternative that had been growing in his mind. "But there is another possibility. One that wouldn't be popular if I brought it up with my boss or it got out to the public."

"Well, Toby's rotten with secrets, but he's not listening at the moment."

Rem stopped in his tracks. Did she just crack a joke with him?

He watched her as she rounded the chest-high row of shelves and headed back toward him in the next section over.

Sure enough, the corner of her mouth tucked just slightly, as if hiding amusement.

Second time in one day she'd joked, actually teased him. Something he thought she'd never do again. Was she softening toward him? Forgiving him? He let loose an answering smile of his own. "As long as Toby's not listening, I guess I can tell you. I'm thinking the bomber could've posed as a civil engineer from the DNR. It wouldn't be too hard to get an authentic-looking ID or duplicate one of our badges. The bomber could've shown up with the ID, claimed to be here for an inspection, and he would've had full access to the turbine room and anywhere else he wanted."

"That's not good." She glanced over the shelves, then turned away to search the other section of the T-shaped store.

Rem trailed after her. "No, it isn't. I've been working to eliminate that weakness since I got this job, but Cal—" He stopped himself before he disparaged Calvin, never mind how satisfying it would be to make him look bad to Bristol. "Certain people within the DNR are fighting me on it."

She sent him a knowing glance, as if she understood what he hadn't said.

He met her gaze, and his pulse thudded with the sensation of their old connection being renewed, like a cord restrung between their hearts.

But she looked away. Then froze.

He traced the direction of her gaze.

A navy-blue backpack lay on the floor next to the bottom shelf of Twin Cities guides and tourist brochures.

She didn't have to tell him what could be inside that pack.

He stepped forward, trying to get between her and the potential bomb.

"Stay back. Toby will tell us if it's for real." She looked at him, her gaze calm and clear. "But you should probably leave."

"Not until you do." His muscles twitched as he watched her move toward the backpack with Toby. Took all his willpower to keep from pulling her back, to let her walk toward something that could kill her. *Help us, Lord.*

Toby smelled the backpack. He sat down beside it and lifted his paw.

The line of Bristol's jaw tightened. "It's real."

Chapter Nine

Bristol stood guard at the suspected device, probably another IED. She tugged the rope toy Toby held in his mouth as she resisted the urge to examine the backpack and see what they were dealing with. She didn't have the authority to do that anymore. Had to wait for the bomb squad, for the minutes to tick by. Hopefully not too many minutes.

If Dickenson or Kennett came this time instead of Stevens, they'd insist on using the robot and probably the mobile X-ray station, wasting too much time if this were another timed detonation. They'd also risk jostling the explosive too much. If it was anything like the bomber's last device, it would be too unstable for handling with a robot.

They would tell her she had no business standing so close to the suspect device, either. But she needed to be within quick reach if the squad took too long or she heard a timer.

Remington reappeared from sounding the alarm and stopped in front of the store's entry. He glanced her way, and she nodded to signal the situation was holding.

Though she stood at the back of the shop, the short shelving units allowed her to observe as Remington waved evacuating people along.

"No need to panic. Just walk to the door as calmly as you can. Thank you." His tone was soothing and solid. He held a smile on his face as he put his hand on the shoulder of a guy dressed in an employee's red polo tee and comforted a panicked woman who asked him what was going on as she passed by.

Contradictory thoughts vied in Bristol's mind as she watched him handle the people. Strange to see Remington Jones take the lead and seem so…dependable. At the academy, he had always wanted to be in charge, but only to challenge rules and do whatever he wanted, not to help people and save lives. But she wasn't surprised he was staying levelheaded in a crisis. He'd always had the skills to be a cop, if only he'd had the responsibility and discipline to go with them.

She drew her gaze and thoughts from Remington and released her grip on Toby's toy so he could lie down and chew on it.

She looked at the backpack, visualizing the device inside. At least there weren't many visitors to evacuate this time, thanks to the early hour.

What was the bomber's intention with this device? Was it planned to go off earlier in the day than last time?

And why plant it in a shop, where it wouldn't likely harm the dam itself if it exploded?

He'd used a backpack this time and hadn't called in a threat first.

Maybe he wasn't going to have a recognizable MO. Maybe he wouldn't follow a predictable pattern.

That would be a nightmare.

But most criminals had some kind of logic, albeit quite skewed, to their actions. Why would he leave a bomb in a public area instead of one meant to destroy the dam? This explosive wouldn't free the river like the bomber had said he wanted.

Unless his professed mission was just a cover for his real desire to destroy lives.

A grim possibility. He'd certainly targeted people in the Leavell bombing. But he could've killed more with explosives here at the Minnesota Falls Visitor Center yesterday.

She stared at the backpack, listening for a timing device she still hadn't been able to hear.

Maybe there wasn't one. Could be a hoax device.

The sound of heavy footsteps entering the store pulled Bristol's attention away from the backpack.

Two technicians wearing full EOD suits headed toward her.

"Bachmann." The lines on Stevens's brow, revealed by his pushed-up face mask, cut deeper than they had yesterday.

Bristol nodded.

The youthful face that stared out from behind the clear mask of the other suit belonged to the same secondary tech. Probably a rookie partnered with Stevens for training, as Bristol had been.

"He alerted?" Stevens looked only at the backpack, but she knew he meant Toby.

"Yes." She stepped to the side with Toby, making room for them to work.

"You know better than to stand that close, Bachmann."

The secondary tech stayed back as Stevens approached the pack.

He kneeled by the suspect explosives, the suit's thick trouser and boot covers positioned to protect him against a blast. "You should leave."

"I'm curious about this one. I'll stick around."

He gave her a hard stare. "You're not in a suit."

"I trust you."

His mouth nearly disappeared in a narrow line. "You were never one to buck the regs, Bachmann. Don't start now."

He had a point. She was slowing him down, though he could've just let her stay.

"Establish the perimeter, will you?" He didn't look up from his work.

She brushed past the rookie, who backed up to stand fifteen feet away, his gaze locked on Stevens.

She stopped another five feet beyond the young officer, then turned around and watched, though her view of all but Stevens's boots was blocked by shelving units.

"Going okay?" The rough whisper sent a tingle down her spine.

She turned her head to see Remington, standing just behind her inside the entrance of the shop. Close enough she could feel his warmth.

"Fine." She kept her voice soft, her gaze on Stevens's boots as she mentally went through the steps she'd have taken to unpack the device. "You shouldn't be here."

"A matter of opinion."

"Is everyone evacuated?"

"Yes."

"There's no detonator." Stevens stood, visible above the shelves as he looked at Bristol. "We're in the clear."

Remington let out an audible breath.

Bristol hurried toward Stevens, her gaze going to the hoax explosive. A white square was attached to the silver pipes. "Is that a note?"

He lifted the loose flap of folded paper with his gloved hand, silent as he studied the contents.

Remington came up beside her, Toby fortunately keeping them at a safe distance with his body between them.

"Looks like it's for you." Stevens glanced at Bristol. He dropped his gaze back down to the note and read, "'Boom. Scared, Bristol? You and your dog will not stop Libertas. Nature must be free.'"

"Are you kidding me?" Anger pinched Remington's voice as he reached for the hoax device.

"Don't touch it." Bristol grabbed his wrist, her heart crashing into her ribs at the sensation of his hot skin under her hand.

He turned toward her, his eyes dark and blazing. "What kind of sick joke is that? To leave a fake bomb at a public place where people can get hurt. And to target you like you're the reason for it. Like it's your fault."

"It's okay." If only her thundering heart would agree and calm down. She released her hold on his wrist. "Toby and I can handle anything this bomber has to dish out." She pushed the hand that had held on to him into her pocket, suddenly unsure what to do with it. "Let's just be glad it wasn't real. Though we can't assume there isn't a real one here or at another dam. This bomber has tried to distract us before."

She looked past Remington to Stevens, who directed the rookie in taking pictures of the hoax device. "Have you heard from Miles?"

Stevens nodded. "We alerted him to the possible device here. He'd cleared the Gellar Dam and was headed for Rocky Falls next."

"Is your other bomb squad team still at the Ceinture Dam?" Remington aimed the question at Stevens. He apparently did have some sort of schedule in his head.

Stevens grunted assent.

"That leaves Crownover as the only dam that hasn't been cleared by the bomb squad or K-9s today so far."

"And the rest of this one." Bristol turned Toby around and headed up the aisle.

"We'll help sweep here after we're done with the device."

She lifted her hand to acknowledge Stevens's remark as she kept moving. The K-9s were faster and more thorough, but she wasn't about to turn down help. They needed to move as quickly as possible now that they knew the bomber had somehow accessed the highest-risk dam. This store was open to visitors, which could mean the bomber had entered as a visitor and hadn't broken into any tightly secured areas.

Remington caught up with her as she exited the shop.

"We'll clear the rest of the visitor floor, then we'll get the galley." She didn't look his way. Couldn't afford the distraction.

Ten minutes into sweeping the main level, he still hadn't said a word, which had to be a record for him. A frown shaped the mouth that creased his beard, and those two vertical lines cut into his forehead by his eyebrows.

She followed Toby as he wound around a children's waterfall and wading pool in the Discoveryland area, trying to shake the odd feeling lodged in her chest. As if she was concerned about Remington. Letting herself feel emotions she shouldn't risk. He was probably just bothered by another explosive being at the dam. Why wouldn't he be?

She was irritated herself. Not her idea of a good time to have a bomber leave a personal letter for her attached to explosives.

She cleared her throat. "They'll have to start searching bags at the entrance before visitors can bring them inside."

Remington took a moment to look at her, as if lost deep in his thoughts. "Yeah. I've recommended that. Metal detectors would be good, too, but I don't know if they'll want to go that far."

"Detectors wouldn't guarantee anything, but it sure couldn't hurt."

He nodded and came to a standstill as she and Toby went

into the corner of the room where Toby had to search large plastic animals apparently intended for children to climb on and through. "Why are you doing this?"

Strange question for him to ask. "What do you mean?"

"Bomb detection. Wasn't being a patrol cop thrilling enough?" He mustered a weak grin.

She bent to point Toby under the shell of a tortoise, curtained by hanging cloth panels.

Toby lowered his body to search the cavern.

"It's not about a thrill. I don't even get an adrenaline high with bomb work. I just want to prevent disasters, keep people from having their lives destroyed."

"So that's why you joined the bomb squad at MPD."

She moved with Toby to the next plastic animal. "As soon as they'd let me. But when I saw Miles and Duke find a bomb before it blew up an office building downtown, I realized I could do even more to prevent disasters if I had a K-9 to find bombs faster and earlier."

"So why didn't you do that with MPD?"

She let Toby follow his nose out of the corner and along the wall. "I wouldn't have had a chance at being on a K-9 team for years if I'd stayed with the squad. But Phoenix contacted me out of the blue one day and asked if I wanted to join her team." Bristol smiled to herself as she remembered her shock that this mysterious woman she'd never met would offer her so much. "And she said she'd give me a detection K-9 if I did."

Toby circled back to the center of the room and looked up at her.

"Good boy." She stroked him under his ears. "This area is clear. Just restrooms left, and then the galley."

She glanced at Remington when he didn't respond.

He watched her with a slight smile curving his lips.

"What?"

"You're amazing."

Heat crept up her neck, headed for her cheeks. She pushed her suddenly wobbly legs to carry her out of Discoveryland.

Remington fell into step beside her. "You're so willing to risk your life to protect others."

She swallowed. "So are you. You stayed to help people evacuate, and you came back to check if the device was disarmed instead of waiting outside."

He shook his head. "That's different."

He fell silent again as they briskly covered the short remainder of the hall.

She shouldn't ask what he meant. But she paused by the doors to the restrooms and made the mistake of glancing his way.

And got caught in that chocolate gaze. Caught by the longing to know this man again. "How is it different?"

"You were there."

Her pulse sprinted.

"I could never leave you in danger."

What about the danger of a broken heart? The rational thought pulled her pulse's race to a halt.

"We're wasting time." She spun on her heel, surprising poor Toby, who hurried to scurry with her into the women's restroom. "Toby, seek."

How could she have let down her guard so quickly? Remington had always known how to get her to ignore her better judgment, melting her resistance with one look from his dark eyes. That's why she'd said yes to going out with him at the academy when she'd known he'd be a distraction, that he wasn't the kind of man she could depend on.

But she had also said yes because she'd thought she could make him into that kind of man. And because he made her feel strong, smart and valued. He made her want to be protected. By him.

The ultimate irony when the man cheated at a police academy. After telling her he was going to change and be responsible.

Biting back a frustrated grunt, she opened the door to a stall for Toby to conduct his search.

Remington Jones couldn't have changed enough for her in six years. Believing that he had would be far riskier than staking her life on a ticking bomb.

Chapter Ten

Maybe Rem should go visit his parents. The brush-off and set-down he'd get from his dad would be what he deserved— what he should've had the guts to face back when he blew everything at the academy.

Rain poured down, finding his head between the beams above as he followed Bristol and Toby across one of the truss bridges of Crownover Lock and Dam. He didn't look beyond the vertical and diagonal posts to admire the view of the river below as he usually would. He didn't have the stomach for beauty at the moment.

Bristol wasn't speaking to him or even looking at him again, and she hadn't for the rest of the search at the Minnesota Falls Dam. She was down to one-syllable answers to his questions.

Just when she'd been warming to him.

He clenched his hand into a fist at his side, glad he'd forgotten his raincoat when they'd left the office that morning. He deserved to get soaked. And she had every right to be mad.

Why had he betrayed her and all he knew she valued?

Why had he thrown away what they had? He'd asked himself the same questions a million times in the six years since he'd cheated and gotten expelled. And the answer was always quick to come.

He'd thought he had no other choice. He'd thought his dad would hate him if he didn't finish the academy and become a cop. Like Dad. Like Grandpa. Like Rem's brother.

Rem had been right about his dad.

But so very wrong about the choices he had made.

Meeting Christ and becoming a Christian had shown him that. Rem knew now that he could choose honesty and integrity, even when doing so might require sacrifice and incur consequences. And he could work hard and respect authority, now that he knew he was actually working for the Lord and under God's authority in everything he did.

But how could he show Bristol he'd changed? That she could rely on him now?

Seeing her again made him want to prove it to her more than anything. The woman was amazing. Smart, skilled, courageous and funny when she let her guard down. Still so gorgeous she could make his heart jump a beat just by looking his way.

And a bomber was targeting her.

The mental reminder drew his attention back to the worry that had been gnawing at his insides since the bomber's note. The terrorist's words made Rem's skin crawl and anger flood his veins at the same time. The guy needed to be caught.

"Remington." Her voice cut through the rain. She stood with Toby at the locked door to the control tower.

He hustled to make up the distance he hadn't realized had grown so much. She'd probably never return to using his nickname like she used to. The sting of the thought added zest to the drops that pelted his cheeks.

She pulled back slightly as he stepped to the door.

He took off his glasses, now blurred from raindrops, pushed them into his pocket and punched a code into the keypad.

He braced himself for a critique of the security system, but she didn't say a word. He glanced at her face, framed under the black hood she'd pulled out of her windbreaker's collar when it first started to rain.

"Is it unlocked?" She met his gaze, but her eyes flashed with irritation.

"Oh, yeah." He pushed the door in and reached to hold it open for her and Toby.

"Look what the whale dragged in." A giggly laugh followed the rib as Harriet Richter peered at him over her computer monitor.

"Just about." He smiled, the action relieving some of the weight on his mind. "How are you doing, Harriet?"

She popped up from her seat behind the long control desk that curved in a half circle back to the wall. Harriet disappeared behind the monitors for a second, then emerged and hit Rem with an air-sucking hug that belied her small size.

She pulled back, gripping his arms to give him a shake, evidently not minding how wet he was. "I've missed you, big guy. Where have you been keeping yourself?" She shifted her green-eyed gaze to Bristol and gave her the same friendly smile. "Don't worry about me, honey." She pointed to the ring on her left hand. "I'm happily married with four kids. But this handsome lug—" she wagged a finger up at Rem from her five-foot-two height "—well, he used to be my friend until he didn't visit for three weeks."

Her long chuckle saved Bristol from having to answer.

Good thing, since she looked as if she'd seen a new planet and didn't know what to make of it.

"I hope you're not insulted if I don't greet you with the

same degree of enthusiasm." Wentworth Felton leaned between two monitors so Rem could see him sitting behind the control desk.

"Hey, Went."

"Rem." He slowly stood, unfolding a skinny body that held together like a tree four inches taller than Rem—a comical contrast to Harriet's short pear, as she liked to call her figure. "Sorry to hear about Leavell." Went's straight lips pressed so thin they nearly disappeared.

Rem nodded, a lump plugging his throat.

Harriet rubbed his arm, giving him a comforting smile like his mother might have.

"What are they doing about it?" Went shoved his glasses back up the bridge of his nose. "I mean, besides sending over the DNR rangers that barely let me in here today."

Rem cleared his throat. "Well, for one, we've got a professional explosives detection team right here." He dramatically swept his hand to Bristol and Toby. At least the glance she shot him looked more surprised than angry now.

"Oh, I know you." Harriet stepped past Rem to stare at Toby. "That's the dog. The one who found that little girl at Whitlow Park."

"And the bomb at Minnesota Falls." Went lightly draped his skinny arms across the monitor in front of him.

"Yes, they did." Rem couldn't help the note of pride that slipped into his voice and broadened his smile. "And now they're conducting searches of all the area dams every day to prevent anything from happening again. Until the bomber is caught."

"Wonderful." Harriet clapped her hands together. "So we'll be seeing you a lot!"

Bristol's eyes widened, but she gave Harriet a small smile. "Us and the K-9 team from the bomb squad."

"Harriet, honestly." Went waved a dismissive hand at his coworker. "Will you let them do their thing before this place blows up?"

"I suppose we better get back to work before Rem reports us." She winked at Rem, then tossed a smile at Bristol. "Wonderful to meet you, honey. If you have any questions, just let me know."

As if they were there for a tour. And as if Harriet would be able to keep from hounding Bristol with questions and chit-chat for more than five minutes.

Rem took the offensive by walking to the control desk and engaging Harriet and Went in conversation while Bristol and Toby searched the tower. The small room didn't take long to clear, and they made their exit with only one more embarrassing comment from Harriet—some inference that Bristol better snatch Rem up before some other girl did.

Only a trickle of rain greeted them as they left the tower, sunlight poking through the receding clouds.

"You certainly know a lot of people." Bristol glanced over her shoulder as she let Toby lead the way across the next bridge. "I mean at these dams. Everyone seems to know you."

He held back a smile at finally hearing her voice directed at him. "Well, I've never liked a desk job, so I try to get out and visit the dams whenever I can." He stretched his stride to catch up, matching her pace at her side.

"You like dams that much?"

He laughed. "No. I like the people who work at them."

"That explains it."

He couldn't read her meaning from her profile. "Explains what?"

"I was surprised to find out you became an engineer."

"Well, after…" He swallowed. No need to bring up the academy again. "I didn't know what I wanted to do for a career. I have an uncle who's an engineer, and he suggested this path. So here I am."

She sent him a skeptical look.

Could she tell he still didn't know what he wanted to do? What his true calling was? He couldn't share his uncertainties and discontentment with Bristol. She already thought he was flaky. He tried for a light tease instead. "Didn't think I was smart enough to be an engineer?"

"Didn't think you'd put in the work for that kind of degree."

He winced inwardly. "I wouldn't have before."

She shrugged, as if trying hard to signal disinterest. "Just an observation." She paused at the stairway that led to the plaza below. "Is this where we go?"

"Yeah." He followed them down, watching Toby's sure-footed navigation of the steps at Bristol's side.

Sunlight and warmer air greeted them as they stepped out onto the plaza. The view of the arch bridge and the rushing sound of water over the dam reminded him of the stunning view to be had at the far end of the plaza. If only they were here for something other than searching for bombs.

He walked closer to the focused team as Bristol directed Toby to smell around the red-painted ship's wheel and the bench beside it.

He followed as they moved on. "If I may be permitted my own observation, you're awfully calm for someone who's just been singled out by a terrorist."

She glanced at him, then focused on Toby. "Comes from being a cop, I guess. You don't expect to win popularity contests."

"I get that. But being targeted by a bomber seems a little outside the norm."

"We'll stop him." She pointed Toby toward the groundcover topping an elevated garden bed that held a tree in its center.

"You and Toby?"

The dog hopped his feet up on the cement wall of the bed and brushed the greenery with his nose as he smelled.

"Sure. Us, Phoenix K-9, the task force. We've got brains and experience on this guy. We'll get him quickly and eliminate the threat."

"I admire your confidence." The image of Leavell yesterday, a flooded mass of destruction and rubble, flashed in his mind. He pushed out a breath. "I know sometimes things don't go as we planned. But that's when I remind myself God is in control."

She paused and looked at him, holding Toby back with the leash. "That helps you?"

"Yes." He met her eyes. "It does."

She turned away, letting Toby have his slack.

Rem's gaze moved ahead of them as he searched for what to say next. Would now be the right time to tell her God was the reason he had changed?

Something dark near the center of the next elevated garden bed caught his eye. He walked closer to the bed and looked hard.

At the trunk of the tree sat a navy-blue backpack.

Chapter Eleven

Bristol kept her gaze locked on the backpack as she approached it with Toby, the groundcover of the elevated garden bed cushioning their steps.

Her mind checked off the possibilities at a calm rate that matched her even breathing. The same style and color of backpack on the same day would be too coincidental to be someone else's. It was likely the bomber's.

Would it contain another hoax device? Or the real thing this time? The one at Minnesota Falls could have been a decoy to distract them from this one. But then why hadn't this device detonated before they got to it?

Toby zeroed in on the backpack, either because of the scent or because it stood out as an odd shape.

Bristol ducked to follow him under the low branches of the small tree, her senses keen to any indication or alert.

Toby smelled the backpack on the top, then both sides. He held his nose close to it, puffing out and in to get a stronger scent.

He lifted his head and pulled her away, continuing his search of the groundcover.

She glanced over her shoulder at Rem. "No explosives."

He let out a breath she could hear ten feet away and pushed his hand through his hair. A few of the wet locks stood on end, darting in chaotic directions.

She pulled her gaze away. "Toby, with me."

Toby swung around and happily joined her under the tree again.

"Down."

He dropped to the ground, panting with a grin that made him look like a kid playing a game. Which was really what this was to him. A game he adored playing every day.

"Good boy." She gave him a treat and told him to stay, then tugged a pair of latex gloves from her fanny pack.

She put them on and squatted by the backpack. The zipper opened easily, the backpack material stiff with a strong vinyl smell like it was brand-new.

A crunch sounded behind her, a second of warning before Remington appeared next to her and kneeled on one leg. Far too close.

She tried to ignore the overreaction of her senses and focused on analyzing the contents of the backpack.

It was stuffed with white tissue paper, like the kind used for gift wrapping. Newspaper would've been better—might have given them some clue about the bomber or something to trace.

A folded square of white paper sat on top of the tissue. She picked it up and opened it. A typed message stared back at her.

"What does it say?" The rough quality of Remington's voice felt oddly soothing.

"'Boom. You and your dog are no heroes. You are the enemy. You will not stop Libertas. Nature must be free.'" She closed the note and placed it back on top of the tissue paper. "Pretty much the same as the other one."

"I don't like this."

She looked at him, and his darkened gaze caught hers. "You mean the hoax devices?" She moistened her lips, chest tightening at the proximity of his face to hers. She looked away. "In reality, it's good practice for me and Toby." She braced her palms in the groundcover as she moved to stand.

But a large hand covered her arm. "Bristol."

Her mouth went dry, pulse fluttering at the warmth of his touch even through her jacket. She forced herself to calmly look at his face, those melting eyes.

"He called you the enemy. Doesn't that bother you?"

The heat of his hand around her arm was the only thing bothering her at the moment. She sat back on her heels, naturally prompting him to release his grip. "I've been called much worse."

"But what if this guy means you're standing in his way? He might..." Remington glanced away, his mouth pulled tight. He swung his gaze back. "He might try to hurt you."

Her heart squeezed behind her ribs at the worry that glinted in his eyes.

But he hadn't been worried about hurting her when he chose to betray her and everyone else at the academy. She got to her feet, wiping her hands on her pant legs to brush bits of greenery and dirt off her palms. "I have the situation under control."

He stood, ducking under tree branches as he walked just outside them to straighten to his full height. "Do you live alone?"

Her gaze jerked to his face. "What's that to you?"

"No—" he lifted his hands halfway between apology and frustration "—I didn't mean it like that. I just don't think you should be alone with this bomber on the loose, threatening you. Maybe—"

"I said I have the situation under control, and I don't appreciate you butting into my private life." The nerve of the man, thinking she needed some unreliable ex-boyfriend to take over her life. She yanked the zipper on the back compartment of her fanny pack and pulled out a rolled-up jumbo bag. She threw Remington another glare. "I suggest you pay more attention to getting this security disaster under control. That bombing yesterday could've been prevented with better organization and security procedures in place."

The pain signaled by the furrows gathering on his brow checked her anger. And gave her a twinge for her unfair words.

She softened her tone slightly as she bagged the backpack. "It doesn't come down to one person, but I'm just saying it was preventable. We have high floodwaters this year—extra precautions should've been taken if only for that reason."

"High waters didn't cause the bombing."

"No, a person did. An ordinary person who knew the greater damage a flood would cause if he attacked now." She stepped out from under the tree, carrying the bagged backpack, and met Remington's gaze. "A person who could have been stopped from killing others if the people in charge had done their jobs."

"Meaning me." His lips held a firm line.

"I mean this isn't a game and it isn't training. You can't goof off or cheat your way through without others paying the price."

A spark flashed in his eyes. "I don't do that anymore."

"I wish I could believe that." She looked at the bomber's backpack in her hands. Under the circumstances, she couldn't afford to take the chance.

★ ★ ★

Rem rubbed his eyes and ran his hands down his face, trying to clear his vision of the computer monitor in front of him. Fatigue from the stress of the last two days seemed to be hitting him as the clock moved toward eight p.m.

A creak came from the hallway of the DNR building.

He looked out the open door of his office, putting on his glasses to see farther more clearly.

The hall was only dimly lit with the low-powered fixture that would stay on overnight. Everyone else had gone home by the time Bristol had brought him back to the DNR.

He listened for another moment but couldn't hear anything other than the buzz of his old computer trying to work.

Probably just jumpy. Finding two fake bombs in one day did that to a person.

Unless that person was Bristol.

Rem shook his head as he clicked through the database of the Minnesota Falls Dam. The image of Bristol's calm, unshakable demeanor as she approached both potential bombs lit his memory.

The woman had nerves of steel. And only coldness for him now.

But that didn't slow his drive to do something about the bomber targeting her. He located the log file from the dam and opened the digital version from yesterday.

He scanned the list of names, recognizing them as employees who ran the dam and visitor center on a daily basis.

Darren Yule.

What would the civil engineer from the DNR have been doing there yesterday? According to the safety schedule, that was much too early for another inspection. It would have been inspected only five weeks ago.

Rem scrolled back through the log to check his suspicions.

Sure enough, Bradley Talcott, another engineer, had logged in five weeks earlier.

Could Calvin have sent Darren out on a different schedule? Calvin did enjoy disregarding regulations Rem put in place, and Rem had implemented a new, higher frequency requirement for inspections after Graham Middleton retired.

One way to find out.

Rem clicked to open a new field and made his way to the digital log of the Leavell Dam.

The list of names was short. Shorter than normal for a full day if there'd been a shift change.

Because it hadn't been a full day.

His throat tightened.

He forced himself to focus on the names, even as they blurred slightly thanks to moisture in his eyes.

Darren Yule.

Same engineer on the same morning. Rem looked at the time of arrival and time of departure. Fifteen minutes. Not long enough for an inspection.

He checked the window he'd left open from the Minnesota Falls log.

Eleven minutes.

The hunch stirring in his belly spun into a vortex.

He looked up Darren's number on his cell and called, willing him to pick up.

"Rem, hey." Noises in the background, like waves and birds chirping, suggested Darren was at a beach somewhere.

"Darren, sorry to call after hours."

"Oh, is it? It's only afternoon here." He chuckled. "Not that I really pay attention when I'm on vacation."

"You're on vacation?"

"Yeah. You didn't remember?"

A vague recollection of Darren mentioning he'd be gone

this week grew clearer in Rem's memory. "I'm starting to. You went to Hawaii?"

"You know it. So great here, man."

A woman, probably Darren's wife, Sabrina, said something in the background.

"So, what can I do for you?"

Rem tapped his fingers against the desk. "Well, I was going to ask if you inspected the Leavell Dam yesterday morning."

"The one that blew up?"

"How'd you know that?" In Hawaii. Suspicion approached like a shadow in Rem's mind.

"Jeanne called me."

Tom's wife. His widow.

"They find who did it?"

"No." Rem's answer came out raw. He cleared his throat. "Not yet." He took in a breath. "I'll let you get back to your vacation. Sorry to bother you."

"Hey, for you, anytime. Just don't let Calvin have this number." Darren let out a laugh that Rem shared as he said goodbye.

The humor faded the instant he ended the call.

It would be easy to verify Darren really had been in Hawaii or en route when he said.

Which would mean someone had pretended to be the engineer. That someone had to be their bomber.

The dam's security cameras might've gotten a shot of him.

The thought sprang Rem from his chair, and he dug in the pockets of his khakis for Agent Nguyen's card. Where had he put it? He needed to let her know what he'd found. Maybe they could take the bomber into custody tonight, and Bristol would be safe.

She also wouldn't have a reason to go with him to the dams anymore.

His chest squeezed at the thought. But she'd be safe, which was far more important. These days, she thought of Rem as something akin to sewage, anyway.

Rem reached for his miscellaneous desk drawer where he'd probably stuffed Agent Nguyen's card. Maybe if he was responsible for finding the bomber's identity and for his arrest, Bristol would at least think of him more fondly.

When she walked out of his life forever.

Chapter Twelve

Twelve dead. Bristol stared at the coffee Cora poured into the green mug marked with the Phoenix K-9 logo as she absorbed the updated death toll her boss had just shared with the team. Bristol had hoped for good news at this meeting at PK-9 headquarters the evening of day two in the search for survivors.

"But thank the Lord we were able to save twenty-one people." Cora turned away from the table along the breakroom wall, holding the pitcher of coffee in her hand. "That's amazing. The water on the shore at the park keeps receding, too, and God put enough distance between Leavell and the next dam that it could handle the extra water."

Bristol rotated to see the others' reactions to Cora's religious statements.

Amalia was the only one of the group who mustered a nod, one hand buried in the fur of Gaston, the huge chocolate Newfoundland sprawled on the sofa and across her lap. One of her feet was pinned on the floor under the head of her German shepherd, Raksa, who took advantage of the safe zone to snooze instead of protect.

Nevaeh rested her cheek against the small head of her corgi–pit bull mix, Cannenta, who sat in the circle of Nevaeh's arms as the two cuddled on the floor by the sofa. Nevaeh's gorgeous head of black curls nearly buried Cannenta's face, but the dog didn't seem to mind.

Cannenta wore her blue service dog vest and gave off a comforting sense of peace and tranquility that made Bristol wish she hadn't dropped Toby off at home before the meeting. But he needed a good rest more than she needed a dog to pet.

"There's always room for improvement." Phoenix wore her usual unreadable expression as she sat in the black armchair. "But you're right, Cora. We did something to be proud of yesterday and today."

Dag's upright ears angled to catch every word she said. He kept his head on his paws as he lay on the floor next to Phoenix's chair, but his sky-blue eyes stayed open and alert.

In laughable contrast, Phoenix's Great Pyrenees, Birger, lay in an open space on the floor sacked out on his back, white feet poking the air as his long, fluffy white fur stuck out all over. He looked more like a giant marshmallow than a dog.

"We'll work on strengthening our SAR strategy and tactics in some drills in the next weeks. But for now—" Phoenix gave a small assenting nod "—you all should feel good about a job well done."

Bristol carried her mug to the open armchair, the reality of twelve deaths sinking to the pit of her stomach as she sat. Only zero deaths could mean a job well done. Twelve people had lost their lives, needlessly. It couldn't happen again.

"We can't have another day like today in the explosives department." Phoenix's dark blue eyes trained on Bristol.

"But both the bombs were hoaxes." Cora slid onto the edge

of the coffee table with her mug, somehow making the movement look graceful. "And Bristol and Toby found them right away." Her golden retriever, Jana, got up from where she'd been lying near Birger and made her way to Cora.

Bristol voiced the truth reflected in Phoenix's gaze. "There could've been armed devices in those backpacks. And if there had been, they could have gone off before I got to them."

"So, what else can we do?" Cora looked from Phoenix to Bristol.

"Remington Jones said he had an idea for figuring out how the bomber got past security yesterday. He was hoping to find out something tonight."

Nevaeh laughed.

"You don't think he can?" Why did Bristol's question have a defensive edge? She should be the last person to defend Remington.

Nevaeh shook her head, one spiral of hair dipping across her smooth, bronze forehead to touch her eyebrow. "Nah, I'm just trippin' over how you blush when you say his name."

"I do not." Even as she said the words, Bristol felt heat rush to her cheeks.

"Nevaeh, don't tease her." Cora smiled.

"Look at her." Nevaeh pointed at Bristol's face. "She's the color of my gram's roses."

"Let's stay on task, ladies." Phoenix's reprimand sounded like a lifeguard's voice must to a drowning victim.

"The reality is—" a smile lingered on Amalia's mouth as she transferred her gaze from Bristol to Phoenix "—this bomber is smart enough that it could be a while before anyone is able to pinpoint his identity and make an arrest." Amalia paused her hand that had been petting Gaston. "We need to figure out a way to predict what the bomber's going to do next, before he does it."

Gaston lifted his head to look up at Amalia and earned a chuckle.

"Oh, did I stop petting you for one second? I'm sorry."

The other women laughed, and even Phoenix's features relaxed, her lips curved upward in the closest she ever got to a smile.

The tension in Bristol's stomach loosened as she watched the women and their dogs, the easy camaraderie they had with each other even in tough circumstances.

"I already know all I want to about this dude." Nevaeh held a hand on Cannenta's chest as the dog continued to sit in front of her. "He's making it personal with one of our girls."

"I don't like that, either, that he's writing notes to Bris." Cora's delicate eyebrows drew down. "And he even tried to call her."

Jana laid her head on Cora's lap, as if sensing her worry.

Bristol's heart warmed. She'd only been with this team for three months. Did they really care about her?

"So why's he so focused on you and not the other bomb detection K-9 with the MPD?" Nevaeh looked to Bristol for an answer Bristol wasn't sure she had.

"I guess because I'm the one who found the other active device he'd planned to explode."

"You're right." Phoenix watched Bristol. "He's taking that personally. But I think there's more to it than that. This bomber is smart enough to realize he can control Miles and the bomb squad's movements."

"Control them?" Cora tilted her head. "Oh…" Her mouth made a small circle as her blue eyes widened. "You mean he can plant another bomb somewhere else."

Phoenix nodded. "Even just a threat, and the bomb squad's K-9 would have to respond, especially if the bomb was at a high-risk location. That makes Bristol and Toby the bomber's biggest problem." She moved her gaze back to Bristol. "He can't make you go where he wants, at least not away from the dams."

"But that means he could get even worse about targeting Bris." Cora angled more toward Phoenix as everyone turned their attention the same way. "What should we do?"

"It's not a safe thing to be targeted, but there is power in being the target."

Bristol waited for an explanation, but Phoenix let her words sit.

"It gives us control."

All eyes swung to Amalia in response to her statement. She pushed her slim fingers through her waves of shiny black locks. "We can isolate his motivations and goals and have a better idea of where he'll be, when. Especially if we get inside his head more."

Bristol lifted her eyebrows. Amalia spoke with the experience and confidence of someone in law enforcement. Had she been a detective or something similar before joining the agency?

Cora had told Bristol that Phoenix had a privacy policy for all her employees. Their backgrounds were between them and Phoenix unless they chose to share with others when asked.

Bristol hadn't gotten up the courage to ask anyone but Cora so far, and her background had been utterly normal. A sweet girl from an upper middle-class family, a computer technology major Phoenix recruited out of college to work at PK-9 as a communications and security technology specialist. A job that led to her also doing narcotics detection with Jana.

Bristol had the feeling Amalia and the others had a little more darkness and mystery in their pasts. Though since Amalia seemed so friendly and open, it was doubtful she'd done anything more mysterious or intense than normal police work.

"So, let's get inside his mind." Phoenix put her hand on Dag's head just as he lifted it beside her chair. "What do his actions tell us about him?"

"He clearly wants attention, supposedly for an environmental cause." Amalia rubbed Gaston's furry shoulder. "That explains why he targeted the Leavell Dam and didn't phone in a threat beforehand, ensuring the bomb wouldn't be found before detonation."

Bristol nodded. "He wanted loss of life for more publicity."

"We know he's not afraid to kill, and he can strategize." Phoenix watched them with the same keenness of the dog at her side. "What else?"

"I think he's looking for a sense of purpose in his life." Cora's mouth dipped in a frown. "He wants to feel important, like most of us do, and he clearly isn't getting that sense of significance or purpose anywhere else."

"Meaning?" Phoenix prodded Cora like a teacher with a prize pupil.

"Maybe he's unemployed or has a menial job he hates. He's probably alone, no family. Or at least no one who loves him." Cora stroked Jana's head on her lap. "It's sad, really."

A snort came from Nevaeh. "Nothing sad about killing people and trying to play with Bris." Her big eyes aimed at Bristol. "That's what he's doing, you know. Playing you. He wants to be in control and make you do what he wants."

"I'm sure Bristol is too mentally tough to let him bother her." Phoenix met Bristol's gaze briefly, but Bristol couldn't tell if she was searching for confirmation or sending an order.

"Absolutely." Bristol spoke with the conviction she felt. "Takes a lot to scare me." Except for one hurricane warning. A flood watch. A dam explosion. She pushed aside the thoughts that contradicted her declaration.

"The challenge is, we don't have much to go on in the way

of facts yet." Phoenix rested her hands on the armrests of her chair. "Katherine and the task force haven't been able to uncover evidence that leads to the bomber or his identity, though they're working around the clock. Thanks to his phone calls, we know he's a man, and we have some stock phrases he likes to use on his notes and verbally."

She scanned the team members with a gaze that seemed to take everything in but let nothing out. "As you know, investigation isn't our purpose. We are first and foremost security and detection specialists."

She tented her fingers in front of her chin, elbows propped on the armrests of the chair. "That said, we'll investigate as is fitting or helpful to further our primary objective. You all need to know Katherine has asked us to keep our eyes and ears open when we're working for the FBI at the dams."

"What are we supposed to look for?" Nevaeh's dark gaze drifted up from Cannenta to Phoenix.

"Anything suspicious. How the bomber is accessing these locations is still unknown. So, Nevaeh and Amalia, keep an eye on even the regular employees when you're patrolling at Minnesota Falls. See if they do anything suspicious, talk to or meet with nonemployees consistently, etcetera."

"You mean like Rem Jones?"

Bristol started at the name. Since when did Nevaeh use his nickname?

And why was Nevaeh grinning Bristol's way as she continued? "The dude talks to every person he sees. Like he took a friendly pill or something. Is he always that way?"

"I wouldn't know." Bristol averted her gaze, willing the heat crawling up her neck to stay out of her cheeks.

"So a nice guy *and* hot?" Amalia's eyes twinkled as she smiled, white teeth gleaming against her warm-toned, sandy brown skin. "Sounds like you got a tough assignment, girl."

Warmth flushed Bristol's cheeks despite her best efforts. She tried to cover with an eye roll. "He drives me crazy."

Amalia's and Nevaeh's toothy grins broadened.

"In a bad way." Bristol gave them a convincing frown. "Seriously, he's always been very..." She held back from saying too much. They didn't need to know about what he'd done or that she'd once dated him. "Very unpredictable. He puts me on edge and makes me uncomfortable."

"Isn't that the fun part?" Nevaeh laughed.

"There's nothing wrong with a steady guy." Cora sent Bristol an apologetic smile, as if she were at fault for the team's teasing.

"Being on edge isn't a bad thing."

Bristol jerked her head to Phoenix, surprised she'd join in the ribbing.

But the serious set of her mouth contradicted the notion. "Stay on your guard. That way you won't be fooled. Especially since you have a history with Jones." Phoenix pierced Bristol with a perceptive gaze.

Did she already know more about that history than Bristol had revealed?

"Katherine wants you to be on the lookout for anything suspicious with Jones. He hasn't been ruled out as a possible accomplice."

Phoenix's words entered Bristol's ears but seemed to get stuck there. Remington, an accomplice? In a bombing? Sure, he was irresponsible and unreliable, but he couldn't be involved in anything that would kill people.

"He's in the best position to make things easy for the bomber." Phoenix watched Bristol as she continued. "Or to be the bomber himself."

"No, he couldn't be the bomber." The response burst from Bristol's lips before she thought.

They all stared.

A fresh wave of heat washed her cheeks. "I mean, he doesn't fit the profile at all." She cleared her throat. "He definitely has his faults. And I don't really trust him completely, but…"

Her throat dried to sandpaper under their scrutiny as her face blazed. Defending him from an accusation of being a mass murderer was far different than admitting she liked him. But she didn't want these women thinking she was too emotionally involved to do her job, either.

She firmed her lips and met Phoenix's inscrutable gaze. "You're right. We can never know what a person is capable of." Remington had proven that to her six years ago. "I'll keep my guard up and my eyes open." And her heart under lock and key.

She caught her breath, trying to slow the rapid beating of her heart under her ribs. She better do exactly what she'd just promised. Because at least where her emotions were concerned, she'd be a fool to imagine Remington Jones was anything but a dangerous man.

Chapter Thirteen

Sunlight pushed through the clouds, seeming to force them back with the strength of rays that streaked down in visible beams.

Rem watched from under the arch of Minneapolis City Hall as the raindrops slowed, then dried up completely.

Still, there was no telling when the clouds would win the battle again, and the rain would recommence. Good thing the 6:30 a.m. press conference was going to be held inside.

Rem turned to enter the historic building.

"Jones."

Calvin. Rem closed his eyes a second before turning to face the source of the sharp voice.

Press members brushed past Calvin as he gave Rem a smug smile.

Lord, give me patience. Rem tried to force a pleasant expression. "Calvin. Don't think I've ever seen you in a suit before." He scanned the engineer's baggy gray ensemble.

"You would talk about clothes at a time like this." Calvin

shook his head like a domineering schoolmarm. "A second evacuation and bomb threat in two days didn't make Franklin happy." He leaned closer, allowing Rem to get a whiff of the man's heavy cologne. "Or the public."

As if Rem had been dancing over it himself. But he bit back the anger he wanted to throw at Calvin. He forced an outward calm that belied the frustration tightening his chest. "I suppose not."

Calvin narrowed his eyes, at least having the sense to scan for reporters within earshot before he continued. "Do you know what this is doing to the DNR's reputation? We're going to have a public panic on our hands thanks to your inability to do your job." He jerked his ill-fitting jacket in a failed attempt to straighten it. The grin that twisted his mouth was just as crooked. "The press will have a field day with you during this conference." Clearly, the man intended to enjoy it.

"Actually, Calvin, you'll be happy to hear Franklin decided Joy Sparrow should do all the talking." Their public relations specialist had initially only been going to provide general information and then Rem was to field questions. "I'm just here to make sure she has all the answers she needs." He was still relieved Franklin had decided the DNR's tenuous position after more bomb scares warranted leaving all the talking to the expert, Joy—who was the only one without her job on the line at the moment.

"Sorry to interrupt."

Rem turned at the sound of Agent Nguyen's commanding tone behind him, not a hint of apology apparent in her voice or expression.

"I need to talk to Jones." She leveled a gaze at Calvin that made him fidget within two seconds and skedaddle within three.

Rem would've thanked the agent for scaring off Calvin,

but there was no more friendliness in her gaze than that of his nemesis. And just how long had she been standing behind him, listening to Calvin's accusations?

"We checked the information you gave us about the engineer and the log records."

Good, maybe this was only an update. He tried to release the pent-up breath from his lungs.

"Darren Yule is confirmed as being en route to and arriving in Hawaii during the time frame in question."

"What about the guy who impersonated Darren at the dams that morning?"

She folded her arms in front of her, scanning the reporters and people who passed them to enter city hall. "We can't be sure the same man who impersonated the engineer is the actual bomber. He could be an accomplice. But we've examined the security footage and pinpointed the individual."

Hope pushed the tension out with his breath. "You found him?"

"We weren't able to identify him from the footage."

The hope crashed. "What?"

"The subject is exceptionally savvy about avoiding cameras, always keeping his face away or blocked."

Was that possible? Rem ran through his mind the locations of the cameras throughout the two dams. Leavell hadn't followed most of his suggestions for updating security. They had only had one camera. But Minnesota Falls was a different matter. "What about the camera at the employee entrance at Minnesota Falls? Or the one at the public entrance?"

The woman's thin eyebrows lifted for a second, as if she was surprised he could think. Seemed to be a lot of that going around. "The suspect entered from the employee parking lot and had a hood over his head that helped obscure his face. The guard monitoring the cameras didn't get suspicious because it was raining at the time and the man had a pass card that worked."

"Didn't he take his hood down when he went inside?"

She lowered her hands to her hips, again scanning their surroundings. "Yes, but there was only one more camera for him to bypass after that, and he turned away from it, appearing to wave at someone off camera."

"So anyone watching wouldn't think he was intentionally dodging the camera."

"It would seem so. We got his hair color. Brown. He's male, probably white, average build. Nothing distinctive."

Another dead end. So much for Rem's lead cracking the case. This bomber was cleverer than he'd thought. He needed to be found. Fast.

"I appreciate that you're doing what you can to help us find the suspect quicker. As the safety and security supervisor, you're in a unique position to offer inside information to assist our investigation." Why did her sudden praise sound like a practice run of a rehearsed speech for the press?

He braced himself for a *but* or a glimpse of the meaning behind her words.

"I want you to keep thinking and keep me informed of anything you come up with." She glanced toward the entrance behind him and nodded.

He looked over his shoulder to see an FBI agent move back inside, probably after signaling Agent Nguyen.

Her dark gaze was ready to meet his as soon as he turned back. "One more thing. Just make sure you don't start thinking you're an investigator on this case. Don't take any action on your own. You could get hurt that way."

Almost sounded like a threat.

"Showtime." She left the word in her wake as she entered the building.

Rem clenched his hands into fists at his sides. This conference should have been filled with news that the bomber was caught and this terror was over.

Instead, the public was still in danger. And so was Bristol.

The last thought was the one Rem carried with him inside, his gut in knots over a woman who probably didn't trust him any more than she trusted the unidentified bomber.

"How did the DNR fail to make the Leavell Dam a secure facility?"

The DNR's public relations spokeswoman smiled as if the reporter's question wasn't meant to be incendiary.

Bristol spotted Remington where he stood in the front row of the crowd of reporters that gathered beneath the first short flight of stairs. His head tilted up to watch the PR woman behind the temporary podium positioned on the landing, but his expression didn't betray any embarrassment or anger, only thoughtful concentration.

The soft lighting in the city hall rotunda seemed to love him. Could be the camel-colored blazer and dark brown shirt he wore that emphasized his tanned skin and strong jawline.

He nodded as the PR spokeswoman finished her careful answer with a statement about their prayers going out to the families of the victims.

The reporters shouted more questions, prompting Toby to lean into Bristol's leg, sensitive to the heightened emotions and tension.

Glad she and Phoenix had opted to stand to the left of the stairs away from the crowd, she stroked Toby's ear, the motion calming her own heart rate. Put her in front of a time bomb, and she was as peaceful as a napping baby. But the idea of getting up in front of this bunch to field questions ranked right up there with a root canal. She wouldn't have to be here at all except that someone unfortunately thought finding an IED before it exploded and rescuing a girl made her and Toby interesting news.

Phoenix stood on the other side of Toby, unflappable and inscrutable as always. Dag sat next to her leg, the mirror image of his handler's steady control and alertness.

One man's voice rose above the other reporters. "But how did the bomber access the inside of the dams? Shouldn't those be more secure?"

"The DNR is in full accordance with the security measures delineated in state policies and federal regulations."

Envy rustled Bristol's nerves at the PR spokeswoman's calm demeanor.

Bristol blew out a breath and moved her gaze up the marble staircase behind the woman, past the two security guards posted there. She tuned out the following questions the reporters launched, hoping they weren't preparing the same kind of interrogation for her and Toby. She smoothed the dog's head again and focused on slowing her breathing. Maybe Phoenix could do Bristol's talking for her.

"...flooding is on the public's mind."

The word she dreaded yanked Bristol's attention to a middle-aged reporter setting up his question. "Given the high water levels this spring, is it true that if the Minnesota Falls Dam were to be bombed, it would cause traumatic flooding?"

"Good question." The spokeswoman nodded. "After the attack two days ago, steps have been taken to make the Minnesota Falls Dam a highly secure facility. It would be extremely difficult to bomb. Also, it's been constructed well and meticulously maintained during the years of its existence. It would take a great deal of explosive power and access, which a person could not easily obtain, to inflict any significant damage."

Bristol glanced at Remington as the spokeswoman explained the partnership with Phoenix K-9 and other security measures.

He already watched her. His mouth quirked with the hint of a smile.

A shiver jolted through her at their first connection of the morning. *Honestly.* They'd only worked together for one day. She clearly needed to do a better job of guarding her heart.

She broke the current that seemed to bind them, pretending to watch the spokeswoman, but letting her gaze wander up the grand staircase that split in two directions, to the stained-glass windows on the wall behind him. She forced herself to focus on the beauty of the architecture, moving her study higher to take in the five-story rotunda with its many arches and intricate stained-glass skylight in the ceiling far above.

Toby bumped into her knee.

She dropped her gaze to see him wiggling at her side.

He looked up at her with his dark eyes and gave a slight whine as he shifted his weight. Did he have to go? He already had on the way in.

He tugged at the leash, pulling in the direction of the reporters and onlookers.

His nose lifted in the air.

He'd caught a scent. But of what?

Explosives? Her heart jumped into her throat. Here, with all these people. A bomb would be deadly.

She slacked the leash slightly and followed Toby.

The spokeswoman answered another question in the background, but Bristol didn't follow the words as her attention locked on Toby.

He plunged into the semiformed rows of standing people.

Excusing herself didn't seem to be necessary as the reporters parted just enough for her to slip through behind Toby's black body, their focus rapt on the chance to ask their questions.

Toby barreled ahead, riveted on the scent. He strained against the harness as she held him back from going full speed so she could keep up without breaking into a run that would cause a panic.

They emerged on the other side of the crowd, and Toby pulled her toward the huge marble Father of Waters statue.

Toby stopped two feet from the statue, his nose hovering over a spot on the stone tiles of the floor. He sat. Lifted his paw.

Explosives.

But there was nothing visible. Just the light brown of the decoration on that part of the floor.

A scent had to be there. From shoes? The bomber could have explosive residue on his shoes.

He was here.

"He's alerting?" Phoenix's voice came from just past Bristol's shoulder.

"Something with explosives residue must have been here."

"Or someone."

Bristol released Toby and rewarded him with petting and verbal praise as Agent Nguyen came up beside Phoenix.

"What's going on?"

"Bristol's K-9 detected explosives here, possibly a scent on the suspect's shoes." Phoenix showed Agent Nguyen the spot. "We're going to track him and see if we can pin him down."

Agent Nguyen waved a hand, and a man wearing a black FBI jacket appeared almost immediately. "Agent Gilson will go with you. I'll begin evacuating the building, just in case."

Phoenix jerked a nod, darting only a quick glance toward Agent Gilson. "Stay behind us." She directed Dag to examine the spot Toby had found on the floor. He would home in on human-related scent, rather than the explosives Toby was trained to find, doubling their chances of staying on the trail. "Track it."

Dag burst into action, instantly hitting the end of his leash in his eagerness to follow the trail.

"Toby, track it." Toby quickly followed behind Dag and Phoenix, absorbed in his own tracking of the explosives scent.

The trail led them toward the front exit.

They pushed through one of the side doors that flanked the revolving one in the center.

Raindrops, noise and pedestrians greeted them past the archway on the wide sidewalk.

Toby looked up at her, seeking her direction on what he should check. He'd lost the scent.

The explosives residue must have washed off the bomber's shoes—if that's who it had been.

But Dag and Phoenix kept going, pushing through pedestrians as they joined the direction of traffic on the one-way street.

"Release. Good boy." Bristol gave Toby a quick pet and hurried to follow Phoenix and the FBI agent who trailed her.

Bristol hopped her gaze across the street, up the sidewalk beyond where Dag tracked his scent.

Some women walked together in a group ahead. A few businessmen types cut a quick pace in the walkway across the upcoming intersection. But no one appeared to be on the run.

Dag slowed at the intersection, his nose in the air as he searched for the scent. He turned right as Bristol and Toby caught up.

Dag walked a few feet farther, moved his nose to the edge of the curb, then lifted his head and looked toward Phoenix.

She touched her hand to the side of his face. "Dead end." Phoenix's tone held a note of disappointment. "I'd guess the person was picked up here."

She glanced up, scanning the area as Gilson did the same.

"Cameras?" Bristol's gaze followed Phoenix's.

"Might have caught the getaway vehicle."

"Could be the traffic camera got it." Gilson pulled out his cell phone, probably to call Agent Nguyen.

"Hard to believe he'd show up at a press conference at city hall—" Bristol shook her head "—with the FBI and cops around."

Phoenix stroked Dag between the ears as she looked at Bristol. "He's taking more risks. Good for us. He'll make a mistake that way."

Hopefully a camera would reveal he'd made that mistake today.

Chapter Fourteen

She took his breath away.

Rem paused, paper cups filled with coffee in both hands, and drank in Bristol's profile as she sat on the old wooden bench outside city hall's security office. The tiny tiles of the hallway were worn and dirty from centuries of use, and the gold and beige walls had seen better days. But Bristol—dressed practically in her usual T-shirt, black windbreaker, loose-fitting cargo pants and sneakers—infused the tired surroundings with life and beauty.

She'd left her hair down today, probably for the sake of the press conference interview she was supposed to have had. She pushed back the waves of mahogany richness, and a lump lodged in his throat.

Bending to pet Toby, who lay on the floor at her feet, she looked Rem's way with those amazing eyes.

He pushed his feet forward, donning a grin he hoped would hide the crazy effect she still had on him. He held out her cup of coffee as he neared. "Coffee, lots of sugar."

Her eyebrows lifted, her hand not reaching for the cup.

"Don't you like it that way anymore?"

She moistened her lips with her tongue and took the coffee. "I do."

His heart sank with his body as he sat on the bench, Toby's position ensuring a professional distance between them. She was so surprised he remembered how she preferred her coffee. Did she not realize how much he'd cared about her?

He swallowed a sigh. Of course she would doubt it. She saw what he did as a betrayal of her, what they'd had. He'd realized that as soon as he'd seen the expression on her face when she had met him outside Sergeant Standish's office at the academy. News traveled fast there. Fast enough to beat him to a chance to explain. Not that he could have. She'd tossed out a bitter, "How could you?"

And all he could think of was the dumbest answer possible. "I didn't have a choice."

But he had made a choice when he'd cheated and partied his way through life. He just hadn't realized what it would cost him until the woman he loved had looked at him with hurt and fury in her eyes, then turned without another word and walked out of his life forever. Or so he'd thought.

"Where'd you find the coffee?" Bristol's voice broke through the pain of the memory.

A question. Something he could work with. He angled a smile. "I'd tell you, but then I'd have to…"

She rolled her eyes, her full mouth settling into a curve that wasn't a smile but wasn't a frown, either. Her hands rounded the cup as if she needed something to hang on to. She stared across the hall at the gold-toned paint.

"Are you okay?"

Her gaze jerked to his face, her blue-gray eyes searching. "Of course. Why wouldn't I be?"

He shrugged but didn't look away. "You've been through a lot the past couple of days. And now, chasing the bomber and having him get away."

She broke eye contact, bending to pet Toby. "I've been through a lot worse."

Probably meaning what he'd put her through. He took a breath to respond, but the door to his right opened, and Phoenix exited, along with Agent Nguyen and other FBI agents.

The FBI gang headed up the hallway while Phoenix stopped in front of Bristol, her hand loosely gripping the leash of her tan dog with startling blue eyes.

"Nothing." Phoenix's even tone betrayed no emotion. The woman was harder to read than an engineering textbook. "The bomber managed to keep his face averted or image blocked from all security cameras here and on the street. Same average body type as the description from the Minnesota Falls Dam. Navy canvas jacket and jeans."

Bristol scooted forward. "What about the car that picked him up?"

Phoenix shook her head. "The location where the vehicle picked him up is a blind spot for the traffic cameras at the intersection."

Rem let out a low whistle.

Phoenix's dark blue gaze landed on him.

"The guy's smart."

She stared at him for a moment, then shifted her attention back to Bristol, leaving Rem feeling vaguely like he'd just been interrogated without a word.

"With the bomber showing up here, hopefully he hasn't had time to plant another bomb today." Phoenix crossed her arms, her black windbreaker crinkling with the motion.

"Miles has been canvassing the dams with Duke and the bomb squad while we're here." Bristol looked up at her boss with a direct, nonjudgmental gaze that gave Rem a twinge of envy. "What do you think the bomber wanted coming here?"

"Gathering information. Maybe planning his next move."

"Or just basking in the attention." Rem's suggestion drew scrutiny from both women.

"Have you a theory on how the bomber got his fakes in place yesterday?" Phoenix asked the question in a neutral tone, though her stare said she was watching for him to blink.

But he had nothing to hide. "Wouldn't be too difficult, unfortunately." He met her gaze. "They were both in areas that allow visitor access but wouldn't have done much damage to the actual dams."

Phoenix watched him. "I suggested security checkpoints and metal detectors be installed at the dams downtown."

Rem chuckled. "I've been suggesting that since I took this job. But the owners are a bit cost-conscious."

No hint of a smile cracked Phoenix's expression. "Well, they're seeing things differently now and will be installing detectors in the next couple of days."

Of course they were. If not from the tragedy that occurred, just Phoenix's fierceness would probably do the trick.

She swung her attention back to Bristol. "You're free to go back to the dams now. Toby might be needed there. Though I'm glad he was here this morning."

Bristol slid off the bench and stood, Toby springing up as if eager for action. "I agree. I can't believe the bomber showed up here. Takes a lot of brass to march into city hall for a press conference when you're the criminal we're all talking about."

Phoenix lowered her arms. "Be careful out there today." She cast a glance in Rem's direction as if he were the reason for the warning.

"I'll take care of her."

Oops. A full-on glare from Bristol and the interrogator look from Phoenix answered that statement, which he should've known better than to utter in front of two capable, modern women. "I mean, I'll do my best to help."

Didn't seem to appease Phoenix, who turned and left at a determined clip without even her dog glancing back.

Bristol didn't look any happier as she started in the same direction, maintaining a silence he was smart enough not to break all the way till they reached the parking garage.

Toby sat between them in the elevator as they rode to the level where she'd parked.

"You don't have to go with me if you parked somewhere else." Her voice severed the silence. "I assume you brought a car?"

Talking to him at last. He stifled a relieved sigh as the elevator doors slid open and they stepped out into the damp air of the shadowed garage. "Mine's still getting worked on. I figured I'd ride with you to the dams from here, anyway, so I hitched a ride with a buddy." He looked ahead but couldn't spot her Jeep.

"Fine. Where are we going first?" She took a left and headed for the next aisle.

"I talked to Miles a few minutes ago to see what he's cleared so far. We'll want to recheck the same dams again throughout the day, but to make sure each has been searched as early as possible today, we'll search the Gellar Dam next. The drive from here will take us through a really cool part of Garden Valley. It'll be fun."

"Fun?" She shook her head. "We're not going to a party." She picked up her pace, apparently trying to leave him and his juvenile ideas behind.

He let her have her space while he sorted out the onslaught of memories and guilt her remark prompted. Thank the Lord they weren't headed for a party. The reckless, careless living that used to mark his days was the last thing he would consider fun now.

How could he get Bristol to see that? To believe he'd changed?

He upped his pace to catch Bristol and walked alongside her.

The angle of her jawline was still set firmly against him, the cold breeze sweeping through the parking lot a match for her demeanor.

"Bristol."

She stopped at the back of her parked Jeep and opened the liftgate without looking his way.

Toby hopped inside, entering his crate.

She waited until Toby turned around, then tossed him a treat and latched the crate door. She finally cast Rem a glance. "What?"

"How can I prove it to you?"

She stiffened, those blue-gray eyes locking on his face. "What?"

"I mean that I've changed. I'm not the person I was at the academy. I'm not a goof-off anymore. I take things seriously now. I never go to parties, and I work hard and do things the honest way. Is there any way I can convince you and... fix things?"

"Fix things."

He took a step toward her. "Yeah. Between us. I know you have a low opinion of me now, and I don't blame you. What I did was wrong. But I wish we..." His throat shrunk. He couldn't say what he'd really like. "Could be friends."

A shadow cloaked her eyes, and she stepped away, reaching up to close the liftgate.

He dodged the gate as she slammed it shut, throwing him a look as if she wished his head had been in there.

"You once convinced me we could be more than friends.

Remember that?" She crossed her arms over her jacket as her eyes sparked. "Because you said you'd start studying and working hard and become the kind of man I'd want to…"

Marry. He remembered. His heart twisted painfully, as if caught between his ribs. Not because of her anger, but because of the hurt that glinted like tears in her eyes. "I'm sorry."

She nodded, but frustrated disbelief, not affirmation, marked the set of her mouth. "You always knew what to say to charm me into believing you." She took a step toward him and lowered her hands to her hips. "But your irresponsibility, your deception—there are consequences. You hurt people. I'm glad you got kicked out, because you had no business trying to be a cop when you can't be depended on to pass a test honestly, let alone protect someone."

He held back a flinch, the desire to turn away from the slap of guilt to his conscience. He'd take his just deserts.

"Being a cop is not a game. Neither is searching for bombs." She started to turn away, then tossed a final shot over her shoulder. "And as far as you and I are concerned? You can't *fix* this. The hurts of the past can never be fixed." She headed to the driver's door, and he followed her instead of going to the passenger side.

"But they can be healed. I'm not going to give up, Bristol."

"If you think I'm going to—"

Her hand jerked to the Glock at her hip.

He looked in the direction of her gaze through the driver's window and the windshield.

A piece of something white—looked like paper. A ticket?

She opened the driver's door with her hand still on her Glock. She scanned the inside of the Jeep as if she expected someone to be waiting there.

Rem squeezed between the open door and the red sports

car parked next to the Jeep. The paper didn't look like a ticket up close. He reached for it.

"Don't touch it." Her snap made him yank back his hand as she shut the door.

"You think it's from the bomber?" Couldn't be. He wouldn't dare get so personal. So close. Heat stirred in Rem's belly at the thought.

Bristol dug latex gloves out of the fanny pack around her waist and tugged them on. Her jacket brushed against his back as she passed between him and the car, shooting electricity up his spine as if she'd actually touched him.

She picked up the folded paper and opened it. Her lips thinned as she looked at the contents.

"What does it say?"

She paused, as if she had to decide whether or not to tell him. "'Libertas is watching you. Don't try to stop me. If you do, you will get hurt. Nature must be free.'"

She lifted her chin so Rem could see the storm darkening the gray in her eyes. "This is real life, Jones. And life isn't a party."

Chapter Fifteen

Bristol turned the knob to open the door that connected her garage to the house.

Toby pushed past her leg to rush into the dark kitchen first.

She chuckled as she flicked the light switch and followed at a slower pace. "Excuse me if I'm in your way. Somebody must be hungry, huh?"

As if to answer her question, Toby sat in front of the lower cabinet that held his kibble.

"Okay, just hang on a second, buddy."

The stillness of the house wrapped around her like a cocoon for her exhausted nerves. Or maybe it was her emotions that needed the break. Another roller-coaster day of unwelcome surprise and frustration.

She opened the coat closet to the right of the door, put the fanny pack and her SAR backpack in their designated bins on shelves and slipped out of her jacket.

At least they hadn't found any IEDs, hoax or otherwise today. Hopefully, between the PK-9 ladies at Minnesota Falls and the other additional security at the dams, the bomber wouldn't be able to plant any new surprises tonight.

She bent to pull off her boots and scooted them under the bottom shelf before shutting the door.

She blew out a breath as she lifted her holster off her hip and placed it with her Glock on the counter. The growing unpredictability of the bomber left an unsettled queasiness in the pit of her stomach.

He could stick with the more obvious targets of the bigger dams located downtown. Or he could decide to do something more unexpected and plant IEDs at dams farther out in the suburbs. She and Remington, and Miles, were canvassing the dams in the suburbs every day, too, but she hated not being able to predict a pattern, not knowing if they were getting ahead of this terrorist.

Toby's whine drew her attention, and she moved to open the lower cabinet. But Remington didn't leave her thoughts as she scooped Toby's food into his dish and filled his water bowl from the sink.

Remington had been much quieter than usual as they cleared the dams today. Lines had furrowed his brow in a way that made him strangely more appealing and tempted her to either try to cheer him up or smooth out the creases with her hand.

She'd thankfully resisted both ideas. And she was home now, where she didn't have to think about Remington Jones or his frustrating unpredictability. Bristol washed her hands and dried them with a towel, rubbing harder than she had to.

She used to think about what would happen if they met again someday. She had never imagined he'd admit what he had done was wrong, let alone apologize for it. When she'd confronted him after he was caught cheating at the academy, he had only said he didn't have a choice.

But now he not only admitted he'd done the wrong thing, but even said he was sorry. And seemed to mean it.

She crossed the small kitchen to the refrigerator next to the water dish Toby drank from and pulled out salad fixings, including the wilted spinach she should've stopped at a store to replace.

She plunked the food on the counter. Remington still hadn't offered a hint of explanation, though. No reason for doing what he had.

She couldn't let her guard down like she had at the academy, even though she'd also never predicted how many of the old feelings he would evoke in her. The same explosion of sensations whenever he got too near, and the same emotional wave her heart rode on when he had swept in and changed her life six years ago.

She had known back then that such inward chaos couldn't end well. She refused to repeat her mistakes now.

She let out a breath, trying to release the tension she blamed on Remington, and got out a bowl from the overhead cabinet. A tossed salad would make a simple, quick and healthy dinner.

Bristol had felt so tired on the way home she had just wanted to eat and get to bed as early as possible. Now, her exhaustion made her crave one of Grandma's home-cooked meals and a good dose of the peace her grandma's presence always evoked.

She placed some carrots on a cutting board on the counter and took a knife from the drawer to chop them. Maybe she could call Grandma again after dinner.

Why was she so uneasy tonight? She usually didn't need handholding and distraction.

The answer loomed before her eyes in the image of a bearded face with golden brown hair and a smile that made shivers run across her arms.

She let out a frustrated grunt and a carrot slipped from her hand, rolling off the counter and hitting the floor.

"Leave it." She got out the command just as Toby reached the vegetable.

He halted and stepped back.

"Yes. Good boy." She picked up the carrot and broke it in half. Walking to his bowl, she dropped one half in the dish. "Release."

Toby sprinted to gulp down the vegetable as if it were a slab of steak.

She washed her hands and went back to prepping her meal, determined not to let Remington Jones get inside her head again. She refused to let an attraction that couldn't be helped lure her into heartbreak a second t—

A noise at the door to the garage halted the thought.

She stepped to her Glock and slipped it from the holster.

Adrenaline surged through her body, but her hands were perfectly steady as she lifted the gun, gaze locked on the door.

Would the bomber dare come to her house?

The knob turned.

If it was him, underestimating her was the last mistake he'd ever make.

Chapter Sixteen

Toby moved toward the door as it began to open, but Bristol stopped him with a hand signal, wordlessly telling him to stay.

She braced her hands on the Glock.

The door opened wider.

Grandma backed in, holding something in her arms.

Bristol jerked the weapon away, quickly shoving it into the holster on the counter as her pulse thundered in her ears.

"Toby! How's my sweet boy?" Grandma smiled at the dog, who broke his stay to go to her, whipping his tail side to side as he blocked her entry with a slobbery greeting.

Bristol dropped a kitchen towel over the gun her grandma preferred not to see.

"And my sweet girl."

Bristol forced a smile and clasped trembling hands behind her back. She'd nearly shot her grandmother. Well, not exactly, but she'd held a gun on her. That was unacceptable. She wasn't sure whether to blame the bomber for his threats making her edgy or Remington for frazzling her emotions.

"What are you doing here, Grandma?"

Round gray-blue eyes looked at Bristol without a hint of suspicion as Grandma set a baking pan clothed in an insulated traveling case on the counter. "You were getting home so late tonight I knew you wouldn't have time to make anything healthy." She unzipped the case. "So, I brought over your favorite."

"Lasagna?"

Grandma slid out the pan, covered in tin foil. "Of course."

After the stress of the day, Bristol didn't mind that her grandmother's idea of healthy was traditional comfort food. She almost shared how much she'd been longing for Grandma's company and cooking.

But then Grandma would know something was up and not let it go until she'd heard everything—and found out a bomber was threatening Bristol. Then Bristol would be smothered with more comfort and hovering than she could take. The less Grandma knew, the better.

Bristol narrowed her eyes. Actually, Grandma was already doing a bit of smothering, showing up with lasagna unexpectedly like this. What had brought that on? Bristol reached to take two plates out from the cabinet. "You couldn't have made the lasagna after I called you. You were planning this, weren't you?"

"Can't a grandma visit her granddaughter when she wants to?" She uncovered the lasagna and easily found a knife and server in the kitchen drawers.

"Nice try. I know you don't like driving at night. And you probably shouldn't."

"Nonsense." Grandma hefted the pan and made her way around the L-shaped counter to the round table in the small dining room. "I refuse to use my age as an excuse to stop enjoying life."

Bristol followed with the plates, a smile turning her lips.

"We use enough excuses to do that as it is." The meaningful note in Grandma's tone made Bristol look up from setting the table.

She met her grandmother's gaze, eyes darkened to more gray than blue, signaling she had something unpleasant to say. Bristol turned away, heading back to the kitchen. "We need forks."

"Your mother called."

Bristol paused, her fingers tight on the handle of the flatware drawer. "I'm too tired to do this tonight." She jerked open the drawer and pulled out two forks. She grabbed a stack of paper napkins from a cabinet overhead and returned to the table, not looking at her grandmother.

"It was her birthday today."

Bristol pulled out a leather dining chair and sat.

Grandma stayed standing.

Bristol finally glanced at her. "I know that."

She moved to the chair by Bristol's and slowly slid it back to sit. "Did you call her?"

Fatigue washed over Bristol at the loaded question. She pressed her palms against her face and slid them back over her cheeks. "If I called her, we'd talk about hurricane season starting soon." She stared at the tin foil on the pan. "I'd tell her to move here, away from the danger. She'd refuse, give me her spiel about moving on and leaving the past behind her."

Bristol lifted her weary head. "If I don't call, neither of us has to get hurt."

Grandma's eyes brimmed with moisture as she reached to cover Bristol's hand with her own soft one. "But when you don't call, you both hurt, anyway."

Bristol stared at her grandmother's hand. Every wrinkle, mole and vein so familiar. "Nothing can change that."

"One Person can."

Great. The Jesus pitch. Better to nip it in the bud. She pulled away. "I know you mean well, Grandma, but we believe different things. I can't believe God is the way you say He is. My life proves something very different."

"You think it does, but—"

"Grandma, no. I can't do this tonight, either." She took a breath, trying to shake the sharpness from her voice. "It's okay for us to believe different things. I just don't want to fight with you about it." She tried for a smile and touched Grandma's fingers still resting on the table. "Okay?"

Grandma nodded, turning her hand to grip Bristol's and give it a gentle squeeze. "I just don't like to see my baby hurting."

Emotion clogged Bristol's throat at the gentle tone she remembered so well, comforting and soothing in her darkest times. She swallowed and forced a bigger smile. "Your lasagna will take care of that." Though, truthfully, the conversation about her mother had robbed Bristol of her appetite.

Grandma's expression lightened as she cut rectangular pieces from the pan and put one on Bristol's plate, then a smaller one on her own.

"It smells wonderful." The fabulous aroma of cheese and Italian seasonings began to reawaken Bristol's appetite. She glanced behind her to make sure Toby had lain down as he was supposed to when they sat at the table.

He watched them from the spot he'd picked on the vinyl floor next to the nearest cabinet, panting and relaxed.

"I'm thinking of serving lasagna for dinner Friday night." Grandma cut into her piece and pierced a small section with her fork, rotating it in the air as if judging it for a competition. "Or do you think I should make my famous noodle casserole?"

Bristol swallowed the first delicious bite. "What dinner?"

"Oh, didn't I mention it? I'd like you to join me and my

special friend for dinner Friday night." A twinkle glimmered in her eyes.

"Special friend?" Had Grandma found a love interest? Impossible. Not after more than twenty years of widowhood and at the age of eighty-four. But things that seemed impossible did sometimes happen. "Is your friend a man, by any chance?"

"He is." Her eyes positively glittered, and a smile teased the dimples that only showed when she was thrilled about something.

"Grandma, are you dating someone?"

"Oh, no." She laughed and waved the thought away with her hand. "He's much too young for me."

Realization switched on like a lightbulb. Her grandma was setting her up. "No matchmaking, please. The last thing I need right now is a relationship."

"You only think that because you've been choosing the wrong men." She slid a piece of lasagna between straightened lips.

"What does that mean?"

Never one to talk with her mouth full, Grandma chewed slowly, then swallowed. "Take the last young man you dated a few months back, for example."

Bristol narrowed her eyes. "Peter."

"Yes, Peter. Do you know *why* you dated him?"

Bristol blinked at the unexpected IED in the conversation. Too bad bomb school didn't cover how to render grandmother-launched explosives safe.

Grandma patted her hand. "Be a dear and bring me a glass of water while you think about it."

"Sure." Bristol stood and went to the kitchen. "But I don't need time to think about it." Though her mind did initially swirl about like the water pouring into the two glasses.

She handed her grandmother a glass and set the other by her own plate.

"Thank you, dear." She smiled sweetly at Bristol. "Did you think of an answer?"

"I know why I dated him." Bristol hid a cringe at the defensive note in her voice. "He's kind, neat, successful, polite."

"That's very nice." If Grandma's expression was any more lackluster, Bristol would be tempted to call paramedics.

"I've never understood why you didn't like him."

"I only met him once, and he seemed like a fine young man." She fingered the water glass. "But that doesn't answer my question."

"You mean, why I dated him?"

Grandma just looked at her, probably aware Bristol was stalling.

Why was the question so hard to answer? She was tired. The day was muddling her brain, that's all. She shifted in the chair. "We were a good fit. He's organized, punctual. Steady and dependable. He's…"

"Safe?"

Bristol's gaze went to her grandmother's. "Yes. He did make me feel safe." Until he abruptly broke up with her. Like the guy she'd dated the year before that.

"I see." Grandma's faded eyebrows lifted like they did when she noticed a wrong stitch in one of her crocheted afghans.

Irritation sparked in Bristol's chest. "That's what you say when you don't like what you see."

"Safety is fine. It's a normal thing for a woman to want in a man. And the man you love should make you feel safe." Grandma's eyes and tone held much more than she was saying.

"But?"

"But I just wonder if you know what true safety is."

The frustration flickered into a flame. "Peter was responsible and dependable. That's what I need."

"But do you know why he ended the relationship?"

Bristol swallowed. "I have the feeling you're going to tell me."

"Because you kept trying to control him. As perfect as you say you think Peter was, even he wasn't enough to meet your standards without you trying to change him into the man you think you want." Grandma held Bristol's gaze. "Sugar, you've tried to control every detail of your life ever since the hurricane."

Bristol shifted, looking away as her heart rate quickened. Grandma was supposed to be her comforter, not accuser.

"You've tried to control your mother and the men you've dated. Especially Rem Jones."

Bristol's gaze jerked back. "I didn't try to control him." She took a breath, struggling to tamp down the defensiveness in her tone. "I tried to change him, but he needed to change."

"In some ways, yes. But, sweetie, the fact is we don't always know what's best, for us or others. If we try to control everything, we end up missing out on what we need most."

Bristol quirked an eyebrow, hoping the apathetic gesture would hide the onslaught of ambivalent emotions her grandmother's words were stirring inside her. "Are you saying I needed Remington Jones?"

"I'm saying if you don't let go of trying to keep yourself safe and protected from everything, you will miss out on real joy. And love. God's best gifts usually come as a surprise, often packaged in problems and trials. They're things we never could have planned ourselves, even if we had known we needed them."

And they were back to the God theory. If He knew what she needed, Bristol wouldn't have to worry about ensuring her own safety or the safety of others. If He was really in control and knew what was best, Hurricane Katrina never would have happened. But it had, and she'd learned she was the only one who could prevent something like that from happening to her again. Whether or not her grandmother thought she was too controlling, Bristol refused to go back on the promise she had made to herself sixteen years ago—she would never be helpless again. Bristol cleared her throat and looked away to feign interest in the food. "I'm happy with my life the way it is."

Grandma slipped a folded tissue out from under the cuff of her sleeve and dabbed her nose, her silence saying more than words. But as she slid the tissue back under her sleeve, her smile slowly returned. "Then you won't have to worry about being at risk when you come to dinner to meet my friend, will you?" She trimmed off another bit of her lasagna and looked up with amusement playing around her mouth.

A chuckle built in Bristol's throat and tumbled out. She could never stay mad at her feisty grandma for long. "Fine, I'll come. If only so you'll let me eat this lasagna before it gets cold."

A pleased glint lit Grandma's eyes. "So, do you think I should make the noodle casserole on Friday?"

Bristol laughed and enjoyed another bite. Whoever the friend was, he had to be pretty special to win Grandma's approval. And whoever he was, he could never put her heart more at risk than the man she had to see every day until the bomber was caught.

If she ever figured out how to render Remington Jones safe, she'd be the best bomb technician in the world.

Don't try to stop him. If you do, you will get hurt.
Rem wrote the words from the note on his whiteboard in green marker.

He stepped back, tightened his jaw as he stared at the threat left on Bristol's windshield. The idea that a man so violent was even thinking about Bristol surged bile up his throat.

It had to stop. There had to be some way to find the guy and put him out of business. Before Bristol or anyone else got hurt. The task force seemed to be getting nowhere.

Rem scanned the contents of the whiteboard he'd been working on since Bristol had dropped him off at his apartment.

He'd taped images of all the dams in the area to the board, taking up much of the space. In the center hung printed photos of the Minnesota Falls Dam and the carnage that was once the Leavell Dam. He'd written out the contents of each of the bomber's notes, as best he could remember, next to each dam where they had been found.

Bristol's name stood at the top of the board, written in blue inside a matching circle. He'd rewritten the bomber's note from today under her name, since it was the first time the guy had left one somewhere other than a dam.

Who's the bomber? The words Rem had written mocked him from the right corner of the board. It was the question that haunted him most, grouped among his guesses and deductions about the bomber in the same corner.

Environmentalist
Attention-seeker
Lonely
Calculating
Intelligent
Nonmilitary
Medium height, build, brown/dark hair

The list went on, infuriatingly simple and unenlightening. If only he could find something unusual, something unique, that could ID the guy.

Rem's stomach growled, roaring in the silence of the apartment to remind him he hadn't eaten dinner. He looked at his watch—nine p.m. No wonder he was hungry.

He walked the five feet from his living room to his one-counter kitchen. Didn't feel like heating another frozen entrée. His mother was right. He should've learned to cook.

He grabbed the box of granola bars he'd left on the counter in his rush out the door that morning. Empty. He tossed the box on the counter and it landed faceup. His gaze fell on the Nature's Energy brand name.

Nature must be free. The bomber loved that phrase. Used it in every note and even on the phone when Rem had talked to him. Why?

And why did it seem almost…familiar? He hadn't given it much notice before, always more focused on the bomber's threats against Bristol. But now…had he heard it or seen it somewhere before?

Rem rubbed the back of his neck. Maybe he was trying too hard. Too desperate for a lead.

Shoving the mystery aside, he scrounged for something else to eat.

A brown banana lay on the counter behind the coffeemaker. At least it was food.

His stomach let out another bear-size growl as he snatched the banana and went back to the whiteboard.

His gaze caught on Bristol's name, as it usually did. Was she safe tonight?

She hadn't even looked scared after she'd read the bomber's note. She'd looked mad. At Rem, as usual.

He could still see the snap in her enticing eyes when she'd said, *Life isn't a party.*

His college adviser had delivered variations on that theme every time he'd met with the woman. But he'd been so committed to living exactly how he wanted, out from under his father's thumb, embracing a life full of fun and freedom, that no voice of reason could get through to him in college or—

College. That was it.

His past sparked to life with visions of students clogging the path through central campus. They'd held up signs and shouted stuff about animals or something. Maybe four or five times a year. Were they an environmental group?

Rem had always been recovering from the night before and too out of it to absorb the chants and calls. But he knew someone who'd hung with that crowd, didn't he? What was his name? Rem searched in the recesses of his mind, the regretful part he usually tried to forget.

Danny... Danny Klikson. The thought of his friend unfortunately brought along memories of Rem's wasted past.

He shook his head and went to the faucet at the kitchen counter, suddenly thirsty.

He stared at the clear water as it filled the glass. He was a different man now. He wouldn't make the mistake of living so selfishly again.

He leaned back against the counter as he downed the cool liquid.

Nature must be free.

He was ninety percent sure that was one of the phrases the group used to shout and write on their signs. Danny would know. He could maybe help Remington get the names of all the members, track them down.

But the phrase could be used by anyone else, too. The words were simple and common enough.

Lord, I don't want to pursue this out of arrogance like I used to. I don't want to fall into the trap of being a rebel again, trying to prove I'm smarter than the people in charge.

He didn't want to make a mistake, either, and end up looking like an idiot or adding to the mess of consequences he already had to live with.

The tension in his gut didn't ease. Nor did the two-timed beat of his heart.

He had to follow the lead. If it could save Bristol from harm, it was more than worth looking like the biggest idiot in the world.

Chapter Seventeen

Something yanked Bristol from sleep. Her eyes popped open, but for a second, she didn't know why.

Her phone rang on her nightstand, probably not for the first time.

She scooted up in bed and grabbed the phone, scanning the screen as she lifted it to her ear. "Phoenix?"

"Bring Toby to the Gellar Dam."

Bristol flung off the covers and stood, snatching her cargo pants off the chair where she'd left them in case of such an emergency. "A bomb?" She glanced at the clock on her nightstand as she pulled on the pants over her pajama shorts—2:16 a.m.

Toby jumped up from the floor with a bark, instantly ready to play whatever game she wanted.

"Not sure. The guard called the police to report he saw someone by the dam, but whoever it was ran off when he called out. Bomb squad's been called and Katherine's going with her people. She wants another K-9 to clear the dam and surrounding area as quickly as possible."

"Got it. On my way." She ended the call and headed for the garage at a jog as Toby sprinted ahead of her with an excited yip.

At least the Gellar Dam was the smallest of the ones they were considering high-risk. It was in a suburb in a park area, like Leavell. But a smaller park with no pedestrian bridge.

Her phone rang as she grabbed her jacket from the closet. She stuffed her bare feet into her tennis shoes as she answered without looking for caller ID.

"Bristol." Remington's voice, rougher than normal, made her pulse leap.

"I know. I'm on my way. Can't pick you up."

"I got a ride hail. See you soon."

Bristol didn't have time to figure out why those words made her breathe easier.

She made record time getting to the Gellar Dam, thanks to the lack of traffic at two a.m. But she was relieved to see Miles's squad car, marked with the K-9 emblem, already parked alongside the dirt road. Unmarked FBI vehicles formed a black line that disappeared into the darkness ahead.

Bristol pulled up behind Miles's squad and reached to the passenger seat where she'd thrown her fanny pack.

"Bristol!" Cora's blond hair caught the moonlight as she jogged across the grass, the beam of her flashlight illuminating the path she cut between scattered FBI agents and MPD officers.

Bristol dropped out of the Jeep and hurried to the back, opening the liftgate as Cora reached her side, wearing a pink fleece jacket under her PK-9 windbreaker.

"So glad you're here." She smiled, her pale skin mostly in shadow. "Miles and Duke are searching the interior of the dam. Phoenix said you and Toby should search the exterior areas."

"Got it."

Toby jumped down from the Jeep, wriggling with extra excitement thanks to Cora's presence.

"You're such a good boy." Cora stroked his face with gloved hands. "You have to go to work now, okay?"

"Where is Phoenix?" Bristol stepped back and closed the liftgate, turning into the cold wind that made her wish she'd grabbed her gloves, too. She forgot the temp would drop to thirty or below again tonight.

"She and Dag are trying to track whomever the guard saw. Agent Nguyen went with her."

Bristol headed up the road toward the dam, its lamps like a row of stars stretching a path of light across the dark river. "Where was the person spotted?"

Cora pointed ahead, following at Bristol's side. "Right at the end of the dam on this side of the river."

"We'd better start in this area, then." She pulled a mini-flashlight from her fanny pack and switched it on. "Toby, seek."

He surged to the end of the leash, his nose dipping to the grass-covered ground.

She swallowed but couldn't manage to hold back the question driving her tongue. "Is Remington here?"

"Take a look." Cora's voice carried a smile.

Bristol glanced up from Toby to see a familiar, tall form walking away from the batch of uniforms clustered by the dam and heading their way. Her heart rate seemed to surge to the end of its own leash.

"Hey." The one word from Remington should not make her pulse skip in the middle of its sprint like that.

"Hello." She pushed out a long breath, willing herself to relax. They hadn't parted on good terms at the end of the day, anyway, with her still seething over his cavalier attitude. About the bomb searches and about their past.

Admitting he'd been wrong and apologizing might be more

than she'd expected, but she couldn't believe he wanted her to just forget what happened without any explanation as to why he'd done it. Without any reason for how he could've so easily thrown away their relationship.

Remington fell into step on Bristol's other side as she followed Toby's swinging path, drawing closer to the border of the river's rushing water.

He wouldn't bring up their past with Cora here, would he? Bristol tensed. Took the offensive. "Has Miles found anything in the dam?"

"A duffel bag." Remington pushed his hands into the pockets of his jacket.

Her grip cinched tighter on Toby's leash. "Did Duke alert?"

"No. Turned out to belong to the guard on day shift. His gym bag. He accidentally left it behind."

"That's a relief."

"Does anyone else think this is weird?" Remington asked the question just as Toby pulled Bristol into his path.

Remington deftly angled out of the way to avoid a collision and readjusted his pace to keep up.

"What do you mean?" Cora gave him a patient smile, while Bristol held her breath.

He better not be talking about the awkwardness between them. "Why would the bomber suddenly show up here, not plant a bomb in the dam and end up being seen?"

A warning flag popped up in Bristol's mind. She hadn't had a moment since scrambling out of bed to think about anything beyond finding potential explosives. But he was right. It didn't match what they knew of the bomber or his pattern.

"You mean because he's been too smart to be seen before." Cora looked at Remington across Bristol as they walked briskly behind Toby.

"Exactly. This guy knows how to evade security cameras and create false IDs. But this…" Remington pulled his hand from his pocket to gesture toward the dam. "This is just sloppy."

Cora nodded. "That's what Phoenix said before she left with Dag. She wanted me to tell you to be extra cautious, Bris. She said she doesn't like the smell of this."

Neither did Bristol.

Just what was the bomber up to?

FBI agents and a couple cops moved aside as Toby wove past, bringing them to the path that turned and led up to the edge of the dam.

Toby smelled a patch of dirt, then something that looked like a blob of mud on the grass near the path. He moved on quickly, still sniffing for explosives.

Bristol followed Toby with her body but twisted to swing her flashlight back over the ground he'd just covered. "Toby, wait."

"What is it?" Remington stopped and followed her gaze as Cora did the same.

Bristol looked at the bump of something dark Toby had left behind. "Is that…meat?"

Remington stepped close to the object and crouched to examine it. "Looks like a hamburger. Raw."

"What would uncooked hamburger be doing out here?" Cora lifted her eyebrows.

"I can think of only one reason." Bristol clenched her jaw hard. "Hey." She called to the officers standing nearby. "Have the lab bag this and test it, would you?"

"You don't think…" Dismay shifted Cora's features.

"I do." Bristol glanced at Remington.

He looked as angry as she felt. "Poison."

Meant for the K-9s.

Chapter Eighteen

Bristol reluctantly followed Remington farther into the diner, already regretting that she'd agreed to stop here for lunch before going to search their fourth dam of the day.

Despite Remington's rave review, the inside of the restaurant didn't look any better than the outside. Faded paint, a flashing neon sign with one letter burned out and decaying brick had given way to a sixties-themed interior that obviously dated back to that era.

Scratches slashed the avocado paint on the wooden chairs that surrounded small square tables covered in checkered cloths. Along the grass-cloth-covered walls, booths with orange vinyl seats clustered together, most of them occupied, despite the off-putting decor and grim prospects for the food.

Remington appeared to be headed for an empty booth, but Bristol made a beeline for a far less cozy table instead.

"Down." She gave the signal to Toby to lie down, and he obeyed, dropping underneath the table and shifting onto one hip in a relaxed pose.

"He's so adorable." The hostess with a heart-shaped face that matched her heart-patterned apron smiled down at Toby as she set two laminated menus in front of Bristol and Remington.

The hostess let out a swoony sigh as her gaze drifted over Remington's grin, despite her having at least twenty years on the man who wore it.

But his charm had somehow worked to get Toby in the door. That and his spiel about Toby being an official K-9 working with the FBI on an important assignment.

All true, but if Bristol had delivered the same story, she doubted the hostess would have let Toby set one paw in the diner. Staring at the jelly stain on her menu, she was sorry Remington had such persuasive powers. She never thought she'd be caught dead in a dive like this—serving greasy, heart-attack-on-a-plate meals and likely ducking the restaurant health code. She still wasn't sure why she'd agreed to try it. Probably because she was dragging from the long night and was tired of Remington giving her puppy-dog eyes.

"Isn't this nice?"

She kept her face covered by the menu in answer to Remington's question.

"You deserve a moment to sit down and relax after last night. Did you get any sleep?"

"Enough." She pretended to peruse the menu's options. He was right, she hadn't gotten much sleep. By the time the Gellar Dam and surrounding area had been canvassed and declared safe, there'd only been about an hour left to grab a few winks before starting the morning searches at other dams.

Finding more deposits of hamburger meat on the grounds around the Gellar Dam, likely all laced with something meant to finish off Toby or Duke, hadn't helped her sleep any better. Thankfully, both dogs held to their training and didn't touch the poisoned food.

If only Phoenix and Dag had been able to find the perp. But the man's trail dead-ended on a road about a mile from the dam. They'd found tire tracks and footprints the lab would analyze. Since other people had walked in those areas, the footprints wouldn't be very helpful, but the tire tracks had more potential. Could lead to the make of the bomber's car.

A long, lean finger appeared in front of her and tapped the onion rings menu item.

She lowered her laminated nightmare and narrowed her eyes at Remington. She wasn't as easy to manipulate as the hostess.

Never mind the somersault her heart performed when he waggled his eyebrows over twinkling irises.

"I'm telling you, best onion rings ever. You have to try them."

"And I told you, I don't even like onion rings."

He sighed and set down his menu. "Look, we're here, so you might as well relax a little and have some fun. I promise you won't regret it."

"I already do." She lifted her menu to see if there was anything remotely healthy to order.

House Salad.

Terrific. Probably a bed of wilted iceberg with some slivered carrots on top, but it looked like the best choice.

The hostess, apparently also their waitress, came back promptly. Probably couldn't stand to be away from Remington longer than five minutes.

Bristol stifled an eye roll as the woman drank in the sight of him while he ordered a bacon cheeseburger and a platter of onion rings.

"And for you, dear?" To her credit, the waitress managed to stop looking at him long enough to meet Bristol's gaze.

"House salad, no dressing."

The woman's smile faltered for a moment. "No dressing at all?"

"That's right."

She turned the smile back up. "Certainly."

Remington chuckled as she left, a soft, deep sound that made Bristol's pulse skitter. "A house salad, no dressing?"

She lifted an eyebrow. "What's wrong with that?"

He held up his hands. "Nothing. It's very healthy." The sparkle in his eyes showed he wanted to say more.

"But?"

His fingers pushed through that thick wave of hair, making it droop more than he likely wanted for the style. But the result of the tendrils touching his forehead was incredibly effective if he wanted to disarm her.

She had to battle the desire to reach across the table and brush the rebels back—

"I just wonder what happened to the Bristol who could let go and do something unexpected now and then. Have some fun."

Perfect timing. She needed a stark reminder of how different they were, how he could never be relied on. A reminder of why she needed to keep her guard up and her mind on doing her job. "You know exactly what happened."

A frown flipped his mouth. He fiddled with the straw in his glass of ice water, bobbing the black tube up and down. "You're never going to forgive me, are you?"

Frustration rose in her chest, pushing into her throat. She met his gaze.

Big mistake.

His eyes, aimed at her under lowered brows, melted into a dark pool of intensity.

But her anger wouldn't be so easily diffused. "How dare you act like I'm the one making this difficult. I'm not the one who threw everything away." Emotion threatened to contort her voice on the last words. She glanced at the cartoon Pluto clock on the wall. Took a breath.

She brought her gaze back to his face, the tension lining his mouth and his widened eyes, full of an emotional swirl she couldn't read. "Why?" The question barely escaped her throat. She leaned forward. "I thought we…" She moistened her lips. Couldn't say that she'd thought they had something special. That they were in love. But she did force out the question burning her heart. "Why would you throw away what we had and tell me you had no choice?"

He pulled back. The chair creaked slightly as he crossed his arms over his chest. He looked away, the line of his beard sharpening as he firmed his jaw. "My dad said he'd never speak to me again if I didn't graduate from the academy." His voice came out rough, raw. "My relationship with my dad has always been…difficult. But I knew if I didn't make it at the academy, he'd hate me." Rem swung his gaze back to her. His brown eyes were filled with aching pain, his features strained with regret.

Her breath caught. "You never told me."

He shifted, lowering his arms to rest on either side of his plate. "It was embarrassing. The son of a second-generation cop, and I was in danger of flunking out of the police academy."

"But you had the skills and intelligence to make it. You just—"

"Didn't put in the work?" A rueful smile touched his lips. "I knew that's what you'd say if I had told you." He let out a light laugh, bracing both hands around his water glass. "And you would've been exactly right, as usual."

"Why not put in the work when you knew you weren't going to make it? I would've helped you."

"I've asked myself that question for the last six years. But I'd heard the lectures and berating from my dad my whole life. He'd groomed me to become a cop—like my grandpa and him—since I was born." He shook his head. "My brother went along with it, but I hated it. Hated having my future planned out for me by someone else, someone who didn't care what I wanted to do."

"You could've done something else, couldn't you?"

"Only if I was willing to lose any chance at my dad's approval. His love. I guess I wasn't willing to go quite that far. But I wanted to get every bit of freedom and fun I could while still giving him what he wanted."

He dragged a hand down his beard. "I'd done the same thing all through undergrad. I thought of all my professors, anyone above me, as just like my dad—people who wanted to force me to do what they wanted with no thought for my desires, so I rebelled against them, too. Goofed off and bucked the rules and cheated when I had to in order to graduate. But I never got caught there."

He sat forward and leaned his elbows on the table. "And I didn't know you in college."

Her heart squeezed at the sincerity and remorse in the chocolate pool of his eyes.

"No reason in the world could excuse what I did. And I've regretted it every day of my life since." He took in a shaky breath. "Believe me, if I could do it over, I would never do anything that would risk throwing away what we had. I think, at the time, I fooled myself into believing it wouldn't matter for us. That you and I could still have the life we'd started to plan. I didn't understand why integrity and responsibility mattered."

Did she believe him? Could she?

She didn't breathe as he held her gaze—

A platter clunked down between them.

"Enjoy." The waitress gave them a broad grin and left the mountain of onion rings on the table as if she'd given them all they needed.

Remington's features relaxed into an angled grin. "Wait till you try these. Your life will never be the same." He grabbed a breaded, greasy onion ring and fit the whole thing in his mouth. A groan escaped his lips. Grabbing another ring, he held it out toward her. "You have to try one."

"No, thanks." She held up a hand.

"I won't let you say no." He pushed it toward her mouth. "Come on, just one bite." Was he seriously going to feed her?

Heat flushed her cheeks as she snatched the offending object from his hand before he could act on the intention. "Fine." She took a quick, small bite.

The flavor started on her tongue, then melted into her whole mouth, exploding in a more nuanced and far better taste than she ever would have imagined.

"See?" His grin broadened as he studied her reaction. "Spectacular, right?"

She swallowed the piece. "Spectacular is a bit strong." She broke off another section of the onion ring, her taste buds already craving more. "But I will admit, it's better than I expected."

He laughed, taking another ring for himself. "That'll do for now. Just don't eat too many or you won't have room left for your salad." He winked, sending her pulse into a spiral that couldn't be healthy.

She wiped her fingers on the paper napkin she had laid across her lap, glad for the excuse to look away. If she didn't get a handle on her emotions, she was in serious trouble. Remington was still not right for her, no matter how much regret he—

An electronic buzz and beep, like a phone alert, sounded.

"Sorry." Remington took out his cell and checked the screen. His eyes widened slightly and his lips parted. Was he excited or worried?

"What is it?"

He shot her a glance. "Nothing. I mean, nothing to worry about. I just got a text from an old friend I've been trying to reach. Haven't heard from him in years." He tried for a smile, but it dropped, distraction obvious in his eyes. He slid his chair back. "I'm sorry, but I really need to make a quick phone call. It'll just be a minute."

He was up and gone before she could decide how to react. He disappeared from view around a corner that a sign indicated led to the bathrooms. He'd even left his beloved onion rings while they were hot.

It was for the best, anyway. His rush exit from the table left her with the space to breathe and think more clearly. She felt badly about his dad and the pressures on Remington she hadn't known about at the academy. But, like he said, that didn't excuse that he had cheated and ultimately didn't change anything between them. He'd proven through his actions that he didn't prioritize her and their relationship above himself. And that he was willing to do something wrong to get what he wanted.

He claimed that had changed. And part of her, the gullible heart she tried to ignore, wanted to believe him. But she couldn't risk depending on a man who would let her down in the end. Again.

She flagged down the waitress, intent on getting her to package the remaining part of their meals in to-go containers. Bristol also wasn't going to risk another emotional conversation or chink in her heart's armor.

★ ★ ★

"Who could ever forget Rem Jones?" Krista Goldman's giggly laugh carried over the phone, sounding every bit like the quintessential sorority girl that Danny had described.

Danny's text message had said she was married now. Used to be Krista Stibbles. According to Danny, she'd been a real partyer at college and president of the Students for the Environment Society, or SES. And though she apparently remembered him from the parties they'd likely both attended, Rem thankfully didn't have a single memory of the woman.

"Well, we all have to grow up sometime, right?" Rem turned around to pace in the direction of the dining area. Where Bristol was waiting for him.

"Say it isn't so." She breathed an exaggerated sigh in his ear.

"I'm actually hoping you can help me out with something."

"Oh, I'm sure I can! I've been a sorority house mom for six years now, so helping sisters and everyone else is really my job, you might say."

Wow. Danny hadn't told him she'd barely left the sorority. "I have a few questions about SES. Do you know how long it existed before you became president?" He might have multiple generations of students to consider if the club had existed for long and used the same motto.

"Um, like a semester. I took over from a senior who graduated midyear. She was my roommate first part of freshman year."

Good. Krista had been one year behind Rem, so at least he didn't have a lot of history to research. He might have to figure out a way to get the names of SES members after Krista graduated, but he'd start with whatever she could tell him. "Did you always use that motto 'Nature must be free'?"

She giggled. "Yeah, I came up with that. Pretty good, don't you think? Everybody loved shouting that at our protests. But they came up with a different motto after I graduated. 'Save the trees.' Pretty sad, don't you think?"

"Definitely lacks the same punch." But the change was perfect for his purposes. If his theory was right, and the motto of this club had informed Libertas's stock phrase, then the pool of possible suspects just shrunk to four school years. Rem paused near the end of the hallway, before he could see Bristol and she could see him. If she hadn't ditched him already. He had the feeling she might not want to continue their walk down memory lane. "I'm looking for a man who used to be a member of your club, I think."

Krista chuckled. "We had a lot of guys in there. Why do you think I was president?"

Terrific. He switched directions and paced back along the restroom doors. "Do you remember if there was anyone who took it really seriously? Like, maybe too seriously?"

"Most of us were in it just for fun. You know, have a reason to protest and be seen on campus, shouting."

"Yeah, I get it."

"There were a couple science majors who were pretty into it."

He stopped. "Yeah? Do you remember their names?"

"Well, one was a girl. Brenda something. She never joined any of the sororities, but I don't know why. I read about her in the alumni magazine the other day. You probably saw the article. About the girl who did some study that helped chimpanzees in Africa? Or maybe it was South America. I don't remember. But she did something cool for the environment."

"And the guy?"

"Oh, yeah, he was sort of cute. Definitely in a geeky way, though."

Rem rubbed the back of his neck, forcing himself to be patient. "Do you remember his name?"

"Um. No, I'm not sure. I think I'm friends with him online. I can get back to you."

"Great. I'll give you my email."

"Or I could call."

He cringed at the interest in her tone. He wasn't exactly in the market for a girlfriend at the moment. At least not one without an explosives detection dog or beautiful blue-gray eyes. "I'm hard to get ahold of via phone. Email's easier."

"Sure." Her tone changed as she seemed to get the message.

He continued before she could end the call prematurely. "I really appreciate your help with this. Can you think of anyone else who was serious about the club?"

"Well, there were a couple others, but they weren't science majors." She giggled. "There was one guy who had a big crush on me. Not real cute, but he had a nice build. Super into the club, even though he was an English major. Maybe Philosophy. Something sort of artsy like that. He had a moody vibe some of the girls were into."

"So he was passionate about the environment?"

"Like me and pledges." She laughed.

He gripped the phone tighter. Passionate enough to become an environmental terrorist? "Could you get your hands on a roster of the club members during the time you were president?"

"Absolutely. I have it in my files. One thing a sorority mom has to be is organized."

"Awesome. Thanks." He rotated back toward the dining area. "And could you mark the names of any other students you remember were especially enthusiastic about the environmental cause? That'd be a big help."

"Happy to do what I can."

"Really appreciate it." He quickly gave her his email address.

"I'll email you tonight." Her tone lifted in a cheerful lilt. "And if you want to get together sometime and catch up, just give me a call."

"Okay, bye." He blew out a breath and headed around the corner.

Bristol was still there, Toby lounging at her feet.

But two Styrofoam containers sat on the table, one open in front of her.

She'd clearly picked over the salad it contained, leaving the wilted lettuce and overly wet cucumbers.

He quirked a smile at her. "Salads aren't really their strong suit."

"Obviously." Irritation darkened her eyes to gray.

How he'd love to have that change to approval if he told her he was working on a lead to find the bomber. But it was a long shot this hunch would pay off. He wouldn't tell her about it until he was sure, in case he was way off base. He couldn't afford to lose even more points in her eyes.

"I hope you didn't pay yet. I'd like to buy."

"Okay." She pushed to her feet. "I'll meet you at the Jeep. Come on, Toby." She didn't look at Rem as she left, passing the waitress on the way out.

He picked up his to-go container and paid quickly, rethinking his decision to make the phone call rather than stay at the table and try to bring the conversation back to them, their relationship. He had hoped his confession might've cleared the air a little and made her think differently about him, but why should it? Pressure from his dad didn't excuse what he did. Not in God's eyes, let alone Bristol's. Wrong was wrong, and there were consequences to making mistakes.

He pushed through the glass door and stepped onto the sidewalk, raindrops pelting his head with the showers that never seemed to stop. He pulled the hood of his jacket over his hair and headed for the Jeep, parallel-parked along the sidewalk a few cars down.

As he passed the black sedan in front of the Jeep, he caught sight of Bristol. Why was she standing outside the Jeep?

Her body was blocked by the open driver's door, but he could see her head, hair getting wet without her hood. Why hadn't she put it up?

"Bristol?"

She stepped back from the door enough to hold out a hand toward him. "Stay back." Her sharp command froze him in place.

For two seconds.

He went to the passenger side and looked through the window.

Something sat on the driver's seat. Raindrops blurred his view too much to make out what it was. "Is it a bomb?"

Through the blurred glass, he could see her gloved hands moving toward the object. Touching it. Moving it.

He held his breath. What if she—

"No. It's a hoax."

Thank you, Lord.

His breathing resumed, but his heart still pounded as he jogged around the Jeep, ignoring the traffic that sped by them with inches to spare.

Bristol glanced at him as he stopped next to her. No fear or alarm flickered in her blue-gray eyes. They held only the steely calm he couldn't fathom.

He looked past her to the driver's seat.

Seemed like a bomb at first glance. Short silver pipes were bound together with wire, and a timer sat on top.

"How'd you know it wasn't real?"

"Toby."

The dog sat calmly in the back, watching them with his tongue lolling to one side.

"He would never let me get this close to explosives without warning me." She grabbed the fake bomb. "The pipes are light, apparently empty. And there's this." She flipped it over, revealing a piece of paper taped to the back.

Words were written in red permanent marker. *BOOM. Stop the search or next time it's real.*

Rem angled so he could see Bristol's face, but she still showed no sign of fear or even concern. The woman had nerves like he'd never seen. Or she was very good at hiding her emotions. "Are you okay?"

Her lips angled in a wry smile. "He'll have to get a lot more creative than bombs if he wants to scare me. I can handle any device he sends my way."

Rem glanced behind the Jeep and in front of it. Both the parked vehicles there were empty. At least they appeared to be. "You know what this means, though, right?"

She pulled out a bag from her fanny pack and started to put the fake bomb inside it.

"There's only one way the bomber could've found you here, right now."

She sealed the bag and turned her head to look at Rem, resolve graying her eyes. "He's following me."

Chapter Nineteen

The roar of the Minnesota Falls crashing down the spillway reached Bristol's ears as she and Toby exited the dam through the door Remington held open. Despite how close and loud the sound seemed, the falls were on the other side of the visitor center and dam complex. Here, down at water level by the entrance of the boat navigation lock, the river was low and fairly calm, lapping gently against its concrete borders.

While Toby searched along the safety rail, Bristol leaned over it to look through the lock. The huge doors at the close end were open, flush with the sides of the tunnel-like passageway. But the other end appeared to be blocked.

She glanced back at Remington, who'd drifted into one of the pensive silences she had never known him to have at the academy.

He stood about six feet away from her, hands in the pockets of his jacket and his eyebrows drawn together in the grim expression that hadn't lifted since she'd found the hoax device in her Jeep.

A strange urge to lighten his expression bubbled in her throat. "At least the sun's out now."

His gaze shifted to the sky, and she also allowed herself a second to appreciate the beautiful sight of the clouds parting, revealing orange rays that streaked the sky like a farewell wave as the orb started its downward departure.

"Yeah." He glanced left and then right, his gaze locking on the bare patch of gravel and sand that bordered the ten-foot chain-link fence on the opposite side of the lock. "We'll have to check over there, too. The fence should keep out trespassers, but a person could maybe get up to the building in the corner with some ingenuity."

"We'll search it." As they had yesterday. She switched her attention to Toby while he darted toward the large, square bins she assumed were used for storage. She followed him around the first bin, a giant orange box.

She glanced back to see Remington had stayed where he was, twisting back to check the door they'd just exited as if he expected someone to appear.

When she and Toby reached the other side of the bin, Remington had taken a few steps ahead to stand near the second bin. His head tilted up as he scanned the extensive stairway that climbed the equivalent of three stories to the top of the dam.

He lowered his gaze again, looking back and forth. He'd done the same thing in the Jeep on the way here, checking for tails as if she wasn't already doing that while she drove. Was the guy that easily spooked?

"I don't think he'd follow us out here. It's too restricted." She let her voice carry without looking as she passed Remington and followed Toby's energetic clip.

Footsteps sounded behind her as Remington closed the

gap between them. "I'm just concerned. Mostly that you're not concerned."

She peered at him without fully turning her head.

He passed a hand through his wave of hair, the front tendrils darkened and damp from the rain that had soaked them earlier even with the hood he'd worn before they'd gone inside the dam. "Is Phoenix still watching your house at night?"

"No." As if she needed someone to patrol her house. "I'm quite capable of taking care of myself."

"I don't doubt that." A hint of humor in his voice drew her gaze.

His lips curved in a small smile that eased the tension she didn't know had been clutching her heart. This was the Remington she knew. Relaxed and smiling. Not wound tight as a spring with worry.

The thought hit her hard just as they reached the other side of the white bin. He wasn't scared for himself. He was worried. About her. Was that possible?

She aimed Toby back toward the six-foot vertical row of lights that looked like a blown-up version of traffic signals. For boats, in this case.

She hurried to keep up with the quick K-9, relieved to move ahead of Remington and have a moment to make sense of this new turn.

When Remington had gotten caught cheating on tests, she'd convinced herself he must not have cared for her at all. She'd once thought he had loved her, but how could he and still do what he had done, knowing his dishonesty and cheating would mean the end of their relationship? But now he was acting as if he did care about her. Always wanting to be sure she was protected and safe.

Her heart started to melt a little, right in the center.

Then alarm seized her chest. What was she thinking? She

could not do this again. Remington was not a safe risk, and she knew it better than anyone.

"Seek." Toby didn't really need the reminder, still pumping his tail as he moved toward the metal framework that provided a rickety-looking base for the tall staircase. But she needed to remind herself what they were doing here. She was searching for explosives.

Remington was her gateway to the dams to get her job done, nothing more.

She directed Toby to the base of the stairs. "Climb." They started the long ascent, her determination to resist Remington solidifying. He should know she didn't need anyone's protection, anyway.

Movement at the top of the dam's wall caught her eye.

She tensed her grip on Toby's leash as they continued to climb.

"That you, Jones?" A man's voice drifted down to them, nearly intercepted by the cold wind that blew stronger the higher they went. "Bringing up the rear?"

"Calvin." Remington's tone communicated his dread without her having to look back at him.

The short man looked smaller from this distance, lounging with one leg slung in front of the other as he leaned against the stairway's railing at the top.

She hadn't liked the guy at the task force meeting, and her opinion of him just plummeted ten more degrees.

He'd struck her as an immature man with a juvenile resentment of Remington, and he was backing up her assessment now.

Sympathy for Remington interrupted her effort to steel herself against him. "Want to go back down?" Still far enough from Calvin that he wouldn't be able to hear, she infused the suggestion with a note of humor she hoped Remington would catch.

His chuckle tickled the back of her neck. "What's the matter—don't you think I can take care of myself?"

She bit back a laugh as she got within range of Calvin's triumphant grin.

The man was apparently still reveling in his attempt at a put-down that Remington probably didn't even care one lick about.

"Toby will run you over if you don't move."

Calvin's smile faded, and he jumped to the side as Bristol let Toby charge ahead, climbing the last step to reach the top of the building.

"Good boy." Bristol reached down to pet Toby, the dog's tongue hanging far out, though his fast movements and excited tail wag implied he had just gotten warmed up.

"What can I do for you, Calvin?" Remington didn't sound winded in the slightest as he crested the top of the stairs and looked at his adversary with a pleasant expression she couldn't fake. He'd certainly stayed in shape since the academy.

Not that she cared. She forced her gaze away from his trim physique.

"I do have work I do at the dams, you know." Calvin sneered. "I don't visit them to see you."

"Glad to hear it." The corner of Remington's mouth twitched almost imperceptibly, but she caught the sign of suppressed humor. "We have work to do, too, so…" He started to walk around Calvin, but the engineer stepped in Remington's path.

"I saw the new security plan you sent out. You can't honestly think the dam owners or the DNR will agree to that. The army certainly won't go along with it at their dams."

Remington met the man's challenge with a softer gaze than he deserved. "We'll have to wait and see."

"You might be happy to wait, but the rest of us want to do something to protect the dams from this—" Calvin waved his hand toward Bristol and Toby as if they were somehow the cause of the bomb threats "—this terrorism."

"We're all working toward a solution, Calvin."

"We'll never get one waiting for you to come up with something in your haphazard way of doing things." Calvin leaned into Remington's space. "I'm starting a committee to handle the security concerns instead."

Remington's eyebrows lifted with surprise she wished he hadn't let Calvin see. "Is Franklin aware of that?"

"Of course. I talked to him about it just this morning."

Remington didn't flinch. "What did he say?"

Calvin's aggressive stance reversed, his body shifting back. "He's considering it."

Remington ran a hand over his chin. "I see. Well, keep me posted."

Calvin's eyes narrowed, his gaze jumping from Remington to Bristol and back again. Clearly not the response he thought he'd get. "I'll do that." He managed to add enough intensity to make the statement sound like a threat.

He turned, hopefully to leave, but stopped and swung back. "You're going to have to do something way more impressive if you want to keep your job, Jones. Franklin's going to see I'm the better man for the position. It's only a matter of time. And not much of it for you. Ticktock." The engineer pulled away quickly as if he wanted to guarantee he got the last word. He hurried across the walkway that spanned the lock and would bring Calvin back to the visitor center, from where he'd likely come.

Bristol let out a breath to release the tension she'd absorbed, though she wasn't even the man's target. "It might just be me, but somehow I get the impression that guy doesn't like you."

Another deep chuckle from Remington shot warmth through her belly.

She glanced at him to catch the grin that curved his lips and tripped her pulse.

"That surprises you?" He quirked a teasing eyebrow.

"Are you going to tell me why?"

"Dodging the question, I see."

She swung away from his angled grin before she was tempted to return it or yield to the charming sparkle in his eyes. "Seek."

Toby launched into action, tail whipping rapidly from side to side as he cleared the fairly open area inside the fence that edged the perimeter of the building.

"Simple answer is Calvin wanted my job." Remington's voice indicated he followed her and Toby. "Still does apparently."

A strong gust of air blew into her light half-zip pullover, making her consider stopping to remove her fanny pack and zip up the open jacket she wore as a top layer. The fifty-degree weather must have dropped into the forties with the lowering sun. But they'd be inside soon. "Does he have a reason to think he should've had it?"

There, Phoenix should be happy. Bristol was investigating Remington just like she was supposed to. But she held her breath as she waited for the answer, hoping she wouldn't hear he'd gotten the job by some underhanded means—like cheating at a police academy.

"In a way, I suppose."

Her chest clenched.

Toby trotted toward the walkway, and she hustled to keep

up, glancing through the slots in the metal bridge to the water in the lock below.

"He has more seniority with the DNR."

Was that all? Her muscles relaxed.

"He was angry when I was hired as the assistant to the previous safety and security supervisor. Graham was very kind to me, showed me the ropes and sort of groomed me to take over for him. So when he retired, I was given the job because of my training and my security experience and background."

Bristol glanced back to see Remington trailing just a couple feet behind her. "And Calvin's never gotten over it."

"If anything, he seems to hate me more the longer I have the job."

She stopped at the end of the walkway, turning to face Remington. "But would Calvin even have the skills to do your job?"

He paused, the fading sunlight giving his eyes a golden hue that spurred a flutter in her stomach. "He's chief engineer, in charge of all the engineers for the Minnesota DNR. He knows a lot about dams, but not much about security, terrorism and criminals."

"That's surprising."

His head angled slightly as his gaze stayed on her face.

"He reminds me of some of the criminals I used to arrest. Except they were friendlier."

A laugh, full and with a scratchy edge as if from a lot of use, burst from his lips. His eyes softened as they latched on to hers. "Is that a smile?" He reached toward the corner of her mouth with a finger, stopping a breath away from touching her. "Careful, Ms. Bachmann. I'll think you're starting to like me."

Toby barked and tugged on the leash. Perfectly timed interruption. That dog had great instincts.

She let him have some slack as she started for the other staircase they'd have to take back down, this time to check the platform on the opposite side of the lock. Toby's eagerness to work functioned as a reality check just when she needed it. Work, not romance.

The whole thing with Calvin had gotten her off track. Maybe as he'd intended?

She halted Toby at the top of the stairway and spun to face Remington, who stopped just in time to avoid thudding into her. She forced herself to ignore his proximity and the sudden shallowness of her breathing as a result. "Do you think…"

"Yep, I was just thinking the same thing."

Was he really? The thought gave her a thrill, summoning memories of when they used to complement each other like that and seemed to pair together perfectly, like they were meant to be.

"But it's so unlikely." He looked away and took a step back, glancing downriver. "Calvin is obsessed with dams."

"Isn't the terrorist, too?"

"No, I mean, he loves them as if they were his children." Remington shook his head. "I couldn't see him ever trying to blow one up."

"But he does have motive. He wants your job. If he could make you look bad…"

Remington laughed. "He wouldn't have to go to all that effort to make me look bad. I do a good job of that myself." The twinkle in Remington's eyes and the humility in his tone were enough to get at her heart again, all too easily.

She turned toward the stairs and gave Toby the signal he was eagerly waiting for to get back to work. They started the downward trek, this staircase running in a zigzag pattern along the wall, which somehow made the distance seem less daunting.

"Does Calvin have the security clearance you do?" She asked the question without looking back, Remington's footsteps sounding on the metal stairs behind her.

"Yes. He can get into any dam in the state whenever he wants to. If Calvin had been the bomber, though, he would've been recognized, here and at Leavell. He wouldn't have pretended to be Darren, our other engineer."

"True. But he could be an accomplice. The inside man." She paused on the first landing to have Toby smell along the edges in case a device had been attached to the outer frame of the stairway.

"I just can't believe Calvin would do that. He's definitely not an environmentalist in any sense. He loves technology and engineering. I just can't see it."

He had a point, but it was possible their bomber was faking the environmental extremism to throw them off track.

One thing Calvin was obviously serious about was getting Remington's job. "Are you worried about his threat?"

"You mean that I'll lose my job?"

"Yeah."

Toby started down the next flight of stairs, and she turned away from Remington to follow.

"A little. I've made a lot of changes to regulations and such since I got the position. That much change makes some people unhappy."

She twisted her head to toss him a look. "Like Calvin?"

"Especially Calvin."

They reached the next landing, and Toby went to work on the perimeter.

"But he has some supporters at the DNR. Hard to believe, isn't it?" That impish grin snuck onto Remington's face.

"What is?" Bristol glanced at him in between watching Toby for an indication.

"That not everyone loves me." He winked, and her pulse jumped into her throat.

Getting harder to believe every day.

Rem rubbed at the soreness in his lower back as he leaned away from the screen of his laptop. He should really get a desk with some comfortable chair instead of using his dining table and a wobbly wooden seat as his home office.

Of course, he didn't usually spend this much time on his computer at the apartment. Krista had already emailed him the list of SES members by the time he and Bristol were done searching for the day. His tired body prodded him to get some much-needed sleep, but he couldn't go to bed until he'd made progress on his own search—for the bomber.

An hour and a half later, he'd finished investigating the first two names Krista had marked as especially committed to the environmental cause.

The first name Krista had designated with a pen-drawn mini-heart was Brenda Adams, listed as a science major. She was unlikely to be the bomber, since the threatening calls had been made by a man, but allowing for Bristol's accomplice theory, Rem followed up on the woman, anyway.

A little research revealed her progress for the environment didn't have anything to do with chimps but was instead making strides toward a possible source of clean energy. An impressive woman with a high-profile job and a ton to lose if she turned terrorist and blew up dams in Minnesota.

He'd crossed her off his mental list.

Second name marked on the alphabetical roster was Jayson Callahan. His college photos and science major made him a possibility for Krista's cute but geeky guy in the club.

Rem doubted the more current pictures he found online would appeal to shallow Krista anymore. Now a biology teacher at a Saint Paul high school, Jayson appeared to be a comfortable family man with a wife and three children.

A social media search found Jayson tagged in a photo with some boys from the basketball team he apparently coached. Dated the same day as the Leavell Dam bombing.

Not likely Jayson could do both in one day or would want to.

A Tristan Doyle was the next heart-marked name. One of three philosophy majors on the list.

Rem typed the name into the internet search bar, along with the Twin Cities location.

A phone number and address came up easily enough. Only one Tristan Doyle in the Twin Cities. Looked like he lived in the Garden Valley suburb.

The man had little else to be found online. No social media accounts, no employment records. At least none that Rem could find.

Was he the same Tristan Doyle from SES?

Rem leaned back in his chair, then stood. Only one way to find out.

He grabbed his cell from the kitchen counter and brought it over to his computer where he could read the phone number to punch in. Eight forty-five at night shouldn't be too late to call.

"Hello?" A husky voice answered on the third ring.

"Hi, is this Tristan Doyle?"

The guy cleared his throat. "Yeah. If you're trying to sell me something, I'm not interested."

"I'm not selling anything. I'm actually a fellow alum of U of M. We were there around the same time."

"You want me to give the school money? I already paid tuition. That's plenty if—"

"No, no. I'm not asking for money, honestly." Rem scrambled for the best approach. "You probably don't remember me, but my name is David Jones." Using his middle name seemed a wise precaution in case he was actually talking to the bomber. His real name and position with the DNR had probably been included in some of the news coverage surrounding the bomb threat.

"I don't remember."

"I was friends with Danny Klikson, who was in your environmental group. The SES, right? Students for the Environment. I remember you used to do protests on campus. I'd watch sometimes." If he could count shooting them annoyed glares as he trudged past.

A pause. "Danny Klikson sounds kind of familiar."

Maybe he'd have more success with the memory of Krista. "I got your name from Krista Goldman, who used to be Krista Stibbles before she got married."

"Divorced."

"Pardon me?"

"She's divorced now. A shame, too. She has two kids."

"Oh. I didn't know. That is a shame." And interesting that Tristan cared. Maybe he was the guy who'd had a crush on Krista and still had one now. "Krista gave me your name because I'm interested in environmental preservation. I've grown up a lot since college and learned to care about the world around us." All true. Even if he wouldn't blow up a dam over it. "I wondered, since you live in the Twin Cities, too, if you know of any groups I could get involved in?"

"Sure. There's always something going on. I'm in the TCES that meets once a month at Springway Park."

Twin Cities Environmental Society, Rem assumed. "Oh, awesome. What day?"

"Sunday nights, third week of every month."

"Oh, bummer. I wouldn't be able to go Sunday night because of church."

"Sunday night?" Tristan's voice lifted with disbelief. "You must be a religious nut or something."

Rem chuckled. "Yeah, you might say that. Jesus Christ is number one in my life. How about you? You go to church?"

"Sure. All the time. I just drive out to Whitlow Park or Springway." Tristan's mirth at his joke carried across the line. "That's my church."

"So who's your god, then?"

Tristan laughed. "I don't know. The sun, I suppose."

Not water. Did that mean he wasn't the river-obsessed terrorist? "The sun is pretty amazing and powerful."

"Yeah. It'll burn us up if humans don't stop creating so many pollutants that destroy the ozone layer. Take me—I didn't even own a car until two months ago. I need it for my work now, but I got a hybrid, of course."

"That's cool. Have you gotten into alternative power?"

"Oh, yeah. Solar power at my house."

"Wow, that's awesome. I'd like to look into getting some of those solar panels myself. Maybe you can give me some pointers on what to buy and all that."

"Sure. No problem. You can come by and see mine if you want."

Interesting. Definitely not the defensive, secretive guy Rem would expect the bomber to be. Disappointment settled in his chest, but he kept it out of his voice. "Really? I'd like that." He should be glad Tristan didn't seem like a terrorist but finding the culprit before Bristol got hurt would've been an answer to his prayers.

Then again, it was easy to act like a person had nothing to hide over the phone. Rem better not pass up the invitation to visit. "How about some evening this week?"

"Uh, depends on the day. I can check my calendar and get back to you." He sounded so normal. Did terrorists keep social calendars?

"Sounds good. Hey, I've really enjoyed talking to you. Let me know if anything comes up for environmental stuff. Like a demonstration would be really cool."

"I'll keep you in the loop. We can use more people dedicated to preserving nature."

Not *Nature must be free*. Would the real bomber have said that?

Rem gave Tristan his number before ending the call. Walking the short distance to his living room, Rem grabbed a marker and wrote Tristan's name on the whiteboard.

At this moment, it seemed unlikely Tristan was the bomber or at all involved. He sounded very even-keeled and normal. Passionate about his cause, but passion for the environment wasn't illegal.

There were still more names to investigate on the roster, but doubt started to weigh on Rem. Maybe he shouldn't have bothered to call the FBI hotline earlier tonight to report the SES motto and his research about the members. He'd used the hotline instead of contacting Agent Nguyen directly, since she'd already warned him once to leave the investigating to the FBI. But the operator hadn't been impressed, either. She'd informed him they were already looking into all the environmental groups at U of M, as well as in the state and the nation.

So far, it looked like she may have been right not to jump on the intel. But no way would he stop his search for the bomber yet. Bristol could've been hurt if that bomb in the Jeep had been real, even with Rem right there with her. He wouldn't have been able to save her, though he was ready to knock her away and protect her with his own body. Almost had before she'd said it was fake.

The bomber was getting more aggressive. Personal. Rem wasn't going to wait around for him to do something worse to Bristol while the task force floundered with no success in tracking down the terrorist. He needed to find the guy.

If Tristan wasn't the bomber himself, he could lead Rem to the terrorist through one of the environmental groups in the Twin Cities. The FBI may be investigating such organizations already, but if Tristan was in the inner circle, he could give Rem insider access to activists the FBI couldn't reach without raising suspicion.

Rem walked back to the table and picked up the SES roster, focusing on the next name Krista had marked—another person who could be the terrorist. Hopefully God would guide him to the real culprit before it was too late. *Lord, I'm not sure if I'm on the right track here or about to make more mistakes. But I pray You'll give me wisdom and lead me to the bomber.*

And please keep Bristol safe.

Chapter Twenty

A squeak pierced through the sleep fog that wrapped around Bristol.

She forced her heavy lids open, vaguely perceiving the dark interior of her bedroom.

The sound seemed to come from elsewhere in the house. Not a squeak. A whine.

Toby.

Did he have to go out? He might be whining by the door. He let out a bark. Then scratched.

What in the world?

Bristol sat up in bed, wide awake.

She swung her legs off the bed and pulled open the drawer of her nightstand. She grabbed her Glock, leaving the holster behind, and hurried barefoot up the carpeted hallway to the vinyl-floored kitchen.

Toby wasn't at the sliding deck door like he should be if he wanted to go outside.

He whined and barked again, standing by the front door instead.

The living room was dark, curtains drawn across the picture window as Bristol had left them. Who was out there?

She dashed to the closet by the garage door, grabbed her tennis shoes and Toby's leash. She set the Glock on the counter as she slipped into the shoes and quickly tied them in case of pursuit. Snatching her windbreaker and the leash, she shoved her weapon into the jacket pocket and went to Toby by the front door, where he pranced from one foot to the other.

His body language signaled excitement, not necessarily danger. But Toby was so friendly he'd be more than happy to welcome a burglar. He and Cora's golden retriever tied for friendliest dogs in the world. Zero guardian or watchdog instincts. Which made his behavior now all the more unusual.

She snapped the leash to his collar and commanded him to go with her—a necessity to pry him away from the front door.

If someone was at the front of the house, she would hopefully surprise the person by exiting through the garage instead.

Toby's heavy panting was the only sound as they entered the garage and walked alongside the Jeep to the door next to the overhead garage door. Diamond shapes of glass patterned the window that allowed her to see out, Glock gripped in her hand.

The driveway was empty. No cars on the street.

A shadow fell on the blacktop, then moved away.

"Wait." The command should stop Toby from bolting.

She switched off the Glock's safety and cracked open the door.

She scanned the ground just outside, checking for wires or other signs of IEDs. If the bomber was paying her a visit, he might've brought some of his toys.

Looked clear. She could have Toby search the area, but

only once she was sure they weren't going to be shot or physically attacked.

She stepped out, still no sound or movement she could detect.

She crept with Toby along the bushes at the edge of the house, her gaze skimming behind the plants, then out to the shadowed yard. The moon didn't provide much light, probably blocked by clouds.

A growl sounded behind her.

She whirled around, weapon raised.

A man?

No. Just the outline of the crab apple tree at the corner of the house.

Another growl, not from Toby.

A figure moved out from the tree's shadow. With a German shepherd.

"Bristol?" Amalia's clear voice floated on the cold air.

Bristol lowered her Glock. "Amalia?" She dropped her gaze to the dog Toby was tugging toward. "And Raksa."

The German shepherd went from high-alert protection dog to playful companion in half a second at the sound of Bristol's familiar voice. He swished his tail and pulled toward Toby.

She took a few steps their way, letting the dogs do a friendly greeting while she tried to make sense of this scene. "What in the world are you doing here?"

Amalia's dark eyes glinted, catching a sliver of light as her wide mouth curved into a smile. "It's my shift tonight."

"Your shift?"

"Yeah." Amalia tilted her head. "Didn't Phoenix tell you?"

"Tell me what?"

"We're taking turns patrolling your property at night. For protection."

The cold breeze seeped through Bristol's cotton pajama tee.

"Because of the hoax device today?" She pocketed the Glock and zipped her jacket.

"No. We've been doing patrols since the Leavell Dam explosion."

Bristol pressed her lips together, not sure whether to be grateful or irritated.

Amalia gave her a knowing smile. "You're new to PK-9, but you'll catch on. When you work for Phoenix, you're family."

Family. The concept sparked warmth in Bristol's chest. She barely had any family left now. But family meant more unknowns, more chances to be vulnerable and more risk of getting hurt. She didn't need that kind of unpredictability in her life. "That's nice, but I'll have to talk to Phoenix about this. I don't need you guys patrolling my house. I've got things under control on my own."

"Sure." Amalia's eyes twinkled again. "Mind if I finish my rounds tonight, so *I* don't have to tell her I didn't do the job?"

"Yes." Bristol sighed, fatigue hitting her as the adrenaline faded. "I mean, go ahead. But I will talk to her about it."

Amalia's mouth angled in a grin. "You do that." She broke off the dogs' mutual smelling session, taking Raksa with her to continue their patrol.

Bristol led Toby back inside through the garage, an odd feeling clinging to her from the knowledge that Amalia and Raksa were outside, patrolling her yard as if she were a PK-9 client. Someone who needed help. Someone who was in danger.

Yet, as she laid her head on the pillow a few minutes later, she had to admit she felt more relaxed than she had in four days.

"You don't have to do that." Bristol let her tone carry an edge as she caught Remington checking the Jeep's side mirror again. "I know how to watch for a tail."

His brown eyes aimed at her, no hint of irritation in response. "But you're also busy driving. It's my way of help-ing out."

Seriously? She gripped the steering wheel tighter and glared at the traffic ahead, glad they only had a half mile to drive to get from Minnesota Falls to the Ceinture Dam downriver. Her interrupted sleep for the second night in a row left her nowhere near rested enough to deal with Remington or the emotional roller coaster he put her on.

The man could be so infuriating. Why did everyone seem to think she was completely unable to protect herself and do her job?

It didn't help her mood that another downpour pelted the windshield, making it hard to see the road. Would the rain never stop? The last thing they needed right now was more water in the Mississippi.

"Have you heard anything from Agent Nguyen about prog-ress?" Remington apparently decided changing the subject was a smart move.

She let out a breath, relaxing her hold on the wheel. She was letting fatigue and stress get to her, which could lead to sloppy searches and vulnerability to danger. "Just the lab re-sults on the hamburger meat left at the Gellar Dam. It had rat poison mixed into it. Enough to kill a dog."

"Yeah, I heard that. But I wondered if they're any closer to finding the bomber."

"I'm sure we'll hear something if significant progress is made."

"Right." Frustration tensed his voice. "I'm thinking they need some help."

She shot him a glance, easily spotting the determination in his taut, bearded jawline. "We need to let the trained investi-gators take care of it. My job is to find explosives before they detonate. Yours is to keep the dams safe. We need to do our jobs and let the investigators do theirs."

She saw his head turn toward her in her peripheral.

"That would make sense if they were getting somewhere. And if your life wasn't in danger until they nail this guy."

She looked at him, regretting the action when she saw the concerned lines bunching on his forehead and the dark shade of his eyes. Her chest tightened, and she swung her gaze back to the road, vulnerable to a different kind of danger—the heart-melting effect of starting to believe he cared.

Softening toward him now would leave her at risk if he hadn't changed and turned out to be as unreliable as he used to be. She swallowed. "The task force is organized to have the best of all the related law enforcement groups. I'm confident they'll find the bomber soon. I just need to keep the dams safe until they do."

"What about the bomber's threat?" The extra roughness of his voice fluttered her pulse.

"You mean to hurt me?" She shrugged. "Likely a bluff."

"Likely." His tone carried his mistrust of the word as he looked out the passenger window, bracing his elbow on the windowsill and stretching long fingers up to the rubber seal at the top.

"This is a dangerous profession, and I'm fine with that." She steeled her jaw, willing her pulse to stop skipping beats. "If you're not, I can get someone else from the DNR for an escort."

He dropped his arm, angling to face her. "It's not *my* safety I'm worried about."

She opened her mouth to respond, then closed it, torn between telling him off and thanking him. She let silence fill the Jeep instead as she avoided his gaze.

She glanced in the rearview mirror to scan for a tail and check on Toby.

He lay in his crate, panting, but not too heavily.

Her phone buzzed in the slot in the console.

She glanced at Rem, who still watched her. "Text message. I shouldn't check it while I'm driving."

"Want me to look in case it's important?"

"It's probably just my grandmother."

A smile tugged his lips. "She texts?"

"Oh, yes."

"You say it like it's a bad thing."

"Only when she uses it to remind me of things."

He shifted in the seat to face her more. "Like something you don't want to do?"

Why did the amusement teasing his mouth have to send a tingle through her whole system? "Sort of. She has a dinner planned tonight that she pressured me into joining."

"You don't want to go?"

"I love having dinner with Grandma, but she's cooked up a matchmaking plan to introduce me to some guy."

A full grin split his beard. Not the reaction she'd expected. Had she wanted him to be jealous? Good grief. Where had that notion come from? She didn't care how Remington felt about her love life. "What's so funny?"

"Nothing." Humor still danced around his mouth. "It's very cute. Do you think you'll like a guy your grandma picks out?"

"I doubt it. She didn't like my last boyfriend."

"Oh. Why not?"

Bristol shifted in the seat, checking the review mirror again. No suspicious vehicle following them yet. "My grandmother can be very picky when it comes to the men her granddaughter dates."

He chuckled. "Smart grandma."

Bristol frowned. "She can be overly opinionated at times."

He lifted his eyebrows and looked at her. "A family trait?"

"Takes one to know one."

"Ouch." He took in a breath, but a smile still curved his features. "Touché."

Her lips twitched with the urge to smile back. But she wouldn't give him the encouragement.

"Well, maybe if your grandmother has found a man even she thinks is right for you, he could be something special."

Her gaze jerked to his.

Warmth softened his eyes as he watched her. Was he that in favor of setting her up with someone else?

She looked at the road, cinching her grip on the wheel again. Maybe she had read too much into Remington's concern for her safety and apologies. Seemed he had moved on romantically. Which was for the best since she could never risk a relationship with him again, anyway.

But the knot twisting in her stomach didn't match the relief she should be feeling. Nor did the weight of disappointment in her chest. She couldn't fall for Remington Jones again. They were so wrong for each other. She needed to remember that. "My grandmother and I have different ideas of the kind of man who's right for me."

"Ah." He looked out the windshield. "I wonder which one of you is right?"

Her phone rang.

"You sure are popular."

Cora's name appeared on the screen.

Bristol punched the button to answer the call on speaker. "What's up, Cora?"

"Hi, Bristol. Can you and Toby come to headquarters right now?" Cora's usually melodic voice trembled.

"Cora, are you okay?"

"I think there's a bomb in my car."

Chapter Twenty-One

Rem didn't know what they'd see when Bristol pulled into the parking lot at the front of Phoenix K-9 headquarters—a small, one-story building with gray siding.

A white Volkswagen Beetle was parked in front of the structure, the driver's door ajar. No signs of an explosion.

Bristol swung left and braked next to Phoenix and Cora, who stood on the sidewalk by the blacktop. Two dogs waited at their sides on leashes, Phoenix's tan one with the blue eyes and the golden retriever he'd seen at the rescue site of Leavell.

Bristol opened her door and dropped out as Rem got out on his side and hurried around the Jeep. "You've got a device in your car?"

"I think so." Cora's eyes were wide and her voice wispy as she answered Bristol's question.

"Pretty sure it's fake." Phoenix's tough-as-nails demeanor contrasted with the clearly shaken woman beside her like steel and water. "But better have Toby clear it."

"Right." Bristol spun to the Jeep and went to the back,

quickly getting Toby out of his crate and clipping the leash to his harness.

Rem stretched his stride to keep up with Toby and Bristol's fast clip as they headed across the sixty-five feet of parking lot to the Volkswagen.

"Don't be ridiculous." Bristol cast him a frown. "You should stay by the Jeep in case this is real."

"We're partners on this whether you like it or not."

Her hardened jaw said she'd love to put him in his place, but she commanded Toby to seek instead.

The dog surged to the car, starting to sniff along the side, then tracking to the front seat where Bristol guided his attention to the floor with her hand.

He didn't sit or raise his paw.

Bristol shook her head. "It's a hoax."

Rem let out the breath he didn't know he was holding.

She stepped back and gave the other women a wave. "Clear!"

Phoenix and Cora headed across the lot.

Rem looked back at Bristol in time to see her putting on gloves. She reached in the car and pulled out a device that looked similar to the one they'd found on the seat of her Jeep yesterday.

Except… "Is that dynamite?"

She shook her head. "Pipes, painted orange to look like dynamite. He must think he gets points for creativity."

"Is that another note?" Rem pointed to the piece of paper stuck to the back of the device, flapping in the breeze.

Bristol flipped the fake bomb over to see the note, reading silently.

"What does it say?" Cora's soft question almost got carried away by the wind as she stopped near them, wrapping her slim arms around herself.

Bristol moistened her lips, gaze locked on the note. "'You wouldn't take the hint. Try this. If you don't care about your own safety, you should think of your friends. Stop searching, or Libertas will hurt them. Nature must be free.'"

Bristol's eyes turned an unfamiliar shade as she lifted her gaze. A darker, bluish gray. Was that worry gathering there?

His stomach clenched. This bomber had to be stopped. Rem wouldn't stand by and watch him torment Bristol. She was stronger than anyone he knew, but a person could only take so much. If he was getting to her—

"I'm going to track the bomber's scent as far as I can with Dag." Phoenix's tone was as calm and fearless as her expression under her baseball cap. "In the meantime, Cora, I want you to check our security footage. The suspect seems to have a skill for avoiding cameras, but he may not have known where all of mine are."

Cora nodded, her gaze moving to Bristol. She touched Bristol's arm. "Thank you so much for coming to help right away."

Bristol smiled, a beautiful expression that made Rem's chest clench painfully. If only he could get one of those aimed at him. "That's what Toby and I are here for."

Music suddenly spilled into the air. A jingling version of a song Rem had sung many times at church—"Amazing Grace"?

"Excuse me." Cora pulled a cell phone out of the pink purse she held.

Curious. Was Cora a Christian, too?

She looked at the smartphone's screen before answering. "Hi, Nevaeh. What can I do for you?" Her face turned the color of snow.

Bristol took a step closer and put her hand on Cora's shoulder. "What is it?"

"She says there's something that looks like a bomb in her truck."

"Give the phone to Bristol." Phoenix delivered the command as she took the fake bomb from Bristol with gloved hands. "See if you can determine if it's another hoax over the phone." Phoenix held the fake bomb lower, letting her dog smell it.

"Track it." She delivered the command in an even tone, and the dog lowered his nose to the ground.

Since Bristol had said Dag didn't detect explosives, Rem assumed the dog must be tracking the bomber's scent instead. The K-9 followed a trail to the car floor, then backed out the other direction, moving away.

Rem watched their progress as he kept one ear tuned to Bristol's conversation with Nevaeh.

"Sounds like another hoax."

"Thank you, Father." Cora's quietly breathed praise echoed Rem's thoughts as relief flooded his chest.

Phoenix and Dag moved quickly across the parking lot, over the patch of grass that separated her lot from the one for an electronics store, and onto the blacktop.

Dag swung to the left, nose to the ground as he tracked to the edge of the street. He halted, lifted his snout in the air as if trying to catch the scent, then looked up at his owner.

Phoenix came back to the Volkswagen as Bristol told Nevaeh to wear gloves to move the hoax device out of the way for driving.

"It will need to be bagged and turned in as evidence along with the other hoax device we found in Cora's car."

Phoenix stopped by them, petting her dog, who looked up at Rem with those surprising blue eyes. "Another fake?"

Bristol nodded, tilting the phone away from her mouth. "She says there's a note."

"What does it say?" Phoenix didn't blink as she watched Bristol.

"Can you tell me what it says?" A pause as Bristol listened, then began to repeat what she was told. "'You didn't listen. So your friends are up next. Stop or they will get hurt.'"

Phoenix's face betrayed no response to the note. "Tell her to come in. We need to meet."

"Dead end at the road?" Cora moved closer to ask the question of Phoenix while Bristol passed along the order to Nevaeh.

"He must have gotten into a car there. He seems to favor that tactic."

Bristol handed the phone back to Cora. "Okay, she's coming."

"Have you checked the Minnesota Falls Dam today?" Phoenix aimed her unreadable gaze at Bristol.

Bristol glanced at Rem, causing his pulse to surge a little under her gaze. "Yes, we cleared it this morning."

"Miles and Duke are searching today, as well?"

Bristol nodded.

"Good, then you can hold off checking the others until after a brief meeting. Take Mr. Jones wherever he'd like to go and then come back here." Phoenix pulled away and walked toward the office building. "We'll meet in forty-five minutes, if I can get Amalia in by then."

"Where is she?" Bristol's question carried a slight thread of alarm. Something Rem had never heard in her voice before. The painful sound squeezed his heart.

Phoenix paused and angled back, checking her wristwatch. "She's sleeping in after her overnight shift. I'll have her check her car carefully before driving."

"Good." Bristol turned her full attention on Rem as Phoenix and Cora disappeared inside. "Sorry. Should I drop you at the DNR?"

Rem forced a smile to cover his disappointment that she was

still so eager to get rid of him. But maybe Phoenix wouldn't allow him to stay even if Bristol wanted him to.

On the other hand, a free moment during the day might be exactly what he needed. "Actually, will you take me to the garage that's fixing my car? It's supposed to be done today." And then he'd have the means to drive himself where he needed to go.

He suddenly had a hankering to look at some solar panels.

A tingling sensation irritated Bristol's nerves as she entered the Phoenix K-9 headquarters with Toby after taking Rem to the garage. It was the feeling that came on with a heavy storm or flash-flood warning. The feeling that people were going to get hurt. And she was helpless to stop it.

She walked through the entry with Toby at her side, the mix of light gray carpeting and steel gray walls doing their best to calm her nerves. Cora's desk sat empty, the glass top clean and clutter-free as usual. Cora must have taken her laptop computer with her to the breakroom since it wasn't on the desk.

Bristol followed the sound of women's voices down the short hall and turned through the doorway to the breakroom.

"Have fun with Rem?" Amalia's twinkling gaze greeted Bristol along with her big smile. Apparently, she had made it and without a trace of sleepiness, either. She picked up a mug off the table by the coffeemaker, another one already in her other hand. She extended one of the steaming cups to Bristol, and the scent of coffee that filled the room sharpened in her nostrils.

"No thanks. I don't want to always need it during the day."

Amalia quirked a shapely black eyebrow. "Wow. A woman who can resist temptation."

"Better leave her alone, Mali." Nevaeh glanced over her

shoulder from the near end of the sofa where she sat, Alvarez lying on the floor against her foot. "Or she won't help you out when you've got the bomb in your car."

"There's decaf if you want it, Bris."

Bristol barely caught the soft words of Cora, who appeared to be sinking into the far corner of the sofa, her knees brought up in front of her chest.

Jana nuzzled her golden head into Cora's lap, between her legs and torso, clearly sensing the fragility of her partner.

A pang tweaked Bristol's heart as she walked around the plush chairs opposite the sofa and went to Cora. She could feel Phoenix's gaze on her from the chair where she sat with Dag beside her as usual.

But Cora had handled Bristol's orientation at PK-9 and even invited Bristol to her home for dinner the week after she'd started working there. She was always tender, always kind and supportive. Someone as sweet as Cora should never feel fear. Or have fake explosives planted in her car.

Bristol crouched in front of her. "Are you okay?"

Toby swung into Bristol, his tail whacking her back, clearly thinking she'd lowered down to play with him.

Cora's pink lips curved in her gentle smile at the goofy Lab's antics. She rested her hand on Jana's head in her lap. "I'll be all right. Thank you."

"Now that we're all here, let's get started." Phoenix waited for Bristol to stand and go to the open chair.

Bristol dropped Toby's leash, since all the dogs were allowed to roam and relax in the breakroom, and he stuck his nose to the floor, smelling every inch of the carpet.

Amalia sat on the floor next to the sprawled body of Gaston. The Newfoundland immediately put his big paw on her leg, no doubt hoping to elicit petting.

"We need to do a little regrouping and make sure everyone's heads are still in the game." Phoenix aimed her gaze at Nevaeh. "Nevaeh?"

She leaned down to give Alvarez a vigorous rub on his broad chest. "I'm good."

"How are you so calm?" Cora looked at Nevaeh with her big blue eyes.

"Don't get me wrong, girl." Nevaeh shook her head. "It was intense. My first bomb. I've been shot and knifed, but never bombed."

Cora blinked while Amalia just chuckled, as if she wasn't surprised. Another reminder of how little Bristol knew about these women she worked with. They each reminded her of icebergs. Only one-eighth visible above the surface.

Could being knifed and shot explain Cannenta, the service dog Nevaeh often had with her? Bristol hadn't figured out a tactful way to ask if Cannenta was her service dog or if Nevaeh was fostering or training her.

Cora had once mentioned Phoenix oversaw a training program at the local prison, where inmates trained dogs to be used as service canines for people in need. Nevaeh could be helping out there, too. Her toned body left no doubt she was in terrific physical shape, and she seemed too tough and fearless to need emotional support from a service dog.

"Gave me a feel for your job for a second." Nevaeh turned her head to Bristol. "You got guts facing this kind of thing every day. I'd be a mess like 24/7." She breathed out a laugh.

Bristol shifted in the chair, which didn't feel as comfortable as usual. She wasn't any braver than the other women here. They all did important work that required courage. Search and rescue, detection, security and patrol were all potentially dangerous jobs. Not to mention the dangers she suspected they had encountered in their pasts. "I'd rather face a bomb than a shooting or knife attack."

"What?" Nevaeh raised her eyebrows with a smile.

Toby chose that moment to return to Bristol, nudging her hand with his wet nose. "Really." She scratched his chin. "Bombs are easy. Any time I find a device, I know it's not likely to go off because I've found it and I know how to disarm it. All I have to do is be faster than the clock on the timer."

Toby walked a couple feet away and circled two times before he plopped down, curling into a ball on the floor.

"What about when it's not on a timer? I didn't see a timer on the one…" Cora bit her lip and looked down at Jana's head, stroking the golden's fur.

"Well, the device in your car was a hoax, and it didn't have any switch in place. The situations without a timer can be trickier, of course, but we still have a good chance of disarming or containing the device before it does damage. As long as we're skilled and practiced, we're in control of the situation."

"Well said." Phoenix watched Bristol. "Thank you."

Bristol wasn't sure from her tone or expression if Phoenix really meant that or was trying to shut her up.

"Bristol's making an excellent point." Phoenix moved her gaze over the other women. "We don't need to be afraid of this bomber or his toys. That's what he's trying to do. He's trying to scare us." Her attention rested on Cora briefly. "Is it working?" She shifted her focus to Amalia, propped against Gaston on the floor.

"No, ma'am." A smile curved her lips.

Phoenix looked at Nevaeh, who shook her head.

"Not a chance, boss."

Phoenix's gaze came back to rest on Cora.

Her eyes revealed the inner battle between fear and determination. But she lifted her chin. "Not enough to stop me from doing what's right."

Phoenix smiled at Cora, an expression of surprising gentleness that Bristol had never seen on her boss's face. The smile vanished as she turned to Bristol. "You're the main target here. You're the one he most wants to frighten with this stunt and the notes."

Phoenix shifted in the chair to angle more toward Bristol, her dark blue eyes piercing. "I know you have tremendous courage when it comes to yourself. But most of us are vulnerable through those we care about." She glanced at the other women, then swung her gaze abruptly back to Bristol. "I wanted you to see our response to this. I wanted you to see that not one of us is going to back down because of threats."

A brace of steel undergirded Phoenix's voice with every word. "All of us are going to support you and Toby and work together to make sure this terrorist doesn't win. We all know the risks in this line of work, but we want to do it, anyway. We need to do it, though our reasons may not all be the same." She turned to the rest of the group. "Am I right?"

They all nodded and added their assent.

"Preach, boss." Nevaeh's comment drew light laughter from the others, relaxing the tension in Bristol's muscles.

"The only thing that's changed concerning our involvement in this case, as far as I'm concerned, is our focus." Phoenix looked at all the women as she continued. "We'll still perform our security and protection duties, and Bristol will continue her searches with Toby. But we're also going to focus on finding the bomber."

Surprise lifted Bristol's eyebrows, though none of the other women looked startled. "Shouldn't we let the task force handle that?"

Phoenix met her gaze. "They're doing their best. But they need help. Sometimes having the room to maneuver outside their stricter regulations gives us an advantage."

Bristol noticed uncomfortably that Phoenix almost sounded

like Remington. She'd just told him they needed to let the task force members do their jobs.

"Let's begin with what we know about today's fake bomb plants." Phoenix looked at Cora.

She lowered her legs and leaned over Jana to reach her notebook computer on the coffee table.

Jana lifted her head out of the way for Cora to set the computer on her lap and open it.

"Our security cameras caught him planting the bomb—the hoax—in my car at 8:15 this morning." Cora tucked a silky clump of blond hair behind her ear, her updo gently falling apart around her face.

"You got him on camera?" Amalia leaned forward.

Cora turned the computer around so they could see the footage on the screen. "He was wearing a ski mask."

Bristol scooted to the edge of the chair to see the small image better.

Libertas.

She clenched her teeth as the video showed him using the old-school hanger method to break into Cora's car.

"He must not have been confident he knew where all my cameras were." Phoenix got to her feet. "Which shows an unfortunate degree of strategic intelligence."

Dag sprang up and followed her in a near-heel position as she went to the table by the wall.

"I asked at the electronics store if anyone saw him or his vehicle, but no one there remembered him." Phoenix grabbed a bottled water from the table and turned to face the team as she twisted the lid off and drank.

Bristol took the pause as a moment to ask the question that had been hounding her. "Why those two vehicles? Why not yours or Amalia's?"

Cora giggled and Bristol turned to her. The smile on her

face was a welcome change from the fear that had tensed her features until now.

"What?"

Cora shook her head. "You haven't seen inside Phoenix's van yet, have you?"

"No." Bristol glanced at her boss, who pushed away from the table and came to stand closer to Nevaeh's end of the sofa.

"Let's just say no one is getting into my van unless I let them."

Impressive. But somehow not surprising given the little she knew about Phoenix. It was as if everything about her was impenetrable. Apparently even her van.

Amalia looked at Bristol. "And I was at my home, which hopefully the bomber doesn't know the location of. Yet. Seems like you're his preferred target, anyway."

"So that leaves me and my girl here." Nevaeh reached across Jana on the middle cushion to pat Cora's leg, prompting a smile from Cora. "I'm guessing he's not my biggest fan since Alvarez and I are keeping him out of Minnesota Falls."

"Probably so." Phoenix looked at Nevaeh. "He likely watched to see your vehicle when you arrived to patrol, then planted the bomb, either before or after he visited here. He apparently wanted to send a personal message to us and Bristol, so he came to our headquarters."

Phoenix walked back to her chair, Dag glued to her side until she sat, the dog dropping to an alert down position next to the chair. "Clearly, you all need security systems in your vehicles. Cora will work on getting those installed as soon as possible, and the agency will foot the bill." She leaned forward to set the bottled water on the coffee table. "I'd like us to review what we know about the bomber from this. Amalia?"

Always the go-to with criminal assessment, it seemed. Bristol still hadn't had a chance to ask Amalia what she did before

PK-9. Must have been some experience that made her skilled at understanding the criminal mind. If Phoenix saw her as an expert, Amalia's background had to be something special. Bristol halted her questions and tuned in to what Amalia was saying.

"...which suggests he's not a serial killer or out to murder people as his primary goal. Clearly, he's not adverse to collateral damage when it suits his purpose, given his attack on the Leavell Dam. So we know he's willing to kill for his cause if he feels it's necessary, which gives credence to his threats with the fake devices today." Amalia rubbed Gaston's belly with her hand as she talked. "Obviously, he views Bristol as a problem, but he's choosing to try to scare her into stopping first." Amalia met Bristol's gaze. "When you don't do what he wants, it's likely he'll decide you need to be eliminated."

Bristol cinched her jaw. "I'm not afraid of his bombs."

Amalia nodded. "But he's shown he may first go after Toby if he can, like with the poison, or attack people close to you."

A shiver tripped down Bristol's spine. *Grandma.*

"Amalia's right." Phoenix's stare locked on Bristol. "Don't be scared, be smart. Just take extra precautions, and we'll back you up. I have full confidence in your abilities to handle this bomber." Phoenix's unusually strong praise chased away the fear growing in Bristol's mind.

Bristol would not be controlled or intimidated by a criminal. The man was still just a bomber. The chances were very slim that he would bother searching for Bristol's relatives when he already knew where to find her friends.

Bristol only needed to make sure she wasn't tailed whenever she went to her grandmother's house. Like for the dinner tonight. She would build in extra time to take an alternate route and circle back to check for tails and ensure she wasn't followed.

Everything would be fine. Everything was under control.

★ ★ ★

Tristan Doyle didn't seem like an out of control maniac or a methodical terrorist. He was either not the bomber or very good at faking ordinary.

Rem assessed the man as he straightened from pointing out the poles that supported his ground-mounted solar panels.

Average height of five foot nine with a medium build, Tristan was neither in great shape nor terrible shape. His teal and dark green plaid shirt was about as ordinary as a man could get, tucked into a pair of relaxed-fit jeans that looked broken in but didn't have any holes. His work boots were scuffed, but presentable. Normal apparel for an outdoor guy in near sixty-degree weather.

"You'll want to install a tracking system along with the pole mounts. I installed a dual-axis system so my panels follow the sun's position throughout the day and can adjust to seasonal variations."

Rem let out a low whistle as he admired the huge solar panels that occupied the majority of Tristan's small front yard. Granted, most people cared more about aesthetics and would've gone for rooftop or backyard installation, but after seeing Tristan's impressive garden, with spring flowers and tilled beds ready for vegetables covering his entire backyard, Rem understood why the panels had to be in the front.

"Increases my production by thirty-one percent."

"That's awesome. And you installed these yourself?"

"Yeah." He brushed back the hair that crossed his forehead in a style that looked like a family member had cut it. "Saved a ton of money."

"I can imagine. I wouldn't know how to install something like this, though. Was it difficult?"

He shrugged. "Not for me, but I've always been handy with things." He pulled an old-fashioned handkerchief out of his pocket and wiped at a spot of dirt on the panel closest to him. "Tell you what, if you decide you want to get some panels, I'll help you install them. Can't guarantee how much time I'll have to do it, but if you wait until the fall, I'll probably be able to get to it."

"Wow, that's really generous of you. I wouldn't feel right not paying you for it. Especially if I was taking you away from your job or something."

"No problem." His brown eyes angled to the panels. "I'm between jobs at the moment."

Unemployed. And free to plant bombs at any time during day or night.

"If I take on something new by fall, I'll work around it to help you with the panels."

"So what kind of work did you do before?" A normal question, Rem hoped.

"Construction." He answered without pause or change in expression.

Interesting. He'd been a philosophy major in college. Rem would've expected something more academic or even artistic.

Tristan started to trudge toward the small blue house he'd already welcomed Rem into. If Tristan were the bomber, he could recognize Rem from following him and Bristol to the diner. But the surprise or suspicion Rem looked closely for in Tristan's expression never showed.

He had eagerly invited Rem to take a tour of his garden and brought him into his home for lemonade afterward. The house was as normal as he was, dotted with pictures of an older couple and a fortysomething woman with a man and children Tristan had identified as his sister and her family.

No bomb-making materials or radical pamphlets anywhere in sight. A lot of nature pictures hung on the walls, but they were tasteful, framed photographs and paintings. Items any nature lover might choose to decorate their home.

Tristan looked over his shoulder as he walked. "Sorry I don't have time to visit longer, but I have to meet a friend."

Rem checked his watch—3:32. Another friend without a day job? He kept that question to himself and asked a safer one. "Somebody from the environmental club you mentioned?"

Tristan stopped and turned to Rem.

Hit a nerve? Or maybe Tristan's friend had something to hide? Rem smiled, easy and relaxed. "I'd love to meet more environmental supporters, get involved in a demonstration or something."

"Yeah." Tristan's gaze moved over Rem's face. "I remember you said that."

A tingle of suspicion tickled the back of Rem's neck at the change in Tristan's demeanor. Rem still hadn't seen the inside of the square garage that stood independent of the house. Could be the perfect place to hide materials for making explosives.

"If you have to go, I won't keep you. You've been awesome to show me your solar power setup." Rem waved a hand at the panels. "This is incredible." And it was. An impressive structure kept in perfect, gleaming condition. Almost too perfect, as if it was an obsession. "Well, I'll get out of your hair. Thanks, Tristan."

He held out his hand and shook Tristan's as he had when he arrived. Tristan had a solid handshake and steady eye contact even Rem's dad would approve.

Rem headed for his car a few feet away on the driveway, then paused and turned back. "Oh, one more thing. I know you have to go, but would you have a second to show me the wiring and control box?" Which were hopefully housed in the garage. "I'd like to see what kind of space I'd need for that."

"Sure, I guess I can spare a few more minutes." He led the way to the separate garage without hesitation, making Rem's hopes fade with every step. He wouldn't be so willing to allow a visitor in the garage if he had anything to hide.

The interior of the garage was perhaps the most ordinary space of all, given his clear enthusiasm for gardening. Gardening tools covered the walls, hung on pegs. The only unusual thing about the space was how organized it was. Tristan clearly didn't favor Rem's controlled-chaos organizational style.

Bristol's garage probably looked something like this. Every tool cleaned and neatly hung in its designated space. At least the guy didn't use a label maker.

Tristan took Rem to the wall next to the back door of the garage where wires connected to a control box.

Rem fought to conceal his disappointment as Tristan talked about the solar power system and listed more advantages. Another dead end in the search for the bomber.

There wasn't a single explosive in this garage. No suspicious extra wires or unusual types of wire cutters. Didn't even look like the guy kept fertilizer on hand or other botanical products that could be used for bomb-making.

The absence of such substances made sense if Tristan was who he claimed to be—a guy who cared about the environment and an organic lifestyle.

At least Rem hadn't told Bristol about Tristan. Imagine trying to live that down now. Hopefully she wouldn't hear about his bum tip to the FBI, if they'd investigated and come up with the nothing Rem had so far.

He'd stayed up most of last night, going over all the names on Krista's SES roster, including the ones she hadn't marked as especially passionate about the environment. When the hour grew too late, he couldn't cold-call the rest of the former students, but he'd done as much investigating online as he could.

Only three stood out as suspicious. Two had felony records but were currently serving time in prison and jail. The third, Ty Jackson, had a history of arrest from protest activities, and his social media profiles showed he still held extreme views and was involved in environmental activism. But he was also living and working in California. Not likely he was commuting to bomb dams in Minnesota.

That left Tristan, who had now turned out to be the least suspicious suspect on Rem's list. And yet…there was something Rem couldn't shake. A feeling he shouldn't rule out Tristan, despite the lack of evidence and abundance of neighborly helpfulness.

Rem glimpsed the watch on Tristan's wrist as he pointed to the wiring to explain something Rem wasn't really hearing.

Tristan hadn't checked the time. Not once during Rem's hour-long visit.

But he'd still said he had to go meet a friend. He was trying to get rid of Rem.

Maybe Tristan wasn't as easygoing as he appeared. His willingness to show Rem the garage and everything else could be intended to put him off the scent. To fool him into thinking Tristan couldn't possibly be the bomber. After all, if Tristan actually was the terrorist, he could know who Rem was and be especially careful.

But, so far, all the evidence except for an ability to tell time without looking at a watch pointed to Tristan being only what he appeared to be—a normal guy with environmentally friendly habits. The FBI would need a whole lot more evidence to go after Tristan. But Rem didn't. And if Tristan wasn't the culprit, maybe he'd lead Rem to where the terrorist could be found.

Rem wouldn't quit until the bomber, whoever he was, stood behind bars and Bristol was safe. He just prayed that happened soon. Before Libertas made good on his threats.

Chapter Twenty-Two

"Grandma, do you want to check if I set the table the way you like?"

"I'm sure it's fine, dear." Grandma's voice carried from the hallway through the doorway to the dining room. "I need to watch for my guest."

Bristol shook her head with a smile as she straightened the china plate on the white embroidered tablecloth that covered the dining table her grandpa had made. As uninterested romantically as Bristol was, she had to admit she was curious to see the young man who had apparently stolen her grandmother's heart. She hadn't seen Grandma this excited for company since Bristol's childhood, when Grandma and Grandpa would watch for the arrival of their grandchildren and rush out the door to greet them as soon as they pulled in the driveway. Bristol would just as eagerly watch from the car window, and Riana—

The memory wiped the smile from Bristol's face. Her sister should be there now. Grandma could be playing matchmaker with her. Or maybe Riana would already have a husband and kids.

"He's here!" Was that a squeal?

Bristol sniffed and wiped at the moisture that started to escape her eyes, wishing she hadn't taken time to apply mascara for the sake of Grandma's dinner. From the compliments when Bristol arrived at the house, she could tell her grandma appreciated the gesture, along with the blue blouse, black slim jeans and black heels she'd donned for the occasion. But maybe she'd gone overboard. The guy was Grandma's friend, not hers. No matter who he was, Bristol was definitely not interested.

Toby jogged into the hallway at the sound of the door opening and Grandma greeting her guest. Bristol dragged in a deep breath, the fatigue she'd ignored before washing over her in a wave. She wasn't up to this tonight. Maybe she could make an excuse and leave early.

A man's voice rumbled in the entry, but she couldn't make out the words.

"Bristol, come say hello."

She rolled her eyes at the line that made Bristol feel as if she were seven years old again. At least such lapses on Grandma's part were rare.

Bristol hiked her shoulders and left the dining room, turning into the hallway and heading to the front door where—

The man who stood by Grandma looked nothing short of gorgeous in a black button-down shirt, trim dark blue jeans with dressy loafers and the camel-colored blazer that emphasized his broad shoulders and brought out the brown tones of his beard and hair.

But he was also Remington Jones.

"Wha—" It was all she could manage as he gave her that heat-sparking grin above the bright bouquet of purple and yellow gladiolus he held in his hand. Her grandmother's favorite flower. How did he know that? And what was he doing here?

"Bristol, I believe you've already met my friend, Rem Jones." Grandma's smile looked positively gleeful. Without a trace of the guilt she should feel.

"Wow." Remington's gaze took in her outfit, certainly a step up from the practical work gear he usually saw her in. "You look amazing."

She reined in her pulse before it could stampede under his warm approval. She wasn't about to be appeased that easily. "*He's* your friend?"

"You think it's impossible for me to make friends with a handsome young man?"

Remington laughed. "Let's not prolong the torture, Jess."

Jess? He called her grandmother a nickname?

"Before you go into shock, I can explain." His crooked grin threatened to douse Bristol's rising irritation. "It's pretty simple—I met Jessica when I visited my uncle at Good Shepherd, the nursing home."

Grandma nodded, resting her hand on Remington's arm as she looked at Bristol. "You know I go there every week to visit Clarice, my schoolmate."

"Of course I know that." At least she'd finally found her voice. She glared at Remington. "You could have told me you were the man she'd invited tonight."

He cringed, though the twinkle didn't leave his eyes. "I'm sorry. Your grandma—"

"I made him promise not to tell you and spoil the surprise." Grandma smiled up at him.

Bristol gritted her teeth as disbelief and exasperation collided in her chest. "Dinner's ready. Let's eat." She spun on her heel and marched past the dining room to enter the kitchen. She whipped Grandma's yellow paisley pot holders over her hands and opened the oven, bending to remove the noodle casserole warming there.

"You're not going to be upset and ruin the evening now, are you, dear?"

Bristol closed her eyes at the sound of Grandma's voice. She set the casserole on the counter and watched her grandmother fill a vase with water. "You know I don't like surprises. And I don't like being tricked."

Grandma proceeded to snip the ends off the admittedly beautiful flowers and place them in the vase.

Bristol checked the doorway to be sure they were alone and lowered her voice to a hiss. "And I don't like Remington Jones. You know that."

"Do I?" She lifted her eyebrows and met Bristol's angry gaze with utter calm. "Perhaps that's why I decided this should be a surprise." She lifted the vase and touched Bristol's arm with her free hand. "Sometimes the unexpected can be good, my darling. If you let it be." She pulled away and turned to leave, the occasional stiffness in her walk more evident than usual.

Was her arthritis worse tonight? Compassion and concern tied a knot in Bristol's chest.

Grandma was only doing what she thought was best, what she thought would make Bristol happy in the long run. She was wrong, but Bristol loved her for caring and always being there.

Bristol hefted the casserole and followed Grandma to the dining room, determined to be civil to Remington for her sake. But if he thought he could win Bristol over by using her grandmother, he was in for a big surprise.

"Remember what your grandpa used to say?" Jessica tilted her head back toward Bristol, who stood behind the sofa.

A smile that nearly stopped Rem's heart curved Bristol's mouth. "'I'm doing women's work today.'" An actual laugh, a joyous sound, tumbled from her lips. "I think he only said that to make you mad."

"It worked." Jess chuckled and looked down at the photo album crossing her lap and Rem's. She touched her finger to the picture of her husband, wearing an apron and the same yellow pot holders Bristol had used tonight. "But the man loved to cook. Had a real gift for it, too."

Her smile faded as she lovingly traced her fingers over the photo. "My Warren."

Rem glanced at Bristol.

She watched her grandmother with concern tugging her eyebrows together. She placed her hand on Jess's shoulder.

The older woman drew in a breath and patted Bristol's hand. "I'm getting tired. I think I'll turn in, but don't you dare let me stop you two from continuing the party." She closed the album and set it beside her as she moved to get up.

Rem held out his hand, and she took it for support as she stood.

"I mean it now." She squeezed his fingers and gave him a stern look that she sent to Bristol, as well. "You two need to have dessert still. I want to see that pie almost gone tomorrow." Her face softened with a smile as she touched his arm and looked at him with eyes so much like Bristol's. "Thank you for coming, dear. You come back soon."

"Yes, ma'am." He smiled in return. "I'll do that."

"Be nice to my company." Jess pointed toward Bristol, then stiffly made her way to the doorway that led to the hall.

"Good night, Grandma."

Rem caught the humor in Bristol's tone and the obvious affection she had for Jess. He angled to see Bristol better as

Jessica disappeared from the room. "I love your grandmother. She's awesome."

Bristol smiled as she watched the empty doorway. Her gaze shifted to Rem's, her beautiful eyes more blue than gray thanks to the attractive blouse she wore. "She apparently feels the same way about you."

"You sound so surprised."

She laughed. At something he'd said.

His pulse thundered in his ears as she made her way around the sofa, Toby intercepting her at the corner with a wagging tail. The dog must love the sound of her laughter, too.

"I forget the size of your ego." She petted Toby as she maneuvered past his squirming body to sit on the sofa, only a cushion between her and Rem. "You're the *special guy*?" She shook her head, her gorgeous smile actually aimed at him. "I can't believe you said that about yourself."

That smile would be the death of him.

"Hello, Earth to Remington." She reached across the empty space and tapped his knee, starting a fire in the spot she'd touched. "What do you have to say for yourself?"

That this relaxed, smiling Bristol was the most beautiful creature he'd seen in six years. But he couldn't say that. "Well, your grandma does have great taste, and she's a very wise woman."

"Uh-huh." The corner of her mouth tucked, beguiling him. "I guess you know I can't argue with those statements, so I'll let you off. This time."

This time. His heart swelled at the implication that there could be a next time—a repeat visit. A future with Bristol.

"What?"

He was staring. At those eyes, her long lashes, the smooth skin. The woman he loved even more now than he had before.

But he couldn't tell her that, either. It was obvious she didn't feel the same way and couldn't forgive him.

She still stared at him with those breathtaking eyes, so he went with something as close as he could get to what he wished he could say. "Really, your grandma is the special one. I'm honored she invited me here tonight. And that she'd consider me good enough for her very special granddaughter." He gave Bristol a smile he hoped conveyed only a hint of what he felt. Not enough to scare her away or make her angry.

She looked down to pick at a loose thread on the upholstered sofa cushion between them. "I admit, you surprised me tonight."

He waited for her to elaborate.

Her lips jutted out farther as she released a sigh. "I mean, you always surprise me, but in a good way this time."

She finally lifted her gaze, her eyes drifting toward gray as she searched his face. "The Remington I knew at the academy would never have sat for an hour looking through old photographs with my grandmother. In fact, that Remington would never have come to dinner at a grandma's invitation, either."

He almost said if it was her grandma he would've come. But he bit back the line, true though it was. Because her point was sadly, painfully accurate. His old self only had time for parties and meaningless activities he'd thought were fun, not visiting and learning from his elders. "I know what you mean." His turn to look away, regret forming a knot in his gut.

"I didn't believe you. I didn't believe you had changed."

Hope brought his gaze back to hers.

"But you are different." Her dark eyebrows drew together. "Why?"

His pulse thrummed in his neck. *Lord, please give me the words.* "When I was caught cheating and got expelled, I hit rock bottom. My dad cut me out of his life, and pretty much out of my mom's, like I'd expected."

Thin lines crossed her forehead. Was she concerned for him?

A lump formed in his throat as he continued. "I was on my own for the first time, financially, emotionally. I'd lived like I didn't care about my family and their support, but I needed it. I didn't realize how much until I blew it and everything got taken away."

He gripped his knees in his hands and took a breath. "That's when I realized how badly I'd messed things up, messed up my life. When I went back to school to get my engineering degree, I met a guy who took me to a Christian group where they talked about Jesus and how He lived a perfect life and died for me, to pay the penalty for my sins."

Rem met Bristol's gaze, relieved she still looked at him, listening. "I couldn't pay for what I'd done, but Jesus did that for me. I asked Him into my life that day. He's been changing me ever since."

"So, Jesus is the reason you're nice to my grandma?"

A small smile pulled his mouth. "Pretty much, yeah. He gave me a new heart when He saved me. A better heart that cares about people without wondering what's in it for me. And He gave me a desire to be honest and responsible. Dependable."

Her grayed eyes watched him, processing, but not allowing him to read her thoughts. "No wonder she likes you so much. You sound just like her."

A compliment, but disappointment sank in his chest. She was putting him off, dismissing the message he'd tried to convey. "What do you believe?"

She propped her elbow against the back of the sofa and tangled her fingers into the thick hair she'd left down to tumble in waves over her shoulders. "There's probably a God. Or was,

I suppose. Everything had to come from somewhere." She slid her fingers through her mahogany locks, pushing the wave back from her face. "But He sure hasn't done anything with it since then. Or He's the worst manager ever. Everywhere you look, there's tragedy, destruction…death."

Her eyes turned stormy, like a window to the turmoil swirling within. She closed the window by dropping her gaze.

His heart lodged in his chest, choking him with desperation to relieve her pain. A debate about God wouldn't do that. But maybe finding out where her pain came from would.

He looked at the album Jessica had set on the coffee table. "I didn't see any pictures of your immediate family in there, other than your dad as a boy."

She lifted her head, surprise lightening her eyes.

"Is there an album of you? Your childhood?"

Her eyebrows dipped. "It wouldn't be a happy one."

Rem frowned, inwardly berated himself for not pressing to know more about her family when they'd dated. She had mentioned her mom a few times but didn't seem to want to talk about her. Since Rem hadn't wanted to share about his own family, he'd been happy to live in the moment with her, just the two of them, pretending they were free from their pasts and difficult relatives. "Rough time?"

Her tongue slid across her lips as she rubbed the sofa's loose thread between her fingertips. "Not at first. But things changed. Life got…unpredictable."

"Life's always pretty unpredictable, don't you think?"

She met the comment with a glare. "Then how can you believe in God?"

"Because it's not unpredictable to Him. He's the One who knows the whole plan. He's got everything under control." Rem tried a smile and a chuckle, hoping to soften his words and the mood. "I know things go very badly when I try to control them, so I've learned to just sit back and enjoy the ride."

Her eyes narrowed. "Not everyone's life is an amusement park, all fun and games."

"No." He frowned. "I didn't mean it was. But I know God's got the bad stuff under control, too. He won't let anything happen without a reason."

"Really?" She pushed off the sofa, looking down at him, her jaw a hard line. "Like when a dad and his twelve-year-old daughter drown in their car? What's the reason for that? I'd love to know." Raw emotion choked her words as she stalked away, Toby getting up to follow her. She headed for the doorway to the hall.

Did she mean her family had died? Pain pierced his chest as if he felt hers, but he forced his lungs to work. "Bristol. Wait."

She stopped, her back to him.

He stood and closed the distance between them, his arms aching to wrap around her. But he forced them to stay at his sides. "I'm sorry. I…didn't know."

A shudder shook her shoulders, sending a sharp jolt to his heart.

He swallowed, calling on every ounce of strength he had to keep from scaring her away by pulling her into an embrace. "Was it your dad? Your sister?"

She sniffed in the pause, drew in a shaky breath. "Yes. They…" She gulped air. "Hurricane Katrina. They were driving to help Mom and me. We were trapped at home. But we made it. They didn't." She turned to face him, wet streaks slashing her cheeks, eyes glistening with tears.

His heart wrenched.

"My mom went to pieces while we waited to be rescued, and I thought I was going to die. I was only ten years old.

How could a loving God let that happen?" A sob escaped, and she buried her face in her hands.

He couldn't hold back any longer. He reached for her, took her into his embrace and held her quaking frame.

Her hands moved to grip his arms, her face buried in his chest as she let out all the pain, the agony, of tragic loss. Things he didn't have a pat answer for.

He could only tell her, promise her, God was good. Even still, even then. Even now.

But God would have to show her that Himself.

Toby trotted into the lit kitchen as Bristol closed the door to the garage behind her and locked it. She went through the motions on autopilot, slipping off her heels and carrying them to her bedroom closet, switching on lights as she went. Her mind was far away, remembering the feel of Rem's strong arms around her as she had cried. Sobbed, really. A woman who'd spent years trying to rise through the ranks of the male-dominated law enforcement profession. She'd never dared shed a tear as a cop.

But stoicism had been easy. She'd stopped crying a week after Hurricane Katrina. Tears only made the pain worse. Better to focus on preventing such pain, for herself and others. Better to build a life that guaranteed she would never be helpless again.

She set her purse on the nightstand and sat on the bed. She leaned forward, holding her face in her hands. She should feel embarrassed, losing control like that. Especially in front of Remington, of all people.

Yet, she wasn't embarrassed. Not even when her tears had dried and she'd realized how tightly she'd been clinging to him.

Maybe because he'd looked down at her with the warmest brown eyes she'd ever seen. He hadn't mouthed any plat-itudes or looked like he didn't know what to do with the weepy female.

He'd simply gazed at her with eyes full of everything she felt, as if he'd somehow jumped into her sea of pain and sor-row, and he was willing to tread water with her there, help-ing to hold her up.

She'd responded stupidly. Telling him she was tired instead of giving in to the wave of gratitude that made her want to throw her arms around his neck and—

But that would have been far more stupid. She'd send the wrong message.

Remington still wasn't the kind of man she needed.

But none of the stable men she ever dated had held her as she cried. Never cradled her with such tenderness and made her feel so…safe.

The ring of her phone, muffled in her purse, interrupted the dangerous thoughts.

She reached in the inner compartment of the purse to pull out the cell.

Cora.

Bristol cleared her throat, hoping for a normal tone. "Hey, Cora."

"Hi, Bristol. Oh, sorry. Did I wake you?"

Great, her voice must sound thicker than she thought. Six-teen years of unleashed tears would do that. "No, I'm just tired. Hadn't gone to bed yet. What's up?"

"I just wanted to let you know the task force has a lead on the bomber."

Bristol scooted to the edge of the bed, her nerves tingling. "What is it?"

"The pipes he made to look like sticks of dynamite were spray-painted."

"Yeah?"

"The spray paint he used is a very specific shade of orange that can be hard to get because most companies don't make it."

Bristol's heart rate picked up speed. The break they needed.

"The FBI was able to isolate the manufacturer, and they're tracking down the online and local distributers. Agent Nguyen wanted us to put you on standby in case they need your help checking for bombs wherever this clue leads them."

"Awesome. That's great news, Cora. Thanks for letting me know. I'll keep my phone close." She got to her feet as they said good night and ended the call. She needed this news, motivation to get her head back in the game, her mind on what mattered.

Being on standby she could handle.

Facing a bomb was straightforward and important.

Figuring out what to do with her emotions and a certain Remington Jones was downright scary.

Chapter Twenty-Three

The phone's ring cut through the night, severing Bristol's sleep.

A night when she was finally sleeping soundly, and it just had to be interrupted.

She cracked her eyes open, darkness seeping under her lids as she reached to feel the top of the nightstand, patting her hand on the surface until it bumped her phone.

The third ring finally woke her brain enough to jog her memory. Standby. Was it Agent Nguyen calling for explosives detection?

She grabbed the phone and propped up on her elbow as she checked the bright screen.

Remington Jones.

In the middle of the night? She put the phone to her ear. "Rem?" She reached for the clock on the nightstand and hit the top button to illuminate the screen—5:02.

A long pause.

"Hello?"

"You called me Rem."

She could hear a grin in his voice, and it did odd things to her newly awakened stomach. "You better have a good reason for calling me at five in the morning." She didn't clear the gritty sound from her voice. He deserved to be growled at.

"I'm outside, ready to get started on our searches for the day."

She pushed up to sit against the bed's headboard. No light sneaked in around the blinds over her window. "Lame joke. It's still dark."

He laughed, sending her belly into a twirl she definitely couldn't handle this time of morning. "I thought you were the early riser. And I'm not joking. I'm in your driveway, with coffee."

"Like that makes it okay."

He chuckled at her mutter. "I'll give you ten minutes, but don't blame me if your coffee gets cold." He disconnected the call before she could protest.

She stared at the screen of her phone. She should be furious with him showing up at her house at five in the morning. Neither of which were planned. She was supposed to pick him up at the DNR even though his car was fixed, because he had said it only made sense to carpool. She'd agreed, so that was the plan.

But a smile tugged at her lips as her heart tumbled, skipping beats here and there as if uncertain how to respond to Rem's surprise arrival. She hurried to get herself and Toby ready, telling herself to calm down and show some irritation when she saw Rem so he'd remember how much she hated surprises.

The flush in her cheeks as she looked in the bathroom mirror called her a liar.

"So what was your plan if it'd been dark when we got here?" Bristol's eyes appeared mostly gray in the twilight as she looked up at Rem, walking by his side on the truss bridge of Crownover Lock and Dam.

He grinned, loving the sound of humor in her tone instead of irritation. "I knew it wouldn't be. Started to get light even before I got to your place. Besides, I've seen how well Toby's nose works in the dark."

She laughed, music that trickled right into his heart. "Better than I do, that's for sure."

"You used to be a morning person." She'd always been the first to class at the academy. Always looked fresh and ready for anything, while he'd stumbled in still half-asleep.

"I am. Not sure why I was so tired today." Her voice dropped in volume as she spoke the thought out loud. The smile was gone.

They both knew why she was exhausted. But he hadn't known how to bring it up. The tears, the loss she'd shared with him. Better to let her talk when she wanted. He would let it lie and keep praying.

He had worried she'd be awkward with him today. Maybe embarrassed. Instead, she was a version of the relaxed Bristol he'd seen last night at her grandma's. So relaxed she was even calling him Rem like she used to.

His chest swelled with hope that his plan for this morning would work. He looked at the orange just starting to tease the sky. Their timing was perfect.

"Let's check out the tower." He gestured to the door as they approached.

"Okay."

He pulled the new proximity card out of his back pocket and held it up to the reader.

"Upgraded the security, I see."

He gave her a smile as the door unlocked, and he gripped the handle to pull it open.

"Are your friends working—"

The question died on her lips as a squeal greeted them.

Harriet trotted over to Rem with a laugh, squeezing him in a tight hug before she let him go and lightly swatted his wrist. "You sly dog, you. What are you doing here this early? You are full of surprises." She leaned over to squeeze Bristol's arm. "Though a surprise from this hunk sure does a girl's heart good, doesn't it, sweetie?" She winked. "Good to see you again, too, hon. Oh!" She looked down at Toby, who wriggled with excitement as if expecting to be petted. "And you brought your dog again!"

Rem chuckled as Harriet granted Toby's wish by stroking both sides of his face and ears.

"They do work together, Harriet." Went moved his narrow head to look through a slot between monitors. "How could she do bomb detection without the dog?"

"Posh." Harriet waved her hand dismissively without looking at Went. "I thought maybe you were here to—" she leaned closer to Rem, lowering her voice slightly "—show her our special secret." She waggled her eyebrows and giggled.

Rem shook his head with a grin. How did this woman have such good instincts about these things? He'd never brought anyone out here before to see the jaw-dropping view. But Harriet was the one who had told him about the incredible sight, who took him to the top of the tower when he'd first started working for the DNR. "You know, I can't believe it, but you have even more energy before sunrise than later."

Harriet laughed, her cheeks dimpling. "Oh, yes. I'm the earliest kind of bird there is. I'm ready to go to sleep by noon. Isn't that right, Wentworth?"

Wentworth probably meant the gentleman of that name was in trouble with Harriet this morning. But they didn't have time to delve into that. And if he knew Harriet, the problem would be resolved by the time he and Bristol returned.

"Harriet, would you mind watching Toby for a minute or two?"

Bristol stared at Rem as if he'd just said he was the bomber.

Harriet gave him a conspiratorial smile. "While you go up top? I'd love to, sweetie."

He took a breath and faced the more difficult challenge—Bristol. "There's something I'd like to show you. Would you come with me for a minute?"

"Without Toby?"

"I just want to show you something up there." He pointed to the watchtower ceiling.

"There's another level to the tower? Why haven't we been clearing that?"

"Went and the other shifts have been clearing it. Nothing can be hidden from view up there. You'll see what I mean when you come with me. But we can only get to it there." Rem pointed to the eight-foot vertical ladder he didn't think Toby would be able to climb.

"I'll watch Toby for you, hon." Harriet reached out her hand for the leash. "I have dogs of my own, and I love them. He'll be happy with me."

Bristol kept the leash. "He's a valuable dog."

Rem sighed. "Honestly, Bristol, you know me and Harriet. Do you really think I'd ask you to do something dangerous?"

Her eyes seemed to go from blue to gray, then back again, as if her thoughts warred against each other.

His stomach clenched as he realized what he'd just said. He'd already shown her just being involved with the old Rem was dangerous. "I promise, it will only take a minute, and you *and* Toby will be perfectly safe. You'll love it." He looked deep into her eyes as they settled into a darkening blue. "Give me a chance. Please?"

Her lips pinched together, then let go. She jerked a nod. "One minute." She held out the leash to Harriet, looking a bit as if she were handing over her firstborn child. "Toby, wait."

Rem went to the ladder before she could change her mind, letting out a breath when she followed him. He stepped to the side. "After you."

"You can go first." So she still didn't trust him completely.

But he'd take partial trust over none. He climbed the ladder quickly, hearing her steps on the metal behind him.

He pushed up the trapdoor at the top, and a vision of orange, pink, red and yellow met him as he climbed through. Thank the Lord for a dry day without the usual rain clouds cluttering the sky. He pulled himself up onto the three-foot square, flat portion of the rounded watch tower.

Bristol's head popped through the opening, and he extended his hand to help her out.

She hesitated, then put her hand in his.

A jolt shot through his arm and ricocheted through his body as he lifted her to stand next to him.

Her gaze locked on the sight he'd awoken her early to see.

The sunrise covered the sky that seemed a limitless expanse, stretching uninterrupted in front of them. Orange and pink dominated, streaking out from the orb that was just starting to appear on the horizon, creating a breathtaking canvas only God could paint.

He'd watched several sunrises from the high vantage point of the watchtower roof, but this was the most magnificent he'd seen.

Yet all he wanted to do was stare at Bristol, the woman who was more amazing than any sunrise. Even the sun seemed to love her, highlighting the mahogany tones of her hair with its mango-colored glow.

"Wow." She whispered the word as her widened eyes took in the sky, her touch still thrilling him as she kept her hand in his. "It's...beautiful."

His throat thickened with emotion as he drank in the sight of her, the feel of her hand. "So beautiful." Something in his tone must have given him away.

She broke her study of the sunrise and turned her head toward him. "Why?"

Why. Did she mean why couldn't he forget her even though she had moved on? His heart ached for an answer. He swallowed, not able to look away from her gray-blue eyes, even if he wanted to.

He took a breath and a step closer to her.

She didn't move away.

"I wanted to see you smile." He lost himself in those incredible eyes. "To see you enjoy something. To see you enjoy the beauty and hope that's also part of this life." He moved closer still, as if some force was pulling, until only inches separated them. "I'd do anything to take away your sadness, Bristol. To make you happy."

Her eyes swirled into gray as she looked up at him, head tilted to meet his gaze. Her lips parted. Then she did it, leaned into him almost imperceptibly, but his senses flew into high alert the split second it happened.

His breathing intensified as his heart pumped in his ears. He touched her fingers at her sides, a test.

Her eyes drifted shut, and she lifted her face to his.

She wanted him to kiss her.

His heart stopped. He dipped his head down as his hands came up to cradle her neck.

No.

He froze, not certain where the thought had come from. But others rushed in with it. She wanted, deserved, someone dependable and committed. He'd kissed her before, when they were dating six years ago, and the memories nearly overcame the resolve forming in his mind. But he shouldn't have kissed her back then. He hadn't been the kind of man she'd wanted and deserved. And though he'd changed now, he hadn't been able to prove that to her yet. Maybe if he could find the bomber or succeed in securing the dams, she would accept he had changed and believe in him again. Or maybe she'd decide he was worth loving despite his failings, like she had thought at the academy. Until that happened, until she wanted a future with him again, he had no right to take anything from her so precious as a kiss.

He dropped his hands and pulled back.

Her eyes popped open as she jerked away, bumping into the guardrail behind her. She gripped it with her hands behind her body, staring at him with confusion in her eyes.

His heart wrenched in his chest. "I'm sorry. I shouldn't have…" He reached a hand toward her, then dropped it, his heart dying a little with the knowledge he might never feel her touch again. "I don't want to hurt you, Bristol. In any way."

Her gaze cleared to stronger blue as she looked at him. "I know." The two words came out in a whisper that seeped into his soul and gave him hope he shouldn't embrace.

She turned to look at the sunrise, and he barely caught what she said last. "I'm sorry, too."

What had she been thinking? Bristol followed Toby's tug on the leash as he searched the mechanical room at Rocky Falls Dam. She wasn't paying as much attention as she should to the search, her mind alternating between consternation and frustration. And avoiding eye contact with Rem, who hung back near the entrance to the room, watching with a furrowed brow and heavy silence.

She'd almost kissed him. Wanted him to kiss her. And he'd been the one to pull away before they'd made the big mistake. Irresponsible Remington Jones had been more responsible than she, stopping them before the fall.

But he'd wanted to kiss her, too. She'd seen it in his eyes.

Toby moved parallel with the dank wall marred by dirt, chips and scratches—evidence of its over one hundred years of existence.

It didn't matter if Rem had wanted to kiss her or not. She'd been a fool to let it go that far. She'd been riding on emotion, conjured by the beauty of the sunrise and residual weakness from her breakdown the night before. She couldn't lose sight of what was best. And that had never been Remington Jones.

Yet, he'd stopped. Pulled his warm hands away from her neck and apologized, aching remorse and longing contorting his features. He didn't want to hurt her, he'd said. Is that why he'd stopped? For her?

Had Rem really changed that much? It's not that he ever wanted to hurt her. She was starting to realize, to admit, that he hadn't meant to betray her when he hid the truth and cheated at the academy. But he was so irresponsible back then that he couldn't, or didn't want to, be depended on.

She wouldn't have believed he could change if she hadn't seen it with her own eyes. Her pulse sped up as she looked his way.

He stood with his arms folded over his chest. The shadows of the dimly lit room crossed his face, masking his features and hiding the direction of his gaze.

Was it possible he could be—

The thought screeched to a halt as her returning gaze hit Toby.

He'd stopped by the wall, attention focused on something

she couldn't see behind a large black tank. And he was sitting, front paw lifted.

"Rem. We've got an alert."

She heard him approach behind her as she went to Toby, digging out her flashlight from her pack. She switched it on and used the beam to illuminate the dark crevices between the tank and wall.

An oddly shaped object was attached to the back of the tank, two inches from the wall and one foot off the ground. A plastic bag. Full of something dark. She leaned closer.

Coffee grounds?

"He's filled the bag with coffee grounds, probably thinking that would stop the K-9s from smelling the explosives. I can't see the device at all, but I trust Toby there's one in there." She touched her hand to the cold wall. "What wall is this?"

"The retaining wall that holds back the water along the whole north side of the arch. If it blows…"

"It won't." The confidence that kept her pulse steady enforced her voice. "I need you to go to the landline phone in the visitor center and call the bomb squad. Don't risk a cell signal anywhere nearby. And tell the staff to evacuate on your way." With only two employees and one security guard at the dam, they'd be able to get to safety quickly.

"Got it." But he didn't move his feet.

She met his concerned gaze. "Rem, go."

"Be careful." He ran toward the opening that led to the galley tunnel. If he sprinted from there, which she was sure he would, it shouldn't take him long to reach the small visitor center set away from the horseshoe-shaped dam that controlled the powerful falls.

"Release, Toby. Good boy." She pulled out Toby's toy and rewarded him for the accurate alert by tossing it and playing tug with one hand. At the same time, she moved closer to the bag. She couldn't see the device or the timer the bomber had likely used again. Didn't know how much time they had.

She couldn't risk waiting. She'd have to at least get to the timer.

She let Toby continue his play alone while she whipped on a pair of latex gloves and crouched in the tight space next to the device. Using her flashlight, she looked over every inch of the bag, then concentrated on the zippered seal at the top. There were no wires or triggering devices attached. And he couldn't have vacuum-sealed an ordinary zippered plastic bag.

Reaching for the bag with steady hands, she slowly, carefully, separated the two sides of plastic along the seal.

No explosion.

"Okay so far, Toby." He didn't look up from chewing on his toy.

She pulled one of her own plastic bags from her pack and began to scoop out handfuls of coffee grounds, transferring them to her bag for evidence analysis. Good thing the bomber didn't realize dogs' noses could easily separate the scent of coffee grounds from explosives.

A few more scoops exposed the first edge of the device.

"Good work, Toby." Another accurate alert.

She kept transferring coffee until she could clearly see the device and timer.

She took in a breath. Twenty-one minutes to go.

Too close for comfort.

But she did take comfort in the predictability of the bomber's MO. The device looked identical to the first IED Toby had found at Minnesota Falls. Same timing detonation, as well. Not a sophisticated or complex device, but still enough unstable explosive power to blow a significant hole in the concrete wall.

One thing was for sure—this bomb was real.

Chapter Twenty-Four

Officer Jim Ulig took off his helmet and nodded to Bristol as he passed. The experienced bomb squad technician had efficiently rendered the bomber's device safe in the five minutes he had once he was in position.

"Are you okay?" Rem's voice drifted to her ear from behind, rougher than normal.

She didn't turn to see him, sensing he was too close for her to risk that. "Perfectly." She took out her phone from her jacket pocket and powered it on, confident it was safe since she and Toby had cleared the rest of the dam. "Ceinture Dam next?" She stepped forward before rotating to face him.

His eyebrows clustered while his gaze traveled her face, as if looking for signs of fear or fatigue.

"I'm fine. I do this for a living, remember? I like it."

The firm set of his mouth relaxed slightly. "Right. Well… what if I need a burger and fries to recover?"

"Nice try."

"Maybe Toby needs a burger?" He tilted his head toward Toby, who stood panting at her side.

A laugh slipped out before she could hold it back.

His answering grin made her heart skip a beat.

Her phone rang in her hand.

Cora.

"Hey, Cora."

"Bristol. Are you okay? We just heard about the bomb at Rocky Falls."

"Yes, we're all fine. It was rendered safe. We've cleared the rest of the facility and there are no more devices here."

"Praise the Lord." But Cora's tone was still tight.

"Did Agent Nguyen tell you about the bomb?" She'd probably been informed after Rem alerted the bomb squad.

"Indirectly, yes." Cora took an audible breath. "Libertas called the governor's office about fifteen minutes ago."

"Oh, no. Another bomb threat?"

Rem's brow furrowed as he gave Bristol a look of concern.

Bristol covered the mouthpiece. "The bomber called the governor."

Rem's eyes widened, probably matching her own.

Amazement lifted Cora's voice as she continued. "Yes, it was a threat. But for the bomb you just diffused."

Bristol shook her head at Rem, signaling there wasn't another bomb. Yet.

"The governor's assistant took the call, and we only have a summary of what the bomber said. He apparently wanted to tell the governor that a bomb would explode in a few moments at Rocky Falls, raising the water level downstream even higher than before."

Bristol's mouth dried to sawdust. "The flood would be worse if he destroys a dam downriver."

"Exactly, but not just any of the dams. He made his target

clear. He said he's going to destroy the Minnesota Falls Dam unless the governor meets his demands."

"What demands?" Bristol blinked hard, trying to chase away the memories that rushed in. The way the floodwaters swallowed nearly everything she'd known and loved.

"He wants the governor to shut down the Minnesota Falls Dam immediately and demolish it within three weeks after closure. He's giving the governor until April nineteenth at four p.m. to do what he says."

Bristol swallowed. "Or what?"

"He didn't say exactly. He said if he didn't hear from the governor that his demands would be met, he would take matters into his own hands because the Mississippi must be freed."

And people must die, was that it? The water level was high enough at the Minnesota Falls Dam now to do serious damage even without successfully decimating the Rocky Falls Dam upriver. High enough to cause a catastrophic flood.

Her breath stalled in her chest as her stomach twisted.

Rem stepped close.

She looked up, and his gaze caught hers. He put his hand on her forearm, the warmth of his touch seeping through her skin to reach her clenched heart. As if he knew she needed support, knew what was bothering her and knew how to help.

The panic starting to course through her veins dissipated as rational thought returned. She'd stopped the bomber's device today. She would do that again. Every time until he was caught.

"Bristol? Are you okay?" Cora's concern reached across the line.

Bristol cleared her throat. "Yeah. We'll stop him, Cora."

"I don't doubt it. I think Phoenix might want you to come in and—hang on…"

Bristol took the pause on Cora's end of the line to quickly fill Rem in on what she'd been told.

"Bristol?" Cora's soft voice sounded in her ear.

"Yeah."

"Agent Nguyen just called Phoenix. They've found a location they think is the bomber's hideout. They're going in and they want another K-9 to clear the scene quickly in case it's booby-trapped."

"Got it."

"We'll text you the location. Be careful."

"Always." Bristol ended the call and turned to Rem. "The FBI are going to raid what they think could be the bomber's hideout. Toby and I need to help clear it."

"Wow. That's...great." A mixture of surprise and worry strained his features as he slid his hands into his pants pockets. "Can you get a ride with someone else?"

"Of course. Please be safe."

She nodded and pulled away with Toby, jogging out of the dam. They might be about to catch the bad guy and stop this nightmare. But all she could think about was the concern darkening Rem's eyes and clouding his voice. The evidence that he cared.

When she pushed that aside, she was left with images of a looming flood, leaving carnage and tragedy in its wake. But that, too, was a foreshadow of something that wouldn't come to pass. She and Toby had shown the bomber they were the ones in control. There wouldn't be another flood or explosion on their watch.

Rem hoped he wasn't on a fool's errand. He blew out a sigh as he turned the wheel to take the corner onto Tristan's street. Stopping by Tristan's house when Bristol was with the task force, about to burst in on the bomber at his hideout, would hopefully give Rem a better indication of whether or not Tristan was involved.

Releasing a longer breath did nothing to rid Rem of the edginess skirting his thoughts, the sense of a red warning flag being waved somewhere in the recesses of his mind.

It was too easy. The bomber was a smart guy. He'd proven that. Would he really use a type of paint that could be so easily traced, with a trail that somehow led to a specific location? Everyone made mistakes, even the smartest criminals, so it was certainly possible. But it just didn't feel right.

Lord, please don't let Bristol be walking into some kind of trap.

He hated this feeling, this helplessness. He couldn't even go with her to the site for the FBI's raid.

But in case the task force was wrong, he could do this. He could continue following the one lead he had. Hopefully find more evidence to show Tristan knew the bomber or was the infamous Libertas himself.

If Tristan was at home and didn't get any sudden, alarming phone calls, that would be strong evidence he wasn't the bomber. Particularly if the task force walked away from their raid with the bomber in handcuffs.

Rem slowed when he neared Tristan's house, easy to spot with the solar panels dominating the front yard. Should he park farther away, so he could observe unnoticed?

No, he'd stick with the approach he'd been using with Tristan so far. Up-front friendship. Whether Tristan was Libertas or not, the nature-loving university alum angle was getting Rem better access to Tristan and potential evidence than skulking around would. He'd have to think of a reason to give for this visit by the time he got to the door.

Rem swung into Tristan's driveway. The garage door was closed tight, and the late-morning sun made it difficult to tell if the interior lights of the house were on or off.

He got out of his car and went to the front door, rang the bell. The tone echoed inside the house.

Tristan sure kept a neat place. The decorative windows in the door and flanking it were free of leaves or cobwebs, while the cement step Rem stood on looked like it must get swept every day. The navy-blue paint accenting the shutters and the paler blue on the siding appeared recent, without chips or fading. The guy clearly spent a lot more time on upkeep than the manager of Rem's apartment building. Or maybe Tristan had bought the house not long ago.

No answer at the door.

Rem's pulse started to beat faster. Of course, Tristan could be anywhere. Though he didn't have a job.

A rapid punching, machinery noise interrupted the birds chirping a song. A tiller?

Rem followed the noise around the side of the house, walking across the mostly brown grass that was smattered with green beginnings of spring growth. The lawn would be more mud than grass with all the rain if not for this neighborhood's higher elevation.

He reached the backyard and spotted Tristan, leaning into a tiller that looked like it'd seen better days twenty years ago. The machine grunted and groaned as it managed to grind up another foot-width of dirt along the garden bed Tristan had just plowed the last time Rem was here.

He looked Rem's direction and stopped. Turned off the tiller. He lifted a garden-gloved hand in a wave. "Hi, Jones."

"Hey." Rem headed toward Tristan, dodging clusters of tulips and daffodils on the way. "Sorry to interrupt." He stopped by the freshly plowed dirt and looked at the tiller that reminded him of the one his dad used to have from the seventies. "Think you'll be able to get it started again?"

Tristan grinned, humor lighting his eyes for the first time

that Rem had seen. "Getting it started is half the fun." He tugged off his gloves and leaned his forearms over the handles, wiping sweat off his forehead under the oddly angled fringe of hair that fell there.

Rem chuckled. "You must like fighting with machinery."

"Eh, it's only a fight if you don't know what you're doing. My old man taught me." A frown replaced the smile as Tristan bent over to pick up a stick from the dirt.

"Was he a mechanic?"

"He was a lot of things. Mostly absent." He chucked the stick hard, landing it fifteen feet away into the stand of trees that bordered his yard.

"That's rough."

Tristan shrugged. "Wasn't great when he was around, either."

"I know how that can be."

Tristan jerked his gaze to Rem, thick eyebrows lifted. "Your old man?"

Rem nodded. "I messed up one too many times. He won't even talk to me now."

A humorless laugh puffed with Tristan's breath. "It was the opposite with my old man. He was the one who messed up. I wouldn't talk to him again, either. But he deserved it."

"Was?"

Tristan smacked the paired gloves into his palm, bracing his other hand on his hip in a fist. He met Rem's gaze for a beat. "He's dead."

Rem's throat tightened as he looked at the man in front of him.

Anger flashed at the foreground of his eyes, but behind that mask, pain swirled.

What if Rem's dad died suddenly now, when they still weren't talking? His chest squeezed. "I'm sorry, man."

"Yeah, well, that's not why you're here, right?" Tristan grabbed the handles of the tiller and turned it, pulling it back out of the dirt as he tilted the blades into the air.

"I stopped by to ask you about your flowers."

Tristan paused, angling a skeptical look at Rem. "My flowers?"

"For my mom. She's been trying to grow tulips the last couple of years, but she only gets one or two bulbs that actually turn into nice flowers. I thought maybe you could give me some tips I could pass along. Yours are amazing." He gestured to the three-foot wide patch of tulips in red, blue, purple and yellow.

Tristan's mouth relaxed close to a smile as his gaze followed Rem's indication to the flowers. "Well, first the location is important."

The next fifteen minutes passed with Tristan giving Rem more gardening tips than he could possibly remember. The guy should write a book.

But Rem's mind was elsewhere, too. Tristan seemed more relaxed than the first day Rem had seen him. If he was the bomber, wouldn't he be worried about the hideout raid? Or, ideally, he was blissfully unaware the FBI had found the location.

He might be an innocent guy who loved gardening, and Rem was wasting his time barking up the wrong tree.

As Tristan explained the strategy for award-winning tulips, Rem's thoughts traveled a greater distance and to a grimmer possibility.

Rem could be looking at Libertas right now, cheerful because he was inwardly triumphing over fooling Bristol and the task force. Maybe because he'd prepared something sinister to greet them.

Rem sent up a silent prayer they were having more success finding the bomber than he was. And, above all, he prayed Bristol was safe.

Bristol entered the condemned building behind Agent Nguyen and another FBI agent, a muscled guy, both dressed in full SWAT gear. Four other FBI SWAT members had breached the heavy door, cleared the hallway and were searching the rooms off it.

Toby strained at the leash Bristol kept shorter than normal to hold him behind the agents.

She scanned the surroundings for any signs of a device as they moved.

Hard to tell what the building used to be. Likely a warehouse of some kind. Many of the walls were partially smashed and gutted, leaving exposed boards and wiring she hoped was no longer connected to any power source.

An out of order sign hung at an angle from one rusty nail in the wall next to an elevator with doors that appeared to be permanently open.

Looked like the rusting metal stairs at the end of the hall would be their only way up to the next level of the four-story building while the first SWAT team finished clearing the ground floor.

Miles had gone in behind the first team with Duke. He would clear the first floor while Bristol went up to the second.

The top two floors were believed to be unsafe for any weight-bearing. Hopefully the bomber had thought so, too, and stayed on the lower levels.

Agent Nguyen paused as she signaled to her partner to wait. She looked at Bristol. "They haven't found any trace of explosives down here so far." Her eyes held a distanced look as if she was listening to coms through her headgear. "Let's go up."

Bristol nodded, and they moved forward. Energy pulsed through her veins. The bomber could be right up these stairs.

Toby tried to pull ahead of Agent Nguyen as they approached the staircase, but Bristol held him back. Until he barked.

"Hold it!" Bristol's shout sounded like an echo of his warning.

Toby never barked on duty. The dog strained at his leash, pushing with all his body weight, ears alert and every muscle straining ahead.

"What's going on?" Agent Nguyen's tense tone said she didn't like the change in command.

"Toby's got something." What, Bristol wasn't sure. He'd never barked as an indication before. He wasn't trained to do that. "Let us take the lead."

Agent Nguyen stared through her clear face mask at Bristol for a second. "Go. We'll cover you." She signaled to her partner, and they smoothly switched positions to flank Bristol and Toby, Agent Nguyen preparing to aim her AR-15 upward to cover the opening above the stairs when they got there.

Bristol loosened her grip on the leash.

Toby shot forward toward the bottom step. He sniffed along the front edge of the stair quickly, then sat, lifted one paw.

"Does that mean…?"

Bristol nodded, glancing at Agent Nguyen. "An explosive device."

That had nearly killed them all.

Chapter Twenty-Five

"Fishing wire stretched across stairs. Talk about old school."
Stevens directed the statement to his rookie partner as they
packed up their equipment, but he sent a glance Bristol's way.

"He's an old-fashioned guy." A fact she'd already noted for
her mental profile of the bomber.

"And determined to give you a very unfriendly welcome.
That much explosive, intentionally made more unstable from
the looks of it... He would've taken down not just your team
but this whole building."

Bristol knew that already, but Stevens saying it drove home
how narrowly they'd escaped the bomber's booby-trap.

She stroked Toby's head, probably the twentieth grateful
hand in the last ten minutes to pet the K-9 who had saved
their lives. She'd also given him an extra lengthy tug and re-
trieve session with his favorite toy as her personal thank-you.

"You guys are clear now." Stevens gave Bristol a nod filled
with more respect than he'd shown her since she'd left the
squad.

Agent Nguyen gave orders to the rest of the SWAT team as she led the way up the staircase. She'd told Bristol to let Toby walk between her and her partner at the front this time. Toby wagged his tail, clearly loving the improved positioning as he charged up the steps.

The SWAT team that had cleared the first floor followed Bristol this time, along with Miles and Duke.

They climbed the split staircase with SWAT keeping them covered, weapons pointed in different directions. The bomber's MO was to use explosive devices only, and always without him present, but there was no predicting when a criminal would change behavior and start shooting, especially when backed into a corner.

Given the present he'd left for them, though, the chances of him sticking around for it to blow him away were slim to none. He was likely gone. Hopefully he'd at least left too hastily to clean up all the evidence behind him.

As they reached the top of the second flight of stairs, the area opened up before them. Only halves of a few walls remained, the rest having apparently been knocked down. Rotting boards angled into each other, the broken skeletons of a structure long gone.

Objects in the farthest corner of the extensive space drew Bristol's gaze.

Were those paintings? And a table, and other items she couldn't make out from here.

Agent Nguyen led the way as SWAT quickly cleared the open space while Miles and Bristol swept for explosives.

They made their way in a grid pattern across the floor, reaching the corner of interest far too slowly for Bristol. Her nerves itched to see the bomber's hideout, if that's what it was, by the time she reached that part of the building.

She let Toby search the corner while she took in what little there was.

A mottled white plastic table on metal legs stood away from the wall, centered on a green tarp laid over the floor. No explosives or equipment that she could see. Just a clean tabletop and tarp. But the lab techs might be able to find traces of something. She had the feeling they wouldn't find anything that could lead them to the bomber's ID, if he was as smart as he seemed.

"Bachmann." Agent Nguyen gave Bristol a quick glance. She'd taken off her helmet, and her straight black hair skimmed her shoulders as she looked up at the two paintings that hung from nails hammered into exposed boards of a former wall.

"Toby, release."

He relaxed out of search mode, and Bristol gave him a scratch behind the ears as she led him over to Agent Nguyen.

"What do you think?"

Bristol followed the agent's gaze to the first painting. A depiction of a river, cascading over rocks in a wide waterfall. A man dressed in Native American clothing sat on the shore in the foreground. Bristol knew next to nothing about art, but an inset in the matting listed the title: *Minnesota Falls, 1849.*

The painting next to the first one was at a different time of day, the oranges and reds in the sky suggesting sunset. But the river was similar, water crashing around a small island in the middle of a rocky waterfall. The second painting was also labeled: *Minnesota Falls, 1848.*

"An obsession or a message?" Bristol murmured the words to herself.

"Good question." Agent Nguyen folded her arms across her body armor, helmet dangling from her small fingers. "Either way, it amounts to the same thing—confirmation of his threat to the governor and our investigation results thus far. His primary target all along has been the Minnesota Falls Dam."

"So you think the Leavell Dam was—"

"A way to get attention drawn to his cause and make sure we're taking him seriously."

"Could've been a test, too."

Agent Nguyen gave Bristol a measured gaze. "Of our response."

Bristol nodded.

"I agree. He could have been calculating our response time and what our response would be." She shifted the helmet to hold it under one arm at her side. "But he's shown too much of his hand now. He's getting overconfident and we're gaining the edge." She looked at Toby, who sat at Bristol's side, panting. "Thanks to you and your K-9, we didn't go up with his bomb like he planned. And we still found this."

Which didn't look like much of anything, unless the bomber had been far more careless than it appeared.

"Our lab crew will find more leads here, I'm sure of it." Agent Nguyen turned away from the paintings and aimed her determined gaze across the open space, where the lab techs had arrived and were making their way across the floor. "We'll find this bomber before his seventy-two hours are up." She gave Bristol a satisfied smile. "I know you and Toby will be able to keep everyone safe until then."

Bristol returned the smile, confidence rippling through her body. Agent Nguyen was right. The bomber was underestimating Bristol and Toby. They could handle anything he had in store.

"This has gotten out of control."

Rem looked up from the paperwork in front of him to see

Calvin march into his office, cheeks tinged red. What was he doing at work on a Saturday? Unless—

Rem's breath caught. "Did something go wrong with the raid? Did anyone get hurt?" His heart wouldn't beat again until he heard Bristol was okay.

Calvin blinked. Stayed quiet for painful seconds. Then: "What are you talking about?"

"The task force. They were going into the bomber's hideout today. I thought maybe—"

"I don't know anything about that. I'm talking about your latest debacle."

Oh. That. Rem's heart resumed operation, and he leaned back in his chair, trying to catch his breath. Maybe he should text Bristol. He hadn't heard a thing from her since she'd gone on the raid. And it had been three hours since he'd left Tristan's place to come to the DNR and catch up on all the office work he hadn't been doing while escorting Bristol to dams.

"...know you've lost Franklin's support." Calvin's face flushed again as he blustered threats. "He's not going to stick his neck out for you anymore."

Rem kept his expression even and calm. He'd missed the first part of what Calvin had said, but it likely had to do with the real bomb Bristol had found at Rocky Falls that morning.

Calvin stepped close to Rem's desk. "The higher-ups are demanding a reevaluation of your position and you." His mouth slid into a smirk. "I volunteered for the job."

"My job?" No surprise there.

"The job of evaluating your suitability as safety and security supervisor."

"You mean like a spot performance review."

Calvin frowned and leaned forward, planting his hands on Rem's desk to stare down at him. "Like a formality before your expedient dismissal." He grinned—one of the nastiest expressions Rem had seen on a person's face. "Franklin won't be able to save you now, Jones."

The words found the chink in Rem's armor that usually held strong against Calvin. But the threat rang with truth this time. Calvin had never gone this far, and Franklin had never been in such a tight spot.

Failure. Again. But what did he expect? Nothing had gone right since he'd made such awful mistakes before he'd come to Christ. The consequences of cheating at the academy had left him with no choice but to pursue a degree he had no passion for and end up here, in a job the bombs suggested he was failing at miserably.

He deserved to be punished, he knew that. He'd done lousy things in his past. Nothing criminal or violent, but in the eyes of God, he knew his past deeds were terrible. But if he were fired from this job, kicked out in disgrace, it would guarantee his dad would never talk to him again as long as they both lived.

He's dead. Tristan's words about his own father echoed in Rem's mind.

What if something happened to Dad while they still weren't speaking? Rem had to try. Had to at least give the apology his dad had never allowed him to deliver.

"Fine." Calvin straightened away from the desk as if Rem's silence had been an answer to something Rem hadn't heard. "But know that ignoring me and the problem won't help your case. Actually—" he donned another smirk "—I don't think anything will." He spun on the heels of his hiking boots and stalked out of the office, disappearing from view.

Rem stood and closed the door, locking it as he pulled his cell phone from his pocket. He selected the speed dial programmed for his mom.

"Rem?" Her voice flowed into his chest in a wave of warmth that seeped around the tension squeezing his heart.

"Hi, Mom."

"Are you okay?" She could tell something was wrong from two words? She'd always known her children well, always been their comforter and listening ear whenever needed. Whenever Dad reamed them out or ignored them completely.

"I need to talk to Dad."

Silence.

"I know he'll say no, but it's important. Would you try again?" The knot climbing up his throat nearly choked his words. "Please?"

"Hold on, honey."

His heart thumped in the ear he pressed to the phone as he waited. His mouth felt like the time he'd swallowed sand on a dare from his brother, Tim. Mom had been so worried about him. But Dad had laughed. Said if Rem was going to do stupid things, he'd have to handle the consequences on his own. Maybe it would teach him to think before he acted.

"Rem?" Mom. Not Dad.

His hopes plummeted. "He won't…"

"No. I'm sorry."

"Di—" The word caught in his dry throat. He swallowed. "Did he say why? Anything?" But Rem already knew why. He didn't need to ask. His desperate heart was grasping at straws.

"You know what he said, Rem." Sadness weighted his mother's voice.

He could almost hear the tears probably pooling in her eyes.

"It's not worth repeating."

He swallowed again. "Thanks for trying."

"I love you, Rem."

"Love you, too." He lowered the phone, made his way

back to the desk where he sank into the chair and leaned his head in his hands.

Yes, he knew what his dad had said.

I'll talk to him when he proves he deserves it.

Chapter Twenty-Six

Rem stared at the words he'd written on the whiteboard in his apartment as if they were pieces in the jigsaw puzzles he used to do with his mom as a kid. Only it was much easier to figure out how pieces fit if you had the whole picture on the box to go by.

Since arriving home this evening, after tiring of Calvin and the office, Rem had been hard at work on the more important problem of the bomber's identity. He'd added more info under Tristan Doyle's name: bad relationship with father—now deceased—passion for gardening and growing things, friendliness, hospitality.

The more facts he added about Tristan, the more Rem had to admit he didn't have a strong reason to keep him on the board meant to help ID the bomber. The evidence—or lack thereof—seemed to show Tristan could never be involved in anything as sinister as murdering innocent people with bombs and flooding.

But Rem couldn't let go of the possibility Tristan was trying to play him. Putting on a good show so Rem wouldn't suspect him.

Trouble was, if Tristan was acting a part, he deserved an Oscar for the performance. Rem would never get any evidence on him to take to the FBI at this rate.

He pushed his fingers through his hair. Maybe he needed to stop trying to force the Tristan piece into this puzzle and reconsider the other pieces he had.

Like the surprise in the news Agent Nguyen had given Rem when he'd called to discuss how the bomber had gotten past security at Rocky Falls Dam. A Homeland Security agent had apparently visited the dam at six-thirty that morning, when no dogs or bomb squad techs were there.

Only the guy wasn't an agent at all. The ID he'd shown the guard must have been as fake as the name he'd given.

The guard provided a description of the man as six foot two, very slim, sandy short hair and a full beard, blue eyes. Agent Nguyen told Rem the database scans had come up empty.

The guy could've used colored contacts for all they knew, and a beard always made an ID unlikely. Maybe he wasn't even in the system.

But the unexpected new wrinkle of information they had now was that the bomber had an accomplice. No one on Rem's list of suspects from the SES club matched the new guy's description.

Rem stepped to the board and wrote, *Tall, bearded guy*, in red marker. He added, *Accomplice*, with a big question mark after the word.

He tapped the back end of the marker against his chin. So Libertas wasn't the lone wolf Rem had thought he was.

The praise and worship song he'd chosen as his new ringtone started to play from his back pocket. He pulled out the phone and checked the screen.

Tristan Doyle.

Tristan was calling him? "Hey, Tristan."

"Jones?"

"Yeah, what's up?" Rem switched the phone to his right ear so he could write with his dominant left hand on the board. *April 19, 4:00 p.m.* The bomber's threatened deadline.

The pause on the line made him stop, lower the marker. "Tristan? Are you okay?"

"How do you think you could make your dad happy?"

Where had that come from? "Make him happy?"

"Yeah, you know. So he'd be...proud of you." Tristan's voice pitched lower than normal, heavy with emotion. With pain.

Rem went to his faux-leather sofa and sat down, dropping the marker on the low coffee table in front of him. "I'm not sure." He moistened his lips, his throat suddenly dry. "Sometimes it seems like nothing will be good enough to do that."

"So why do you keep trying?"

His breath stuck in his lungs, nearly making him cough. How did Tristan know he was still trying? Maybe the same way Rem knew the emotion thickening Tristan's voice was identical to the pain that choked his. One recognized a fellow sufferer.

He let out the raw, honest truth. "Because I want him to love me, I guess."

Silence. Tristan cleared his throat over the line. "What if he never will?"

Rem ran his hand over his beard, seeing Tristan for the first time as something other than a suspect. Seeing him clearly as another hurting person like everyone else.

Rem silently prayed God would give him the words to help when he was weighed down by hopelessness himself. "I believe God does everything for a reason. He has a purpose in what He allows to happen in our lives."

"You think God is in control of everything."

"I know He is. He has a plan tha—"

"He's not in control of anything." Anger shifted Tristan's tone. "Nothing has a purpose. This world is chaos, and we need to learn to accept that. People create destruction and misery when they try to take control of what's impossible to control."

Was he talking about his father and his death or something else? Rem carefully chose his next words. "You mean like with the environment?"

"Sure. And other things. People have majorly botched things. They try to control everything, subjecting nature to bondage of the worst kind. The whole world is in jeopardy because of what they've done. Someone has to fix it." His voice solidified into steel with his last words.

Rem's senses perked.

Tristan was sounding more like the bomber. Would he give himself away while he was upset?

Rem thought out his next question before he asked it. "How can it be fixed?"

A pause. "The chaos people are so afraid of has to be restored. Chaos isn't bad, it's natural. It's the only way this world can be free."

This, from the man who spent hours tilling up grass to plant a garden. Rem could point out the inconsistency, but that would end this conversation in a hurry.

"I guess you can believe whatever you want, though." Tristan's tone lightened as he spoke before Rem thought of something safe to say. "It's supposed to be a free country."

Rem pushed out a chuckle. "Sure is."

"Let's hope it stays that way. Good night, Jones."

"Have a good one."

Tristan ended the call quickly.

Too quickly for Rem to lure any incriminating statements out of him. Did this conversation mean Tristan wasn't Libertas?

The real bomber wouldn't call Rem to chat about his relationship problems, would he? Or risk revealing the radical nature of his views?

But Tristan had done so without giving Rem so much as a string to hang him with. No evidence to share with the FBI or to pursue on his own.

Rem picked up the marker and went to the board.

I'll talk to him when he proves he deserves it. His father's words overlaid the scrawled facts on the board.

He let out a frustrated grunt and tossed the marker at the board. It clattered to the floor as Rem walked away, wanting to ask God why He'd brought Tristan into his life, Bristol into his heart and a terrorist to their city. But he feared the answer.

Bristol washed her hands at the kitchen sink, the two eggs she'd cracked now cooking in the frying pan on the stove. No yellow morning glow lit the sky through the window above the sink. Gray and clouds created a patchwork of shadow, promising more rain soon to come. Which meant higher water in the Mississippi.

Her breathing shallowed.

A whine came from behind. She turned to see Toby's dark gaze locked on her face. She chuckled, her tension easing. "Your turn for breakfast, huh, buddy?" She scratched his perked ears as she opened the low cabinet behind him and scooped out a measured amount of kibble from the lidded pail.

Her phone rang as she plopped the food in Toby's dish, and he dove in.

She pulled out the device from her jeans pocket and looked at the screen.

Janice Pollenta.

She stared at the phone, throat shrinking. She could let it go to voice mail. But then her mother would leave a message, and Bristol would have to return her call. Better to bite the bullet now.

She tapped the green button and switched to speaker. "Hi, Mom."

"Bristol." A mixture of relief and surprise lifted her voice. "So glad I caught you."

Perfect way to put it. Bristol set the phone on the counter and washed her hands again. The eggs sizzled in the pan.

"How are you?"

Great. They were going to do the small-talk thing? "I'm fine." She pulled out a spatula from a drawer. "You?"

"Good, good."

Bristol flipped the eggs yolk-down, prompting more sizzles.

"Are you making breakfast? I'm sorry, I shouldn't have called this early."

"It's after six here." And Rem hadn't shown up yet. Apparently the sunrise surprise wasn't going to be an everyday thing. That shouldn't leave her with disappointment sinking in her stomach. But it did.

"Right. You always were a morning person. I remember—"

"What did you want, Mom? I'm about to eat breakfast." And she did not need to start the day with her mom pretending the tragic past hadn't happened.

"I just wanted to find out myself how you are. I'm worried about you with the news about those bombs."

So that was it.

"I saw online that another one was found yesterday. Your grandma told me you found it."

"That's my job."

"I know, but I still worry about you. I wish you hadn't picked such a dangerous profession."

"My profession is safer than living in New Orleans." Bristol shoved the turner under the eggs with a thrust that was too hard and tore one of the eggs. Irritation at the mistake fueled her rising frustration, sharpened her tone. "You should know the danger there. But you never seem to think about me having to worry about *you* every year." She transferred the eggs to the plate on the counter.

"Honey, people can die anytime, anywhere. I'm not going to live my life in fear."

"Or acknowledge what happened apparently." Bristol flipped the knob to turn off the burner.

"What does that mean?"

"It means you live like they never did. Like none of it ever happened!" Bristol snatched the phone and stalked around the U-shaped counter to the dining room side, needing to move. Her breath came in short bursts as she tried to tamp down the emotions rising to the surface.

"How could you say such a thing?" Hurt strained Janice's voice.

"You remarried five months after they died. *Five months*, Mom." She lifted a hand and let it smack down against her leg. "And you still live there. You'd probably live in the same house if it hadn't been destroyed."

"Moving on with my life and trying to be happy again doesn't mean I forgot your father or Riana. I could never forget them."

Bristol's chest heaved. She needed to calm down. Focus on something else. Breakfast was a wash. She could head out early, call Rem and see if he was on his way since they'd planned to meet at her house. She had everything ready to go, her Glock resting on the far counter by her keys, ready to grab on her way out the door.

Going back around the counter to the kitchen where Toby drank from his water dish, she set the phone next to her un-eaten breakfast on the counter while her mom said something she didn't want to hear.

"...you're hiding from it."

Bristol tuned in just in time to catch the words probably better missed. "I'm hiding from what?" She didn't care that heat fired her voice. She jerked the plate off the counter and dumped the untouched eggs into the garbage under the sink.

"You're hiding from what happened. From their deaths."

Bristol bit back the reply she wanted to let loose as she dropped the plate in the sink and grabbed a damp cloth. She stepped back to the flat-topped stove, scrubbed at the egg yolk splatter. And Grandma wondered why she never called—

A smash burst behind her.

She spun around as glass shards exploded inward from the kitchen window. She threw her arm in front of her face and lunged for her weapon across the room, pricks of pain darting her neck. "Toby, come!"

He instantly ran to her as she ducked into the small protected space between the closet and the door to the garage.

She swept him behind her with one arm as she pulled out the Glock, let the holster drop. "Stay."

Her mom screamed something through the phone.

A small object flew through the shattered window. Landed in the center of the kitchen.

A grenade.

Four seconds or less till death.

Toby barked.

"Stay." She shifted to block him with her back.
Lifted the Glock in both hands. Aimed.
Fired.

Chapter Twenty-Seven

Bristol jerked at the sound of a car door slam.

Cora rested a calming hand on her shoulder.

Bristol stroked Toby's head, the dog sitting next to her in the open back of the ambulance at the end of her driveway. Aside from a small cut on one of his footpads, he was unharmed and much less unnerved than Bristol seemed to be.

She looked past the paramedic who finished cleaning the cuts on her forehead.

Agent Nguyen, the new arrival amid the swarm of emergency responders and FBI agents, marched toward them.

Phoenix stepped away to shake hands with Agent Nguyen as she approached in a dark FBI jacket.

Bristol winced as the paramedic tweaked a cut.

"I'll need to bandage this one, as well." The woman gave Bristol a small smile probably meant to be comforting.

"Will she need stiches?" Cora rubbed Bristol's shoulder lightly—a motherly gesture that somehow started to reconnect and relax Bristol's frayed nerves.

"No. The cut on her temple is the most severe, but all of them should heal if they're kept clean."

Bristol barely heard the paramedic's response as the attack replayed in her mind. The glass breaking, the grenade landing so near, so fast.

It was an explosive. She knew explosives. Knew shooting a grenade would keep the blasting cap from going off. She could handle it, no problem.

But what if he'd attacked when Grandma was visiting? What if Bristol hadn't been in the kitchen and Toby had gotten hurt?

She ran her tongue over her lips. The bomber was becoming unexpected. Unpredictable.

"Word is a frag grenade." Agent Nguyen stopped in front of Bristol and pushed back her jacket hem to brace small hands on her hips. "That right?"

Bristol nodded.

"Tell me the story."

Bristol moistened her lips again, gave Toby's head another stroke. "I was on the phone and making breakfast in my kitchen. The window shattered. He must've used some sort of heavy tool to break it all at once like that. Then the grenade flew in. I took it out. That's it."

"You took it out?" Agent Nguyen cocked an eyebrow.

"She shot it." Phoenix watched Bristol with an unreadable gaze as she answered for her.

"You shot it." The agent's lips twitched, her dark eyes shifting to look at Phoenix. She swung her attention back to Bristol. "Learn that on the bomb squad?"

She nodded. "Some of the boys and I tried it out when we had time on our hands. Doesn't work with a high-powered weapon, but a handgun stops the blasting cap from even going off, renders the grenade inert."

Agent Nguyen cast a gaze at Phoenix. "You sure know how to pick 'em."

Phoenix crossed her arms over her open black windbreaker and widened her stance. "Only the best."

Agent Nguyen shook her head, a smile playing on her lips as she took out a notepad from her jacket pocket, along with a golf pencil. Her gaze lifted and aimed at Bristol. "Did you go after the suspect or walk where you might have contaminated evidence?"

"No." Bristol had wanted to, but she was keenly aware Toby was a target as much as she was and couldn't be left alone. Certainly not in a house with broken glass. And she wasn't about to risk his life chasing a bomber who might be packing another grenade. "Toby and I waited at the front of the house until Phoenix and the agents got here."

"Evidently the bomber is trying to kill you now. Any idea why?" The intelligence in the agent's dark eyes showed she already had her own theory but wanted to hear Bristol's, anyway.

"I assume it's because I didn't stop looking for his explosives like he wanted me to."

Agent Nguyen jotted a note on her pad. "You mean in the threatening messages with the fake bombs?"

Bristol nodded.

"And maybe because you found the bomb at Rocky Falls that he had planned on going off." Cora's soft blue gaze transferred from Bristol to Agent Nguyen. "Phoenix said that wouldn't make him happy."

"You're right." Phoenix's deep voice drew their attention. "But there's one more reason." She paused as she looked at Bristol, seeming to gauge something. Whether or not she could handle what Phoenix was about to say? "He wants you out of the way for whatever he's planning next. You're too good, you and Toby. He sees that and he hasn't figured out a way around you. You wouldn't be scared off, and he apparently knows he can't accomplish whatever he wants to with you and Toby in the picture."

Bristol met her boss's gaze, the twist in her stomach tightening. He'd hit too close to home this time. What if he did worse next time? Grandma could be with her when he tried again.

"Katherine, we're going to need to kick Bristol loose for now." Phoenix turned to Agent Nguyen. "The bomber might be planning to attack a dam today since he was obviously trying to kill her this morning."

"I'm pretty sure he isn't going to do anything until he sees if his demands to the governor are met." Agent Nguyen matched Phoenix's commanding gaze, then seemed to yield. "But better safe than sorry. The bomb squad is still canvassing the dams today, too."

"Agent Nguyen?" A young, skinny guy approached, his gloves indicating he was a lab tech. "We've found something."

Agent Nguyen swung to the paramedic. "She okay to go?"

"Sure." The paramedic had just been standing there while they talked, anyway. Probably waiting to get her ambulance back.

"Come with me." Agent Nguyen's invitation seemed to encompass all of them, so Bristol slid down from the ambulance, and Toby jumped out beside her.

She followed Phoenix, Cora keeping step with Bristol and Toby as the lab tech led them past the yellow crime scene tape and around the house.

He stopped at the kitchen window and pointed to the ground beneath.

A footprint was outlined in the wet dirt next to the rosebush that had been there when she'd moved in.

"Finally made a mistake we can use." Agent Nguyen's mouth curved in a smile as she looked at the print. "His supposed hideout was cleaner than a hospital. Like he'd already abandoned the place and made sure he didn't leave anything behind we could trace to him." She looked up at the window. "I see he cut the screen out. Probably the night before so he wouldn't be heard."

"We patrol at night." Phoenix studied the sliced edges of the screen.

"Must've come during the day, then." Agent Nguyen squatted to get a better look at the footprint. "Looks like a pretty common brand athletic shoe, but maybe we'll catch a break and it'll be imported."

"You and Toby better get to work." Phoenix nodded to Bristol. "We'll stay and close up the house after Katherine and her team leave."

"Maybe Bristol should take some time off." Concern colored Cora's eyes. "Since someone just tried to kill her." She looked at Phoenix for permission. "Like Agent Nguyen said, it's unlikely the bomber will do anything until the nineteenth."

Phoenix shook her head, though her voice softened a tiny bit, as it seemed to when she spoke to Cora. "I don't know that we can be so confident the bomber will stick with that itinerary. He tricked everyone with his first diversionary bomb threat." She turned her gaze to Bristol. "It's up to you, though. I won't send you out where you're not ready to go."

Bristol swallowed, tension contorting her stomach.

Agent Nguyen's radio crackled, and a male voice emerged. "There's a Remington Jones out here by the perimeter who says he's okay to come through."

She lifted the radio off her belt. "Roger that, let him in."

Rem. How stupid she'd been to wish for him earlier and now here he was, an hour later. If he had come sooner, he could have seen the bomber, maybe prevented the attack or at least identified him.

She had only herself to depend on. And only she could stop this bomber and keep him from hurting people. The memory of the little girl in the woods pressed on her mind—the way she'd clung with her arms strangling Bristol's neck as she'd carried her to safety, leaving the dead body of her mother behind for others to take care of.

Bristol could prevent that kind of tragedy from happening to anyone else. She could keep the loss she'd tasted in New Orleans from happening here. And she would.

She met Phoenix's gaze squarely. "I want to make sure this terrorist doesn't get away with hurting anyone else. If he wants to stop me, he'll have to find a better way to kill me."

A smile, the first Phoenix had ever given her, brightened her eyes for a quick second that let Bristol see how stunningly beautiful she was. "Then get out there and make him sorry he picked you."

"Bristol." Rem's voice shot straight through to the soft part of her heart, the part she hadn't had time to harden to him yet.

She closed her eyes briefly, then turned to look at him.

His eyes melted into dark chocolate, lines bunching his brow as he leaned toward her, though feet away, as if he wanted to take her into his arms.

Right there in front of Phoenix and everyone.

"I'm fine."

"They said a grenade—"

"I'm fine." She added ice to the words. "We need to get to work. He might be trying to plant a bomb, thinking he got rid of me."

Rem's eyebrows pulled together, and pain filled his eyes as if the words, the idea, hurt him physically.

Her heart thudded against her rib cage, hard enough to bruise. They needed to get out of here before the whole world knew he liked her and she—

No, she wouldn't give in to it. She brushed past him with Toby, rounding the house as quickly as she could at a controlled walk.

"Bristol."

She didn't look back as she kept going toward her garage, opened the door that had already been dusted by the lab.

"Bristol." His voice carried an urgency that made her heart ache.

But she couldn't look at him, those eyes so full of concern and…something more. She couldn't face it and hang on to her resolve, to her better judgment that told her he wasn't the right man for her. He couldn't be depended on when she needed him most.

She loaded Toby in the back of the Jeep, feeling the heat of Rem's gaze. Then she realized her mistake. She'd have to walk back toward him to go into the house and get her fanny pack, Toby's harness and the rest of the supplies.

She lifted her chin and turned his direction, but he didn't move. Just stood in front of her, blocking the way until she jerked her gaze up to meet his. "What?"

"I'll drive." His voice cut low, firm.

Not what she'd expected. The traitorous sinking sensation in her chest said it wasn't what she'd hoped for, either. "I'm perfectly capable—"

He stepped into her space, inches away.

She stared at his broad chest, the blue fabric of his jacket, instead of his eyes.

"Bristol." His tone gentled, reaching past the independence and courage she'd just rediscovered to touch her inside, where vulnerability and worry still vied to control her. He lowered his voice more, dipped his head so his breath brushed her cheeks as he spoke. "Let me drive, please?"

She slowly pulled the keys from her jacket pocket, held them out.

His fingers brushed hers as he took the keys.

Her breath seized at the sudden urge to fall into his arms, those strong arms that had held her that night at Grandma's as she'd cried. The worry and fear she thought she'd brought under control surged to the surface in an overwhelming wave.

And he just stood there, so close, waiting for her to look at him.

But if she did that, she'd be undone.

Somehow, she kept from reaching for him. Somehow, she kept the emotion bottled, and managed to speak. "I have to get our gear."

"I'll wait here." He stepped away, heading for the driver's door.

She gulped in air, eyes pricking with moisture. Frustration, not sadness. She would not depend on Remington Jones for anything. She would get ahold of herself, this situation, again. The bomber would not beat her.

Then get out there and make him sorry he picked you.

Bristol grabbed Phoenix's words and used them like a dam to halt the flood of emotion as she hurried to get the gear. She'd stop the bomber and end this. Go back to the safety and peace of her ordered life.

If the bomber's threat was true, there were only two more days left before she won, chaos was defeated and life went back to normal. No fear, no Remington Jones.

No more pain that threatened to drown her heart.

Rem fluctuated between wanting to punch something and the urge to break down in unmanly tears. But he couldn't do either while driving, Bristol sitting silently in the passenger seat. The fact she'd let him drive said a lot about her mental state. But it probably wasn't half as bad as his.

He could've lost her. Could've arrived to find nothing but a shell of a house and her body—or what was left of it—amid the wreckage. The thought propelled horror through his bones.

The shudder was followed by a tremor of fear. Why did he have to love her so much? But he knew the question was ridiculous. Might as well ask himself why he had to keep breathing.

From the moment he'd met her at the academy, he'd started to fall for her. It had been puppy love at first, then grew stronger when she became the only person he'd ever met who made him want to change, to become the better person she saw he could be. And when he found out she cared for him in return, his heart became hers forever.

After she broke up with him, he had tried to move on, but it was impossible. He'd had an immature, self-centered affection for her then that matched the person he was. But now that emotion had blossomed into a deeply rooted, full-grown love. The kind that could destroy him if anything happened to her.

He took in a breath as he adjusted his hold on the wheel. How ironic that she didn't love him anymore. But that was just one more consequence he deserved for messing up so badly in the past.

He glanced at Bristol, the sight of the small cuts smattering her cheek giving him a twinge of pain.

The worst of them warranted a bandage apparently, on her left temple. Her jawline was rigid as she avoided looking his way.

But he caught a tremor in her chin.

His chest squeezed. Phoenix or the FBI, whoever had made the call, shouldn't have sent Bristol back out to work so fast. She should be resting somewhere, recuperating.

She suddenly turned her head, her gaze crashing into his.

An unexpected flash sparked in her gray-blue eyes. "You know you don't have to come to my house all the time now. I can pick you up at the DNR on my way."

He looked at the road, breathing evenly as he chose carefully how to respond to her anger. Was fear driving the emotion? "I thought we'd agreed on your house today, since the DNR is out of the way for the first dam we'd planned to search. Seemed silly to make you go all that way and waste the time." Just as silly as this conversation. Disagreeing about something so trivial in light of what had just happened.

Maybe she was still upset about yesterday. Rem sucked in a deep breath and cast a look at her, in profile again. "I hope you believed me when I said I was sorry."

She turned her head his way.

"For yesterday. The sunrise. When we…when I almost…" When he'd almost kissed her. But it was too awkward to put into words.

She apparently thought so, too, since she jerked away, facing the passenger window instead.

"You've made it clear you don't want a relationship with me. Which I get because you can't forgive me. I never should've let things…go in that direction." He wove the Jeep around slower traffic in the center lane of the freeway.

Toby panted in the back as usual.

Rem's breath sat in his chest as he waited for her response. Braced for anger or accusations, which he deserved.

"You were late this morning." The words, soft and thick, seeped behind his rib cage, infusing his heart with the disappointment they carried.

"I guess I was." Only a few minutes, he'd thought. But he hadn't checked the time when he had arrived and seen the emergency vehicles and FBI agents on the street and in her yard. Only concern for Bristol was on his mind from then on.

"I got stuck in traffic on the way." He wouldn't have been there early enough to catch the bomber, even if he'd been more punctual. But the thought he had disappointed Bristol again dropped like a weight on his shoulders.

The weight was heavy with familiarity. How many times had she scolded him for being late to class at the academy or late to a date with her? Her frequent anger at him back then blurred with her expression now in his mind, dredging up a forbidden, dark thought he'd once had years ago and quickly buried in the recesses of his memory. The thought that, maybe, she had never loved him at all. That she'd loved only the idea of the man she wanted to make him become.

As he looked at her implacable, disappointed profile, he knew it was true. But he had no right to blame her for that. He had only himself to blame for his inability to be the kind of man she deserved.

Nothing but his shortcomings were responsible for the truth of his new realization, too. He could never be perfect enough for her. He still failed. Failed to secure the dams, failed his parents, and he would be sure to fail Bristol again, too. No matter how much he tried not to. He could never be the man she wanted.

Which meant she would never love him.

He swallowed and forced out the words ricocheting in his soul. "I'm sorry."

Silence stretched between them as memories of their past, the good times when they were happy together and the times when he'd let her down, danced in his mind as if to a swan song.

"Me, too. Having a grenade chucked through my window definitely puts things in perspective."

Meaning him. Their relationship. His failure to be there for her and do the right thing when she needed it. Again.

Surprise cut into his guilt when she turned her head and looked at him, her eyes void of the accusation he thought he'd see there.

"I should've seen it coming."

Was she talking about his failure or the grenade? Either way, he couldn't allow her to blame herself. None of it was her fault. "You can't see everything coming."

Her mouth pinched downward.

Oops. Wrong thing to say.

"Oh, right. I forgot. Only God can control everything, right?" Anger steeled her tone as she looked out the windshield again. "Think He saw that grenade coming? The bomber about to throw it before it happened?"

She whipped her head around to shoot daggers at him with her eyes. "Or how about at the Leavell Dam? Did he see that? The little girl and her mother? They were just out for a walk together in the park. They weren't bad, weren't hurting anyone. Neither were the other eleven people who died."

She wrapped her arms around herself, crossing them over her chest. "Or your friend, the dam operator. Did he deserve to die that day?"

He looked from the road to her face. His rib cage felt like it was being crushed under the look in her gray eyes, the pain there reflecting his own.

"If your God was in control that day, why didn't He stop that?"

Rem's throat thickened as if coated with pitch. He couldn't find his voice, couldn't move his tongue. He'd lost that day, too. And he had seen Bristol carrying that little girl, tracks of mud outlining the path of tears on the child's cheeks from when she'd sobbed over her dead mother.

He had thought the same question in his heart. Why?

And God answered it with the truth Rem had already known. God is in control. God is good. All the time.

That was enough.

But would it be enough for Bristol?

Rem had to try. It was all he could do. Whether or not she could ever love him was nothing compared to the importance of Bristol coming to know God.

He cleared his throat, gripping the wheel hard. He glanced at her.

His breath hitched at the sight of moisture glistening on her cut cheek. His heart knotted, but he still had to push aside his own turmoil to offer the best answer, the only hope there ever was. "I don't know why, not all the details. But I do know this—God is good. He will bring good, something better than we can possibly imagine, out of all this. Even out of the bombing at Leavell."

He felt the pressure of her gaze as he managed to spot their exit just in time and took it.

"Something good. From a mother dying right in front of her daughter?"

He swallowed. This was where the rubber met the road. But God met him there, too. Filled him with conviction that chased away his doubt and calmed his pulse. "Yes. We can't always see what He's doing right away. Sometimes we won't see it until we get to heaven. But He promises He'll use even the worst things that happen for good." Rem looked at Bristol. "That's why He allowed it. So something better can happen in the end."

Her eyes were a shade darker than the cloud-cluttered sky as she stared at him.

Until he had to look back at the traffic in front of him.

"Nothing so awful can be used for good. Nothing can make it right." Her voice faded with each word. "Nothing."

And he knew she wasn't talking about the girl in the park. She was talking about the little girl that was Bristol. Who lost the people, the family she loved most, in one horrific flood.

The little girl who was still waiting to be healed.

There was only one Person who could do that. *God, please let her see the good.*

Chapter Twenty-Eight

"I'm sorry to impose like this." Bristol followed Amalia into the hallway of her house from the attached garage as Raksa's bark sounded from somewhere inside.

Toby entered at Bristol's side, tail wagging in his excitement of getting to explore a new place. "I told Phoenix there was no reason I needed to stay with you."

Amalia chuckled, her black wavy hair swishing across her gray PK-9 windbreaker as she looked over her shoulder at Bristol. "I'm sure that went well. When Phoenix says you need to do something, that's it, girl."

She tossed her keys into a cup on a small table by the door and called out to Raksa. "That's enough, Raksa. Just me and some friends."

A deeper bark made Bristol start. Gaston jogged toward them, his jumbo paws padding on the wood floor as his jowly grin and excited body language showed he'd decided they were friends.

Amalia laughed as the big Newfoundland made a beeline for

Bristol, greeting her with slobbers and nudges for petting, despite Toby nosing the dog's furry neck in an effort to say hello.

"You're a little late if you meant to scare off the intruders, buddy." Amalia's dark eyes glimmered in the dim light of the entryway as she glanced at Bristol, white smile bursting onto her face.

At the reminder of her voice, Gaston switched to rubbing his body against Amalia.

"A guard dog he is not. But he likes to pretend sometimes."

His people-greeting taken care of, Gaston finally switched to Toby, and the two dogs smelled each other thoroughly, wagging their tails.

Bristol watched them with a grin. "Looks like he's fine with Toby on his home turf."

"Oh, yeah." Amalia took off her jacket. "Raksa should be, too. I have him crated, though, so we can do a more careful introduction."

"They were good the other night at my house."

"Yeah, but he might be more territorial at home. We should play it safe."

"Sure, good idea."

Amalia held out her hand. "I can take your coat and hang it in the closet with mine. Unless you want to keep it with your stuff in your room."

"I have my own room? I don't mind sleeping on the sofa."

"Pshh." Amalia dismissed the suggestion with her hand. "I have a guest room, girl."

"Right, okay."

"Just dump your duffel here on the floor for now, and I'll get Raksa so we can do the introduction."

Five minutes later, Toby and the German shepherd jogged behind Amalia and Bristol to the guest room, the two dogs giving each other playful swats and nips like fast friends. Gaston lumbered beside Amalia, practically glued to her leg.

The hallway that led to the bedrooms was decorated with professional-quality photo prints of people. A dark-haired woman with a young girl and boy. Another photo with a young couple holding kids that might've been the same youngsters. The third featured a middle-aged couple in a light embrace, the man holding flowers between them as if caught on camera giving them to his love. "Nice pictures. Your family?"

"Uh-huh." Amalia led the way into the guest room, her gaze running over the tidy space decorated in neutral gray and beige tones. "Well, looks like everything's in order. You have an attached bathroom to use. Towels and everything you should need are in there but let me know if you think of anything else."

She looked at Bristol, her gaze seeming to stop on the bandaged cut. "Do you need anything special for your injuries?"

Bristol shook her head. Her stomach chose that moment to growl. Loudly.

Amalia laughed, a hearty sound that tumbled from her beaming smile. "Dinner, we can do. You haven't tasted anything until you've tasted my pasta. Homemade, family recipe."

"Wow. Didn't know you cooked."

"I'm full of surprises." Her long lashes dipped as she winked.

A jangle resonated from somewhere nearby. Sounded like the latest pop song Bristol had caught on radio stations.

"Hang on." Amalia pulled her cell from the pocket of her slim black jeans and silenced the ringtone. She looked at the screen. "We've got a lead."

"A lead?"

"Text." She flashed the phone screen toward Bristol so fast she couldn't actually see the message. "I put out some feelers after the grenade showed up."

Amalia had contacts to reach with feelers? Bristol blinked at her.

"I'm sure you thought about the grenade being different than everything the bomber's used before."

She should have. But between worrying about Toby and Grandma since the grenade landed in her kitchen, she hadn't. "He had to get it from someone."

"Exactly. He didn't make a homemade one."

Bristol could've thunked her forehead. She was the one with bomb squad experience. Why hadn't she thought of that right away? Grenades were illegal to obtain and own in the state, making them hard to get. Their homemade bomb-maker had gone out of his element. "We thought he didn't have military contacts because he wasn't getting C-4 or other military grade explosives."

"Right." Amalia typed a text on her phone, maybe an answer to the message she'd received. "Phoenix thinks he probably doesn't have good military or black-market contacts of his own, or he'd have used them before."

"So he got scared into taking a risk."

Amalia looked up. "And hopefully making a mistake."

"Is the text from Phoenix?" Bristol nodded to the phone.

Amalia shook her head. "She put out some feelers among her sources, too, but it looks like I've got a bite with mine."

"Who?"

Her mouth curved halfway up. "He'll meet us in ten."

"Us?"

The smile grew full-width. "Phoenix told me not to let you out of my sight, and I ain't messin' with that *chica*."

What kind of sources would either Phoenix or Amalia have? More questions about their pasts surfaced in her mind. "But how do you and Phoenix—"

"Will you come?" She beckoned with a grin as she headed

for the bedroom doorway to go into the hallway, the dogs jogging after her. "We can play twenty questions on the way, but it takes fifteen minutes to get there, so we better vamoose."

Fifteen? "Then how will we get there in time?"

She laughed.

And Bristol started to suspect she was in for an experience she wouldn't soon forget.

Rem stared at the whiteboard until the words started to blur. There had to be something there. Something he wasn't seeing. He'd listed all the facts he knew about Libertas and the attacks so far.

Rem pushed off the sofa and walked to stand closer to the board.

He needed to get inside the bomber's head. Had to figure this out. The guy was trying to kill Bristol.

The thought lodged like a rock in his gut as it did every time he reviewed the events of that morning. The grenade thrown in her window, nearly killing her. He could see it as if he'd been there.

He shook off the image, the way it caused an ache in his chest. She was fine. Staying with Amalia tonight, thankfully. Though he was skeptical the petite woman could actually offer much by way of protection.

He puffed out a breath. He had to trust God to watch over her.

And he had to stay focused on finding Libertas. The terrorist would try to kill Bristol again if he wasn't stopped.

Why? That was the question Rem needed to start asking if he was going to understand the twisted mind behind all this.

The motive for the Leavell Dam attack seemed clear—the bomber needed something big to grab the attention he wanted for his cause and give legitimacy to his future threats.

He'd also tried to bomb the Minnesota Falls Dam that day, but Bristol had stopped him. Why that dam on that day?

Rem thought back to where Bristol and Toby had found the bomb. In the hydropower room by a turbine. If the bomb had exploded there, the dam itself probably wouldn't have been damaged, at least not enough to cause a breach.

But a portion of the visitor center might have been hit, and certainly the hydropower function of the dam would have been crippled, likely destroyed.

That was probably the goal. In the mind of Libertas, mankind taking the river captive was bad enough, but using it to generate power likely seemed akin to abuse. So a double blow had been intended, and an end to the supposed abuse of the resource.

Until Bristol and Toby had interfered.

Libertas seemed to switch his focus then, aiming to frighten Bristol and make her think he was unbeatable with his fake bombs and threatening notes.

She couldn't be scared off, so he must have decided he needed to kill her. But why now? She must be standing in the way of his planned attack, supposedly on the nineteenth.

Or maybe the bomber was lying about that date and actually planned to attack earlier or later. Maybe he even had a different actual target and the whole thing was a misdirect.

But then why tell the governor that date?

Rem reached up and circled the date—*April 19*—in blue. Why April 19?

An odd feeling, almost like a shiver, snaked up his spine. There was something familiar about that date. Something to do with one of the dams. The Minnesota Falls Dam.

His pulse picked up speed as he spun away from the whiteboard and went to his dining table where he'd left his notebook computer.

He flipped it open and slid onto the chair. Tapped his fingers on the table as he waited for the computer to wake up.

Could it really be what he was thinking? He'd studied the history of many area dams when he was apprenticing to Graham because he thought he should know what he was going to be overseeing. And that date was familiar. Like something he might've read, known for a time.

The computer screen came to life and let him log in. He used the touchscreen to quickly reach the DNR database and typed his password to gain access.

The program seemed to move at a snail's pace compared to his racing heartbeat as he accessed the history of the Minnesota Falls Dam.

He froze, staring at the screen.

April 19, 1935.

Same date, over eighty years later.

Libertas hadn't randomly picked that date at all. He must have been planning it. Probably for a very long time.

Rem sat back, his pulse thumping in his throat.

It wouldn't matter whether the governor agreed to the bomber's demands or not.

This was all far too planned to abandon now.

On April 19, the date construction had begun to build the Minnesota Falls Dam, the bomber was going to blow it up.

Chapter Twenty-Nine

Amalia was still laughing, this time at the expression on Bristol's face, by the time she screeched her car to a halt in some dark alley on the same side of Minneapolis as the bomber's warehouse hideout.

Bristol took a moment to catch her breath now that the car was finally still instead of swerving at breakneck speeds. "I don't even want to think about how many traffic violations you just committed."

Amalia's throaty chuckle bounced between them in the car as her teeth flashed. She thumbed to the back seat. "Raksa isn't bothered by it. I can tell you used to be a cop."

Bristol looked at the woman beside her—the iceberg with only the tip showing. "And you used to be somebody much different than I thought. Am I right?"

She kept her smile, the twinkle in her dark eyes, no sign Bristol had or hadn't hit the mark. "Come on, we have two minutes." She reached behind Bristol's seat and pulled out a pair of black winter gloves—the small and stretchy cotton kind. She slipped them on quickly, then dropped open the glove compartment in front of Bristol, reached in and came out with a black winter hat.

Wasn't that cold out. Probably the forties, which was like a heatwave to most Minnesotans after the long, freezing winter.

"Not that Ramone is known to be punctual, but it's always better to expect the unexpected."

Expect the unexpected? Bristol couldn't live with that philosophy. Better to be prepared and know exactly what to expect. Though what Amalia was preparing for with the burglar's outfit was beyond her. Unless she was trying to disguise herself?

"You have your piece?" Amalia's mouth still held a curve when closed, as if she found that question light and amusing. Even though she used the word *piece* to refer to a gun. Just what was this woman's background?

"Yes. My Glock."

"Good. Not that we'll need more protection than Raksa, right, buddy?" She grinned at the German shepherd in the back, then faced forward again to open her door. "Let's do this."

Do what exactly, was the question that started to tingle Bristol's nerves as she exited the car and waited for the five seconds it took Amalia to get Raksa out.

Amalia's trademark smile vanished without a trace as she kept her body and gaze moving, headed to the street. Her posture was relaxed, but she was ready, on alert. She checked the peripherals just as much as Bristol was doing.

But Bristol was an ex-cop who had sometimes had her beat in this neighborhood. What was Amalia's reason?

A dog barked somewhere in the distance as they emerged from the alley, Raksa leading the way slightly, his leash hanging loosely between him and Amalia. Just after 7:45 p.m., it was early enough for people to be out on the streets. Too early for the clandestine meeting Bristol had the distinct impression this was.

Kids, mostly teenagers, hung out in groups of three to five. Some adults sat on the steps of the run-down apartment buildings, chatting or getting high.

All eyes followed Amalia and Bristol as they passed. Probably thanks to the striking German shepherd. He also ensured the mini-gangs of men kept their distance. Along with the keep-back glare Amalia had suddenly adopted.

If Bristol didn't know her as the smiling, fun-times Amalia, she'd back away from that fierce stare, too.

"Here." Amalia jerked her head to a set of stairs that cut into the ground along a building, leading to a door. "Cover the rear." She marched down the steps with Raksa while Bristol angled to do as she said.

Bristol stopped at the top of the stairs, watching for anyone coming up behind them.

A few of the pot smokers from two housing units down watched but didn't make a move to approach. Wasn't Amalia's source worried about neighbors seeing them come here?

"Bristol." Amalia nodded to her, then looked at the door just as it cracked open, no light coming through the opening.

Bristol hurried down the steps, her cop instincts tipping the hairs on the back of her neck.

Raksa wasn't growling. Hopefully a good sign.

Though his tail wasn't wagging, either—it was nearly rigid as Bristol followed him and Amalia through the door into a small, dark room that smelled of pot and rotting pizza.

"Who's the *mujer*?" A man's voice grunted out of the black corner of the room next to a window covered in short, thick curtains.

Bristol tensed, unable to see the speaker as Raksa leaned forward with a low growl.

Amalia spewed something back in rapid Spanish. She was fluent in Spanish?

The man responded. His voice sounded older, but she could only make out the worn sheepskin slippers on his feet, touching the floor as he sat in what appeared to be an armchair.

Bristol had picked up a little Spanish on the streets, but not enough to translate what the man said. She only caught the word *policia* in there.

Amalia answered again, fast and smooth.

Bristol held her breath.

A chuckle drifted from the corner, then a heartier laugh.

"What was all that?" Bristol whispered out the side of her mouth to Amalia, not shifting her gaze from the dark corner.

"He said you smell like a cop. But I assured him you'd left all that for a much better offer."

Great.

Amalia's smile flashed in the darkness. "Turn on some light, would you?"

The man said something in Spanish, and a light flicked on—a lamp—at once illuminating a gray-haired man and a younger male, standing at his elder's side behind the end table.

The older man, probably in his eighties, looked up at the youth and whispered something.

The young guy's black hair shone in the lamplight as he came out from behind the table and headed for a closed door to Amalia's left.

Raksa growled as the young man passed them on his way to the door.

Bristol could see why.

The guy was carrying, the butt of a gun jutting through his shirt that overhung the waistband of his low-slung jeans.

She released her held breath when he closed the door behind him without incident. But for all she knew the old guy could be packing heat, too. Probably tucked beside him in the faded blue armchair.

"Are you still happy here?" Amalia stepped closer to the man but didn't move to sit in either of the two dining-style chairs that angled toward the armchair. As if the old man held court or meetings of some kind in this room.

"I love this country. It is my home now." His English was heavily accented as he opened his arms wide, his fingers kinked with arthritis. "Will you go home soon?"

"I have no home."

Bristol looked at Amalia.

No smile. Just a relaxed yet steady gaze locked on the man in the corner.

"You should find one, *chica*." The old man's thin lips opened to reveal more than one blackened tooth when he smiled. "You were smart to leave the CIA."

CIA? Bristol jerked her gaze to Amalia but saw only her unchanged profile.

"You have a dog now, good. Now you find a nice *hombre* and have babies. Be happy."

Amalia put a hand on Raksa's head, and the dog sat beside her, his silent gaze locked on the man. Her mouth curled into a close-lipped smile. "I'll be happy when you tell me about the grenade buyer."

He chuckled. "I live to make you happy, so I will tell you."

Bristol held her breath.

"An *hombre* came, bought one grenade."

"Only one?" Amalia watched the man, her fingers touching Raksa's neck.

"*Sí.*"

"Do you know him?"

A sly smile tucked the man's mouth. "Marita, would I tell you?"

Marita. Was that a nickname Amalia had?

She answered his smile with one of her own, tilting her head slightly. "You might." Something in the gaze she kept on him, or something Bristol couldn't possibly guess—some hold Amalia had on him?—made the man nod.

"*Sí*. But I don't know his name. And he has never been seen before or again."

Amalia shook her head. "Not good enough, Ramone. I need more. And you have more, don't you?"

He watched her with eyes just as dark as hers. "There was suspicion. This man no one knows buying only one grenade. And he was so worried about the money."

"So you checked him out?"

"He drove a van. Green. Fake name on the side."

Amalia glanced at Bristol, a gleam in her eyes that timed with a hopeful jump in Bristol's pulse. "And somebody checked for the real name, right? What was it?"

"Kid didn't remember the whole name. A construction company. Started with F."

Hard to tell if Ramone was lying about knowing the name, but it was still more than they'd had. A certifiable lead.

"Thanks, Ramone." Amalia nodded to him. She turned with Raksa, signaling they should leave.

"Marita."

They looked back at Ramone.

"He says he'll be back. For big buy. Didn't say what."

Amalia looked at him with no hint of a smile. "You know how I feel about that, Ramone."

"*Sí*, and you know how I feel."

She jerked a nod, turned back to the door and led the way out, Raksa alert and ready at her side.

The overcast sky seemed to have made the sun disappear faster than usual. Shadows hid more than Bristol would like outside the patches where light from streetlamps hit the sidewalk.

Bristol kept her gaze moving, nerves still on edge, ready for anything as they retraced their steps to the car. Hopefully it would still be in the alley, hubcaps intact. "Going to tell me who that was?"

"Somebody I used to know."

"When you were in the CIA."

Amalia gave her a glance as they kept walking. "Now you know."

"Does Phoenix?"

"Of course."

"Who else knows?"

"You do." She flashed the smile Bristol was used to, all fun and open without a care or concern. Without secrets. But apparently that smile hid a lot more than Bristol had realized.

"So can you tell me why we just left an apparent arms dealer without calling the cops or your CIA people?"

She laughed, even as her gaze locked on a group of three male gangbanger types swaggering toward them on the sidewalk. "I can't tell you as much as you'd like to know, I'm sure. But suffice it to say, Ramone is better for us on the outside than behind bars."

The men looked them over as they passed, but the combined effect of the women's dauntless stares and the low-throated rumble from Raksa was enough to deter any ideas.

"And he doesn't sell the weapons himself. Not anymore. But his information is always reliable. He's not a fan of terrorism, which makes him a friend to us."

Us. Amalia suddenly sounded like a CIA agent, speaking on behalf of the United States.

"That's why he talks to you?"

"Partly."

They swung into the alley, Amalia's black car parked where they'd left it, apparently unharmed. The car beeped as she pressed the remote to unlock the doors.

"One thing I know for sure—" she looked across the car at Bristol as she opened the back door for Raksa "—he wouldn't tell me about the guy who bought the grenade unless he thought it was leading to something bigger, something like terrorism on a large scale."

Like blowing up a dam in the middle of Minneapolis.

Chapter Thirty

"We're about to go off duty, ladies."

All eyes turned to Phoenix as the PK-9 crew, minus Nevaeh on patrol, sat in the breakroom, surrounded by several of their dogs. Most of the ladies held coffee, helping them wake up for the Monday morning, 6:30 a.m. meeting.

"Starting at seven tonight, Katherine and her task force are taking over security at the Minnesota Falls Dam. Thanks to Jones's intel, tomorrow seems almost positive for the bomber's attack, so Katherine will be bringing in a large presence of agents and officers to protect the dam overnight and tomorrow."

"Did the governor give a reply yet?" Bristol dangled her hand off the sofa where she sat, touching Toby's head with her fingers. He lounged on the floor at her feet and chewed on a wishbone-shaped toy—a gift from Cora—that he held between his paws.

"He will tomorrow by the deadline." Phoenix looked at Bristol. "He'll say he doesn't negotiate with terrorists. But given the significance of the date Jones pointed out, I agree it seems likely the bomber will go through with his plans no matter what the response."

"What about detection? Are they handling that?"

Phoenix rested her hands on the arms of the black arm-chair she always sat in. "You'll do your usual searches today, then Miles and Duke will be at Minnesota Falls overnight. Katherine wants you and Toby to come in the morning to relieve them."

Phoenix moved her gaze to take in all the team. "It's been a long haul, and you've all done an excellent job. But our work isn't quite over." She focused her attention on Amalia, as if expecting something. "We have some more news."

Bristol raised her eyebrows. Amalia hadn't told her anything new this morning before they'd left her house.

Amalia looked up from petting Gaston, her small fingers buried in his neck fur as he rested his head on her lap, his body sprawled on the cushion between Bristol and Amalia. "I heard from one of my sources that our grenade buyer also bought large amounts of explosives early this morning, some of it military-grade, from two different black-market arms dealers. He's stockpiling for something big."

The nausea in Bristol's stomach that had been there all morning churned again. A collection of explosives? That wasn't his MO. He used simple, homemade devices with timers. They had the potential to be unstable, but she could still beat them.

With a stockpile of explosives, there was no telling what he would do. How could she be sure she could stop him?

"We should be able to track him down from the name on the van." Amalia's optimistic statement stalled the panic clambering up Bristol's throat.

She looked at Amalia. "I thought we handed that over to the feds."

"We did, but that doesn't mean we can't still assist them." Phoenix nodded to Cora.

Her beautiful golden sleeping on her feet, Cora leaned forward slightly in the armchair. "I did a search." She kept her soft voice lowered, as if worried she might be in trouble if someone overheard. "I was able to narrow the list down to three possibilities in the greater Twin Cities area. The Fentworth Construction Company, Flickson Construction, and the Ferris and Dawson Construction Company. Fentworth appears to be the only one with green vans for company use."

Phoenix nodded. "The FBI will of course investigate those companies themselves, but we'll see what we can find out with our connections, as well." Her gaze shifted to Bristol, locking on her. "We will find him and stop him. Before he can try anything else."

Her meaning was clear: before he tried to kill Bristol again.

But it wasn't the thought of a grenade in her kitchen that caused the fear churning in her belly. It was the little girl, screaming over her dead mother at Whitlow Heights Park. It was Riana, submerged in floodwater, unable to escape the car. It was Bristol, feet slipping closer to the edge of her home's wet roof as she fought to keep from plunging into the depths that would swallow her whole.

It was Grandma, on the border of the Mississippi River, in the path of the catastrophic flood.

He had to be stopped.

A bittersweet sense of nostalgia, which even the rare visit of sunlight shining on them couldn't lift, settled over Rem as he followed Bristol and Toby out to the courtyard at Crownover Dam. Or maybe it was something else...a sense of impending loss.

From what Bristol had told him, this could be their last

day of doing this. Not that he wanted to search for bombs the rest of his life, but being with Bristol—that he wanted to do forever.

She was more distant today, quiet. He couldn't tell if she was mad at him after their conversation yesterday or just bothered in general.

Despite the firm set of her jaw, she seemed nervous, on edge. She jerked at slight noises and didn't praise Toby as much as normal. Didn't even seem to watch him closely. It was as if her mind was elsewhere, which seemed dangerous given what they were looking for.

Maybe, like Rem, she felt searching today would yield zero results. The bomber's plan was to attack tomorrow. At the Minnesota Falls Dam, not here at Crownover.

On the other hand, he could've planted something here today as a diversion. Something to throw them off. It was still good to check.

And it was still good to be with Bristol, to be near her, one last day.

His chest tightened. Their conversation yesterday seemed to have built a wall between them again.

No, that wasn't true. The wall had already been there. Everything that happened yesterday had merely revealed it to him—the insurmountable wall he'd refused to see ever since he fell in love with Bristol Bachmann. The wall of her ideals and his failings that meant they could never have a future together.

His heart sank into his stomach as he watched Toby sniff around the base of the elevated garden beds.

She'd developed the pattern of having him jump on top of the beds and search there, too, since the day they'd found the backpack. "Up." She patted the top of the cement wall and

Toby easily hopped over it. She climbed up behind him and walked over the groundcover with the dog.

"Rem."

He started at her voice. She'd barely said three words to him all day.

She pressed the edge of her hand against her forehead, shielding her eyes from the unusually bright sun. "I think there's somebody by my Jeep."

He jerked his gaze over the water to the shore on the other side. He spotted her Jeep parked where they'd left it.

Movement near the tires caught his eye.

"Stay here." He took off at a sprint, taking the stairs up to the walkways three at a time.

His breathing deepened, holding even as he ran across the truss bridges, taking the shortest route to cross to shore and reach the parking lot.

Terry, the security guard at the entrance to the dam, startled as Rem raced toward him.

"Something weird in the lot." Rem shot out the words as he hurried past the guard. "Stay here to protect the dam."

"Yes, sir."

Rem dashed across the walkway but slowed as he hit the edge of the lot at the end of it. Didn't want whoever was out there to hear his steps. He couldn't see the Jeep in the line of cars in the employee-designated row from this angle, which meant the person who was messing with it couldn't see him, either.

He walked past a Suburban on the end, pausing as he reached the rear. He peeked around the SUV. Couldn't see anyone.

He quietly made his way up the row behind the vehicles, straining to spot the Jeep.

Its silver bumper protruded past the tan sedan he remembered on the left when they'd parked.

Still no sign of a person. But the movement had appeared to be on the far side of the Jeep. Whoever it was could still be there. If he wasn't too late.

Adrenaline kicked through his veins. What if it was the bomber himself?

Doing something to Bristol's Jeep. The second thought doused his excitement with apprehension. Was it another attempt on her life?

Something dark moved on the ground behind the Jeep.

He froze.

A man? On the blacktop under the Jeep. Tampering with it.

Fury spiked his adrenaline, and he took off, aiming for the killer under the vehicle.

The guy turned his head Rem's way as he barreled toward him. Nothing Rem could ID through a ski mask, black jacket and jeans. He scrambled out from under the Jeep just as Rem crashed into him.

The guy flew several feet, falling on his side.

Rem closed the distance between them, reached to grab the thug.

He popped to his feet, dodging Rem's reach. Surprisingly agile for a lanky guy two inches taller than Rem.

Sunlight flashed off something in his hand.

A knife.

The guy slashed at Rem.

He jumped back, safe by inches. He let the guy take another swipe, gauging his movement.

The attacker led with his right shoulder.

Rem watched the shoulder, waited for the next move.

The shoulder started forward.

Rem grabbed his arm at the wrist, rotating it up and bending it down to his elbow.

The attacker dropped the knife, locked in Rem's hold.

A dog barked.

Rem glanced up to see Bristol and Toby running toward them.

Big mistake.

The guy punched him in the jaw with his free hand, hard enough to make him step back.

The attacker jerked loose, grunted as he darted away.

Rem took off after him.

The guy flew fast, disappeared around the cement pillar of the open gate at the edge of the parking lot.

Rem was two seconds behind him. He swung around the pillar to see the man jump into the front passenger seat of a black two-door that was already running.

The tires squealed as it took off.

He ran toward it, getting an angle to see the license plate before it disappeared.

"No!" Bristol puffed out a heavy breath, stopping at Rem's side with Toby. She braced her hands on her hips as she watched the car cruise onto the road and vanish behind trees.

"I got the license." He breathed hard, squinting against the sunlight behind her as he reviewed the plate number in his head.

"I'm sorry. You had him."

He shook his head. Though the near miss scraped like a rock in his chest. "My bad. I know better than to get distracted during a fight. Guess it's been too long since I've been in one."

She lifted an eyebrow. "Where'd you learn to fight like that? They didn't teach us that much hand-to-hand at the academy before you…left."

Before he got booted out. Nice of her not to say it so bluntly this time. "Like I said, my brother and I were raised to be cops. Dad started me on hand-to-hand combat training before I was five years old." Another thing he hadn't learned well enough apparently.

If he had, the bomber might now be in custody. And Bristol would be safe.

"He didn't look like the bomber, did he?"

Rem glanced at her as she still watched the road where the car had disappeared. "Not the guy we thought was the bomber. Fits the Rocky Falls suspect."

"I guess you're right. We don't actually know which is the bomber and which is the accomplice."

He lifted his shoulders and let them drop. "Could be him. Or could be the bomber was the one driving the car."

Her gray-blue eyes widened. "What if we've been looking for the wrong man this whole time?"

"Amounts to the same thing, I suppose."

She looked at him, question in her gaze.

"The bomber's still out there."

Chapter Thirty-One

Bristol pulled up next to Rem's parked car in the DNR lot. The receding sun cast blue and purple shadows over his vehicle and streaked the sky orange and pink behind the office building.

Rem sat quietly beside her, Toby's panting from the back the only sound in the Jeep.

Except for the pounding of her heart.

Her gut still twisted when she remembered the sight of the masked man, slashing at Rem with a knife. She'd spotted the weapon, seen what was happening, when she paused for a second on the walkway bridge, on her way to help.

Her breath had ripped out of her chest.

Then as they'd watched the attacker get away, she should've been upset. But relief had flowed through her limbs in a hot wave instead. Rem was all right.

Her heart still squeezed with the realization of how much she cared. She didn't know when it had happened, but despite her resistance, she'd ended up caring for Remington Jones again.

And, maybe, that wasn't such a bad thing.

He'd more than shown up today when she needed him. He had risked his life to stop the attacker, who was probably trying to cut her brake lines or plant an explosive device. She could've died. But thanks to Rem, she hadn't. They were all fine because he had come through when it counted.

She couldn't ask for more than that in a man.

Didn't hurt that her heart zinged every time he looked her way, and she sensed the heat of his closeness just when he was sitting in the Jeep with her.

She turned to face him. "I wanted to—"

He looked at her, and her gaze collided with his, drying up her voice.

She moistened her lips. "Thank you."

His mouth curved in a slow smile that darted a shiver up her spine. "You have nothing to thank me for. I wish the license plate had turned up something useful, other than a stolen car."

"You came to the rescue, scared away the bad guys." She smiled. "Like a hero."

He chuckled, the deep sound making her stomach do a cartwheel. "I'm no hero." His smile lowered. "I'm just sorry I couldn't catch the guy."

He stared at her for a long moment, her breath growing shallow under his gaze. He reached out, cradled her cheek ever so gently in his hand. "I'd do anything to keep you safe." His voice lowered to a thick whisper, and he trailed his thumb along her cheek.

She closed her eyes as his touch somehow seeped through her skin and flowed toward her heart where it skirted her defenses and found the soft vulnerability there.

Her muscles tensed. Did she dare risk giving him that kind

of power? The power to make her dependent on him, to make her feel all the chaotic emotions that churned inside her every time he was near, and to put her at risk of pain again.

She opened her eyes.

He watched her, softness in those brown depths, as he lowered his hand.

Could he see the battle that raged inside her?

His lips curled in a smile that looked almost sad. "I better go." He shifted away.

Without thinking, she reached across the console to grab his jacket sleeve. "Rem, wait."

He paused, looked back.

Words caught in her throat. What could she say? That she was starting to care about him, but the thought scared her to death? The idea sounded lame even in her own head.

He looked down at her hand, still gripping his jacket sleeve. He gently covered her hand with his own.

She loosened her hold as warmth seeped from his touch, through her arm and into her heart, spawning a cascade of emotion that made her believe more was possible. More of this heroic man Rem had become. More of a present and a future with him—his partnership, support…love.

Maybe that was worth the risk.

"I think—" Fear nearly closed her throat and halted the words she couldn't believe she was about to say.

His gaze looked into hers, deep emotion turning his eyes into dark melting pools.

The love she saw there infused her with courage to give voice to the words. "I think I'm falling in love with you again."

His eyes widened, then shuttered as he lowered his hand, leaving hers cold.

She brought her hand to her lap, staring at him as confusion circled her exposed heart.

"You don't know how much I've wanted to hear you say that." His words grated over his vocal chords, raw with a pain she didn't understand.

She moistened her lips, staring at his features as if a study of them would explain his response. "I am saying it now. I'm saying I want to be more than friends again. I'm saying... I love you." Her heart pounded as she said the words.

"Don't." He shook his head and turned away, but not before she caught the agony contorting his face.

"Rem, what is it? Why don't—"

"You don't love me, Bristol." He looked at her, briefly, as if seeing her hurt too much for him to bear more than a second. "You never did."

What was he saying? Her heart twisted painfully. "Of course I loved you."

"You loved the idea of the man you wanted me to be. You pushed and prodded and scolded me to try to make me become that man."

You've tried to control your mother and the men you've dated. Especially Rem Jones. Grandma's words sounded in her mind like an echo to Rem's accusations.

"Are you saying I was too controlling?" Anger singed her tone as she glared out the windshield.

Rem sighed. "I needed to be a better man. And I thank you for trying to show me that. But what I'm saying is that you never really loved me because I wasn't good enough for your love." He paused, drawing her gaze to his profile.

Her hackles lowered as she recognized the sadness touching his face, thickening his voice. "But all that matters is that you've changed now. I didn't believe you before, but now I know you've changed." She reached for his hand where it lay on the console between them and squeezed it beneath hers. "You are the man I want now."

"Bristol—" he turned toward her, his eyes moist with sadness nearly overflowing their boundaries "—I will never be that man. I will never be perfect. I fail." He pressed his lips together. "I will always fail, and I will always let you down. I can't pretend anything different."

She shook her head slowly. "I don't believe that." But the fear speeding her pulse and shortening her breath made her doubt her own statement.

"I would never be enough, Bristol." His gaze went to their hands, and he pulled his away. "We can never be together."

He turned away and pushed open his door, stepping out of the Jeep and closing the door behind him without another look.

She stared, frozen, as she watched him walk to his car.

He still didn't turn back.

Tears spilled onto her cheeks as she tore her gaze away. She put the Jeep in Reverse, backed out of the stall and shifted to Drive. She resisted looking behind for a last glimpse of Rem as she pulled onto the street, biting back a sob that lurched up her throat.

Why had she taken the risk? Why had she let herself love him again? She knew she would only get hurt. And it had happened sooner than expected.

You don't love me, Bristol. You never did. Rem's words burned through her mind.

It wasn't true. She had loved him at the academy, or it wouldn't have hurt so much when he'd betrayed her. And if she didn't love him now, she wouldn't need to fight back tears as she drove away.

Would she?

The traitorous question swirled with Rem's accusations and his claims he would fail her again.

Hadn't she been saying that ever since she saw him at Minnesota Falls the day of the first bombs?

She sucked in a shaky breath. He was right. He couldn't be the dependable, safe, reliable man she needed. He'd proven that in his response to her declaration of her feelings.

She should probably thank him for being so blunt. And for reminding her of what she'd already known, before she had let a wave of gratitude carry her away. She and Remington Jones could never be together.

Bristol let out a long sigh as she set her phone and keys on the nightstand in Amalia's guest room.

Toby trotted to the rug beside the bed, circled twice and laid down in a curled position, ready to sleep now that he'd had his dinner.

If only she were as adaptable as he was.

She looked at the bed—clean, comfortable and hastily made by her that morning, but it wasn't her own bed in her own home.

Phoenix would brook no arguments about Bristol returning to her house yet, especially after the attempt to sabotage her Jeep today. And Amalia said she enjoyed having Bristol stay over.

Which made losing control of her living space a tad more bearable. She had to admit, it was nice they cared.

Her phone rang and vibrated against the wood of the nightstand. She picked it up, glancing at the screen for caller ID.

"Hi, Grandma."

"Sweetie, are you all right?" Her voice washed over Bristol, soaking into all the frazzled cracks to make her a steadier whole again.

"Yes, Grandma, I'm fine." Wait. She couldn't know about what had happened with Rem. Why was she asking? "Did someone tell you something?"

"Your mother called. She said she was talking to you yesterday when a bomb went off in your house?"

Bristol pushed back her hair. Leave it to her mother to give Grandma a heart attack. "No, it wasn't like that. Nothing so scary."

"What was it, then?"

Bristol pinched her lips together, then let out a sigh. She had to tell her now. "You know that bomber who's been threatening the dams?"

"Yes, it's all the news reporters talk about lately."

"Well, someone threw a grenade into my kitchen yesterday morning, and we think it was probably him."

She gasped. "A grenade? Are you all right? What happened? How did you—"

"Grandma, I'm fine." Bristol kept her tone ultracalm. "I was able to deactivate the grenade in time, so no one was hurt."

"You can do that?"

A smile found Bristol's lips. "Yes, I can. Toby and I only got a few little cuts from the glass of the window when it broke. Nothing else. We're really just fine."

"Praise the Lord. I prayed for you, as I always do. The Lord answered my prayers for your safety."

Bristol bit back the retort she'd like to make, that her being unharmed had nothing to do with God and everything to do with her quick thinking and marksmanship. "Thanks."

"I'm going to bring some of your favorite chicken dumpling soup over. Have you eaten yet?"

The idea of Grandma coming anywhere near Bristol after what had happened sent a tremor through her body. "You

can't." She took a breath, softened her tone. "I mean, I'm staying with a friend tonight."

"Oh, well, maybe I'll stop by tomorrow, then."

Bristol moistened her lips. "I think it's best if you don't
come over. Just for a little while."

"You mean until the bomber is caught?"

"Yes."

"You don't have to hide things from me, dear. I know
what's going on. I know you've been in more danger than
usual. That's why I've been covering you in even more prayer."

Bristol smiled. Should've known she couldn't get anything
past her grandma. "Okay. I'm sorry." Bristol sat on the edge
of the bed. "I just didn't want you to worry."

"I don't worry. God has you in His arms." She said the
words so simply, brimming with unshakable confidence.

For some reason Bristol couldn't explain, moisture pricked
her eyes. Likely just emotion from the difficult day. She took
in a breath, trying not to sniff into the phone. "Whatever you
say, Grandma."

"That's more like it."

A laugh pushed out, and Bristol wiped her eyes. She was
apparently more tired than she realized. Weepy and emotional was not her.

"I'm glad you talked to your mother."

Bristol's smile dropped. "Did she tell you we had our usual
blowup, too?"

"No. I'm so sorry to hear that." She paused. "About the
hurricane?"

"Of course."

"There's something you need to understand about your
mother. She may have moved on much more quickly than
you would have liked, maybe more quickly than she should
have, especially for your sake. But she loved your dad very

much. As his mother, even I never doubted that. And she loved Riana as much as I loved my son. As much as she loves you, the daughter she still has."

A lump balled in Bristol's throat, clogging any words she might try to get out.

"I would give anything to hold my son again, so I know how your mother feels."

A single tear dropped onto Bristol's cheek, trailed down to her chin.

"She just wants to be close to you."

"I can't." Bristol's lips trembled. "I can't even…see her."

"Oh, sugar." The soft, compassionate words wrenched Bristol's heart. "She wasn't in control that day, either. It wasn't her fault your dad drove back with Riana to try to get you and your mom out. He did that because he loved you both. So much, he'd risk his life for you. It was his choice to do that, and he made the right one. He couldn't leave you there or your mother. But it wasn't his fault or your mom's fault, or yours. Not one of you is to blame."

Bristol barely held back a sob. "Then who is?" She sniffed, trying not to blubber into the phone. "Just God is left."

"Yes, my darling. Just God is left. And He was holding you then like He's holding you now."

"No." She swiped at the tears that fell down her cheeks. "If He cared about me that much, He would've stopped it. He never would've left me so helpless. He wouldn't have let Riana and Dad…"

"His ways are not our ways, honey. He loves bigger than we can understand and has plans we could never imagine. He had something better in store."

Something better. The same words Rem had used. And they stuck in her belly like a knife. "How can you say that?" Anger bubbled around the knife. "How can you say there can be something better than my childhood being safe and free from trauma, than Dad and Riana being alive right now? I thought you loved them."

"Oh, sweetie." Injury twisted Grandma's voice, sending a pang through Bristol's heart for being the cause of it. "I love them more than you can imagine. Just as much as I love you. But God loves you and them even more. So I know I can trust Him and everything He does. Because He is always, *always* good. Only God can take things that are bad and make them into something good, something beautiful."

"I'm sorry, Grandma." Bristol took in a shaky breath, her tears drying as ice froze her heart. "I don't mean to hurt you, but I just can't believe that. I can't see it." She could only believe what she knew—the hurt and pain, the tragedy she'd give anything to change.

"I know. I love you no matter what, Bristol. Do you believe that?"

The lump fought to block her throat again, but Bristol managed to answer around it. "Yes."

"Good. Don't ever forget that."

"I won't."

"I'll be praying for you. And I'll miss you until we can see each other again. Soon."

"I hope so."

"Get some rest, sugar. I'll call you tomorrow."

"Okay. Good night, Grandma."

"Sweet dreams."

A click signaled Grandma hung up, still using a landline phone at her home.

Only then did Bristol realize she hadn't said *I love you* back.

Cold pulsed through her veins as she remembered what else she'd forgotten to tell Grandma. She hadn't told her of the flood, the one that could happen if the bomber succeeded in breaching the dam. A shudder ran through her at the thought.

No. It would not happen. She would stop the bomber, find whatever explosives he planted in time. No flood would happen on her watch.

She'd call Grandma tomorrow, anyway, just to tell her she loved her, too. She was sure Grandma already knew, but not having said the words left an uneasy, empty feeling in Bristol's heart.

The bomber would not rob her of her peace. She wouldn't allow him even that much. She'd bested him ever since she'd found his Minnesota Falls bomb.

If he really attacked tomorrow, she'd be ready. This time to end the terror.

Chapter Thirty-Two

Dread curdled in Rem's stomach as he knocked on the closed door of his boss's office, responding to his early-morning summons.

Two voices talked on the other side, then paused.

"Come in."

Rem opened the door and stepped inside, taking in Franklin behind his desk and Calvin, sitting in a chair by the wall.

That left the chair opposite Franklin's desk for Rem.

He couldn't shake the feeling as he sat down that his was the execution chair. But Franklin liked him. Might just be another reprimand or encouragement to make more changes.

The tight smile Franklin wore, hints of sadness around the edges, did little to confirm the optimistic theory.

"I'm sorry to have to call you in here today, Rem." Franklin shook his head, folding his hands together on his desk. "We've just learned of your past."

Heat crawled up to Rem's face. Which part of his past?

Franklin met his gaze. "I was shocked, personally, to learn

that you were expelled from the police academy for cheating on an examination."

Shame surged more fire to his cheeks, even as anger ignited a different kind of spark in his belly.

He looked at Calvin, the sure source of this information.

Calvin wore the smirk that made Rem want to grab him and—

But that thought just added to his shame. It was his mistake, his very costly mistake, that had landed him here, in this painful moment.

He swallowed, meeting Franklin's disappointed gaze. "It's true. Six years ago, I cheated on examinations at the police academy, and I was rightfully expelled for doing so. It was a horrible mistake, one I've paid for ever since." He scooted forward on the chair, earnestly searching his boss's face. "Please believe me when I say I have never repeated such a mistake since then and never would again."

Franklin studied him a moment. Glanced at Calvin. He cleared his throat. "I think the worst of it is that you never disclosed that…mistake when applying for the job with the DNR."

"I didn't think it was relevant. It wasn't a criminal offense." But was that true? Even as Rem launched the excuse, he questioned it. He hadn't mentioned the cheating or getting expelled because he knew he might not be hired if he told them. Sure, it wasn't required and there was no question on the application that would've covered such a situation. But if he'd been one hundred percent honest, shouldn't he have put it down? Or at least mentioned it to Graham at some point so it was known? Then he wouldn't be sitting here, looking like he had purposefully deceived them about a sordid past.

"I'm afraid, Rem—" Franklin glanced at Calvin again "—I'm afraid that in light of all that's happened, it's become very relevant." He separated his hands and flattened them against the desktop. "We can't have someone with the slightest appearance of dishonesty or untrustworthiness in charge of dam safety and security at a time like this."

"The press would be all over it." Calvin's tone was cheerful as he added what must have been the part of his argument that had convinced Franklin to do what he was about to.

The writing on the wall was clear. Rem knew what came next.

"I'm going to have to dismiss you from employment with the DNR."

Still hurt. Rem closed his eyes.

"I'm sorry." Franklin's burdened tone suggested he really was.

Rem opened his eyes, catching the triumphant gleam in Calvin's gaze. Franklin was apparently the only one with any remorse over the situation.

Rem didn't have the energy to feel anger toward Calvin. His mind was too busy swirling with the ramifications of what had just happened.

"The termination is effective immediately. Right, Franklin?" Calvin's voice barely registered through the cloud descending on Rem, the haze that seemed to surround him.

"I'm afraid so."

Rem pushed out of the chair, walked quickly to his office. Though it was no longer his now. He went through the motions of gathering his things, putting them in a box Calvin immediately provided.

How little he actually had here. Didn't even fill up the box.

A desk calendar he never used. A picture of his mom and dad. One of him and his brother.

His favorite pen.

The Vikings paperweight Mom had given him for Christmas years ago.

The office was bare in a few minutes. As if he'd never been there.

Maybe in a way he hadn't. Maybe not really loving this job, this career, had materialized into nothing that was difficult to leave behind.

And yet, as he walked out of the building into the cool air under a gray sky, his stomach was in a knot and a weight pressed on his shoulders. He put the box in the back seat of his car and straightened, looking across the roof of the car at the DNR building.

Another failure.

What would his father say? Not that he'd ever hear him say it. This would seal his father's silence forever.

His chest singed with the burn of yet another consequence from his past mistakes. He knew he deserved punishment, but he'd already spent years in a career he hadn't wanted and even more time cut off from his family because of his wrongdoing. Wasn't that punishment enough?

He kept trying to make up for it, live the better way now, but it seemed like God didn't care. Like it would never be enough, and he'd never be free of having to live down his past.

The sound of a vehicle slowing drew his attention to his right.

Bristol's Jeep paused there, perpendicular to his parked car. For a moment, he'd forgotten she was picking him up to search for bombs at the Minnesota Falls Dam.

His heart sank even further. He still hadn't figured out how he was going to face her after yesterday, after leaving her alone with hurt and confusion filling her beautiful eyes. He didn't think he'd ever heal from the pain of hearing her say she loved him when he knew it wasn't true. When he knew it didn't matter, that they couldn't have a future together because of his own failings.

At least getting fired would prove his point to Bristol. Probably would've made her withdraw her declaration of love now, anyway.

The passenger window of the Jeep rolled down.

He slowly walked over, ducked his head to see in.

Bristol watched him with cloudy eyes.

"Hi." A totally inadequate word for the heavy emotions stretching between them, but he had to say something.

She raised an eyebrow when he didn't get in. "Are you planning to walk to the dams?"

"I have some bad news." He winced. "I just...they just fired me."

Her lips formed a hard line. "Calvin." She shook her head. "He can't get away with that."

Rem gripped the door, the rough edges of the window track digging into his palms. "He had a good reason. He found out about my cheating, getting expelled from the academy. Franklin had to fire me."

She looked out the windshield, then turned back to him, her gaze stormy. "No, he didn't. You've done a good job for the DNR."

Hope sparked in his chest. Approval from Bristol? But her distanced, grim demeanor signaled he had better not read too much into the compliment.

"Well, we're wasting time. Hop in."

"Um, I'm not technically with the DNR anymore. I can't enter the dams."

She looked forward again. Her finger thumped the wheel. "I don't work for the DNR. You can come along as my assistant."

His hands slipped off the door, nearly making him pitch

forward in his surprise. Did Bristol want him to come along? Some of the weight of the morning began to lift as he opened the door and slid onto the seat. "Are you sure?"

Her gray-blue eyes found his gaze and locked on. "We should finish this together."

He nodded, throat tightening. His job at the DNR and even the immovable obstacles between him and Bristol didn't matter much in light of the bomber's threat and the attempts on Bristol's life.

He looked at the clock in the dash as Bristol swung the Jeep around to exit the lot—*6:11.*

They were to relieve Miles and Duke at seven, checking for anything new or missed. Would the bomber try to kill Bristol before his four p.m. deadline? And what would he do after four o'clock?

Rem looked at Bristol's beautiful profile. *Please, God. Whatever happens, keep Bristol safe.*

He only hoped God was still listening to his prayers.

A low-level buzz lined Bristol's veins as she turned the Jeep onto the road that would lead them to the Minnesota Falls Dam. And the clock moved closer to the deadline.

The adrenaline was much better than the nerves that had nauseated her belly since she'd awoken. Until she had seen Rem in the DNR parking lot, looking like a lost little boy.

Her heart had surged with a powerful, almost painful desire to fix whatever had hurt him. A ridiculous urge, since he'd just hurt her again yesterday, when he'd rejected her. But Rem had always been a temptation to go against her better judgment.

She'd been afraid he'd bring up yesterday's conversation on the drive to the dam, but his silence was a welcome surprise. Today had enough at stake without needing to add their relationship issues.

Part of her wanted to swing the Jeep around, head for the freeway and get away. Somewhere away from darkness and threats to destroy the dam and hurt people.

That part of her just wanted to be happy. To escape the foreboding cloud that hovered in the back of her mind like a premonition of impending doom.

Or maybe just a manifestation of her past. She was probably projecting her fears onto this situation, which was actually very different. There was no reason there would be a flood.

The task force had the combined resources of the FBI, MPD, Homeland Security and probably other agencies she didn't know were involved. They should be able to beat one little self-made terrorist.

Especially with Bristol and Toby to help. And Miles and Duke. If the abundance of law enforcement personnel at the dam overnight hadn't been enough to prevent the bomber from planting explosives, the K-9s would find the bombs before anything happened.

The worst thing to occur today would be Rem getting fired. Which was ridiculous. She couldn't believe the DNR would fire someone who had nothing to do with the bombings. From everything she'd seen, he'd been doing his job well and trying to make improvements that the dam owners had resisted before the terrorist showed up. That wasn't his fault. And they had no business holding a six-year-old mistake over his head.

Though she had done the very same thing.

She swallowed, glancing at Rem, who stared out the windshield, furrows clustering on his brow.

A quarter of the parking lot was filled with law enforcement vehicles as she pulled in and took an open stall in an unused row farther from the visitor complex.

Uniformed MPD officers patrolled the exterior of the center, along with a few agents wearing FBI jackets. There would be more indoors, as well. She couldn't see Miles and Duke, but they were likely rechecking the structure's interior before Bristol and Toby took over.

She glanced at the clock as she killed the engine—6:32.

Still hours until the deadline. But, realistically, she didn't see how the bomber could imagine he'd get a bomb planted here now past the significant law enforcement presence. And with Miles and Duke already having cleared the place overnight and into this morning, she and Toby would have an easy job to do today.

As long as she didn't let herself be distracted by Rem and the chaotic feelings he stirred in her.

She exited the Jeep and went to the back.

Rem met her there, looking at her with those chocolate eyes she could melt in. "I need to clarify something. In case today doesn't—"

"Today is going to go exactly according to plan." She tensed her jaw against the buildup of emotion she couldn't explain that threatened to escape. "We're going to eliminate the threat, and everything will be fine."

His mouth softened around the corners. "I like your plan."

The gentleness in his eyes and his tone seeped behind the defensive wall around her heart, prompting her to do what she shouldn't. She stepped toward him, her fingers reaching to touch the softness of his beard along his angled jawline.

His eyes darkened. "Bristol, I—"

A flash lit the sky behind him, and a massive boom exploded the air.

Tremendous force threw her backward, one horrible thought blasting through her mind.

She was too late.

Chapter Thirty-Three

Hands reached for Bristol, pulled her to her feet.

Rem.

"Are you okay?" His deep voice got lost in the sounds of horror around them—yells, moans, a scream.

She looked past him as she gripped his forearm, braced in front of her for support.

A tan cloud ballooned above the dam, the visitor complex.

What was left of it. Half the building appeared to be missing—a pile of debris, wires and...was that someone's jacket?

Her stomach wrenched. How many people were in the explosion?

Sirens screeched nearby—first responders on their way.

Something crunched under her feet as she took a step.

Glass and bits of debris littered the ground. All around the Jeep.

Toby.

She pulled away from Rem to open the liftgate.

Toby hunkered down in his crate, tail swishing along the floor as he let out a whimper.

Looked like the front passenger window had blown in, shattered.

But no glass around Toby. He looked okay, just scared.

"Good boy. It's okay." He'd be safer inside the Jeep until she figured out what was going on.

"I want to see if I can help over there, but are you sure you're okay?" Rem touched her arm, turning her toward him. "You hit your head when you fell. I think you were unconscious for a few seconds." Concern lit his eyes as he ran his fingers over her forehead as if looking for a bump.

"I'm fine." She looked past him, her heart pinching at the sight of survivors making their way through the destruction and entering the part of the visitor center that remained. "We should help them."

He nodded.

She closed the liftgate and jogged after Rem, their shoes crunching on glass from other parked vehicles and debris from the building.

Two fire engines squealed into the lot, sirens blaring, adding to the chaos.

FBI and MPD personnel darted around, shouting to each other and directing first responders to where they were needed.

Ambulances arrived within seconds, along with more fire trucks.

Bristol stopped, dodging the rescue workers who jumped from their vehicles. She didn't want to get in their way.

A petite woman in a white shirt and dark pants pointed a paramedic toward a pile of rubble on the north side of the visitor center.

"Agent Nguyen!"

She turned at Bristol's shout, and Bristol hurried to her, Rem keeping pace. "What happened?"

The agent pushed back her hair, revealing cuts along one cheek. The sleeve of her shirt was torn, bloodied from a long gash in her arm that matched the length of the tear. "A boat." She made a sound that stretched between grief and rage. "We should've thought of it."

"But he'd always used time bombs inside the dams."

Agent Nguyen nodded. Her eyes pooled with moisture. "He must have loaded it with an incredible number of explosives. I don't know. I was inside the center, but they said he aimed the boat at the dock and bailed."

"Was he caught?"

She shook her head, gripping her black hair on top as if she wanted to pull it out. "He dove into the water before our guys knew what was happening, and the boat went up a second later. We don't know if he survived."

"What about the MPD detection team?" Bristol braced for bad news. "Are they hurt?"

Nguyen looked around at the chaos. "I saw the handler being carried to an ambulance. The K-9 was limping. But they're alive."

Relief undid a portion of the knots in Bristol's stomach.

Until a different sound she hadn't heard when farther away pushed through the other noises. A thundering, steady, powerful noise. "What is that?"

Her heart knew before Rem answered.

"Water."

They rushed to the river, the old access through the building now a mound of broken debris. She scrambled up behind Rem, avoiding sharp points of metal, bricks and wires.

The sight sucked the breath from her lungs.

Water gushed through a massive hole in the dam, creating

a waterfall that dumped excessive amounts of water into the river below. The waterline crawled up the banks on both sides.

Her pulse jumped into her throat, nearly choking her. This couldn't be happening. Not a flood. She was supposed to stop it.

"It's not destroyed." Agent Nguyen spoke from beside her. She sounded relieved, while Bristol's heart pounded in her ears. "He failed." She headed back down without explaining herself.

Bristol's gaze returned to the water pouring through the breach. She tried to breathe above the rising panic in her chest.

"It's okay." Rem wrapped warm fingers around her elbow.

She leaned into his gentle touch. "No. It's not. The river's going to flood." Grandma. She jerked toward Rem. "I have to get Grandma out. She's by the river."

He put his hands on her arms. "But Agent Nguyen was right. The bomber didn't manage to wipe out the dam. This won't be like Leavell."

She lifted her gaze to his face. "It won't?"

"Not likely." He lowered his hands and looked over the edge at the hole. "With a breach that size, the water flow is slow enough that the Ceinture and Crownover dams should be able to hold the excess and keep the levels safe downriver. That's part of the reason there are three dams so close together here. The operators will let the overflow through the next dams at a controlled pace, so the breach won't lead to flooding. The level should just go up a number of feet."

Her pulse slowed only slightly. "Should? What aren't you telling me?"

A flicker of hesitancy touched his eyes. "I don't know the extent of the structural damage. If it's worse than what I can see from here, it's possible more of the dam could give way."

Her pulse picked up speed again. "I've got to get Grandma." She spun and started down the rubble.

Noise behind her signaled Rem was following. "Agent Nguyen will be starting to evacuate the areas at risk, just in case. The engineers briefed her on the risks and flood radius."

The ring of Bristol's phone startled her tense nerves. She stopped and pulled the cell from her pocket. Had Grandma heard the explosion?

No caller ID. Could be someone from the task force.

"Bachmann here."

"Hello, Bristol."

A man's voice she didn't recognize. But he used her first name. "Who is this?"

"How do you like my work? Stunning, isn't it?"

Realization turned her blood cold. Libertas. Without a voice changer this time. That had to mean he no longer cared about the risk of discovery. What did he know that she didn't?

Rem touched her free hand. "What is it?"

She took the phone from her ear and switched it to speaker.

"Do you have me on speaker, Bristol?"

"Just so I can talk to you… I cut my hands."

"Oh, tsk tsk. I'm sorry to hear that. I hope the injury won't interfere with your…work."

Anger pumped through her veins, pushing out the surprise that had frozen her moments before. "Not a chance."

"I suppose you think you've won, don't you?"

She glanced at Rem.

His skin was nearly white despite his tan as he stared at the phone in her hand.

"You mean because you didn't completely destroy the dam?" Still injured and maybe killed people. Still threatening to flood hundreds of civilians downstream. Didn't feel like a victory. But to his demented mind, anything but making good on his threat must seem like failure.

The bomber laughed. "You can stop your celebrating. You all underestimated me, every step of the way. When your dog made things difficult, I admit I had to change my plans. But I knew having to use a boat might not produce the results I wanted."

"You mean you have a backup plan?" More bombs.

"The Mississippi will be freed, Bristol. I promised."

She met Remington's widened gaze, realization lighting his eyes at the same time it hit her. "You're going to blow up the other two dams."

Libertas chuckled. "Knew you'd figure that out. But you can't stop me."

She steeled her jaw and started forward again, heading for Toby in the Jeep. "You've made the mistake of underestimating me before."

He chuckled. "No, Bristol. This time, I'm ready for you. I took out some insurance."

Her pulse ricocheted, testing her bravado. "What do you mean?"

"I knew you'd figure out what I planned to do while everyone else was distracted by the damage of my masterpiece."

She swallowed the bad taste in her mouth. The guy fit the definition of *terrorist* to a T.

"So I built in a fail-safe."

She walked faster. No time for playing games.

"Don't you want to know what it is?" His voice grew clearer as she got away from the noise of the river and rescue efforts, but she almost wished she couldn't hear him.

She glanced back at Rem, who was looking blue around the edges. Had he gotten injured? "Whatever you say, I'm still going to stop you. I'm going to find and disarm your bombs at the other dams. Mark my words."

"Oh, I'll do that." The bomber's voice cut low, deadly. "I'll also tell you my fail-safe is named Jessica Bachmann. Sound familiar?"

Bristol froze.

Rem bumped into her shoulder.

"What?" She barely got the word out her rapidly closing throat.

"Yes, I have your grandmother. Don't worry, I'll take care of her as I would my own grandmother. So long as you don't go anywhere near my other bombs or try to disable them in any way."

She couldn't speak, couldn't move. Could barely think. Her world was imploding around her. *Grandma.*

"Do you understand me, Bristol?"

The question reached for her past the panic closing in.

"Please don't hurt her. She hasn't done—"

"I'm sure she's a wonderful person. But collateral damage is often necessary for positive change. We've hurt the environment so much, you know. Maybe it's payback that we should hurt, too. But enough of that. I don't want to miss any of the show. Remember what I said, Bristol. And don't tell anyone about me or my other bombs. If you do, the next time you see your grandma, she'll be in pieces."

Words crossed the phone's screen. *Call ended.*

He'd hung up.

Rem rested his hand on her shoulder.

She turned into him, burying her head in his chest as her whole body trembled, the helplessness she'd promised herself she would never feel again rushing at her like a tidal wave. This is what it felt like to live a nightmare. The city was about to

see the destructive power of a massive flood. Innocent people would die. Like Riana. Like Dad.

With the MPD detection teams out of commission, she was the only one who could stop Libertas. But if she made a move, she'd lose Grandma. Bristol would never survive that.

"Bristol—" Rem took her arms, gently pushing away "—I have to tell you something." A pain she didn't understand swirled in his eyes.

His tongue ran over his lips. "I know that voice. I know who the bomber is."

She stepped back.

"I was looking for the bomber, found a guy named Tristan Doyle. I went to his house a couple times, talked on the phone."

Confusion jammed her mind. She couldn't be hearing this. "You…went to his house?"

"I thought he could be the bomber, but I didn't have any evidence. He acted so normal, like he wanted to be friends, and—"

"Friends?" She felt as if he'd just kicked out the ladder she'd been hanging on to to keep her head above water. When oxygen returned to her lungs, it brought a wave of fury. "How could you not know who he was? Did you tell him about my grandmother?"

"No." He shook his head adamantly. "I'm not that stupid. I just—"

"It was stupid to befriend a bomber and not tell the authorities about him! Not to tell me!" She didn't try to lower her voice or calm her rocketing pulse.

"I told the FBI, but I wasn't sure about anything." His voice contorted with frustration, desperation. "There wasn't any evidence. I'm so—"

"Are you sure now?" The shout caught in her throat as

emotion swelled in the passageway. "Because I am. I'm sure I never want to see you again!"

He just stood there, staring at her. As if he had a right to be stunned. A right to wonder why she was angry and hurt.

Her grandmother was being held hostage, might lose her life because of him. And Bristol was stuck between a rock and a breached dam. Because he just couldn't be responsible, wouldn't do things the right way, the safe way. "Why did I ever start to think I could depend on you? You haven't changed. You still always do everything your own way. Look where that leads!" She lifted her hands out from her sides.

He flinched, as if her words had cut deep. But he deserved to feel a fraction of the pain he'd inflicted on her breaking heart.

"Just go!" The scream tore from her throat.

He dragged his gaze away and turned, shoulders slumped as he walked across the parking lot toward the street.

Her chest squeezed despite her anger. Despite that she had every right to be angry over his mistake, over his catastrophic unpredictability.

She clenched her jaw, opened the liftgate of the Jeep.

Then stopped. She couldn't. If she got Toby out, looked for those bombs, the bomber would...

She couldn't even finish the thought. The world spiraled around her.

Bris! Her sister's voice, screaming as she probably had when she died. Had Daddy clung to her as they waited for death under the water? Had they struggled? Suffered?

Bristol gasped for air, as if drowning herself.

She'd dedicated her life to preventing a disaster like the one that was about to happen.

But she'd give her life itself to save Grandma.

She leaned into the Jeep as the horror, the panic, washed over her in waves.

She gripped the metal door of Toby's crate, her fingers curling around the bars as her heart gave out and she went under.

Chapter Thirty-Four

Rem wasn't sure how long he walked or how far he went. Despite putting one foot in front of the other on a road somewhere, he was paralyzed. He couldn't do anything to help Bristol or to stop the other bombs.

And don't tell anyone about me or my other bombs. If you do, the next time you see your grandma, she'll be in pieces. Tristan's words pummeled Rem's mind.

Even if he could find Agent Nguyen, Rem couldn't tell her a thing. He couldn't live with the mistake he'd already made about Tristan. How could he live with himself if he shared information that terminated Jess's life? The life of Bristol's grandmother? That wasn't his decision to make.

But if he didn't tell someone, so many other lives could be lost in the ensuing flood.

Phoenix. Since she and her team weren't law enforcement, maybe they could do something under the radar so Tristan wouldn't know anyone had been told. From what Rem had seen, Phoenix knew how to keep a secret and had the judgment and skills to know how to act. He hoped.

He stopped walking and reached into his jeans pocket to take out his cell. His fingers trembled as he lit the screen and searched for the number Cora had given him days ago to reach Phoenix K-9 if needed.

The first ring cut short.

"Rem?"

"Hello?" His voice came out raw. The feminine voice seemed familiar. But he couldn't place it in the darkened recesses of his mind.

"Rem, this is Cora. Where are you? Bristol isn't answering her phone. We heard the explosion, felt it from headquarters."

Where was he? He looked around, tried to see where he was, tried to clear his mind. He seemed to be about a block away from the dam, near the historic bridge. "We're not hurt. The dam is breached, and the bomber's going to blow up the Ceinture and Crownover dams."

"What? How do you know that?"

Rem somehow stumbled through telling her everything, the terrorist's threatening phone call, how he was holding Bristol's grandmother captive. "And you should know it's my fault."

"Your fault?" Doubt hung on her question.

"I know the terrorist. A man named Tristan Doyle. I found him when I was looking for the bomber, but I couldn't get any evidence to show he was anything but a normal guy in love with the environment. When I heard his voice on Bristol's phone, I knew it was him. I'm sorry."

The apology fell ridiculously short. He knew that. But it was all he had to give.

"Jones." A deeper female voice. "Phoenix here."

He'd been on speaker?

"I want you to stay where you are. Cora's going to pick you up. Don't worry about Bristol. We'll take care of her and her grandmother. Don't go anywhere."

"Tha…" His voice choked. "Thank you." His eyes pricked with moisture.

They ended the call, and he sank to the ground, landing on the curb alongside the road.

He leaned forward and dropped his head in his hands. He hoped they could do what Phoenix said. But it wouldn't change the one fact he would never be able to erase.

He'd made the worst mistake of his life. One he couldn't live with.

I'm sure I never want to see you again!

Bristol's scream ricocheted in his head, the hatred and despair that had twisted her features plunging like a dagger into his heart.

The death blow was, she was right to hate him.

He could've prevented all of this. The lives lost at the Minnesota Falls Dam. How many people was he responsible for having killed?

He pressed his hands against his mouth. *Dear God, please forgive me.*

But would God even do that?

Rem hadn't changed. Bristol was right about that, too.

He still thought he always knew best. He hadn't wanted to make a bigger deal out of Tristan to the FBI because he didn't want to falsely accuse anyone or overstep Agent Nguyen's boundaries. There hadn't been any evidence to prove he was the bomber. But maybe Rem hadn't acted just so he wouldn't make another mistake. To save face. To save his pride.

It was still all about him, just like the way he used to live.

And then he had made the worst mistake of his life, anyway.

A mistake Bristol and Jessica would pay for. Maybe hundreds of people would pay with their lives if Bristol didn't find the other bombs because of the terrorist's threat to her grandma.

Rem knew better than most what would happen if both the other dams were breached. The university was in the path of the massive flood that would result. Residential areas, hundreds of homes.

His stomach lurched. He bent over as vomit threatened to come up.

He managed a shaky breath as the feeling passed, the bile sliding back down to his stomach.

How could he make such a huge mistake? The consequences this time were beyond belief. Even God wouldn't be able to forgive him for this kind of devastation.

If the punishment for his wrongs before he came to Christ was still ongoing and getting worse, as his firing indicated today, what would the punishment for this mistake be? Bad choices had consequences, he knew that.

This time, he was already tasting the worst possible consequence. Worse than losing Bristol, worse than the deaths. He felt a stabbing pain as if his soul was being torn in half as he realized what the punishment would be. What it was. He'd lost God's love.

That's why this had happened. It was an extension of the punishment for everything wrong he'd done. Now the world was falling down around him, and he had no one to turn to. He couldn't go to God. The never-ending punishment for his mistakes made that clear. Only God's wrath now remained for Rem, and it was hitting everyone around him.

Don't go anywhere. The irony of Phoenix's command cut deep.

He had nowhere to go. No one would have him or forgive him. Not Bristol. Not himself. And not God.

★ ★ ★

Bristol sat in the closed cargo area of the Jeep, staring out the side window at the rescue efforts still in progress at the destroyed dam. Rain pounded on the Jeep's roof, numbing her ears along with her senses as she stared at the carnage. This was only the beginning of the damage, the horror and loss that would ensue if she didn't find those bombs.

Toby whined as he leaned into her.

She had let him out of the crate beside her and held him in her arms now.

He didn't wiggle or wag his tail with his usual energy. He seemed to sense her heart was breached, her stomach lurching as memories resurfaced, flashing before her eyes at intervals.

Her mother's wails as they waited on top of the house.

Bristol's terror as she watched the water climb higher, leaving them only three feet of roof. She'd searched the horizon for rescue. For Daddy, Riana. She'd prayed they would somehow be saved.

She had looked for a place to grab hold besides her weeping mother. But there was nothing. Only wet, slippery shingles, rapidly disappearing. She couldn't do anything to save Mom or herself, their house or the happy, safe world that was all she'd ever known. She'd been helpless.

That wasn't supposed to happen here in Minnesota. There were no hurricanes, no strong weather that could cause this kind of flooding.

But here she was, the same terror taking hold of her heart and wringing it out. The same helplessness sinking into her soul. The worst was about to happen, and she couldn't do a thing to stop it.

If she and Toby didn't find the other bombs, they would explode, and more people would die in catastrophic flooding. Like New Orleans all over again.

But if she searched for the bombs, Grandma, the person she loved most, would die.

An impossible situation. An impossible choice.

If there was a God, He must really hate her. Or maybe He was like she'd always thought—a God who got the world started and then let it spiral into chaos on its own, not caring what happened.

But Bristol cared. She didn't want anyone else to die or to feel the fear and pain she'd felt the day her world was destroyed. What was she going to do?

You can't save everyone. Grandma's voice reached for her.

The words, so familiar. The sweet sound of the voice Bristol knew by heart.

Only God can, and that's a good thing because He is good. The memory of Grandma's face, the truthful, loving light in her eyes as she'd said those words, was too much.

The pain, the worry, the love welled within Bristol until she couldn't hold it back. She stopped fighting and let the tears free. They rushed down her cheeks, flowing unchecked as she buried her face in Toby's neck.

Only God can take things that are bad and make them into something good, something beautiful.

How was that possible? How could good come out of any of this?

"God...please." The words barely emerged from her mouth, a small whisper under her tears. "If you can do that, please do it now. I can't..." A sob hitched her voice. "Things are so out of control. Please...help me."

A ring jangled in the silence. Maybe she should answer this time.

She sniffed, reining in the tears as she pulled her phone from her jacket pocket. She kept one hand on Toby's damp neck. "Bachmann."

"Bristol, where are you?" *Phoenix.*

Bristol tried to wipe the moisture from her face, hoping her voice didn't carry the evidence she'd been crying. "Minnesota Falls. The parking lot. But I can't—"

"We know the situation. Jones briefed us. You need to search for those bombs."

"My grandma—"

"Will be fine. We've got your back, Bristol."

Her breath caught in her chest. "You mean you'll look for her? But the bomber said—"

"I mean we'll find her and get her safely away from the terrorist. Trust your team. We've got this." Phoenix's strong voice was steeled with confidence, determination, certainty.

All the things Bristol didn't have at the moment, but exactly what she needed to hear. There was someone else to shoulder the load. She didn't have to do it all. She had help.

Air filled her lungs as if Phoenix had reached into the water and pulled her out just before she drowned.

Like the man who had stretched out his hand from the boat sixteen years ago and lifted her off the roof, taken them to safety, to dry land.

Like the people from the local church who had welcomed Bristol and her mom into their home until they could find a new place to live. And the mother of that household, a pastor's wife, had fed and cared for Bristol while Mom spent days in bed.

Is that what Grandma meant by God using bad for good? By caring for her in the midst of the flood?

Bristol cleared her throat, finding her voice. "Thank you, Phoenix."

"No thanks needed. Just find those bombs." Phoenix ended the call before Bristol could respond.

But the best response was to do as Phoenix had said.

And she suddenly felt like she could.

The PK-9 team was good but finding Grandma and rescuing her in time was a long shot. So was discovering and disarming the bomber's devices before they went off. Bristol knew that.

Yet, for the first time in her life, the thought of facing the uncertain didn't scare her. Instead, a strange peace she couldn't explain flowed through her body, loosening the tension in her chest, her taut muscles, and freeing her to breathe deeply.

She remembered how a whole community, starting with the churches and extending to the entire city of New Orleans, banded together to rebuild after the flooding, to make something better than what had been lost. They rebuilt neighborhoods and residences that had been crumbling before the hurricane, making them stronger, cleaner, safer—making something beautiful. God, bringing good from the bad.

Had God built her life into something more beautiful, too? If that hurricane, the flooding, hadn't happened, she wouldn't be here now. She wouldn't have spent these wonderful years growing closer to Grandma. She wouldn't have friends and coworkers, the PK-9 crew, who were willing to risk their lives to help her and others.

And she wouldn't have fallen in love with Rem, the best man she'd ever known besides her father. She knew she loved him from the horrific pain that had ripped her heart when she thought he'd let her down, making Grandma pay the price. But she should've believed he'd done the right thing. The best that could be done. She should have heard him out.

He'd been right yesterday. She had expected him to be an idyllic, perfect man of her imagination, and she'd tried to control him like everything else in her life. He was also right that she had loved that imaginary Rem more than the real thing six years ago.

But she should have listened to Grandma. Because Bristol was the last one to know what she really needed. Who she needed.

The look on Rem's face when she'd told him to go away, that she never wanted to see him again, pierced her chest. But she'd have to leave Rem and their future in God's hands, too.

For once, the thought didn't bother her. Her pulse continued at a normal beat when it should've been pounding.

She reached into her pocket, took out the keyless remote and opened the liftgate.

Light streamed into the Jeep as the world opened before her.

Rain poured down like a waterfall, and shouts of rescue workers and moans from the injured reached her ears, along with the roar of rushing water, still bursting through the breach.

The peace didn't let go.

She couldn't handle this one on her own, so thank God she didn't have to.

"Come on, Toby. Let's go to work."

"Rem?"

He slowly lifted his head.

Cora leaned over from the driver's side of her white Beetle. The way her eyebrows drew together said it all. He must look as horrible as he felt.

"Can you get up? Or are you hurt?"

He pushed with his hand against the curb, slowly stood. Was he hurt? His heart felt like it was being sliced by a hundred shards of glass.

But that was likely not what Cora meant. "I'm fine." Bristol's favorite response fell from his lips, cinching his chest even more.

He pulled open the passenger door and slid onto the clean front seat.

Cora looked over her shoulder before pulling out onto the road. "You were sitting along the road in pouring rain. You're not fine."

Rain? He hadn't noticed. But sure enough, his hands and jeans were soaked, droplets beaded on his waterproof jacket.

He didn't look her way, couldn't begin to apologize. He couldn't even see anything past the cloud of guilt and regret that surrounded him.

"Phoenix wants you to help us figure out where the terrorist took Bristol's grandmother. Dag tracked her from her house to the driveway, but the scent stopped there. We think she must have been put in a car and taken somewhere. Can you think of what you learned about him? Anything that might tell us where he would take a kidnapped victim?"

Rem pressed a wet hand to his aching forehead. "I can't do that. I'll just make things worse."

"What happened, Rem?"

He lowered his hand, blinked slowly at the rain blurring the windshield, the wiper blades fighting a losing battle to keep the deluge at bay. "He blew up the dam, probably killed people. And I could've stopped him."

"You think that was your fault?"

"I talked to him a bunch of times. I was trying to find something…anything real I could take to the FBI to prove he was the bomber. And I failed. Let everyone down."

"What did Bristol say to you?"

He looked at Cora then, peering at her from under eyelids too heavy to open all the way.

Her rosebud mouth pursed in a serious cluster, but her eyes were filled with compassion.

That he didn't deserve. "The truth. That I messed up." He

swallowed but couldn't sink the emotion plugging his throat. "She said she never wants to see me again." He dropped his gaze to his hands, glistening with water, clutching the darkened knees of his drenched jeans.

"Are you a Christian, Rem?"

"Yes."

"Then don't you know God has forgiven you?"

Not the direction he'd expected her to go. He moistened his lips. "Of course I do. But that doesn't mean there aren't consequences to the bad we do. There's still punishment."

She turned the car at an intersection. "Do you think God is punishing you?" There was no condemnation in her tone. Just a simple, quiet question.

"Isn't it obvious? I've lost God's love. Messed up too many times."

"Why do you think that?"

"Look what's happened because of my mistakes. Bristol still won't trust me, and my family basically disowned me. Now I lost my job. And, oh yeah, I didn't do anything about a bomber because I wanted to be right. Didn't want Bristol... anyone to see me as irresponsible again."

"And because you didn't want to accuse an innocent man without proof?"

Nice of Cora to try to make him feel better, but he couldn't deny the truth. "It doesn't matter why I did it. What matters is, I brought this on myself and everyone else. You have to pay for your mistakes. But it's so much this time. So terrible." He ran his hands down his face. "This isn't the kind of punishment He'd give me if He still loved me."

"Let me ask you something, Rem."

He waited as she made a left turn.

"Do you believe God is just?"

He'd told Tristan as much. "Yes."

"Then you're wrong. Horribly, horribly wrong about Him punishing you."

Rem turned his head to see her profile, her hair falling out of her bun in wisps around her small neck. "How do you figure that?"

"Because God already punished Jesus in our place."

"Yeah, but—"

"No, Rem, there's no *but*. That's it. It's done." She gave him a smile, her eyes moist. "He doesn't look at you and see your sins anymore. He sees Jesus and His righteousness." She sniffed as she looked at the road. "So if God punished you, that wouldn't be just, would it?"

The truth arced in his soul like a rainbow after the storm. She was right. The scripture verses he'd read that said the same thing moved into the clarity of light in his mind. Why hadn't he seen it before?

Had he been so hung up on his own mistakes that he'd thought he had to somehow correct them? It was as if instead of fully believing in Jesus's payment for his sins, he'd kept some of those sins on a list for himself to take care of. Mainly the ones his dad still held against him. Maybe the need to earn his dad's forgiveness had made him believe he needed to earn God's, too.

But that wasn't Dad's fault. Rem should've known better. Should have opened his Bible and trusted what it said. Like when God said nothing could separate him from the love of Christ.

Rem only hoped Bristol would be able to forgive him, too. But even that thought couldn't keep the burden from lifting off his shoulders or halt the renewal of his soul as a refreshed awareness of God's amazing love coursed through him.

Rem could finally let go of the mistakes he'd been carrying with him through life. Dropping the weight made him feel lighter than air.

"Thanks, Cora." He smiled at her, a testament to the joy God was able to pump into his soul despite the circumstances and the wound from Bristol's rejection that still cut his heart.

"You're welcome." Cora returned the smile as she slowed for a stoplight. "Now let's figure out where Bristol's grandma is. Do you know if he has a house or another place he goes to?"

Rem nodded. "He has a house out in Garden Valley. But he's been so careful to hide his identity and not use anything that could be tied to him. I don't know if he'd risk bringing her there."

"Is there anywhere else he might use?"

The environmental group Tristan had mentioned met at Springway Park. But that location would be too public and exposed for hiding a hostage. "The house is the only place that would make sense." He looked at Cora. "Out of the little I know."

"Then I'm guessing Phoenix will want to try there." She turned the car in a sudden U-turn.

He gripped the armrest next to him. He never would've pegged Cora as an aggressive driver.

She typed in the code to unlock her cell phone, attached to a magnet holder on the dash. "I'll tell Phoenix where to meet us. Hopefully Bristol's grandma will be at his house. But keep thinking in case she isn't. And maybe you'll remember something that will help us nab the bomber if he isn't with her."

"You really think Phoenix is taking my word for it? That Tristan is the bomber?" He wouldn't blame her for doubting him.

"You'll see." Cora accelerated as she tapped Phoenix's programmed call button.

Phoenix answered almost instantly, her voice on speaker.

"Tristan Doyle is confirmed as the suspect. Dennis Fentworth at Fentworth Construction wouldn't talk to the FBI, but we just got intel from another source that he often loaned a company van to his brother-in-law. Tristan Doyle."

Rem closed his eyes. Confirmation just when he most needed to be trusted. Almost like a sign, a reminder that God was indeed still on his side. *Thank you, Father.*

"We're going to his house now. Rem's been there before." Cora looked at him. "What's the address?"

He gave her the address, and they agreed to meet a block from the house.

Cora threw Rem a worried glance as soon as Phoenix ended the call. "I think we better pray the rest of the way there."

Exactly what he was already starting to do.

Chapter Thirty-Five

Wind whipped raindrops under the hood of Bristol's jacket to hit her cheeks as she let Toby lead the way across the walkway on top of Ceinture Dam. He had already cleared the interior, and some uninjured FBI agents and bomb squad technicians continued to search inside. The human crew had also searched this walkway before Toby had gotten to it. But without success.

The canine nose was far superior, but how much more time did they have before the terrorist detonated this dam?

She didn't know what had stalled him this long. Unless it was the water level. She'd been watching the level against the Ceinture Dam rise higher and higher as the water rushed through the breached Minnesota Falls Dam upriver. The operators of Ceinture were letting some of the water through, but slowly, so as not to cause a flood downriver in the more vulnerable area.

The bomber was confident he had a foolproof strategy.

Probably the perfect strategy to maximize flooding when he destroyed the two remaining dams.

Her heart skipped a couple beats as apprehension stirred in her belly. What if they were too late?

She let out a long breath, raindrops pelting her lips. God was in control. It would take her a while to remember that. But comfort lowered her pulse every time she did.

Please help us find the bomb in time. And please keep Grandma safe.

Rem hunkered down in the stand of trees behind Tristan's backyard. The rain didn't reach him as much here, but he still shivered from the drenching when he'd sat on the road before.

Phoenix and the three other ladies of her crew moved like a veteran combat team, surrounding the house silently as they cased it, peering inside.

They whispered their findings into earpieces connected to the one Phoenix had let Rem borrow.

"Kitchen empty."

"Blue hybrid in garage. No occupants."

He wasn't always sure who was saying what, but he recognized Phoenix and Cora when they talked.

"Bedroom is vacant." Cora. She crouched below the window at the end of the house, where he'd told them the bedroom was. It was crazy how relaxed and normal Tristan had been about welcoming Rem into his home, showing him the whole place. As if he was a man with nothing to hide. As if he wasn't a terrorist.

"Dove found." Phoenix's deep, intense words struck Rem in the chest. "Living room, southwest quadrant."

"How is she?" Rem held his breath for the answer.

"Appears alert, conscious. No visible signs of injury. Hold it…"

Rem's heart thudded against his ribs.

"Crocodile is in the house. Repeat, Crocodile is here, with Dove."

Rem froze at their chosen code word. Tristan—Libertas—was here?

"Should we raid him?" Sounded like Nevaeh, but he wasn't sure.

"He has an alarm system." A voice he didn't recognize. Maybe Amalia. "Pretty sophisticated digital one with sensors."

"Regroup at start," Phoenix ordered. "Nevaeh, hold position with eyes on Dove. All others, return to start."

His pulse raced as he watched Cora make her way back, darting from tree to tree in Tristan's yard. Could they somehow get in without Tristan hurting Jessica? His mind grabbed at possibilities, ran through scenarios.

There were five of them, if he helped. They might be able to do it, entering by the back way. But it depended on whether or not Tristan was armed and with what kinds of weapons. And how ready he was to use them.

Cora smiled slightly as she approached, her skin pale beneath the black winter hat that completely covered her upswept hair. "Thank the Lord we found her."

"We're going to breach the place."

Rem started at Phoenix's voice next to him. When had she gotten back? And Amalia, crouching next to her in the brush. He hadn't heard either of them.

"But we'll need to eliminate the alarm system first."

"What's the situation with the hostage?" Amalia reached glove-clad hands to adjust the soaked black hat she wore, her dark hair tumbling out onto her black turtleneck in wet strands.

"Libertas is sitting in an armchair two and a half feet from Bristol's grandmother, also in an armchair. An end table with a lamp on it is between them. He has a nine mil Glock. It was on the table, but he picked it up once while I was watching." Phoenix faced the house, keeping an eye on it as she listed the facts, rapid-fire. "Chairs are angled toward the southeast corner where there's a TV. He had on a local news station."

Cora pursed her lips. "You don't think he's watching it to see the results of his bomb at Minnesota Falls, do you?"

"Very likely." Amalia looked at Cora, her dark eyes grave. "And probably watching to make sure his next bombs detonate."

"Which means he'll notice if Bristol disarms them and they don't go off when they're supposed to." Rem wiped at the raindrops that had gathered on his forehead.

"Exactly." Phoenix kept her gaze locked on the house. "He has two cell phones on the end table by his gun. One is a smartphone, and the other is a cheap flip phone."

"Oh my." Cora's pale skin whitened more. "He could be using a phone to detonate his next bombs."

"He's always used time bombs before." Amalia looked at Cora. "We can't be sure that's what the extra phone is for."

Rem's thoughts clicked into place, clenching his stomach. "It makes sense."

The women brought their attention to him.

"His plan is to maximize the force and water levels for maximum flood damage. To do that, he'd have to wait about forty or forty-five minutes after the first breach for the pressure to build before blowing the Ceinture Dam. Then he'd wait a little while, I think about twenty minutes or so, before blowing the last one, the Crownover. He couldn't do all that with preset timers because of the boat and whoever he used to pilot it. He wouldn't have been able to predict the exact timing of the explosion or the degree of damage." Rem rested his hands on his hips. "My guess is he's also using the news coverage to show him the water levels so he can make sure his timing is right."

Cora's eyes widened. "He could explode the next bomb while Bristol is trying to disarm it."

The observation pinched his oxygen. *Dear Lord, please protect Bristol.* "Should we take the risk and call Agent Nguyen? Or the police?"

"No." Phoenix watched the house, not Rem.

"Even with the bomber here?"

"Especially with him here. They wouldn't arrive in time, and they'd send in SWAT. SWAT would prioritize the 'greater good'—higher collateral damage numbers from a possible flood—over Bristol's grandmother." She angled halfway toward him and the women behind her, passing her unreadable gaze over them. "I told Bristol we would keep her grandmother safe, and that's what we're going to do."

Rem couldn't deny the truth of what she said. He knew the priorities SWAT would have to follow in this case. Taking out the bomber before he detonated bombs would be the primary objective. And Jessica could get hurt. Phoenix was right about the timing, too. If Rem's timeline was right, they only had minutes to spare.

"But we're going to accomplish both objectives." Phoenix turned back to face the house completely. "We're going to protect the public and Bristol's grandmother." Her jawline was as hard as her tone. The woman had more confidence than anyone he knew.

He had no choice but to rally behind her. And he was itching to get inside, to grab Tristan himself before he triggered the bomb and hurt Bristol.

She could die. The thought squeezed his chest in a vise.

"How about I go up to the door, pretend like I'm here for a visit." Rem's words tumbled out as the idea formed in his mind. "I've stopped by before, and he's worked hard to convince me he isn't the bomber. He might want to keep up the act if he can manage it. Either way, I can distract him to keep him from detonating anything while you get inside from behind."

Phoenix turned her head to look at him, as if considering his idea. "You're not going in. We can't have someone else in danger."

He opened his mouth to contradict her authoritarian denial, but she interrupted him. "Stalling him is a good idea, though. You have his number?"

Rem nodded. "In my phone."

"Call him. Keep him busy talking. That might be enough to delay him, at least while we disconnect the alarm and breach the house."

She stepped over to the other women and formulated a plan with them while Rem removed his earpiece and slipped his phone from his pocket.

He selected Tristan from his contacts and desperately prayed this would work.

Still no find. Bristol kept her eyes locked on Toby while they crossed the top of the Ceinture Dam one more time.

His nose pointed in the air, then lowered to the ground. He was working hard. But the rain and wind were working against them.

Or there was nothing to find.

The thought seemed far too naive at a time like this. The bomber had admitted he planned to blow up the Ceinture and Crownover dams. There had to be at least one device here.

But she'd had Toby search the inside of the small dam a second time. Nothing.

It had to be out here somewhere. Toby didn't miss explosives.

The Lab stopped, swung back around. He moved toward the rail along the edge, reached under with his head.

"Whoa, don't jump, buddy." She tightened the leash and moved closer to him.

Just as he pulled back and sat. Lifted his paw.

Adrenaline kicked through her veins. He'd found it.

"Yes! Good boy, Toby."

She leaned over the rail to look down, rushing water below creating a dark backdrop. But something moved against that background.

An object, swinging in the wind.

Had to be attached to something.

She looked closer at the rail. A clear wire wrapped around the base of a supporting pole. Fishing wire.

She gently pulled up the wire, trying not to create jostling as she watched the object, likely an IED, nearing her.

She winced as it bumped the concrete wall of the dam. Paused.

No explosion.

She pulled again.

She reached for it at the top, her fingers grasping plastic. A shopping bag, spray-painted beige to match the dam, surrounded what was almost certainly the explosive device. She set the object on the walkway, kneeling beside it.

She carefully opened the bag, peered inside.

A new kind of device for Libertas. No timer. Instead, the explosives were wired to a cell phone.

One call would detonate the IED.

No time to send a runner for a bomb squad technician. She'd have to disarm it herself.

She opened the back pouch of her fanny pack with wet fingers and took out her wire cutters.

God, I'm new to this whole praying thing. But please help me.

The image of Grandma's face, the love in her eyes, appeared in Bristol's mind. Along with her voice, telling Bristol that God cared, that He was good.

She took a deep, steadying breath before she began. No timer to beat. No guarantee she'd render this one safe in time. All she could expect was an unpredictable detonation by someone she couldn't see.

This one could blow up in her face.

"The kind of environment you grow them in makes all the difference."

Rem couldn't believe Tristan was taking the time—while holding a hostage and waiting to blow up two more dams—to give Rem advice for his mother's tomato plants.

But it fit Tristan's strategy to avoid being considered as a suspect. He was very good at normal. He somehow segmented the two parts of himself so well that no one would imagine they could coexist in the same person.

"Thanks, man, my mom will love you for this."

Tristan chuckled, as he had several times during the brief conversation. Seemed almost giddy over the explosion that made Rem feel sick.

It took all his willpower to keep his own voice even, normal, and to infuse it with cheerfulness. He had to distract Tristan for a few minutes longer as Phoenix and her team silently breached the house.

Amalia and Cora had disappeared along the side of the house somewhere. To dismantle the security alarm, he assumed.

He had to come up with something more to talk about. "Hey, I wanted to ask you about something else."

"Shoot." Funny.

Rem's stomach wouldn't settle down. Nor would his accelerated heart rate. This plan seemed too risky. If Tristan heard any of the team as they entered, he could shoot Jess and detonate at least one bomb before they got to him.

"Did you see what that environmental bomber, Libertas, did this morning?" Rem stood and walked out from the cover of the trees.

A pause.

Only a sprinkle dotted Rem's face as he made his way around the perimeter of Tristan's yard. From what Phoenix had described, Tristan wouldn't be able to see Rem in the yard from where he was in the living room at the front of the house.

Tristan finally answered. "Yeah."

"Got me thinking. Maybe we need to do something like that. You know, if we really want to make a change for the good of the environment."

"You think so?" Tristan's voice lifted, as if he was smiling.

Rem swallowed down the bile that started to crawl up his throat as he played Tristan's game. Tristan knew who Rem was, so that's what this had become. A game of cat and mouse. And right now, Rem had to play the mouse, trying to trick a cat who thought he knew every one of the mouse's tricks.

Tristan probably assumed Rem had phoned to try to discover, as a last-ditch effort, if Tristan was the bomber. But, Lord willing, he didn't know the real reason for the call.

Rem forced himself to continue. "Yeah. I mean, it's pretty impressive the attention he's getting. And he almost did it. Almost freed the river."

"He will do it."

"What do you mean?"

"Libertas isn't done yet. Turn on the news. And wait."

"Really? But what else could he do?" Tristan had no idea Rem had listened in on his call to Bristol, and Rem planned to keep it that way.

"There are two more dams downtown on the Mississippi, just below the one he already destroyed."

"Whoa." Rem tried to infuse his tone with admiration rather than the disgust that threatened to choke him. "You mean he's going to take out those two?"

"That's exactly what I mean."

"Wow. But he couldn't do that with all the cops and FBI there, could he?"

"Libertas is smarter than they are. I'll show you. The news helicopters are covering the explosion at the first dam. Turn on your TV and you'll see them switch where they're filming. In forty-five seconds."

"Hey, I'm here." Rem didn't know where those calm but quick words came from as his heart launched into overdrive. He took off at a sprint for the front door, darting past Amalia and Cora crouched by bushes at the end of the house.

"What?"

"I was going to surprise you. I'm here. Decided to drop by." He swung the speaker of the phone away from his mouth to hide his panting breath.

"But I can't have visitors right now."

Rem knocked on the door as he forced a laugh. "Right. It'll only take a sec. I wanted to give you something." A sock in the jaw for starters.

His heart beat out the seconds of Tristan's threat. "Come on, man. Open the door, would you?" He took a risk, leaned over the railing along the cement step by the door to peer in the picture window with a friendly wave. He'd force Tristan to have to deal with him.

Tristan jumped up from the armchair, headed for the door. Worked.

The door started to open.

Rem threw his body into it.

Tristan yelled as he flew backward into the side of his armchair.

Rem went for him.

But stopped at the sight of the gun pointed at his chest.

"Rem!" Jessica gasped as she watched him from the armchair farthest away.

Tristan must've brought the gun to the door with him, maybe tucked under his shirt.

"Tristan." Rem lifted his gaze from the gun to the bomber's face. "Why are you doing this?"

He shook his head, slowly. Anger and pain layered in his eyes. "Well, Remington Jones. As in Remington Jones, security supervisor. I saw you with Bristol and her dog."

"I know you did."

A flicker of surprise registered in his gaze. "But you didn't know, did you? Not for certain."

Rem worked to even and slow his breathing. To stay calm. "You didn't give me much to act on, I'll give you that. You fake friendly very well."

"You were the only one who connected me with SES. I knew if I convinced you and anyone watching that I was an average nobody, you and the feds couldn't touch me."

Rem needed to cut past the bravado, get to Tristan's emotions somehow. "But those talks we had about your dad—was that all part of the act?"

Tristan's mouth flattened in a hard line. "For a spy, you're easy to talk to."

So that had been real. Maybe Tristan had been so desperate for someone to talk to, he'd called up the one person he figured wouldn't tell anyone. A tug of compassion pulled in Rem's chest. "I feel the same way about you, Tristan. You're a nice guy. I never would've guessed you're a terrorist."

"That's a filthy word. A label for anything the powers of this country don't like."

"No, it's for people who spark terror in others by their actions. Who cause pain, death and violence. You've done that. You're doing that right now."

"You don't know anything." Tristan's volume raised as red flushed his face. "You're a traitor. You wanted me to think you were my friend when you were spying on me all along. But I knew what you were doing."

"I am your friend, Tristan."

He sneered, backing in front of the chair toward the end table. He picked up the flip phone, opened it with one hand. "Then you won't mind if I make a quick call."

"No." Rem stepped forward, his hand out.

"Don't move." Tristan lifted the gun higher.

"Don't detonate the bomb, Tristan. Please. You're going to hurt…" Bristol. "You're going to hurt innocent people that had nothing to do with the river being restrained."

"You mean taken captive into bondage!" The gun shook with Tristan's shout. "You don't understand. You're just like the rest of them. If you had your way, nature would be destroyed."

"I wouldn't do that, Tristan. Put the phone down and we can talk about this."

"I'm through talking." He moved his thumb to a button on the phone.

"No!" Rem lurched toward him.

Tristan switched the gun to Jessica.

Rem froze.

"I'll kill her." He pressed the button.

Rem's heart stopped. He couldn't breathe.
The bomb had been detonated. *Bristol.*
The lights went out.

Chapter Thirty-Six

Bristol sucked in a breath, air returning to her lungs as she looked at the cut wire.

No explosion. And the device was now safe.

She'd never know how close it might have been to going off before she disarmed it. Only God knew.

And only He knew what would happen to Grandma now. What if the bomber realized his device hadn't detonated? He would know Bristol hadn't listened to him.

He could kill Grandma.

God, please let the PK-9 team save her. Let them have reached her already.

Bristol got to her feet with the safe device in her hand. She needed to trust God and trust her team. She still had work to do.

As long as this was the only IED at Ceinture—and Toby's search made it almost certain it was—then this dam, at least, was now safe. Preventing a breach here should work to prevent a catastrophic flood, even if she wasn't able to find and disarm the bomber's device at the Crownover Dam downriver.

But she better hustle there to prevent another explosion and more damage if she could. The Crownover still held back a lot of water that the Ceinture operators had allowed through, raising the water between the two dams. She didn't think it was enough to cause extensive flood damage without the added water the Ceinture Dam now held back, but better to be safe than sorry.

She hurried to leave the dam with Toby, realizing for the first time that the rain had stopped. Should make searching Crownover easier. She switched on the radio Agent Nguyen had given her before returning to the rescue effort.

"Bachmann to Agent Nguyen and Bomb Unit. Device located and disarmed. Proceeding to help with Crownover search."

"Roger that, Bachmann." Crackles spattered Agent Nguyen's voice, and other people talked in the background. "Received new intel Ceinture Dam is not safe, won't hold."

Bristol stopped at the top of the stairs that led them down from the walkway over the dam. "Repeat that?"

"DNR's chief engineer informed us Ceinture's owners had not made repairs to structural weakness. He agreed to give them more time to do so."

Calvin. He'd given someone a pass on a safety requirement? How much had they paid him for that? And he dared to get Rem fired for withholding information on his résumé. Anger stirred in Bristol's stomach.

"The structural weakness means it may not hold with the excess amount of water from the Minnesota Falls Dam breach."

"Roger that."

They needed the Crownover Dam to hold.

Bristol jogged with Toby down the steps. She only hoped there was enough time to find the bomb Libertas had planted.

Or the flood of her nightmares would still happen.

Rem never should've doubted the Phoenix K-9 team's skills.

They must have cut the power to Tristan's house right when he'd detonated the bomb. Or tried to.

Rem prayed Bristol had disarmed the bomb in time.

But with the TV off, Tristan had no way of knowing if his device had worked. No way of knowing Bristol had gone ahead and searched for the bombs, anyway. So Jess was still safe. For the moment.

He gave her smiles when Tristan wasn't looking, trying to comfort her however he could. Though she didn't seem to need it.

She looked at Rem warmly, her gray-blue eyes filled with a peace he never saw in Bristol's as she watched him with inexplicable calm, as if she'd invited him over for dinner and didn't have a rope around her body, tying her to the chair.

Tristan had relegated Rem to the floor beneath the picture window, where he sat with his knees propped up in front of him.

Tristan searched for something on his smartphone. Probably something Rem didn't want him to see.

"What are you looking for?"

He glanced at Jessica instead of Rem, then returned his gaze to his phone. "News coverage."

"I told you, the power outage means your bomb went off. You must've blown the power circuit when the explosion caught the hydropower plant." *Please let Bristol have disarmed the bomb in time.*

Tristan looked at him, distrust in his eyes.

Rem didn't look away. "Why else would the power go out?"

Tristan moistened his lips. "I don't know."

Rem shrugged. "The only explanation."

"I still want to see for myself."

Rem needed a longer play. Something to stall him while Bristol got to Crownover and disarmed the bomb there. Assuming she was still all right.

He swallowed. *Father, please help me.*

That was it. Father.

"You know, I owe you an apology, Tristan."

That got his attention. He lowered the phone, and the gun swayed slightly as he looked at Rem.

"I didn't give you a good answer when you asked me that question. You know, about your dad."

Tristan glanced out the window above Rem. "I don't want to talk about that now. Not with you."

"Well, in case this ends badly for me, I need to tell you what I should have then." Rem leaned forward, hanging his arms over his knees as he looked intently at Tristan. "You asked me what you should do if your dad will never or *can* never give you his love, his approval. I know the answer now."

"Really." The tone sounded like he couldn't care less, but Rem caught a glimmer of hope in his eyes.

"All you can do—what you need to do—is forgive him."

Tristan snorted.

"I'm serious, man. If you don't forgive him, you'll never have the peace you're looking for. It'll eat you up."

"My old man doesn't deserve forgiveness."

"I get it." Rem knew his dad didn't deserve it, either. He'd never ask for it. Didn't want it, certainly not from his black-sheep son. But conviction seized Rem's heart—he needed to forgive his dad as Christ had forgiven him. He needed to stop trying so hard to earn his dad's forgiveness and instead offer forgiveness to his dad. "Do you want to be free like you want to free the Mississippi?"

Tristan met Rem's question with silent attention.

"Forgive your dad. With God's help, I'm going to forgive mine. I want to let it go. Be free." He lowered his arms, looking up at Tristan. "What do you say?"

"I say you're trying to con me again. I don't even care what my old man thought about me. He's in the ground where he belongs." But the moisture in Tristan's eyes as he raised his voice shouted the opposite of his words.

He aimed the gun at Jessica as he backed away from Rem a few steps. He tapped something on his phone's screen, and his face whitened. "It didn't go off. She found it." He lifted his head, gaze shooting daggers at Rem. "She didn't listen to me!"

He threw the smartphone onto the empty armchair and swung his focus to Jessica, then back to Rem. "She killed her grandma. But I'm going to kill her and that dog first." Tristan kept the gun trained on Jess as he picked up the flip phone from the end table.

Bristol. Rem's heart dropped to his stomach.

"I hope she's trying to disarm my Crownover bomb right now." Tristan gave Rem a sickening grin as he opened the phone. "It would be sweet justice to take her with it."

Rem's muscles tensed as Tristan watched him, waiting for a reaction.

The only reaction he'd get would happen when Tristan risked looking away.

Tristan moved his thumb over the buttons. Looked down to check.

Rem hurled himself at the bomber.

The world was silent and dark, deep in the belly of Crownover Dam.

Bristol moistened her lips as she took out her wire cutters to disarm the bomber's IED. The last one, she hoped.

She couldn't believe how quickly Toby had found it after they'd arrived. She'd figured the bomb would either be hanging near the buttresses on the outside or buried in the interior on a wall of the dam. The latter proved true. Toby had found the large device tucked in a dark corner where it would destroy the base of the dam wall.

She clamped the flashlight between her teeth, giving her some light to see the IED.

Same setup as the last one, but with more explosive power for the larger dam. It was rigged to a cell phone, ready to detonate with the bomber's call.

Which could be any second.

Yet peace still flowed through her veins, her limbs. She'd never known how calming—wonderful, really—it felt to realize everything didn't depend on her. That Someone good had control when she didn't.

Please help me, God. No matter what happens, keep Grandma and Rem safe. And the PK-9 team. Thank You for them all.

A sense, like this might be her last prayer, came to her. Maybe the bomber was about to make the call, detonate the explosives in her face.

But even that feeling didn't bring fear. Somehow, she knew it would be okay.

God is good, Grandma had always said. He had good planned for the future. Bristol would rest in that.

"Here we go, Toby."

He sat at her side, wagging his tail with a grin on his face, seeing the good as he always did.

She reached for the wire that had worked to disconnect the previous device. She hoped the bomber hadn't built in a surprise she couldn't see.

And that God kept him away from a phone until she could render this device safe.

★ ★ ★

Rem landed on Tristan, grabbing his arms as he scrambled to reach the phone that had fallen on the floor.

Rem swung, landed his fist on Tristan's jaw.

The bomber jerked back with a yell.

"Don't move!" Phoenix leveled a Glock at Tristan as she came swiftly into the living room behind the armchairs.

Amalia moved in beside her, weapon aimed at the bomber.

Rem pushed off him, lunging for the phone. He scooped it up, closed the lid. Let out the breath he'd been holding. *Thank you, Lord.*

Rem grinned at Phoenix and Amalia. "Nice timing."

"Our pleasure." A hint of an uptick, like the shadow of a smile, tweaked the corners of Phoenix's mouth. "Cora," she said into the radio, "call Katherine."

Bristol halted her Jeep as near as she could get to the bomber's house. Emergency vehicles, FBI SUVs and cars lined the street and driveway. The whole road was blocked off in front of the house.

"Be right back, Toby." She dropped out of the Jeep and jogged toward the perimeter.

An FBI agent held up his hand as she neared. "Hold it."

"My grandma's in there." She gasped out the words, tempted to deck the guy to get past.

"Let her through." Agent Nguyen yelled to the agent from the walkway that led to the front door.

Bristol jogged around the barrier, spotting Phoenix, Nevaeh and Amalia with Agent Nguyen. "Where is she?" Bristol slowed as she reached them.

"Inside." Phoenix gestured to the front door.

Bristol sprinted toward it, stopping to wait for another FBI agent who exited through the open doorway. Her heart pounded as she strained to see past him into the living room. "Grandma?"

"Bristol?" Grandma's voice. "I'm in here."

Bristol's breath hitched.

She was alive.

Thank you, God.

Gratitude expanded her heart as tears heated her eyes, blurring the sight of Grandma sitting in a chair, arms open to Bristol with a smile.

Bristol fell into her grandmother's hug, disregarding the paramedic who had a blood pressure cuff around Grandma's arm. Tears burst free, cascading down Bristol's cheeks as she cried into her grandmother's soft shoulder, the smell of her lavender soap like the scent of heaven.

"Shh, shh. It's okay, my darling." Grandma gently stroked Bristol's wet hair. "The Lord took care of us. Thank You, Jesus. You saved my precious girl."

Bristol took in a shaky breath and slowly sat back into a squat. "He did, Grandma. I think I finally understand what you meant. That God is in control and that's good. Because…"

"He's good," Grandma finished with Bristol, her eyes glittering with tears of joy above a giant smile. "Oh, my precious girl, you have no idea how long I've prayed for this day. For you to know our good, good God."

Bristol gave her a watery smile. "Maybe that's the good He's bringing out of this."

A sniff reminded Bristol they weren't alone.

Cora smiled down at her, tears tracking her smooth cheeks.

"Thanks, Cora. To you and the whole PK-9 crew, for saving my grandma."

She shook her head. "It wasn't just us."

"What do you mean?"

"God sent your young man."

Bristol met Grandma's gaze. "My… Rem?" Her pulse skittered.

"Yes, sugar. Your Rem." A twinkle glinted in Grandma's warm gaze. "He risked his life to tackle that evil man and save me. And you. Before the man could set off his bombs." She rested her hands on Bristol's shoulders. "He's a real hero. A man you can always depend on."

Bristol's chest squeezed so hard she thought her ribs might break. "Where…"

"Right behind you." Cora gave a nod as her gaze focused on the door.

Bristol rose, turned, heart in her throat.

There he stood. The unpredictable, frustrating Remington Jones. His hair was a mess, locks of golden-brown teasing his forehead, his dark brown button-down halfway untucked from his jeans, and he sported a purple bruise on his cheekbone.

But she'd never seen anything more gorgeous in her life.

She didn't think, only acted on instinct. She crossed the divide between them and sank into him, her arms wrapping around his torso as she buried her face in his strong chest.

His arms came around her, squeezing tight, as if he didn't want to ever let her go.

And she hoped he never did.

But then his hands moved to her arms, and he gently pushed her away.

Her heart plunged into her stomach. He didn't believe she loved him. She couldn't blame him, not after the things she'd said to him, yelled at him.

She looked up, her gaze colliding with his chocolate eyes. "Rem, I'm so sorry. I blamed you unfairly, and you still came here to save Grandma. How can I…" Her inadequate words drifted off as he gently brushed his fingers against her cheek.

His gaze searched her face. "Did you mean what I heard you say? About God?"

Tears flooded her eyes, spilling out as she nodded. "Yes. I want what you and Grandma have. I want to know God like that and…to be able to always depend on Him like I could today."

A smile stretched Rem's lips—a smile of pure joy and happiness that radiated through her body and stopped her heart. "He's the perfect One you've always been looking for, Bristol. He'll never let you down." Rem tucked Bristol's hair behind her ear, his touch sending a shiver down her spine. But his smile faded as he pulled his hand away and took a step back.

She reached for his arm, closing the gap between them as she moved close again. "He showed me something else. That you were right—I used to love the man I wanted you to be."

His head lowered, but she tightened her hold on his bicep so he wouldn't pull away.

"But I found out today, I don't need that imaginary, perfect man. I need you."

His gaze shot up, finding hers.

"I love you, Rem. Surprising, unpredictable you."

He gripped her arms as his dark eyes searched her face, her soul. "Are you sure? I'm still going to fail, you know."

A laugh escaped Bristol's lips as she tasted the saltiness of her own tears. "And I'll fail along with you. But I'll count on you and God to forgive me. It's no use trying to get rid of me, because I will always love you, Remington Jones. Whatever comes our way."

"And I will always love you, Bristol Bachmann." Rem slipped his arms around her and dipped his head. His lips found hers, and she leaned into his strong embrace.

As she returned his kiss with all the love she felt, her heart filled with a wild, boundless joy that was greater and more powerful than she'd ever imagined. Like a flood in her soul.

Epilogue

Bristol nearly burst with pride as she watched her fiancé receive his award for his role in identifying and apprehending Tristan Doyle.

The lights of Minneapolis City Hall loved Rem just as much as last time. She'd advised him to wear his camel-colored blazer, since it made her pulse sprint whenever she saw him in it, the tan tones accenting his hair and eyes.

This time, she stood on the landing with him, enjoying her great view from only five feet away. He made a lighthearted comment, effectively lifting the mood from earlier in the press conference, when MPD's chief had related the fate of Tristan and his accomplice. Tristan's future would take some time to decide as his case moved through the court system. He would surely get a long prison sentence, if not the death penalty.

His accomplice had already tasted death, thanks to piloting the boat packed with explosives. The body of the man who had apparently been a proselyte of Tristan's extremism had washed up on the banks of the Mississippi.

The news was heavy, but a certain comfort came from knowing justice was being done, and the terrorists would no longer be able to hurt people.

Toby got up from his sit at Bristol's side and wagged his tail.

Probably because Grandma was waving at him from the front row of seats below the staircase.

Bristol smiled at her and switched the award she'd just received from the governor to her other hand. An award for finding and disarming the explosives, saving the Twin Cities from catastrophic flooding. But really the whole Phoenix K-9 team deserved to be up here with her, receiving the award. She wouldn't have been able to do any of this without Phoenix hiring her and without the team's support in rescuing Grandma.

Bristol laughed with the crowd at Rem's closing joke, her heart swelling when he came to her side and intertwined his fingers with hers.

She barely heard the rest of the governor's closing remarks, since Rem chose to give her that grin that made her heart tumble over itself.

They stood together for the final applause, and Rem turned to face her the moment the clapping dwindled. "He actually talked to me."

"Your dad?"

Rem's eyes glistened with joy and unshed tears as he nodded.

Her heart swelled as she leaned into him, wrapping her arms around his firm torso. She still couldn't believe his parents had shown up for the awards ceremony. But it was about time Rem's father realized he had a very special son.

Someone pushed between them.

Rem reluctantly drew back, laughing as he dropped his gaze to Toby, who wriggled between their legs. "Are you jealous, mister?" He rubbed Toby behind the ears. "Can't say I blame you." He looked at Bristol and gave her a wink that curled her toes.

He straightened and scanned the people who lingered from the audience, now standing, clustered in small groups. "Is your mom here?"

Apprehension clutched Bristol's chest. "I didn't see her, but she said she was coming. With Roger." The idea of rebuilding her relationship with her mom, and maybe even restarting one with her stepfather, had seemed easier when she'd thought of it long distance. "Maybe she changed her—"

Bristol's gaze found Grandma, talking with a couple she didn't recognize and her mom. She looked very much the same as the last time they'd been together, though time was tinging her mahogany hair with gray. "I see her."

Rem gave Bristol's hand a squeeze. "God's got this, re-member?"

Warmth cloaked her anxious nerves at the reminder.

"Congratulations, you two." Cora's voice and soft touch on Bristol's arm made her turn to see the PK-9 crew on the landing and the top few stairs. The human members of the team, at any rate. Dag and Cannenta were the only dogs in the group, Dag fixed at Phoenix's side and Cannenta sitting in front of Nevaeh's feet as she stood on the third step down.

"Thanks." The remnant of Bristol's anxiety vanished under the smiles of her friends, her partners. "Though you should've all been up here. The whole PK-9 team deserves to get an award."

"And we did."

Bristol met Phoenix's unreadable gaze. But this time, she knew what Phoenix meant. A win for one of them was a win for the whole team. Bristol smiled for them both.

Cora looked past Bristol at Rem. "We heard Calvin Bestrafen is facing charges for accepting bribes, and the DNR offered you your job back."

Rem nodded. "Nice of them to offer, but I'm not planning to take it."

Amalia laughed from where she stood on the second step down. "No surprise there."

"What will you do?" Cora's gentle smile was full of the encouragement she always gave to others.

"Private investigations." Rem grinned. "I like finding the bad guys."

"Welcome to the club." Amalia flashed her big smile as she glanced at Phoenix.

Rem looked at Bristol's boss, too. "But I don't intend to step on your toes or compete for business. You run an amazing organization—" he glanced at all the ladies "—with an incredible team."

"We don't specialize in investigations." Phoenix held his gaze. "Who knows, maybe we'll take advantage of your investigative talent again in the future."

Pride and gratitude flowed through Bristol, and she gripped Rem's hand tighter.

"Guys, maybe they need to talk to their family." Nevaeh had lifted Cannenta and held the dog in her arms. "We shouldn't hold them up."

And that's when Bristol knew. She looked at these four women who had her back in the toughest of times, who cared about her just like she cared about them.

"That's okay." Rem glanced down at Bristol and voiced the same realization that was flooding her heart. "We're with family right now."

And it was very good.

★ ★ ★ ★ ★

Lex Fielding drove, cutting down the narrow dirt path between the towering trees. Branches slapped the side of his park ranger truck, and rocks spun beneath his wheels. All the while, words cascaded through his mind, clattering and colliding in a mass of disjointed ideas that didn't even begin to come close to what he wanted to say to Poppy. Years ago, he'd had no clue how to explain to the most incredible woman he'd ever known that he didn't think he was ready to get married and have a family. He might not have even had the guts to tell her all his doubts, if she hadn't called him out on it after he'd left a really unfortunate and accidental pocket-dial message on Poppy's voice mail admitting he wasn't ready to get married.

Something about being around Poppy had always made him feel like a better man than he had any right being. Even standing beside her made him feel an inch taller. He just hadn't thought he'd been cut out to be anyone's husband. Something he'd then proved a couple of years later by marrying the wrong woman and surviving a couple of unhappy years together before she'd tragically died in a car crash.

He heard the chaos ahead before he could even see it through the thick forest. A dog was barking furiously, voices were shouting, and above it all was a loud and relentless banging sound, like something was trying to break down one of the cabins from the inside.

He whispered a prayer and asked God for wisdom. Hadn't been big on prayer outside of church on Sundays back when he'd been planning on marrying Poppy. But ever since Danny had been born, he'd been relying on it more and more to get through the day.

Then the trees parted, just in time for him to see the two figures directly in front of him dragging something across the road. His heart stopped.

Not something. *Someone.*

They had Poppy.

Don't miss
Wilderness Defender *by Maggie K. Black,*
available June 2021 wherever
Love Inspired Suspense books and ebooks are sold.

LoveInspired.com

For readers of *Lilac Girls* and *The Lost Girls of Paris*

Don't miss this captivating novel of resilience following three generations of women as they battle to save their family's vineyard during WWII

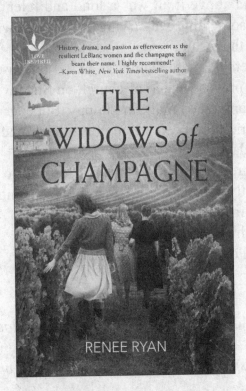

"With complex characters and a stunning setting, *The Widows of Champagne* will sweep you into a wartime story of love, greed, and how one should never underestimate the strength of the women left behind. I couldn't put it down."
—Donna Alward, *New York Times* bestselling author

Coming soon from Love Inspired!

LOVE INSPIRED
LoveInspired.com